M *and* M

Also by John A. Peak

Mortal Judgments

Blood Relations

Spare Change

M and M

JOHN A. PEAK

THOMAS DUNNE BOOKS
ST. MARTIN'S MINOTAUR ✖ NEW YORK

For Eloise M. Peak

1915–2001

First, last, and always a teacher of children

THOMAS DUNNE BOOKS.
An imprint of St. Martin's Press.

www.minotaurbooks.com

Design by Susan Yang

Library of Congress Cataloging-in-Publication Data

Peak, John A.
    M and M / John A. Peak.
        p.   cm.
    ISBN 0-312-27674-5
    1. San Francisco (Calif.)—Fiction.   2. Infants—Crimes against—Fiction.   3. Women physicians—Fiction.   4. Women lawyers—Fiction.   I. Title: M and M. II. Title.

PS3566.E157 M13   2002
813'.54—dc21

                                                                    2002068135

First Edition: November 2002

10   9   8   7   6   5   4   3   2   1

Acknowledgments

I owe enormous thanks to the many physicians, too numerous to list, who have patiently discussed various aspects of this book and others, trying to keep me close to the right track in any technical descriptions and explanations. Any errors, of course, are my own. I owe special thanks to my agent, Julie Castiglia, for encouragement and occasional prodding and to my editor, Ruth Cavin, for her unfailing insight and dependably accurate comments and suggestions. Finally, I owe more than gratitude to my wife, Maggie Durham, and to my progeny, Heather, Shelby, and Lauren, for putting up with my early-morning schedule (occasionally overlapping with the late-night schedule of one of them) and all of the vagaries of the habitual teller of tales.

One

Vicki Shea came into Gunnison Memorial Hospital through the Emergency Room entrance, thinking that she could go through the waiting room incognito and, as she passed by her, get a look at the patient's mother. It was raining and cold and a small hospital, so she didn't expect there would be many people waiting at three A.M. There weren't. The one woman sitting and staring at the carpeting had to be the mother.

The young woman glanced up as Vicki came through the door, seemed to decide Vicki was not who she was looking for, and then looked away. Even in a lined trench coat over her sweatshirt and jeans Vicki was small and slight enough to be mistaken, at a quick glance, for one of her pediatric patients. Her blaze of red hair was half combed, still flattened by her pillow on one side, making her a little wild-looking, an effect that was not diminished by the blood in her eye as she scowled at the woman in the waiting room and then down at the floor when their eyes met. Vicki didn't stop.

The mother's appearance barely registered as young-looking, blonde, frightened, and tired. No one was attending the triage desk and Vicki didn't bother the nurses she could hear at the back, near the microwave. Popcorn smell. She was looking for Tom Boyle, the ER doc that had this shift, or Magdalena, the nurse who had called her. She found Magdalena first.

"In here, Dr. Shea. I'm sorry. I know you're not on call tonight."

"Forget it." Vicki scowled into the newborn warmer, pulling off her coat and reaching for the box of disposable gloves. "Where's Tom?"

"Radiology. He knows you're coming."

The baby girl in the warmer was naked, on her back, limp. There were blue marks on both upper arms and another, high in the center of her forehead, right at the hairline. There was a small catheter plugged into the femoral vein, slow-dripping normal saline, waiting for Vicki's orders. As Vicki watched, the right hand twitched, then twitched twice more.

Vicki didn't move her eyes from the baby, taking in all the marks, watching the hands and feet for spontaneous movement. "Like this since she came in?"

"No change. Got here about two-thirty. She's seventeen weeks old, normal gestation, vaginal delivery. Mom says she slipped and fell while she was carrying her."

Vicki snorted. "Right."

Vicki's hands were small and the gloves universal, so there were boggy tips on her fingers as she reached through the portals on the warmer. Oh-so-gently, she probed the little abdomen, felt the ribs, the long bones in the arms and legs, the shoulders, the hips and ankles. Nothing obviously abnormal or out of place so far, except the baby didn't respond. The twitch was not connected to anything in the outside world, it was in response to a spontaneous firing of motor neurons that shouldn't have been firing. Vicki touched the area around the mark on the front of the scalp. Nothing much there, to palpation anyway. She slid her fingers around the cranium until she felt the soft, spongy texture of swelling at the back of the head. Okay, there it is. Wait for radiology.

Magdalena pushed an instrument tray near Vicki's elbow and opened a sterile package, exposing a tiny clear plastic catheter. Vicki lifted the tent from the incubator and, with deft, smooth maneuvers, drained the bladder into a sterile cup. Dark yellow. No obvious pink.

She passed the specimen to the nurse. "Look for occult blood along with the regular panel."

"Sure."

Using a funduscope, Vicki looked carefully at the retina in each eye. The eyes reacted to light equally. The retina on the left looked hemorrhagic. She looked again. Yes, a small but definite retinal hemorrhage. Using two hands now, she felt the phalanges behind the spinal column on the back of the neck. Grossly normal.

Vicki stood over the warmer and stared at the little girl. From what Magdalena had told her this had been a normal baby. Just yesterday, this child had been squawling, smiling, reacting to faces, gripping toys, turning her head to noises. A little girl.

Vicki couldn't let it show but it was impossible for her not to react. A little girl. A brain injury. She'd seen her own Mary like this, the seizures, the unresponsiveness. It was just like it was yesterday. Twenty-five years and it was still that clear—so clear that if she let up just a little she would be in tears now over this new baby. She would not let up. It had taken her twenty years to be able to take these problems on, to be able to look at them as she thought a doctor should. Mary had been born with the mysterious injury built into her brain. This one had not.

Vicki could hear Tom Boyle snapping films into the view box behind her in the examining room. She glanced at him and then continued watching the baby, watching for the twitching. She pulled off the gloves.

"What'd you find, Tom?"

"AP and lateral of the spine look okay, but there's a stellate skull fracture in the occiput."

"Left side?"

"Yes, left side. That ecchymosis you see in front seems to have a little epidermal hematoma under it. There's probably a subdural clot under the fracture in back. Can't see it here, but that's my guess." He kept staring at the films. He glanced at Vicki and then looked back at the view box. "Want me to call for transport to Moffett?"

"Yes, thank you. I'll call Neurosurgery, tell 'em we're on the way."

"Transport's waiting in the hall, Neurosurg is expecting you, got an MRI open in twenty minutes. They'll hold it for you if they can." Magdalena's voice was decisive, firm, with maybe a little defensive anger behind it.

Vicki looked at her, saw the defiant look back. "Don't worry about it, Mag. You did right. Who's on call?"

"Dr. Jacobs."

"Oh. Who's the baby's regular pediatrician?"

"It was Dr. Holmes."

Vicki looked at her again. "Mike Holmes? The guy who died last week?"

"Yes." She nodded for emphasis. "Dr. Jacobs will miss the chance to pick her up as a regular, now."

Vicki waved it off. "Don't worry about it. I'll call him right after I talk to the mother. He'll understand."

It would not be all right, of course. Jacobs would be pissed that somebody else got his call, but Vicki was the only pediatrician who had also been an assistant DA in her past life, before she went back to medicine late and completed her residency. Not all of the nurses, but certainly a veteran like Magdalena, would call Vicki first when there was any suspicion of child abuse. Five years earlier, as a new resident at San Francisco General, Vicki had caused a stir by calling in a child abuse report on her own without waiting for the attending faculty pediatrician. Nobody criticized her because of her background, and besides, she was older than the attending. She had called in two more on her own, and then other residents called her if they thought they might have an abuse case, which turned out to be fine with the attending. He was squeamish about cops.

Tom was still staring at the films, his voice offhand over his shoulder. "Tell Jacobs I called you. He can't stand me anyway, so it won't hurt a thing."

"Okay." Vicki stood at his shoulder and looked at the skull series, immediately dismissing the concern about Jacobs's feelings. "Nondisplaced, huh?"

"Looks like it from here."

Vicki was already moving toward the door. "What's the mother's name?"

Magdalena handed her the newly minted and growing chart. Patient name: Charlotte Sanderson. Responsible party: Francis A. Sanderson. Scrawled in Magdalena's pen next to that typed entry: Julia Wilkins-Sanderson.

Great, thought Vicki, squeaking down the hall in her running shoes. *Still don't know what to call her.*

The mother was standing with her back to the ER, ostensibly looking at a poor reproduction of a good painting on the wall. Vicki noted that she was tall, but then everybody looked tall to Vicki. She was wearing an expensive, full-length, soft leather coat. She turned at the sound of Vicki's shoes and her face looked openly frightened for a second before she composed it with an effort.

"Ms. Sanderson?"

She nodded. "Julia."

"I'm Dr. Shea, Julia. I'm a pediatrician." Vicki heard her own voice sounding flat, shallow, unsympathetic. "Charlotte is very sick. We have to take her to UCSF, to Moffett Hospital, where we can do an MRI. She may have to have surgery."

Julia's hand was inside a slick black leather glove, clenched in a fist as she brought it up to her mouth and held it there. It was as though all of her tension was in her hands, acting independently, while her face remained wide-eyed but composed, calm, the expression of someone trying to be helpful. She was nodding her head, seemingly eager to agree to whatever was being told to her.

"All right. Will she be okay?"

"I can't tell, yet. I'm sorry." Vicki added that last almost involuntarily. In spite of the calm expression, the young woman was literally shaking with fear. Vicki immediately regretted her hard tone, her hard face. "Here. Sit down a minute, okay?"

Obediently, Julia lowered her backside to the very edge of a chair and quivered there, her eyes wide and moist, her mouth a white straight line. Vicki sat in the chair next to her and plopped the chart on her knee for something else to look at.

5

"She has a skull fracture—"

"Oh!" The word squeaked out of her and the hand opened to cover her mouth. The other hand, acting on its own, came up and crushed a car key against her upper lip. The tears she had been restraining seemed to pool in her eyes. She blinked them back, refused to give way to them while she continued to stare at Vicki, waiting for her to go on. Vicki was struck by how young she seemed. In spite of the grip she was trying to keep on herself she looked vulnerable and hurt. Then Vicki thought about the flaccid baby, the unconnected twitching that betrayed the damaged brain tissue. She had to make a conscious effort to soften her voice a little.

"That's not the real problem. Bones heal very quickly in a baby. The problem is, there seems to be a blood clot underneath the bone where the fracture is." Vicki put her own hand on the back of her head to show where she was talking about. "So, we need to use the MRI to see how big it really is and if it's pressing on the brain. If it is, they can take it out pretty quickly and see if that doesn't solve the problem. She might be just fine in a couple of days, but I can't really tell right now. Understand?"

The mother nodded, so tense she couldn't make her neck work smoothly. "I need to take her up to UC?"

"No, we're taking her by ambulance. You just need to meet us there." Vicki saw a minimal amount of relief that she didn't have to do it herself. "They won't let you ride in the ambulance but I'll be in the back with her, okay?"

Again, the jerky nod, agreeing to anything and everything. "Where do I go? I mean, I know how to get to the hospital . . . you said Moffett?"

"Yes, Moffett Hospital." Vicki fumbled in the pockets of the lab coat until she came up with a card with her name on it. "The nurse is going to make you sign some consent forms, then you can come on over. Have me paged and I'll tell you where we are, okay? Julia? Take a cab."

More vigorous nodding, then the recognition of what she'd been told. "Oh. Yes, I'll take a cab."

"Can your husband meet us there, too?"

"We're not living together——" She stopped herself, then went on. "I'll try, but I think he's out of the country."

Finally, Vicki couldn't control it. She had to reach out, put a reassuring hand on the woman's arm. "Forget what I said. Do what you want about that. Listen, they're the best in the world up there and we'll be doing everything that can be done, okay?"

Julia nodded, and again she seemed to struggle to control herself. Her whole being was concentrated on Vicki's face, staring at her eyes, trying to read real answers behind the words.

"Can you . . . do you have privileges at Moffett, too?" She was no dummy.

Vicki finally allowed herself a small smile. Whether this woman had caused these injuries or not—and Vicki thought it was likely that she had—she was still the mother of her patient and all Vicki's instincts were to help her as much as humanly possible to get through this circumstance. The old prosecutor buried in her somewhere wanted to toughen up and put the bitch away. The mother in her, not always so firmly buried, wanted to wipe away her suffering.

Through the small smile, Vicki said, "Actually, I teach a course up there. On babies' brains."

She knew it sounded good, but Vicki was not sure this baby would even make it to the other hospital. Probably she would. Pressures, pulse, and spontaneous respirations were holding up okay. All you could ever really do was to run with the probables and hope for the best.

Two

"Vicki? You the one that called?" The on-call social worker at Moffett Hospital was Penney Alvarez and Vicki was grateful to see somebody who had been around the block a few times. "Somebody said you got a battered child?"

"Looks like it. Come on, I'll show you what we got."

Vicki had called for Social Services while she was still in Radiology looking at the scans with a radiologist and the attending neurosurgeon. She brought Penney back to where the scans were. "See that? That's a skull fracture. See that? That's a subdural hematoma." Her voice was flat, just a touch of the returning anger. "It's about a hundred cc's and that's a whole lot for a baby."

Penney nodded, taking notes, all business. "This is an infant?"

"Seventeen weeks."

"Oh, lord."

"She's also got some ecchymosis on her upper arms that looks like finger marks and a small retinal hemorrhage on the left."

Penney nodded decisively and made a note. "Confirmed the retinal hemorrhage?"

The neurosurgeon turned around. He was not much taller than the women. "I'll confirm it." His voice sounded grim, more angry than either of the two women.

"Good morning, Dr. Chin."

"Good morning, Penney. Going to arrest this broad?"

"I won't, but somebody might. Is it fresh? The hematoma?"

"I can tell you that when I drain it."

"Okay, make me a good note." She turned to Vicki with a sigh. "I brought a camera in my bag. I suppose I better see the baby before we talk to Mom."

They talked as they headed for the elevator, Vicki bringing the social worker up to date. "The patient was comatose in the Emergency Room at Gunnison Memorial with right-sided seizure activity in the upper extremity and hypertonic on the right lower. That's mostly gone away now with a little phenobarb. She actually woke up for a minute in the ambulance before we medicated her."

"That's a good sign, huh?"

"Very good, but not conclusive. She had a weak, high-pitched cry. That's bad."

The pediatric ventilator made soft, sighing noises while they stood and looked at the small, still being. She had been intubated, the breathing tube taped to the little face, the eyes shut and puffy. She was heavily medicated to stop the seizures and so she wouldn't fight the endotracheal tube. She lay very still, the diaphragm rising and falling under the notch in the ribs, obeying the rhythm of the machine.

Penney shot frame after frame while Vicki gently turned the child to make sure the evidence was photographed and preserved. As she held the baby between her hands, Vicki thought she felt disturbingly limp. She knew it was mostly the medications but it bothered her, a deep furrow between her eyes the only outward sign Vicki would allow.

With the endotracheal tube taped in place and the bruises in the light for the camera, this child was clearly a trauma victim, not so much like Mary now.

Completely irrationally, Vicki had a sudden urge to try to go back in time, just a little, just a day, to stop this, to see this baby whole and keep her like that.

She knew it was an emotional reaction and she tried to stop it, but for a moment she couldn't. Feeling utterly powerless, she had a sudden, overwhelming urge to fight, somehow, to make her own body a shield, to protect this child, to guard her from this catastrophe, to make her the way she must have been just a few hours ago. Vicki was so startled by the thought, the realization that she was reacting so emotionally, that she forgot to turn the baby for the next picture. She tried to force herself back to the moment, the job at hand, but for a few seconds she simply stood there, bent over, her two hands on the child's chest and back. She tried to push the feeling aside but, instead, humiliatingly, Vicki heard herself make a low groaning sound, a kind of muted grunt.

"Exactly my opinion." Penney snapped the next picture, the strobe instantaneous and brilliant and gone all at once.

Gratefully, Vicki turned the child once again. Okay, she wasn't going strange. Vicki had felt this way before with little children with brain injuries, but Penney was an old hand at battered babies and she felt the same way.

Finally, Penney removed the roll of film, dropped it into a plastic bag, and wrote on a label.

Vicki waited until she looked up. She was all business again, a little stern. "You ready?"

"I guess so."

"Well, let's do it."

They went back down the hall to the waiting room in silence, both thinking about the upcoming interview. Vicki felt a little of the old prosecutorial, predatory rush. But then she remembered the mother's face, the key unconsciously crushed against the lip. This woman surely loved her daughter.

Okay, Vicki thought, anyone could feel like losing control under stress, the extreme demands of a new baby, the breakup with her husband. But there were so many services available and, for someone like this, friends, professional help in abundance. But even so, in the middle of the night, left to cope by herself, somebody could feel over-whelmed and helpless, blaming the baby for all the problems. . . . Still, Vicki's first loyalty was to her little patient and somebody had certainly shaken this baby, banged her head on something, gripped her by the arms. The question now in Vicki's mind was, who else was there?

An older couple was in the waiting room, sitting with the mother. The man was wearing a camel sport coat, his wife bore a huge rock on her wedding set. They looked well-dressed, well-groomed, as though attending an appointment in the middle of the day and not sitting in a hospital at four-thirty in the morning. No, on second glance, they both looked stricken, clearly very frightened.

Julia rose as soon as she saw Vicki and the social worker come through the door.

"Is she going to be okay?"

Vicki smiled automatically, her professional, sympathetic smile. "There's at least a good chance. I can't give you any more than that until after surgery. Actually, it will probably be a few days before we know very much for sure." It would be more like months or years, but Vicki wasn't going to hit her with all of it at once.

"So, she definitely needs surgery? The blood clot . . . ?"

"Yes, that's right. Dr. Chin will remove the collection of blood to get the pressure off. Then we'll just have to see if she improves, but I'm ninety percent sure that she will. It's just a question of how much."

"How much? What . . . ?"

"Well, I've seen cases where they looked a lot worse than this when they came in and wound up with no brain damage at all. I've seen other cases where they did have damage in the long run. No guaran-tees. We just have to do what we can and then wait it out."

"But it looks good? I mean, you think she probably won't have damage, right?"

"I can't tell, but it never hurts to be optimistic and it never helps to assume the worst outcome in advance. Okay?"

The older couple were standing, hovering, eyes wide, taking in everything. Vicki smiled at them and wished that she'd stopped to comb her hair. "Hi, I'm Dr. Shea. This is Penney Alvarez from Social Services here at the hospital."

"We're Charlotte's grandparents, Jack and Cynthia Wilkins." The grandmother spoke first, taking over since her daughter didn't seem to be able to focus at all and her husband, in spite of decorously buttoning his jacket when he stood, was wearing a look that was close to despair. "Doctor, if there's anything we can do at all . . . I mean anything that insurance doesn't cover, we'd be happy to cover it, so . . ."

Vicki waved a hand, dismissing the topic. "I'm sure that will be appreciated, Mrs. Wilkins, there's always something, but I don't have anything to do with that. You should probably have a word with the hospital administrator before you leave if you want to set something up." She tried to turn her attention back to Julia.

Mrs. Wilkins was insistent, raising her voice slightly—subtly but unmistakably stepping in to take over. "The hospital administrator? Is that his official title?"

Vicki stopped and turned to her, giving her a new appraisal. People reacted very differently to bad news. Some were stunned into immobility, some sweated through the bureaucracy, meekly doing the best they could. Others seemed to kick into high gear, turning the nervous anxiety into belligerence, in an effort to gain control over events that were mostly out of their control, no matter what they did. Vicki thought that her diminutive patients sometimes needed a strong advocate and didn't mind them, although they could upset the younger members of the staff.

"Yes, that's his title. Any of the nurses will be happy to—"

"I can take you up to the duty officer." Not about to be intimidated, Penney spoke up. "My office is right next to Administration so you can come with me after we've talked to Mrs. Sanderson for a minute." Penney looked back at Julia, already turning to the door. "Mrs. Sanderson, can you step this way, please?"

Vicki followed them a short way down the corridor to a small conference room. Vicki hated hospital conference rooms but she couldn't have said why. They were all alike, she thought. The same laminated, blond wood tables, the same upholstered plastic chairs, the same handy box of tissues, the same bad news. You could give people good news in any corridor. When the door closed, Vicki was so uncomfortable she couldn't make herself sit down.

Penney had no such inhibitions. She took over a chair and opened a folder in front of her containing some printed forms. She already had a copy of the admission sheet so she had the basics of identity and relationship in front of her.

Penney's voice was directed, at first, toward the folder. "This will just take a few minutes." Her manner said it would take as long as she decided it would take. Penney was dark-haired with gray streaks, a delicate mustache. She was not Hispanic like her husband but she looked as though she could be. As Penney raised her gaze to look at the mother, Vicki thought she looked tough for a social worker.

"Mrs. Sanderson—"

"Could you call me Julia? I'm sorry. It doesn't matter, go ahead."

Vicki shoved her hands in the pockets of her lab coat and leaned one shoulder against a wall, watching. Penney's eyes didn't waver from Julia's. Julia could not look directly back at her.

"Mrs. Sanderson, I'm sure you understand I'm required to ask you some questions. About how this happened. You understand, don't you?"

"Yes." The voice was small. She was either terrified or trying to appear to be to gain sympathy.

"Just tell me in your own words what happened, okay?"

"I must have slipped on something. I don't know. I was carrying her and I fell and I guess she hit her head or something. I don't know, really, how it happened exactly." She began to cry softly, without making any noise but unable talk for a moment. Vicki shoved the obligatory box of tissues in front of her and sat next to Penney, still just watching.

Penney made notes. "Anybody else in the house with you?"

Julia hesitated. "You mean living with me?"

"I mean just there. Living with you, visiting, whatever."

"Oh. No, just the two of us."

"Cats or dogs?"

"No, my mother . . . I don't have time to deal with a pet or any-thing."

"Okay, no pets." Penney made another note. "So you just slipped and fell down while you were holding her?"

Julia could only nod, the tears still falling. Penney was looking over her forms, about ready to close her folder and give it up until later.

Vicki's voice was quiet. "How did you happen to be up? Did she wake you up?"

"Charlotte was hungry so I got up with her—"

"Does she usually wake up at that time for a feeding?" The question was a pediatrician's question, about the baby.

"No. Usually it's later, but sometimes she still wakes up twice."

"Okay, go ahead. You got up with her . . ."

"I carried her into the kitchen in the dark. I guess there might have been some water on the floor, or—"

"Water on the floor?"

"I guess. I—"

"Where did the water come from?" Now Vicki's voice was a little sharper.

"I . . . I don't know, really, I'm not sure if it was water or—maybe something else had spilled and I didn't see it. I don't know . . ."

Vicki's voice was quieter again. "All right. So you went into the kitchen?"

"My feet just seemed to slip out from under me and I fell—"

"Which way did your feet go?"

"I don't know. I don't know which direction my feet went, I just fell." She was crying again.

Vicki acted as though she didn't see the tears at all. "Well, did you fall forward, backward, what?"

"I don't know!" She seemed about to get angry but then didn't. She controlled her voice. "I guess I went kind of sideways."

"You slipped and fell sideways?"

"I don't know. I don't remember exactly."

"Did you drop the baby?"

"What?"

"Did you let go of her when you fell? You know, drop her?"

"No, I kept hold of her." Her eyes were wide a moment then she looked down again, not returning Vicki's flat stare.

"Julia, how did she hit the front of her head *and* the back of her head in this fall?"

"I don't know! I don't know how that happened. I must not be remembering exactly or something . . . I can't . . ." She was really sobbing now, having trouble getting her breath.

Vicki didn't wait. "Julia, is there anything else you want to talk about? Anything you want to tell us?"

No answer.

"Was somebody else there?"

"No." She shook her head quickly, suddenly calmer. "No, nobody."

Vicki stared at her, her eyes unblinking, her face expressionless. After she gave it a moment, she spoke again and her voice was quiet, nonthreatening. "Did someone come by? Maybe even earlier? Somebody besides you and Charlotte at the house?"

Julia did not react to the persistence of the question. It was almost as though she had expected it. When she answered, her voice sounded subdued but a little stubborn.

"Nobody else was there." She would not look up.

Three

Gloved and gowned, Vicki watched as a resident, a young woman Vicki thought had a lot of potential, held a retractor in one hand, delicately pulling a section of scalp away from the target area on the little skull. Chin had parted the periosteum with a spread clamp and the resident held that steady with her other hand. Chin burred a hole in the thin bone and then carefully enlarged it. He probed gently and got a return of blood, red and fresh. Using a tiny suction tip, he cleared the rest of the hematoma, rinsed with saline, and stepped back to watch. A small amount of cerebrospinal fluid leaked out, but it was clear.

Still watching the resident's hands to make sure they were steady, Vicki spoke up. "That was bigger than we thought, huh?"

Chin didn't seemed concerned. "Yeah, maybe . . . maybe closer to a hundred-fifty cc's. How we doing, Garrett?"

Garrett McDonald, an old buddy of Vicki's whom she had called out of bed for this task, was the anesthesiologist. She couldn't say so, but she had wanted a friend. Garrett knew how important this patient would be to her. His voice was cheerful.

"Steady as she goes. No change. Ready for the pressure catheter."

Chin was definitely relaxed, his gloved fingers moving gently, almost caressingly over the fontanels. "Ah, let's give her a minute. I want to lavage, make sure there's no more blood, then I'll stick it in."

He looked at Vicki. "Feel that."

Vicki's fingers traced gently over the gaps in the immature skull. "Soft and flat. Good pulse." She smiled behind the mask.

The smile crinkles were in the corners of Chin's eyes, too. "Shoulda been a surgeon, Vicki. You could still do it."

"Just what I need, another career change. I keep hoping for a well-baby practice."

McDonald snorted. "Yeah, me, too."

Chin looked mildly amused. "You want to be a pediatrician?"

"No, I want Vicki to have a well-baby practice so I can get some sleep."

"Hah! You think you've got it bad. Vicki thinks this whole damn building exists just to keep her babies out of the M and Ms." It was an old joke. M and Ms stood for the hospital's morbidity and mortality tables, the statistics for bad outcomes.

Vicki was finally relaxing, too. "Laugh all you want, guys. Just keep doing it."

Chin concentrated as he performed his lavage, a rinse with warm saline into the burr hole, then he suctioned a small amount of clear liquid back out into a container where they could look at it. He held it up to the light.

"Ten bucks says in a year you won't have any detectable signs this kid was ever hurt."

"Don't bet, Vicki. Kid looks good from here."

Vicki felt relieved and satisfied but would not let herself accept the news completely. It was too early to tell and would be for a long time. The hematoma had been too big. "We'll see."

Four

The cop was sitting and reading in the physician's lounge. Vicki's first thought was that he was there on some other business. Then she remembered what her case was about and she knew he was probably there to see her. If she'd thought about it in advance, Vicki would have predicted a woman in plain clothes, not this buff, fair-haired man in a uniform. He looked young, leaning over a photocopy of a medical chart, his cheek on one hand as he concentrated.

Absently, Vicki pulled off her cap and rubbed at her scalp, already thinking about the shower at home.

"Looking for somebody?"

The cop continued to read from the chart in front of him. "I'm waiting for Dr. Shea."

"You found her."

He raised his eyes to look at her without moving his head. "You're Dr. Shea?"

"Last I checked. Who are you?"

Quickly, he shook his head, grinned, and came to his feet, sticking out one hand. He wasn't all that young. "Sorry. Tim Murphy. Psych Police asked me to come by and pick up what you got." He kept looking, staring almost.

Vicki knew there was a special unit at SFPD for handling psychiatric cases, making arrests or carrying out 5150s, protective holds when someone was out of control. To her understanding, though, they weren't in uniform. "You're with the Psych Police?" She made a vague gesture to indicate the uniform, paraphernalia, all of it.

Murphy kept grinning. "Yeah, well, I'm in the middle of a transfer. Long story. Can I ask you a couple of things about this Sanderson baby?"

"Sure, go ahead."

Vicki wished she had Penney there with her. While she'd been in surgery she'd lost the anger that had pushed her earlier. Now she was mostly just tired.

"In your professional opinion, has this baby been abused?"

Vicki hesitated, but not long. She thought she had to go through with it now. She'd get angry again later. "To a reasonable medical certainty, I believe she has been abused."

Officer Murphy took his time, dutifully writing down the magic words of medical-legal jargon that would satisfy a judge on the issue of probable cause.

"Can you give me the basis for that opinion?"

"Yes, I can." Vicki thought, mustering the words. "This baby has bruises on her upper arms that appear to be consistent with finger marks where someone has grabbed her by the arms very forcibly. She has a bump on her head in front, at the top of her forehead, that appears to be from recent trauma. On the back of her head she has a skull fracture and a subdural hematoma under it. That means—"

"That's okay, I know. A subdural hematoma . . ." He didn't look up from the pad where he was writing.

"She also has a retinal hemorrhage. That means—"

"Which eye? Both?"

"On the left."

"Okay." He finished writing that much down and looked up. "Okay, and your conclusion?"

"Subdural hematoma accompanied by retinal hemorrhage is diagnostic of abuse."

"Pathognomonic?"

"Absolutely. Textbook."

He nodded, wrote a few more notes. "Okay, just a couple more questions. You were present when the social worker interviewed the mother, right?"

"Yes, I was there."

"Can you tell me what she said so I've got confirmation?"

Vicki quickly ran her fingers through her hair again, distracted, trying to remember so she could get this over with and go home. "She said she slipped and fell in her kitchen while she was holding the child. I asked her what she slipped in or something and she was very vague, couldn't remember exactly how it happened, couldn't remember details like which way her legs went. I didn't believe her. That explanation is not consistent with the injuries on the child, and the mother herself did not appear to be injured. She said she was there alone with the baby but I didn't believe that either . . . I don't remember what else."

"That's okay. You got the essentials."

The cop folded the pad into a folder, looked up at her, and grinned. "Thank you." Once again, Vicki thought he was staring at her, watching her with a look of mild amusement and interest.

Vicki did not smile back. "You going to arrest her?"

"Yeah, I guess so. Why?" He gave it a very short pause. "You want to prosecute her yourself?" He grinned.

This time Vicki slowly smiled, surprised. "You know me?"

"Sort of. I know that you are also a lawyer, used to have a private practice before you went back and finished med school. And I know, before that, you were an assistant district attorney for a long time."

Vicki nodded, feeling flattered. "Shouldn't make you notorious, should it?"

"Oh, of course it does." He kept on grinning as he walked toward the door. "You're still one of ours. Any cop with a brain would want to at least meet you once. Thanks for the help." He gave her one more long look before he seemed to catch himself and then make himself go on through the door and down the hall.

Five

This was a Thursday, supposedly Vicki's day off. She was still low enough in seniority in her practice group that she had to cover the weekends and a lot of the on-call schedule. She showered in her condominium and thought about trying to take a nap, but she didn't feel particularly tired, now that she was home. She kept thinking about that cop. "Pathognomonic." Even most doctors didn't use that word. They would just say "diagnostic" when they referred to signs and symptoms that pointed, inevitably, to a certain particular diagnosis.

So, who was this cop? Vicki knew that there were three or four licensed psychologists, Ph.D.s, who were San Francisco cops. There were also a few CPAs and nine or ten licensed attorneys. The psychologists tended to wind up in the Psych Police, naturally enough, and Murphy either had been or would be one of them. He certainly seemed old enough—mid to late thirties was her guess. So what was he doing in a plain old Q2 uniform? Not even a sergeant. And why would the Psych Police be involved, anyway? Usually Vicki dealt primarily with social workers to report an abuse case and they turned everything over to the cops later. Vicki still had a number of friends in the PD. She thought she might ask one of them about this guy.

The phone rang while she was making herself breakfast.

"Dr. Shea."

"Hi, Vicki." She recognized Jacobs's voice, and only then remembered that she was supposed to try to schmooze him after she'd been summoned to take a patient on his shift.

"Hello, Luke. How are you?"

"Did you happen to take a call last night?" Luke Jacobs didn't really have the nerve to sound angry when he spoke to her. For one thing, there was the discrepancy in age, he being about fifteen years younger than she was. Even when they went through residency together he was a little awed by her, if not outright overpowered.

"Yeah, sorry about that. I guess it seemed like it was right up my alley with a head trauma and probably a criminal situation and all that."

"I *am* a trained pediatrician, Vicki." He was whining. He was probably furious, but he would take it out on the nurses, not on Vicki. "I mean, geez, you know how hard it is to build up a practice."

"I know, I'm really sorry. You want to take my next call?"

"Oh, that just gets so complicated."

"Yeah, it does. I owe you one, Luke. I'm serious about that, okay?"

He sighed. "Yeah, okay."

"I'll tell you what. You want to take the follow-up on this patient? I probably burned my bridges with the mother this morning, when I turned her in to the police. She was one of Mike Holmes's patients, so they'll be needing a regular pediatrician."

"Really? Another one of that guy's patients?"

"That's what the nurse said."

"For a guy in his seventies, he had a lot of patients. Well, sure, I'll take her over for you." Now he acted like he was doing Vicki a favor.

"Great. That's one thing I won't have to worry about, then."

"No, don't give it another thought. I'll go see her this afternoon."

Vicki sat for a moment, sipping coffee, after she hung up. It bothered her to turn over this patient to somebody else. Up at UC with all the bright, shiny residents running around, the absolutely brilliant neurosurgical staff to look in on her, there was plenty of expertise on head trauma. For the long term she thought they would transfer the baby back to Gunnison, the hospital closest to her home and the hospital Vicki used most of the time. The mother would undoubtedly be out on bail. She would see her in the corridors. Well, she thought, it couldn't be helped.

She knew that wasn't the primary reason she was troubled. It was the child herself. Seeing a baby like that, one who had been hurt so badly, was a hazard of the profession, but Vicki still wasn't good at keeping a professional distance. She knew it was probably related to her own early experience, her own daughter who had never been injured after her birth but had been born with an injured brain, nevertheless.

Later, if little Charlotte Sanderson survived this initial critical period, it wouldn't make any difference how the destruction of brain cells had occurred, it was just a matter of degree, of "the severity of insult" in the ironically understated medical jargon. The stilted language, the words of learning, actually helped to maintain the distance, turning an injured child into a professional, intellectual problem to be solved, instead of a repository of disappointment, a receptacle for all the broken hopes for the future.

Oh yes, Vicki remembered that part well. She'd had her daughter when she was nineteen years old. Mary had been afflicted with cerebral palsy, so severe that she had died when she was four. It had taken Vicki twenty years after Mary sixteen years after her death—to decide that she could go on. She had finally realized that she would not get over it, that Mary was a part of her and always would be. After twenty years she finally had been able to look at other children without anguish, and that's when she went back to do the pediatric residency.

In the interim she had gone to law school, and was well on her way to a successful career as a partner in a small defense firm. There had been a crisis, a major trial that had turned into a nightmare, with witnesses murdered and Vicki herself badly wounded. Since then, Vicki had managed to pour herself into this new career, this new identity as a physician, with precious little of the old swagger surviving from her past success. She had at least stopped being so much of a loner, but all of her time seemed to disappear into the practice, very little left over to call a person anymore. But maybe it wasn't that bad. It was only when she paused occasionally to look around that she missed having a sex life. When she did pause to think about it, she was surprised that it had gone and she didn't even seem to notice it was missing.

By now, or tomorrow at the latest, Social Services would have official custody of the child and who knew what would happen after that? Maybe they would pass it off to the grandparents. They seemed to be a responsible enough couple. For the next few days or weeks, though, this child would have a rough time and, although she didn't doubt the competence of the other professionals, Vicki felt left out. She wanted to be there, not because she would do anything different, but so that she could be sure, deep down, that this child had every possible chance for survival intact.

Vicki looked around her apartment. She had a stack of journals that she needed to get through. She was working on a paper on prenatal hydrocephalus that was getting close to the deadline. She and a couple of residents had painstakingly examined the records on a hundred cases up at UC, and she was trying to draw conclusions about risk factors to either confirm or contradict a similar study in Boston, but none of it was coming very clear. She wondered if all that work would produce anything that would even be worthy of publication.

What journals wanted from Vicki was medical-legal stuff, but she didn't want to do it. She'd been a lawyer for thirteen years when she went back to her interrupted residency and took up pediatrics. She was thoroughly jaded on the law and happy to leave it to others, except that other people expected her to keep going back to it. She'd wasted valuable time keeping up with the mandatory Continuing Legal Education requirements so her license would stay current. She supposed that she probably hadn't abandoned it entirely. Inevitably, though, when she started working on any medical-legal project, she started thinking too much about that last big trial, the pain of dead friends, at least one good friend, and the smashed femur in her own leg that had seemed to take so long to get any better.

Vicki had met Garrett McDonald on that case and they had been a pair, a couple, for a while afterward, almost a whole year. At that time, Garrett been a divorced man with two daughters, one an adult in college and one in high school. He wanted more children, a second family, for God's sake. He wouldn't admit how important it was to him, but Vicki could see it in everything he did, every decision he made. Vicki was forty then, and after much agonizing she admitted to herself that she was not willing to have another child. Vicki had not wanted to face the issue of other children of her own but, at forty, it was make or break time and she had not been willing to make.

Garrett had protested that it wasn't important but his protests were weak, feeble. He had eventually married a thirty-year-old. Two years later, two kids. No surprises. In spite of all her rationalizing about it, Vicki had taken a year to decide to like the new wife, to decide that it was okay that Garrett was happy with someone else. She spent time with them socially, as a kind of offshoot of the time she spent with her former client, Arnold Jones, and his wife. She watched all their kids grow, untroubled by the intermeshed relationships of the big people around them, bored by anything that had to do with the adults.

Vicki had not sworn off men. If she'd taken the time to ask herself, she would have thought the idea was bizarre in the extreme. Men had always been an important part of her life, from her husband onward. Sometimes they were nearly anonymous, some clearly more important than others, but men, as a concept at least, had always been important. On the rare occasions that she took the time to think about it now, she only supposed she was busy, that nobody had really interested her, lately. She wasn't preoccupied with the subject, but that didn't mean that it wasn't still important somehow, in the grand scheme. It just wasn't urgent.

Now, here she was at forty-five. Periods were coming about every two months, and soon, in the next couple of years at the latest, she would begin to feel hot when everybody else was cold. It wasn't so funny. It was going to get worse but it would get better, too. She decided the best way to deal with it was to ignore it, to stay busy and try not to think about it.

The staying busy part was easy. Vicki had discovered that it was difficult now to make a decent living as a doctor. Insurance payments for a physician's work were not only lower than they had been ten years ago, they were incredibly slow in coming. The paperwork was so complicated that there was no way to avoid the overhead of hiring people to do it. Even in a group practice, with the cost spread out, it was expensive.

Her oldest nephew, Wesley, was sixteen years old and an honor student. Cody, Vicki's brother, was a policeman and a sometime cowboy with four sons, a daughter, and no savings. Vicki was determined that Wesley was going to the best college that would take him. That was going to be expensive with his 4.0 grade point average and SAT scores at 1600. There were three more nephews and a niece behind him, but Wesley was the Ivy League candidate. Vicki was forty-five years old, owned an apartment with no equity instead of a house, drove a five-year-old Volvo, and she still had to hustle.

Vicki sipped her coffee and tried to relax. She tried not to look at the telephone. Maybe it wouldn't hurt to check.

Vicki called the Pediatric ICU at Moffett and got the charge nurse on the phone.

"Hello, Dr. Shea." The nurse sounded troubled.

"Hi, Jill. I just wanted to let you know that I'm going to be off that Sanderson baby's case. Luke Jacobs will be taking over this afternoon."

"Oh." Jill sounded relieved. "You heard already?"

"Heard what?"

The nurse's voice lowered, confidentially. "The grandmother was by here about ten minutes ago, like totally on the warpath."

"Oh. Angry at me?"

"To put it very mildly. I guess the baby's mother got arrested and she blames you."

"They arrested her already?"

"Right here in the hallway. Huge scene except that the cop was pretty good, got everybody calmed down after a few minutes and took her away."

"A uniformed cop?"

"Yeah, sure was. If I were you I'd avoid the grandmother for a few days, at least."

"Don't worry. Why was there a big scene? Were you there?"

"After it got started, we all were. She was all yelling and crying, you could hear it all over."

"Who was?"

"The lady getting arrested. She just went bonkers."

"Oh. Really angry?"

"Well, she was more like all hysterical about the baby and everything. Poor thing."

"Yeah, poor thing. Speaking of which, how's the baby doing?"

Jill sighed. "Not good, I'm afraid. Chin's been up here, brought up Dr. Carter. They would have been calling you if the arrest thing hadn't happened and the grandmother said you were not to be called. Shall I call Dr. Jacobs?"

"Yes, right away. What's wrong with the baby?"

"She's still comatose. Looks like seizure activity in spite of the meds. Don't worry, they're all over her."

"The pressure up?"

"The intracranial pressure? Yes, it is."

"That's cerebral edema. It would begin about now."

"Well, they're all over it."

Vicki sat back and stared vacantly out her window. "Oh, I'm sure they are. They know it's brain swelling, don't they?"

"I'm sure they do."

Vicki hesitated, but not long. "Is Chin there now?"

"Yeah, you want to talk to him?"

"Would you mind?"

Vicki waited impatiently, listening to a recorded message about all the reasons to choose Moffett Hospital/UC Medical Center. She should leave it up to them now, but she just couldn't until she was sure they were doing it right. She heard the recording cut off and then a woman's voice.

"Vicki?"

"Yes."

"Cheryl Carter." Dr. Carter was head of Pediatric Neurology, a department of one full-time faculty and three residents. Dr. Carter was short, stocky, with iron gray curls that looked like a helmet. Most of the residents were afraid of her. She talked to Vicki about pressure readings, diuretics, oxygenation, sedation, dosages for a baby of that size. Vicki realized that Dr. Carter did not believe she really needed Vicki's input. She seemed to be deliberately trying to make her feel better about being bumped off the case. Fine, okay. They could handle it. She was grateful to Cheryl anyway, hoping she would remember to do that for someone else if she were ever in the same position. Other members of the faculty would not have characterized Dr. Carter as being a particularly caring individual, but Vicki knew better.

She thought about calling Liz Abrams, Arnold Jones's wife who had gradually evolved into Vicki's best friend. With the phone in her hand, she decided not to call until she was in a more cheerful mood. Maybe she would try to pry her out of that house full of kids to go to dinner or something this weekend.

Or, for that matter, she could call Elaine Cohen. Elaine was a lawyer in a mostly business-oriented firm whom Vicki had known distantly when she practiced law. She had become a good friend after Vicki had gone back to medicine. Elaine had gone out of her way to retain Vicki as a consultant on one of her cases that had some medical issues, exactly when Vicki had needed the extra income toward the end of her residency. Elaine had been in the middle of working up a major case for trial in the hopes that she could second chair it with the senior partner at her firm, but at the same time she was separating from an alcoholic, verbally abusive husband, another lawyer, and dealing with a new baby. Vicki had been filled with admiration for the woman and Elaine, in turn, had thought that Vicki was the greatest thing since medium heels. Over the course of a year they became close friends. The case was settled out of court, so Elaine didn't get the trial experience she wanted, but she managed the divorce with all the ruthlessness of self-surgery, riding over the pain and focusing on her bright, delightfully healthy baby, who, of course, became Vicki's patient, as well.

Vicki decided she would wait and call one of them later, at home.

Vicki ran errands. She picked up the laundry, bought groceries, went to the post office and stood in line, realizing that she was putting off working on her paper with a deadline next week and then feeling guilty about it until she couldn't wait to get home and get to work. She checked to make sure her pager was on. It was.

There were no messages on her voice mail at home, either. Okay, that's what she insisted on when she had a day off, wasn't it? Okay.

At seven o'clock she called Liz. Liz was at a Brownie meeting. Oh yeah, Thursday.

She called Elaine, caught her in the middle of dinner, and told her she would call back later.

By nine o'clock Vicki had forgotten she'd called either of them, and when the phone rang she leaped for it.

"Dr. Shea." She realized she could hear the tension in her own voice.

"This is Nurse Abrams." Liz pitched her voice as low as she could get it in imitation of the business voice Vicki used whenever she picked up the phone. She laughed raucously at her own humor and Vicki could feel her shoulders lower as the tension went out. Then Vicki could hear the whining voice of a tired eight-year-old in the background.

Liz quit laughing. "What's up?" The whine in the background got louder, turning into a cry.

This problem was so common, they had a code. Vicki said, "Friday?"

"Saturday's better." Vicki could hear the ten-year-old joining the fray, demanding attention, ratcheting up the volume.

"Okay, Saturday."

"Your place at seven?" Liz was yelling over the noise.

"Good. See ya."

"See ya then." Vicki could hear Liz's voice rising in pitch as she was hanging up the phone. "What did I tell you about bothering me while I'm on—" Cut off in mid-tirade. Vicki had to smile.

At eleven Vicki turned off the computer and put away her folder of notes. She picked up the phone just to make sure she had a dial tone before she went to bed. The call came at ten minutes after midnight.

Vicki was instantaneously wide awake. She had known it was coming and her subconscious had not let her forget it.

"Dr. Shea."

"Sorry, Vicki, I hate to—"

"It's okay, Cheryl. What's happening?"

"Grand mal about forty minutes ago. Pressures are not looking good, bulging fontanels, the works." Vicki noticed Cheryl hadn't even bothered to identify the patient. "The senior Mrs. Wilkins is calling the shots, and I guess she decided to fire Jacobs and bring you back in as their regular pediatrician, if you're willing to do it."

Vicki blinked her eyes, forcing them wide open. "Really?"

"No, I thought a good joke—"

"Okay, okay. Sure, that's fine. You want me to come down now?"

"No, I just want to be able to tell her I called you. Are you awake? We can run down what we're doing and see if you got any other ideas."

"Sure, go ahead." Vicki kept a yellow pad and a pen on her bedside table just for this purpose. She picked up the pen and began to write as she listened.

Vicki knew that the problem was the swelling. Brain tissue, like any other soft tissue, swelled with an injury, complicated by the fact that the brain was confined in a closed, hard container. If it swelled enough, the brain surface would be trapped against the inside of the skull and squeezed. Eventually blood flow to a large area of the brain could be severely diminished or cut off entirely. If the swelling was bad enough, the lack of blood supply injured more tissue, because oxygen, normally delivered by the blood to the brain cells, couldn't get to them. This new "hypoxic" injury would cause more swelling as a deadly spiral wound down, the prognosis increasingly grim. The brain swelling could begin twelve to eighteen hours after the initial injury and continue to get worse for thirty-six to seventy-two hours.

Vicki reminded herself that babies in this setting had a slight advantage. In the first place, the hard confining space of the skull was not entirely rigid. There were immature joints, suture lines that could expand a little but not much. In the second place, a baby's brain was tougher than an adult's because it tolerated the lack of oxygen for longer periods without permanent damage. Both advantages, however, were only relative and limited. The doctor's task was to try to control the swelling, and that, Vicki knew, could be a bitch.

Six

The next morning Vicki was at Moffett by six A.M. She went over the medications, talked to the nurse, and then sat for a long time, looking at her bruised little patient, the marks she came in with, the new ones from the IV lines, the bandages on her head from the surgery. So far, the medical attention had made her look worse.

For the rest of the day she spent every break between clinic patients on the phone to Moffett. The seizure activity was still there, small ones, twitching, rhythmic vibrations in the right hand, even with the medications. One nurse thought they were more frequent than they had been at the beginning of his shift. Still, the EEG was showing some normal sleep background behind the spikes of the seizure activity.

Two of Vicki's afternoon patients were behind in their milestones, patients referred to her by other pediatricians in the group to see if they needed a full-blown neurological workup. One of them was lagging significantly, so Vicki ordered a long line of tests and a referral to a neurologist. The mother went from blissfully ignorant to completely distraught. Vicki loaded her down with information booklets and support group data but felt that she was somehow not doing enough. The young mother would have a long trip down this road once she started, and there was not one thing that Vicki could do that would significantly lighten the burden for her.

When Vicki had a chance to call again, the word from Moffett was almost encouraging. Charlotte's pressure seemed to have plateaued. The readings were the same as they had been two hours previously.

At four o'clock a couple showed up with their one-year-old, the mother obviously pregnant again. When Vicki saw that the father was there, too, she braced herself for a tearful list of symptoms. Wrong. Brimming with apparent satisfaction, they both just wanted to be there for the checkup. Vicki looked in the child's eyes as best she could with a curious toddler, and then the ears, evoking a squalling protest that didn't last. She moved all the limbs in a full, relaxed range of motion. She listened to the chest when she could get the stethoscope away from the baby, who wanted to pop it into her mouth but just as cheerfully chewed on a tongue depressor instead.

Vicki stood the child on the padded examining table and slowly let go of her to watch her stand, steady and confident, still curious about the stethoscope, turning over the listening end of it in her wet, pink fingers, and then looking up at the doctor, eyebrows raised in cheerful curiosity.

Impulsively, Vicki laughed out loud, hugged the baby, and then sat back and grinned. She looked over at the startled parents.

"You have no idea how good it is to see a normal child!"

At six Vicki was back at Moffett, talking to a neurosurgical resident she hadn't met before.

"Look at this." He was nervous, talking to Vicki. "Intracranial pressure is nineteen-point-eight. It's been exactly the same for four hours." He was pointing to the nurse's notations of the pressure readings from the catheter Dr. Chin had placed through the burr hole next to the baby's brain.

Vicki nodded, not sure why he was nervous. "So?"

"I think it's plugged up."

"Oh." Vicki hadn't thought about that. "You want to replace it?"

"As soon as possible."

"Call Chin."

The resident hesitated. "Okay."

"You want me to call him?"

"No, that's okay, I'll do it."

Chin was somewhere on the premises so Vicki sat and talked to the resident in the doctor's lounge for half an hour, waiting for Chin to arrive at the Pediatric ICU. The young man seemed to relax as they talked, finally realizing that Vicki was not a potential threat. She was not even a seasoned veteran pediatrician in spite of her age and clinical faculty status.

Then it was back to surgery, Dr. Chin acting as the assistant this time while the resident carefully but confidently replaced the pressure catheter with a new one. He took about twice as long as Chin would have, but to Vicki's mind careful was better than fast. They waited in the OR, watching the readings.

Vicki spoke first. "Twenty-three. It's up."

Chin nodded "A little bit. Not significant."

"You sure?"

Chin thought about it. "Well . . . could be. Worry about it closer to thirty."

Vicki lingered in the doctor's lounge after she'd changed out of her scrubs. She kept thinking about Chin's opinion on the numbers. Oh, yeah. The problem with listening to Chin was what the neurosurgeons thought was a good result. She went back to the ICU, looked at the medications list once more, ordered another CT scan for the morning. Satisfied only that she couldn't think of anything else to do, she finally went home.

Vicki got a call from the ICU nurse just before midnight. The intracranial pressure was up, over twenty-eight now. Vicki slept fitfully for a while, then drowsily called the nurse back at two.

The nurse sounded tense. "I was just going to call you."

"What's going on?" Vicki could feel herself surge wide awake, the tension infectious even over the phone.

"Grand mal a few minutes ago—"

"I'm on my way. Call Chin."

In the car, Vicki forced herself to focus on driving. The streets were empty, lights blinking four ways at the major intersections; everything told her she should be in bed asleep like a normal human being.

She would not let herself think about the baby until she was actually in the hospital, going up in the elevator. The lights were dimmed only slightly, a minor concession to nature, balanced against the nurses' need to stay awake and reasonably cheerful.

A nurse Vicki did not know had a hand on the baby's forehead, the bare spot between the tape holding the endotracheal tube and the tape of the head bandage. The baby's back arched as Vicki watched, the legs spasmed and went rigid. Vicki held the chart in one hand and ordered a change in the medication which the nurse promptly carried out, porting into the piggyback on the femoral line. The convulsions stopped before the medication had a chance to reach the baby's brain.

The two women watched. The child seemed to be asleep. Vicki glanced at the heart rate; it was about fifty percent higher than normal sleep but seemed to be coming down. The respirations were controlled by the machine, but Vicki focused on the sternal notch at the center of the base of the ribs, watching the ebb and flow of air by the rise and fall of the little diaphragm. She put her stethoscope on the chest, one side then the other. Lungs clear at least, heart rate settling down a little more. No murmurs. Oxygen saturation was near one hundred percent, the toes and fingers pink, mean arterial pressure holding okay. Suddenly not trusting the numbers, Vicki squeezed a toe and watched the blanched spot quickly pink out again. Okay.

The baby was still. Even the right hand was still. Then it twitched. It twitched again. Vicki swore under her breath.

"Where's Chin?"

"He asked for you to call him when you examined the patient." The nurse was Asian and Vicki recognized a Filipino accent. She was young, wearing too much makeup, but clearly concerned about this patient, her fine brows drawn together in worry.

"Okay." Vicki wasn't surprised. Chin was only about twenty minutes away, and she wasn't sure what he could do, anyway.

She looked at the pressure readings from the intracranial catheter. Thirty-two. She swore again. She called Cheryl Carter, ran down the symptoms, the medications, the random ideas in her head.

"I'd give her at least an hour or two. Let's see how the increase in phenobarb handles it."

"Okay."

"Not good."

"Yes."

"Does the family know?" Carter asked.

"I haven't talked to them yet. I'll do that now."

"Call me."

"Okay. Thank you." Vicki hung up. With her hand still on the phone, she took a deep breath, held it a moment, and then blew it out through pursed lips. "Okay." She headed down the hall to the waiting room.

Jack Wilkins's sport coat had changed. This one was a blue worsted that looked as though it had been pressed an hour ago. The top button of his shirt was buttoned and his tie was knotted in place.

Vicki had a glimpse of him staring at the television screen, his eyes only half awake until he became aware of her and quickly got to his feet, smiling, doing his best to be friendly, probably to make up for his wife's recently controlled hostility. No one else was in the waiting room and he stepped over quickly and switched off the television.

"Here by yourself?"

"Might as well. Cynthia and Julia went home to get some sleep."

"That's probably a good idea." Vicki smiled, took a deep breath, and looked around at the empty chairs. She realized that she was avoiding looking at him and forced herself to meet his eyes. His eyes were anxious and patient all at once.

"Have a seat, Jack. Things are not going well." She pulled a chair around so she could sit facing him. He was waiting, holding his breath.

"She's started having major seizures."

"Oh." The hurt flooded his eyes, his mouth going flat and rigid, the lips suddenly almost white.

"I've raised the level of anticonvulsant medication but we can't just keep cranking it up. It may work, it may not. We'll have to wait and see."

Jack nodded, trying to show his understanding. It took him a moment to find his voice. "Is there anything else you can do?"

"Not much."

"But something?"

"The problem is pressure. I've talked to Dr. Carter and I'll be talking to Dr. Chin in a few moments. We might consider another surgery to drain fluid off the brain just as a means of reducing pressure. It's called a shunt procedure. There's also the possibility of a craniotomy as a sort of last gasp if we're desperate."

"You going to do that now?"

"No, not right now. Either one of those is a drastic step to take. We're going to wait and see how she does on the medications first and talk about it again in the morning. We'll talk to you all again before we do anything like that, okay?"

He nodded again, almost continuously nodding. Vicki wished he would stop that bobbing of his head, but then realized he probably didn't know he was doing it.

"This is a pretty bad sign, huh?"

"I'm afraid it is."

"It's not hopeless, is it?"

"No, it's not. She's going to have ups and downs for awhile. She could still come out okay."

He kept nodding, then stopped abruptly. "I better call."

"You could just wait until morning. There's nothing to be decided right now and I know they need to get some rest. All we can do right now is to watch and wait. I know that's hard."

He nodded and nodded until Vicki realized he literally could not speak. She patted his shoulder. "Hang in there, okay?"

He nodded and nodded and nodded.

Back at the nurses' station, she looked at the phone. Okay, call him.

She woke up the neurosurgeon at home and told him what was going on. She could hear the huskiness of sleep in his voice when he spoke.

"Probably ought to give her a few hours, huh?"

Vicki could picture him looking at a clock. "I guess so. You coming down in the morning?"

"Saturday? I'm not scheduled, but call me if you want me."

"Okay, thanks." Vicki didn't know why she'd called him. She wanted reassurance that she'd thought of everything, that there wasn't another step out there, another procedure that she hadn't thought of, another medication she could try.

She looked at the young nurse. "This your only patient?"

"I have one other."

"I can watch this one for a while."

"I have charting."

"Go ahead, I'll be here."

Vicki dimmed the lights in the room, leaving enough to see her patient clearly, but wanting to at least make it look like she was sleeping normally. She vaguely reasoned that the lights could bother even an unconscious child, interrupt normal sleep. . . . She shook her head. She found a stool, pulled it over next to the crib, and sat on it, her feet on the crossbar. After a few moments she reached out one hand and placed it on the baby's abdomen. The child's skin was warm and soft, the motion of the diaphragm small and unobtrusive and alive under her palm. Very gently, Vicki patted her and then left her hand where it was.

On Saturday morning Vicki was at the clinic on schedule, seeing children who needed to be seen without appointments. Now that the sun was up, Vicki hardly felt tired. Jacobs came in at ten and they had time to sip coffee and gossip for a few minutes before the next unscheduled patient came in the door, the third or fourth flu case of the day. Luke examined the patient. Vicki was glad she'd had the chance to halfway patch things up with him. He didn't seem resentful, but it was hard for her to tell with him. Luke's wife, Martha, made it awkwardly obvious that she didn't like Vicki at all. Vicki thought that told her more about what Luke thought than whatever he would let her see himself.

The phone rang and Vicki talked to a mother about medications for a few minutes while the phone rang twice more and her beeper went off. She finished the first call and checked with the service. One of the new calls was from Moffett, the same number that she had on her pager. The other call was from Tim Murphy, the uniformed cop who was transferring in or out of Psych Police.

She called Moffett first, the nurse's station in the Pediatric ICU.

"Dr. Shea, this is Kathy. Wanted to let you know your patient is looking a little better. The Sanderson baby?"

"Really?"

"Dr. Carter wanted you to know. She said to tell you the intracranial pressure had dropped off a little."

"Is she there?"

"She had to see some other patients but she said you would want to know right away."

Vicki grinned. This news didn't mean much. The pressure could fluctuate a bit and continue to keep going up overall. Still, Vicki had been so braced for bad news that a favorable sign, no matter how faint, made her disproportionately cheerful. She relaxed, even putting her feet on the desk in front of her while she dialed her next call.

The number Murphy had left was a beeper but he called her right back.

"Vicki, when's the last time you talked to Julia Sanderson?"

"I don't know, Tim." She deliberately used his first name since he had used hers. She had become so used to people addressing her as "Doctor" that it was almost a relief to remember that she preferred the more informal approach. She was thinking about that and only half focusing on what Tim was asking. "Probably not since before the surgery, before I talked to you. Why? Is she missing?"

"Not now." He was serious.

Vicki quit smiling. Something in his voice brought her feet off the desk as she sat forward, frowning. "What?"

"She's dead. Looks like suicide."

It took a few seconds before Vicki could move at all. Then she put her elbow on the desk and rested her forehead against the heel of her hand.

Her voice was almost a whisper. "Oh, no."

She couldn't think what else to say. Vicki's mind was racing: the bad news this morning with the grand mal seizures, Julia's arrest coupled with the desperate feelings of a mother with a child hurt this bad, her court date, the pressure just too much. Then the word just came out.

"How?" Vicki couldn't have said why that was a pertinent question, but it was the first one that came into her mind.

"Shot herself."

"Shot herself? A gun?"

"That would appear to be the case. Left a note." He paused while Vicki stared at the blank desktop in front of her. Then he asked, "But you hadn't talked to her, huh?"

"No." She finally realized he was expecting her to say more. "I talked to her father early this morning up at Moffett. He said everybody had gone to get some sleep so I assumed that included her."

"Was that the last you talked to any of the family?"

She had to think for a minute. "Yes, it was. I was going to talk to all of them again tonight . . ."

"Was it bad news? This morning?"

"Yes. Terrible. The baby was having grand mal seizures."

Murphy seemed to think about that for awhile, or else he was writing it down. "So she was significantly worse?"

"Yes."

"Well . . ." He seemed to think that was important. Vicki could see the reasoning, feel it in the pit of her stomach—the rising pressure of more bad news on the young mother, already desperate with fear and guilt.

"What did the note say?" Vicki realized she didn't want to hear it, even as she had to ask.

"Said she was sorry."

"Sorry?"

"Her exact words were, 'I am so sorry.' That was the entire note."

"That was it?"

"That's it. Right there on the bed next to her."

Seven

Liz had quaffed her first glass of wine while they were waiting for their table. She was chattering, bleating about the insanity of "group learning," because in her view, her son, Matthew, had to do all the work for the whole group of goof-offs that he had been saddled with, and then they all got the same grade. Such a gross injustice could not be allowed to stand. She would bring down the house if her son would just let her talk to his English teacher, which was another problem because although the kids liked him, Liz thought he was a closet pervert. . . .

Vicki was only loosely following the thread of it. She stared at her menu without seeing it at all, her mind deep in the mysteries of suicide, hopelessness, and death. She realized Liz had quit talking. She glanced up, thinking she had missed some question. Liz was regarding her gravely over the top of her own menu.

"Some guy?"

"What?"

"Some guy got you zoned out?" Liz could be perceptive but she could be oblivious, too. Sometimes she was half-accurate, like now. She was expressing concern but also her own chronic voyeur's interest in her single friend's sex life.

Vicki finally realized what she was asking about and shook her head. "No chance of that, I'm sorry to say."

"What's the deal? You look like somebody died."

Vicki nodded. "Somebody did."

Liz's voice dropped to a confidential, sympathetic level, finally completely focused on Vicki and ready to listen. "Oh, I'm sorry. I was blabbing away. A patient?"

Vicki took a deep breath and let it out. "Patient's mother shot herself this morning sometime."

"Eeew! Shot herself?" Liz seemed to be commenting more on the mode than the outcome. "With a gun?" She realized what she had asked. "I mean, you don't hear about . . . I don't know . . ."

"No, women don't usually do that. They take pills or something."

"Sure she did it?"

"Left a note. I guess they're sure. One of the cops called me and told me, wanted to know—" Vicki's voice stuck and she had to clear her throat.

Liz leaned forward, putting the menu aside. "The cops called you?"

"Not like that. The cop was somebody I know, somebody who had already talked to me about her. . . . Oh, Liz." She waved her hand as though it was all just too complicated.

"Take your time. I got all night."

"Liz, she was hardly more than a child herself. Maybe twenty-one or two. I accused her of child abuse and—" Tears welled up in Vicki's eyes and she hadn't expected that. She had to stop and look down.

"Vicki, you must have had a good reason. I know you. You wouldn't have made the accusation without a very good reason."

"I did. A classic case, just textbook, but—" She stopped and took a deep breath and then another.

The waiter was suddenly hovering. Without looking up, Liz waved him off. "More wine and keep out of the way."

"I had a very good reason, but Liz, it never felt right. It felt funny. It was like, okay, skull fracture, subdural hematoma, retinal hemorrhage, right down the checklist, even marks on the arms where somebody grabbed her—"

"Grabbed the child?"

"Right. Marks on the upper arms that looked like finger marks where somebody grabbed her and shook her."

"How old?"

"Seventeen weeks."

"Oh, Vicki! What choice did you have?"

"I know." Vicki blotted her eyes with her napkin, feeling foolish now that she had started talking about it. She was exhausted, ought to be in bed asleep, but she had thought she needed to talk to a friend more than she needed the rest.

"Look, Vicki. Since I started working the triage desk at General I must have called in a hundred of those things."

"Really?" Vicki stared at her. "I hadn't thought of that." She suddenly grinned tearfully, gratefully. "I knew there was a reason to call you."

"After the first twenty I quit worrying about it. Who the hell's going to protect these kids if the doctors and nurses are afraid to do it?"

"Oh, I know. I was supposed to be the tough guy in pediatrics when I was a resident. I've said the same thing."

"Besides, you don't really take any action yourself. All you can do is to get the family into the system and hope, for once, it works like it's supposed to. Usually, at least, the kid gets some protection, if nothing more than scaring the hell out of the parents. Right?"

"I guess so."

"But this one bothers you because of the suicide."

"It's more than that. It bothered me before that." Vicki had to stop and think about what she'd said. She hadn't mulled this through. "She was . . . she was too passive or something. She had this story about slipping and falling in her kitchen that didn't fit with the injuries. She was so vague about it that I didn't believe her for one minute, but still . . ." Vicki didn't know what it was. She had to try to think it through, to decide what had bothered her.

Liz watched her thoughtfully. "Go ahead. 'Still' there was something about the injuries? About the baby?"

"More about her, the mother. She just didn't seem capable of that kind of anger."

Liz sat back in her chair and watched. Her face had a knowing look, a little cynical, a look that said, "Yeah, right. Not the type."

Vicki finally waved a hand as though to brush off the look. "I know, there's no 'type' for child abuse. You just don't see it that much in somebody that's educated, well-off financially."

"A rich kid?"

"Looked like it, yeah."

"A little arrogant? Superior?"

"No, not at all. She just seemed terrified for her baby. Very normal, really. Scared to death. Kept asking if the baby was going to be okay, like . . . like a normal mother with a seriously injured child, that's all."

"Anybody else around that could have done it?"

"We asked her that. She said no."

"You didn't believe her?"

Vicki stared at Liz, thinking it through. "No. I guess I didn't."

"You thought she was protecting somebody? Her husband?"

"They were separated." Vicki was thinking hard now.

"Somebody else? A boyfriend, maybe?"

This was a harder question. "Well . . ." Vicki's voice dragged the word out. "I don't know. I just now realized, while we were talking . . . just remembered that I didn't believe her when she said nobody else was there."

"Yeah, but now . . ." Liz moved her head to catch Vicki's eye. "With the suicide . . ."

"Yeah, now . . ."

"I guess that answers that question, doesn't it?"

Vicki looked at her, thinking. The suicide, the note. "I guess it does, doesn't it?"

Liz nodded, firmly confident. "Of course it does. What did she say in the note?"

"Just said she was sorry, nothing else."

"She was sorry?"

"Yeah."

Liz spread her hands, eyes wide. "Well . . ."

"Seems obvious, doesn't it?"

Liz nodded vigorously, eyes still wide. "I would say so."

Vicki thought about it some more. Finally, she sighed. "Yeah, I guess it does."

Vicki got home early, before eleven, and called Moffett. No more grand mals, but the focal seizures, visible in the hand, had appeared for a few minutes at about nine. Nothing since then.

Vicki set her pager to audible, made sure it was on the bedstand next to her head, then plunged deep into sleep.

At four o'clock Vicki had to sit up and blink her eyes repeatedly in order to read the clock. She checked her pager but it had not gone off. The phone was not ringing. She closed her eyes and snuggled under the covers again. Her eyes popped open on their own. She tried again, but her eyes would not stay shut.

Finally, she sat on the edge of the bed, switched on the light, and called Moffett.

"Any change?"

"Well . . . ICP went up a little to twenty-nine, down a little. It's hovering." It was a different nurse.

"Any more seizure activity?"

"Myoclonic on the right side. Last time about midnight. No grand mals."

"Still got that twitching, huh?"

"Yeah, doesn't seem like it's as often as it was yesterday, though." Vicki could hear the nurse flipping pages in the chart as she read. "Well, actually nothing since midnight. She might be a little better. It's hard to say."

"Okay, keep me posted."

"You bet."

Vicki stepped into her shower, intending to take a long one to help her relax and go back to sleep. Within a couple of minutes, though, she found herself rushing her shampoo and impatient with the whole process. In the middle of toweling down, she stopped herself and stared at the mirror, the misted-over image. What was she hurrying for? If she was going to the clinic about nine, she had tons of time to go to Moffett first, if she wanted to. She had absolutely no reason to hurry. But if she left now, she had time to go over everything at Moffett.

The baby hung limp between her hands as Vicki turned her, listening with the stethoscope. The lungs were still clear, eyes were doll's eyes, rolled up and unseeing. They reacted equally to light, though, and Vicki allowed herself a small feeling of triumph at that. She wrote an order for another full EEG as soon as someone could do it. It was Sunday morning. Probably wouldn't get it together before Monday. She couldn't think of a good reason why somebody would have to come in and do it now. She pulled up the stool and watched the baby. She only meant to give it a few minutes, just make sure there was no more of that twitching. She sat there watching until it was time to go to the clinic.

Luke was writing in a chart when she walked in. He looked up at Vicki with a mildly surprised expression. "Thought I was on today."

Vicki blinked. "Oh." She laughed awkwardly, feeling the blush turn her face a deep red. "I don't know what I was thinking."

"Get some rest, Vicki."

Back in her car in the small parking lot, Vicki felt her face glowing in embarrassment. What was she thinking? She and Luke alternated Sunday clinic because, unlike Saturday, flu seemed to usually take that day off. For once, Luke was probably right. She was simply exhausted.

People learned during residency not only how to stay awake for two days running, but how to sleep during the day when they could. Vicki thought it was because she hadn't done her residency while she was still young enough to learn that trick, but whatever the reason, she had a hard time with daytime sleeping.

Late in the day she was back at Moffett, carefully reading each entry that had been made by the nurses over the last twenty-four hours. She called Cheryl Carter.

"No seizure activity since midnight last night."

There was a short pause. "You want to start weaning?"

"I'd like to try it if you agree." The idea was to try to find the least medication they could give her and still prevent the seizures.

"Let's wait until midnight, give her twenty-four hours."

"Okay." Vicki was not going to let her voice reveal it, but she was excited and filled with dread at the same time. They needed to see if Charlotte would wake up, but another round of seizures might cause even more brain damage. "I thought I'd cut back just a little at first." They discussed the exact dosages and the time line for testing the little brain. Vicki wrote the orders and went home.

At 2 A.M. she was at the baby's bedside again. The effect of the reduced dosage would take a while to show up. The nurses in the ICU were perfectly capable of watching her and calling if any twitching showed up, but Vicki found that she was not capable of waiting at home to hear. She scolded herself for doing it, but she pulled over the stool, turned the lights down a little, and put her hand on the baby's abdomen.

She had to cover her share of clinic on Monday, then she slept from 7 P.M. to 2 A.M. and was again at bedside. No seizures, no twitches, lower the dosage again. She sat and watched, a little calmer about it now.

On Tuesday, Cheryl suggested a switch in medications, so they did that. Still no seizures, but the baby wasn't waking up, either.

At 3 A.M. Wednesday, Vicki was on her stool, her hand on the baby, when Chin dropped in.

"How's it going?" He raised an eyelid with his thumb and peered at the baby's eye. He raised an edge on the bandage and then removed it when he saw the surgical scar was smooth and dry. He looked hard at Vicki. "Anything going on?"

"No seizures. EEG looked fairly good this morning." She knew what she must look like with the lack of sleep and the etched lines of worry in her face, but she decided she wasn't going to get concerned about that with Chin.

He kept looking at her. "I saw the EEG." He glanced at the baby again but then looked back at Vicki's face, trying to make up his mind about whether he was going to say anything. But he was a surgeon. He was going to say whatever he wanted.

"You know, you're not doing any good."

She knew exactly what he meant. She realized she'd even known he was going to say it. Her voice was quiet and flat. "For whom?"

He watched her, maybe a little amused. "Okay. That's a point. You need to get some sleep, though. Well, you can do without the sleep, but you need to get a little distance. She could take another week."

Vicki didn't say anything. The longer the baby stayed in a coma, the grimmer the prognosis, although it didn't always work that way.

Chin reached out as though he did it all the time and tousled Vicki's hair. Then he turned and walked out of the room. Vicki could hear him talking to the nurse, just a few words, and then he left. She almost smiled. He was right, of course, but it was hard. She doubted he understood it very well.

Eight

The phone number on the note had a 553 prefix. Police department. The rest of the number looked familiar, too, but Vicki couldn't quite place it. Murphy? Yes, that's most likely what the indecipherable scrawl at the top of the note meant to convey. One of the other doctors must have taken the message after the clinic switchboard closed at 5:15. Vicki remembered that she had meant to call somebody to find out what the story was on this cop, but she hadn't done it yet.

It was 5:30 Wednesday afternoon and Vicki was getting ready to leave the clinic to make late rounds over at Moffett. She wanted to take a look at Charlotte Sanderson before her day off. Tonight it would be exactly one week since the initial injury.

Vicki had been lecturing herself all day that she was going to actually sleep all night at home and spend Thursday finishing her paper. She was out of time, and besides, Chin was right. He hadn't said anything that she hadn't already thought about. If she hadn't thought of it herself, the looks she was getting from the nursing staff would have told her. She needed to quit acting like this child's mother, for Christ's sake.

She called Murphy back first, cradling the phone with her shoulder while she punched in the numbers because she was holding her pocketbook and lab coat in her other hand.

"Homicide, Murphy speaking."

"Hi, it's Vicki. You call me?" *Homicide?*

"I did. Just wanted to let you know we got some autopsy results on that Sanderson woman."

"Yes?" Vicki wondered why that would concern her, but she did want to know.

"Heroin."

Vicki had to take a moment to let that sink in. "Heroin?"

"Pretty good hit just before she died."

Vicki dropped the lab coat and pocketbook on top of the desk and sat down. "I am amazed."

"Why? Not the right class?"

"I suppose so. I would never have guessed. Sure they didn't mix up the samples?"

"Yeah. It's not just that."

Vicki only had to think a second. "Tracks?"

"Between the toes. She had a recent venipuncture in the arm, but there were old tracks between her toes."

Vicki sat back in the chair and winced. At the same time, she felt so relieved that she almost smiled until she caught herself, guiltily. "So she was an addict?" Somehow, that information seemed to shift the blame for the suicide off of Vicki's shoulders.

"That's my thought. Like you say, you never know."

Vicki almost wasn't aware of the pause in the conversation while she considered the idea, a complete surprise, but it explained a lot when she thought about it. She was about to thank Murphy to end the conversation when he cleared his throat and actually sounded a little nervous, a slight change in the timbre of his voice.

"Listen, can I buy you a cup of coffee? A beer, maybe?"

Vicki stared at the phone as if she could see his face in it, trying to see the meaning clearly. Then she realized she had hesitated too long. His voice rushed to fill the gap.

"You might give me some ideas about a couple of questions I have." He'd lost his nerve.

"Oh. Sure, okay. I'm headed up to Moffett to look in on a few patients, but it won't take long. You meant now, right?"

"Yeah, that's fine. I got just a couple of things to take care of here."

"Meet you at the cafeteria at Moffett? About an hour?"

"Sure, that's fine."

On the drive across town, Vicki realized that enough time had passed since she had dealt with the people in Homicide that she hardly knew anybody there now. Her old friend, Marty James, had long since retired, and Augustus Kane was now a deputy chief, ready to retire this year or next. In fact, Vicki couldn't think of anyone up there she knew well enough to just pick up the phone and find out gossip.

She felt vaguely disappointed that they could go on without her and change so much in so short a time. Wasn't it just a minute ago that she knew everybody in that department, and it seemed like it would always be like that? Now if she went up to the fourth floor of the Hall of Justice, it would be filled with strangers. Worse than that, they would all look like adolescents, all of them impossibly young.

In the Pediatric ICU, baby Charlotte was still showing some hypertonicity on the right, muscles and tendons in the arm and leg on that side just a little too tight for normal, but Vicki thought she detected some improvement. She hoped she wasn't just seeing what she wanted to see. Vicki made her notes in the chart, then looked in on a newborn with a heart defect who seemed to be recovering well from surgery. Vicki congratulated herself again for choosing pediatrics. Wounds that took weeks to heal in adults practically scarred over in front of your eyes in a newborn.

No blue uniforms in the cafeteria. She helped herself to coffee and sat down at an empty table with a chart in front of her to wait. Murphy, wearing a sport coat, got up from where he had been sitting and only then did Vicki recognize him.

"Hi! I didn't know you without the uniform."

"I'm working undercover, disguised as a police inspector." He grinned, enjoying his own humor, and dropped a large envelope on the table as he sat across from Vicki.

"Are you actually assigned to Homicide?"

"Right."

"Well, what . . . ? You were in a uniform the other day, weren't you?"

"It's a long story. I agreed to do a year in Homicide, then I get to go back to Potrero Station."

"As what? Lieutenant?"

He shook his head quickly, trying to get off the topic. "Patrolman."

"A Q2? You call that progress?"

"I do, yeah. See, the trick is to pick a career path that nobody else wants. That way it's not so competitive." He grinned again, trying to put her off. "It's a long story."

"I'll bet. You were in Psych Police, though?"

He sighed. "For one year. The department paid for a good part of my Ph.D. so I figured I owed 'em at least that much, plus the year in Homicide."

"You're a psychologist?"

"I'm a cop. I have a license as a psychologist but I'm probably going to let it lapse. It's a long story, very boring, I promise."

Vicki couldn't imagine for a moment why anybody would do that, completely forgetting her own experience.

"That's a long time in school. You must have wanted to be a psychologist pretty bad at some point."

Murphy looked at her with his head cocked, as though to emphasize his warning that this was a long, uninteresting story. "I thought I did. Then once I got close, I had to finish it up just to show I could do it."

"You got disillusioned or something?"

"You would, too."

Vicki had to grin, suddenly fascinated. The guy had to be either terribly complex or a flake. He didn't look much like a flake. Except for the gun under his jacket he looked normal, not even like a cop. There didn't seem to be that hint of a metallic edge to him that she was used to seeing in cops, no matter how much she might consider some of them to be nice guys.

"This is not my favorite topic of conversation." He was smiling, but Vicki could see that he meant it.

She stared at him, thinking, then said, "You must have to explain it all the time, huh?" Certainly that had been her experience as a forty-year-old resident.

"Uh . . . yes."

Vicki remembered that most of her fellow residents had considered her a flake at first. Thirteen years as a lawyer and then going back to the voluntary slavery of a residency at that age. Only she hadn't resented the other residents' view. It *was* pretty flaky.

"Okay." She shrugged happily. "I just think it's terribly interesting. It's something beyond normal experience, that's all." The questions she wanted to ask were the same kinds of questions that had been put to her all the time when she started her residency. He didn't see the similarity, didn't take the hint. She shrugged again, deciding to let him off the hook.

"All right, tell me about Julia Sanderson."

"Okay." He seemed relieved. "First of all, let me ask you a few things, all right?"

"Sure."

"You still the child's doctor?"

"Yes."

"Who have you been dealing with?"

"You mean instead of parents?"

"Right, who do you talk to for permission to do procedures?"

"The grandmother. The grandfather's always there, too, but she's the one making decisions."

"Has she told you anything else? Any discussion of what happened with her daughter or anything?"

"Actually . . ." Vicki sat back and thought about it. "No, she hasn't. It's been a rather strained relationship. At first, it seemed like she wanted to communicate through the nurses, but I told her I couldn't do that. Since then, she's been very cooperative."

"But no good talks?"

"No. It's all been strictly business, in a very businesslike tone of voice. Not very friendly. I actually asked her at one point if she wanted me to recommend another pediatrician for her. She said she had done her research and decided that she wanted me to be the baby's pediatrician because of the head injury, if I was willing to keep doing it. Of course, I agreed."

"Why of course?"

"Well . . ." Vicki had to think a moment how to explain it without sounding unprofessional. She distrusted the word, the concept of cool, impersonal detachment, but most of the world she moved in seemed to think it was important.

"The child is my patient, not the grandmother. My concern with the family is that she needs to have a good home she can go to later—clearly, the grandparents are good, decent people, whether they like me personally or not."

"What about the father?"

"I was going to ask you about that. He has never shown up. He wasn't even mentioned until I finally asked. Mrs. Wilkins just said I didn't need to worry about him for now. Where the hell is this guy, do you know?"

"Belgium."

"Belgium? He didn't come home for his wife's funeral?"

"He came for the funeral, then he turned right around and went back. I talked to him while he was here."

"Didn't he want to see his daughter?"

"He did. I talked to him in the hallway upstairs here. He didn't try to call you?"

"No. I never even knew he was around."

Murphy shrugged. "I guess he thought he had all the medical information he needed from his mother-in-law."

Vicki shook her head. "Weird." She looked up at the cop. "Is he weird?"

"Just chauvinistic."

"Chauvinistic? I'd call it pretty damn cold."

"Well, maybe, but I didn't think so." He looked at Vicki until he caught her eye. "He's fifty-six years old."

Vicki's mouth opened in surprise, then she caught herself and closed it. She half grinned, knowing that he had been watching for her reaction.

"Oh."

"Yeah, 'oh.'"

"Rich?"

"Very. Some kind of import-export broker for commodities. He started to explain it to me but lost me in the first or second sentence."

"That's why he's in Belgium?"

"Right, brokering some kind of deal for very large quantities of sugar from Louisiana."

"An honest-to-God sugar daddy."

Tim laughed. "Everybody up at Homicide said that."

Vicki laughed out loud, picturing Marty, then caught herself, realizing he wasn't there. She wouldn't know any of them. Her laughter died to a wistful smile, then she frowned, suddenly remembering the topic. "He's as old as her parents!"

"Yes." Tim looked down at the coffee cup in front of him for a moment, then looked up. "He's her father's partner."

Vicki squirmed in her chair, scowling now. "This is too weird."

"It gets better."

"Oh, no."

"They were married about eight months."

Vicki's scowl deepened as she thought that over. "Now, let's see. The respectable little girl gets herself in trouble. She won't or can't name the father and won't or can't get an abortion, so instead they sell her to the highest bidder, huh?"

Murphy looked at her with a kind expression. Vicki thought his eyes looked kind, not like a police officer at all. More like a psychologist. His voice even sounded kind.

"It may not have been that bad."

"You think she had a torrid love affair with her father's partner and they had to get married?"

He shrugged, smiling a little now. "You never know. Everybody could have been conspiring to accommodate the baby, give her a name and an explanation of who her daddy was when she's old enough to need to know."

Vicki was immediately remorseful. "I didn't think about that. Boy, I am getting cynical. Is that what they told you?"

"No, I didn't ask."

"Well, you met him. Does it seem likely to you?"

He shrugged. "Seems as likely as the other idea." He paused, looking at her again. "There's more."

"More?"

"Two years ago Julia Wilkins was a serious suicide risk. She was twenty years old and—"

"I thought she looked young."

"Young, but bright. She was a junior at Cal. Anyway, she was put on a 5150 hold at Presbyterian for awhile."

"As a danger to herself?"

"Right. Before my time, but that was why Psych Police had an interest in her, wanted to follow up when this child abuse business was reported."

Vicki nodded. "Sure, I see. That's why you came by to talk to me yourself, instead of just getting the Social Services file."

"Right. I was between assignments, waiting for my slot to open in Homicide, when they called me and asked me to go see her."

"Because they were short?"

"They're always shorthanded."

Vicki nodded. "Sure, okay. So did you already know about the heroin?"

"No, in fact, I didn't. Her old file had her on speed."

"Amphetamines?"

"Yeah." He shrugged. "Maybe they had it wrong, then." Vicki saw him look away.

There was a young Hispanic woman several tables over, trying to supervise two young children, one about five, the other younger, maybe three. The five-year-old girl, a child with beautiful, long black hair, was making noise, teasing her little brother by hiding her face behind a chair and then popping up with her tongue out. Both children shrieked with laughter. Vicki smiled, used to families in the cafeteria, usually waiting while adults visited upstairs.

When she glanced back at Tim, he was staring at the children. It wasn't exactly the distracted stare of looking at whatever was making noise, and he wasn't amused. He seemed to be incongruously disturbed. It wasn't as if he were angry at the children's normal raucous behavior, it was as if seeing them, just looking at that little girl, had upset him. He couldn't seem to look away.

Vicki tried to bring him back to the conversation. "You think your old department made a mistake?"

For a moment he didn't respond. He stared, his mouth partly open as though he had forgotten Vicki entirely. Then, abruptly, he seemed to remember where he was, snapped his mouth shut, and looked back at her.

"Sorry. You said something?"

"Did they make a mistake about what drug she was using?"

"Yeah, could be."

There was something about the way he came back to the conversation—maybe the casual way he had assumed that his old department had made a mistake—that didn't seem quite right.

No, it was something about that child that bothered him. She watched his eyes being drawn, almost involuntarily, back to the little girl. He had to make an effort not to stare at her. He seemed so uncomfortable that Vicki finally stood up.

"Shall we take a walk? It'll be less noisy in the hallway."

He actually seemed relieved. "Yeah, let's walk."

As they took their time, strolling idly toward the doctors' lounge, Vicki glanced at him. He seemed to have relaxed again.

"Did you talk to Julia after the arrest?"

"Quite a bit. I spent about an hour with her." She could see him almost transparently thinking about it, troubled again. When he spoke his voice was quiet, thoughtful.

"I did not think she was suicidal. They talked to her up at Presbyterian and they didn't think she was, either." Murphy took a deep breath and let it out. His eyes were a pale, faded looking blue, the sclerae a little red-tinged as if he were tired. Vicki realized she wasn't the only one feeling guilty over this case.

"If you ever figure out a way to accurately predict human behavior, I want in on it."

He heard her but he wouldn't let the conversation run to tired excuses. Instead, he said, "I wonder if you could help me with something?"

Vicki looked up at him. "Sure, if I can."

"I wonder if you could look at the newborn chart on your patient and tell me if you think she could have been addicted when she was born and they just missed it."

"Missed the diagnosis?"

"Right."

Vicki shrugged. "All right. She's my patient, I can order her chart. Where was she born?"

"Here, at Moffett."

"That makes it easy, then. I've already got it, just never read through that part. Sure, I'll be glad to take a look. What's the point?"

"If Julia had a long-standing addiction, one that she couldn't break, it makes suicide more likely."

Vicki took a couple of steps and then looked at him again. "Why is there still an investigation going on? Hasn't the coroner made up his mind?"

"I don't know. Probably. There won't be a report from him until he gets one from me, and I want to be a little more sure."

"What's to be sure about? You got a note, right?"

He stopped walking and leaned forward, lowering his voice. "An unsigned note that doesn't specifically say she's about to kill herself."

Vicki turned and continued to look up at him. "Any other problems with it? Handwriting?"

"No, it's her handwriting, all right."

"Let me see if there's anybody in the lounge." She opened a door and found the room empty.

"We can sit in here and talk." She took a chair across from him at a small table.

"So? What's the question, if she left a note?"

"It was an unusual method for killing herself."

"You mean because it was a woman, using a gun?"

"Well, there's that, but the wound itself was . . . odd." He seemed to be reluctant to describe it.

"In what way? Go ahead, I was an ADA, remember?"

"She shot herself through the mouth."

"The most effective way."

"But her mouth was closed."

Vicki looked puzzled. "Closed?"

"Entrance wound in her upper lip, took out her front teeth, palate, brain stem."

Now Vicki leaned forward, keeping her voice low, too. "Yuck!"

"That a technical medical term?"

"It's the right one. Yuck!"

"And it wasn't in contact."

"What wasn't?"

"The muzzle of the gun. If the muzzle is held against the flesh, when it's fired it leaves a distinct ring of powder residue concentrated around the edge of the hole like a stencil. This one had powder residue sprayed all around her mouth. The gun was at least several inches, maybe a foot away from her face when it fired."

Vicki was frowning, concentrating, picturing the act. It didn't make sense. "How about on her hand?" If Julia fired the gun, it should have left traces of residue on her hand.

"Residue on both hands. But on the palmar surfaces only. It was concentrated on the radial side—thumbs and forefingers."

Vicki held her hands up in front of her, curled, trying to picture how she might hold a gun pointed at herself, thumbs on the trigger. She looked doubtful. "Well, maybe like this."

"Or else like . . ." Murphy held both hands up, palms out as though trying to ward off a blow to his face. There was plenty of space to shoot between the hands, through the gap between the outstretched thumbs and forefingers.

Vicki looked down at her own hands, curled around an imaginary gun, tried to picture how the traces of powder would be sprayed out of the chamber onto the hands. "Nothing on the backs of the hands, the thumbs, maybe?"

"Nothing. The residue was only on the palm side."

"Is it possible it could have been wiped off in transit?"

"Sure. Anything's possible, but it doesn't seem very likely. The coroner's office is pretty good about that kind of thing."

Vicki kept looking at her hands. She opened them and turned them to face out, turned them over again to look at the palmar surfaces, thinking about it. Suddenly, Vicki realized what she was doing. She was surprised. No, she thought. Not really surprised. All the time that had passed was gone in a flash. She was a prosecutor trying to fit the pieces of evidence together and she recognized it, realized she was doing it as though it was normal. She knew she wasn't really surprised. It was part of who she was. She looked up at Murphy. He was watching her with that kind expression, a waiting, patient look, calm, letting her think about it and knowing in advance what she would think about it.

"Why are you telling me this?" She knew he wanted something but couldn't think what, at first. Then she knew, even before he said it, spoke the obvious.

"You're going to be in contact with this family for a while. I thought you ought to know about the rest of it, that's all."

She started to smile but stopped it. She knew it wasn't going to be a pleasant smile and she didn't want to overreact. "You want me to question these people?"

He shook his head. "No." He looked at her, and she was aware that he was watching her expression as he spoke. "I just wanted you to know."

"But you want me to tell you if I find out anything from them, right?"

He shrugged, the barest movement of his head and shoulders to pass off the suggestion without denying it outright. "Use your own judgment about that. There may not be anything at all. They may not know anything else to tell."

Vicki stared at him, waiting for him to go on. "But . . . ?"

"Well, yes. There's always the chance. I think we could use a few more facts than we have here." He was studying her, his mild, friendly eyes watching her, and she was self-consciously aware of him watching. She wondered if too much time in Homicide would change that open expression into something less naïve, more like the flat, neutral face she usually saw on homicide inspectors, who seemed to wear a kind of psychic metal shield behind the neutral expression like street cops wore their body armor under their shirts. Right now, this guy seemed too open, too transparent for a cop. When he spoke again, she knew it was in response to what he was seeing in her face.

"I'm not going to quiz you on what they say to you or talk to you about. That's privileged and probably not any of my business." He hesitated, and Vicki knew that he was reading her reaction as though it were written out for him. He was good. "I just thought it was best, overall, if you knew about this. Does that make sense?"

Vicki looked down at her hands, turned them over, looking at the surfaces. She stared at her hands but she was thinking about the older man she hadn't met, the husband who was old enough to be Julia's father's partner. She thought of the entrance wound, the spread of the powder residue, and barely kept herself from actually picturing the minute burns on Julia's face, thinking involuntarily of that face behind hands thrown up in front of it in a reflexive gesture of self-protection, seeing the gun pointed between the hands in the instant before that face was mutilated and that consciousness obliterated.

"Yeah."

Vicki sighed. He had said she was still "one of ours." She supposed she must be.

"I guess that makes sense."

Nine

Cynthia Wilkins no longer seemed quite so formidable. Vicki had found herself thinking about the older woman a lot. Vicki knew what it was like to lose a child, but not like this. She had an unexpressed empathy for her—for any mother who lost a child—but she thought she couldn't imagine it entirely, what it would be like to lose a child who was an adult, a child who should have been old enough to have been safe from those dangers of illness and accident that seem so threatening to children.

But this particular adult child had been very badly flawed. There were the drugs, an old story these days, but one that would be new to them, to these parents who had to live with it now, personally. Then on top of the drugs there was the new allegation that the daughter had done violence to the granddaughter. Vicki could not imagine the double horror of the injury to the little baby who should have been a source of nothing but pure joy, and the awful knowledge of the guilt and then the death of the daughter, who should have been the source of such pride. So what would be worse? What could be? Hope died, if it ever did, only after great struggle.

In the two or three days immediately following her daughter's suicide, Cynthia Wilkins had stubbornly spent her time at the hospital, watching mostly through the window while others cared for her granddaughter. Vicki had heard from the nurses that a nonreligious memorial service had been held for Julia and that Cynthia was back at the hospital in her mourning suit immediately after the service. She hadn't even gone home to change.

Vicki had seen her and spoken to her the next day. Cynthia had been so stricken with tragedy that she almost seemed to forget her grievance against Vicki, but she had not dropped her shield, her iron-hard determination not to give in. She waited and watched.

She still dressed well, as if incapable of leaving her home without proper grooming and meticulous attention to her appearance. If Vicki watched her face long enough, she saw the stamp of Cynthia Wilkins's personal grief, worn hidden like a second face that would slip from behind the shield of self-control and betray her if she wasn't on guard. In those first few days she was frequently not on guard. But she wouldn't go home and stay there, either.

Vicki held to her resolution to regain some "professional" distance from this patient. She slept until 7:00 A.M., tired enough that it was surprisingly easy. When she looked at the clock she immediately sat up, rubbed her face, and called Moffett. No seizures, no twitching. The change in medication had gone smoothly and Dr. Carter would be there shortly to look at their mutual charge.

Vicki told the nurse to call her pager number instead of the clinic if there was any change. Okay, that would have to do. Period.

She looked at the mass of data in the folder for her article and went to work. She would just have to skip running errands this week and get the damn thing out. By noon she was caught up in it, making excellent progress, and thought she ought to be able to finish by early evening.

At three o'clock her pager went off. Moffett. Punch the numbers. Sound calm.

"This is Dr. Shea. Somebody paged me?"

"Guess what!"

The nurse's voice was as excited as a schoolgirl's. Vicki stood up. "What is it?"

"Your patient is feeding!"

"My . . . which . . . ?"

"The Sanderson baby!"

Vicki blew her deadline.

She came out of the elevator at Moffett almost running, barely managing to restrain herself to a fast walk. Cynthia Wilkins was in the hallway, both hands on the glass window to the ICU. Vicki paused next to her and looked in. A nurse was holding a bottle for the baby, and the baby's eyes were open, watching the nurse's face and suckling like there was no tomorrow.

Vicki glanced up, and Cynthia's face was rigid with attention, eyes wide, mouth a straight line. Vicki looked back at the baby and her vision blurred in a wash of tears that she didn't know was coming. She tried to be discreet as she wiped at her eyes but Cynthia noticed and looked straight at her. Then, suddenly, tears poured from her eyes, too, and her mouth twisted in an agonizing, vain attempt at control.

Why now? Vicki wanted to shout at her. It's your granddaughter, it's all right to cry, you don't have to be stoic! But at the same time Vicki realized she was doing it, too. Her face was hot with the effort, the struggle to keep from breaking down completely. She wiped her cheeks with the flats of both hands and laughed, an odd squeaking noise, her face hot in embarrassment.

Cynthia Wilkins's mouth twisted with a tortured smile, her body rigid as she struggled for breath. Then she whispered, almost as though she were afraid to say it out loud, the whispered words throaty and choked.

"Thank you, Vicki Shea."

Over the next week Vicki forced herself to keep to a normal schedule, making rounds at Moffett morning and night before and after her rounds at Gunnison. Charlotte Sanderson improved steadily until on the following Wednesday, two weeks after the injury, Vicki allowed the transfer back to the hospital closer to home, to take place the next day.

The problem with a day off in the middle of the week was that it was still the middle of the week. The business of normal people went on and they expected you to have the same normal schedule. In consequence, Vicki discovered that she sometimes did not get a day off at all, and at other times only a part of one. This time, she left her apartment at midmorning to go to Gunnison without being called.

The baby had been transferred and installed in her new room in Pediatrics. She was in with the newborns where she could be watched closely but without the obsessive zeal of the ICU at Moffett. Now, Vicki thought, she needed the active participation of the family.

When Vicki had talked to her about the transfer to Gunnison, she had seen Cynthia Wilkins' face relax, almost a smile tugging at the corners of her mouth, quickly controlled. Vicki realized she would be grateful to leave the haunted halls of Moffett. The woman had spent probably the worst moments of her life standing there in the hallway, looking helplessly through windows, isolated with her ghosts, barred from the actual work of caring for the baby. Yes, of course she would be glad never to set foot in there again.

On Thursday morning Vicki walked briskly into the nursery at Gunnison and saw Cynthia sitting next to the baby's crib. Her husband's arm was across her shoulders but he moved it when Vicki came in, as though it were a breach of decorum to be caught in an attitude of affectionate, mutual support. Always the excessive decorum. He stood and grinned at Vicki, his eyes dancing.

Cynthia was holding the baby, looking up at Vicki. "I thought this was your day off." As it had been since the baby came out of the coma, her greeting was friendly to the point of affection.

Vicki pulled a visitor's chair over and sat down, smiling. "It is, technically. I had some stuff to do up here, though, so I wanted to check on her. How's she seem today?"

They both stared at the child, concentrating their attention on her. The right hand was fisted and drawn in toward the shoulder. The toes on the right side curled downward.

Vicki reached for the little fist. "Is she using her right hand?" As if in response to the question, the fist opened and grasped Vicki's finger, but then the left hand came across as the baby took Vicki's finger, and pulled it toward her mouth while her right hand curled back into a fist.

"Let me show you something." Vicki worked her finger free and took up the baby's right hand again. She pulled on it and met resistance. "See how that's a little tighter than the other arm?"

Cynthia took the hand from her and pulled gently, then tried the other hand. "I think so . . ."

"It's subtle. That's a good thing that it's subtle. But you can see how she wants to hold it all curled up like that, right?"

"I noticed that, but she does use it. Is it abnormal?"

"Well . . ." Vicki cocked her head and shrugged as she answered, trying to soften her words. "It's a little spastic. Just a little. You can see the same thing in the way she curls her toes on that side, see?"

"Oh. Yes, now I can see it."

"Okay, here's what we need to do." Vicki went through a routine of instructions on how to do passive range-of-motion and stretching exercises. She noticed that the grandfather got in on this part, too, eagerly asking questions and reaching in to try his own hand at it. The two of them instructed each other, correcting each other easily, arguing naturally and earnestly, learning this together. They seemed eager to have something active that they could do to help.

Vicki realized that she felt relaxed and comfortable with these people. After Charlotte came out of the coma it was as though there had never been an atmosphere of tension between them. She thought it was sweet, seeing them in a personal moment as she walked in the door, and she wished they weren't so inhibited about it, so stuck on appearances.

As the baby's doctor, she needed to clear away the uncertainty of who she was supposed to be dealing with. Although Social Services could tell her who technically had custody, this family had to tell her who was really going to be in charge. Vicki was certain now that this baby had brain damage, but it would be a long, tedious, maybe heartbreaking few years before they could try to predict how much it was going to affect her later in life. Damage to the part of her brain that controlled motor responses did not mean she would have any cognitive deficit, but if she did, then how they handled the early training could be important. Vicki knew she needed to begin dealing with the long-term, and for that she had to ask.

"I still haven't met Mr. Sanderson."

The Wilkinses looked at her with the same blank expression, as though they didn't have any idea who she was talking about.

"You know, the father?"

"Oh, Frank!" Jack Wilkins looked sheepish and amused at their momentary lack of comprehension. "Well, sure, of course."

Cynthia was smoother in covering it. "We're very close to Frank. We knew him for many years before he and Julia got together."

Vicki nodded and smiled, joining in their laughter at not remembering who she was talking about, but she was more than a little puzzled that they obviously had not expected her to ask.

Jack was still grinning. "Frank is actually my partner."

Vicki smiled with them, trying to be agreeable. "Yeah, somebody told me that."

"Really?" Cynthia Wilkins was suddenly not laughing. Then she seemed to catch herself and shook her head, smiling again, as though she had inadvertently said something rude.

"I mean, what did they say?"

She really did want to know. She was being friendly, but she was serious about the question, as though someone had been discussing matters that were supposed to be private. Again, Vicki thought the response was a little odd. Were these people really that private?

Vicki did not want to admit that she had talked to the cops or that they had talked to her. "I don't remember who said it. Probably one of the nurses. I guess he came up to Moffett? I was surprised I hadn't heard from him and somebody said he was your husband's partner." They were watching her. "I don't really remember how I heard it, but something like that."

They seemed to accept it. This time Jack spoke, as though on business matters he was allowed to say something.

"We've got Frank in Europe a good bit of the time, now. No way to avoid it, really, or we would have just brought him home for good when all this happened. He's the one with all the languages."

Cynthia broke in as though she had been quiet for as long as she could stand it. "Charlotte's going to be living with us. Frank's not really . . . well, he's not really equipped to take care of a baby even if he were home all the time. We've already talked to him about it and he's in complete agreement. Seemed relieved, actually."

Vicki realized that she had wanted to hear that. She'd been assuming that was the way things were going to be but she was glad to hear it confirmed. She assumed that somebody in Social Services would talk to Frank separately and make sure there wouldn't be a problem with it, but never having met the guy, Vicki found it easy to assume that some unknown man would not be able to take care of a small baby by himself.

Ten

As Vicki left the hospital she heard a car horn honk. She glanced up and saw a nurse waving at her from her open window as she drove by. Vicki grinned and waved back. All was right with the world. She crossed the street mid-block and exchanged greetings with two more nurses and another doctor before she got to her car. She was in a great mood, beginning to think about having the rest of the day off with nothing to do after she got the laundry and picked up some groceries.

Her pager went off. Murphy. Oh yeah, she was supposed to call him or something after she looked at the newborn chart.

She returned the call from her cell phone, sitting in her Volvo in the garage.

He sounded cheerful. "You got time for lunch?"

She thought about laundry, groceries. She was suddenly starved. "Sure."

They met at a restaurant in the Marina that Vicki suggested. She saw his eyes as they looked at the menu and knew she would be picking up this one. This guy may have chosen a career path he liked but it wasn't because of the money.

"I didn't forget to look at the newborn chart," she told him. "I just forgot to call you about it."

"Anything there?"

"No, I don't think so. She seemed to cry a lot, but a lot of babies do that. There are other things, jitteriness, hypersensitivity, things that are hard to miss. None of those things are charted. Besides, she gained weight in the nursery. Usually they lose a little the first couple of days of life. If she was sick she almost certainly would have."

"Could the mother have been addicted and not the baby?"

"I don't think so, on an opiate. It crosses the placental barrier pretty freely."

He stared at her and thought. "Interesting."

"If you want my opinion . . ."

He nodded. "Sure."

"It doesn't prove anything one way or the other. I've seen plenty of mothers quit smoking as soon as they knew they were pregnant and go right back to it after delivery. Tobacco's not quite as addictive as heroin, but close."

Murphy shrugged and looked out the window, lost in thought for a moment. He was better looking than she remembered. His blond hair was too short but his eyes were a nice blue, pale, almost the color of sun-bleached denim. He leaned forward, his elbows on the table and the fabric of the inexpensive dress shirt he was wearing stretched taut over his shoulders. No missing the fact that he was buff, overall in good shape, and yet he didn't seem particularly aware of it.

As she watched him, Vicki realized that she had been thinking about him off and on since their last conversation. Several times she had wanted to call him after she looked at the newborn chart, but there was always something else to occupy her and she hadn't done it. Now she realized that she had put it off, maybe on purpose, as though not sure if she wanted to simply give him a report over the phone.

She realized she had been making excuses. She was interested in him, period. She didn't even know if he was married. As though the thought had never occurred to her, she wondered if she were considering him a candidate. . . . No way. He was at least five, maybe seven or eight years younger than she was, and she wasn't going to let herself start thinking of him as even a possible—she realized they were staring at each other. *Say something.*

"Did you turn in your report to the coroner?"

He nodded. "Had to. I couldn't see any more leads . . . out of ideas."

"So he decided it was a suicide?"

"Yes, obviously."

"But you're not happy with it? Really, Tim. Don't you think she did it?" Vicki realized as she was asking the question that she wanted to believe that it was a suicide. She wanted to believe it because that would make her original judgment right, that the mother was drowning in guilt because she was a drug addict, and had lost control and battered her own child.

"I guess . . ." Vicki could see him struggling, trying to articulate the inexpressible, the vague sense that something didn't quite fit. She was familiar with the feeling, had felt it herself during criminal investigations. Even when there was a confession, there frequently seemed to be something that didn't quite add up, that didn't quite fit. She had decided a long time ago that it was because you were trying to deal with human behavior and human behavior frequently defied logical analysis.

Murphy's voice sounded tentative. "I guess I don't like the way she did it, the physical act seems . . . unlikely is the only way I can put it. The physical evidence of the wound, the powder residue, is more consistent with somebody shooting her."

"What about the heroin, though?"

"See, to my mind that works against the suicide theory." When he saw that Vicki didn't get it, he looked out the window again, thinking of how to explain.

"I worked Narcotics for a while, years ago. What addicts have told me is that the high is this super-euphoric feeling that's supposed to be better than anything else, better than sex. This one woman told me that if she had to be stranded on a desert island, as long as she had enough heroin she'd be happy. Not just satisfied but truly happy. It's not like coke or speed or even booze, where you might get high and all hyper and nasty—with heroin, they say it's pure euphoria. People commit suicide when they're addicted and can't get it, not when they've just taken a big hit. And she had just taken a big hit."

"It's not impossible. A little self-anesthesia maybe, when she was already determined to do it in advance."

"You're right, not impossible. Just . . . it just seems unlikely to me."

He suddenly turned and looked directly at her. "Didn't you say yourself that you didn't believe her when she said nobody else was there when the baby was injured?"

Vicki looked at him and blinked, as though startled. "I did?"

"I thought you did. Something about when you and Penney Alvarez interviewed her. She said she was alone and you didn't believe it."

Vicki had to sit back and give it some thought, staring at him, suddenly remembering. "I did, didn't I." It was not a question. "I'd forgotten that." She concentrated. "Do we know for sure that the husband was in Europe?"

He quickly nodded his head. "Oh yeah. Passport checks out, several telephone calls that night between the Wilkinses' phone and Antwerp."

"Antwerp?"

"In Belgium."

"Oh. What about her friends? Talk to any of them?"

"I would if I could identify any. Her parents didn't know the names of any close buddies."

"They don't know her friends?"

"That's what they say—"

"The parents live right in the same town and they don't know who their daughter's friends are? They never met any of them?"

"They say she was shy, didn't make friends very easily. Her husband wasn't any help either."

Vicki stared, open-mouthed. Then she plunged in. "Wait a minute. You believed this?"

"You don't?"

"No. Not if we're talking about the same woman."

"You got to know her?"

Vicki saw his point and hesitated. "Well, not really."

"But you had a different impression?"

"Well, sure. I guess that's all it is, but this was not some retiring little wallflower."

"How do you know?"

She had to stop and think about that question, too. "How do I know? I don't know—her coat? Her shoes? It just doesn't fit."

"Doesn't fit?"

"I don't mean her clothes didn't fit. How do you explain this to a man?"

"Try."

"Somebody who doesn't have any friends at all, who doesn't have anybody to confide in or talk to, just doesn't dress like that. It's not just clothes—"

"How she presents herself?"

"Exactly. If she was that shy, that afraid of human contact, she wouldn't wear that coat."

"Her coat was stylish? I don't—"

"Okay, forget the coat. Tim, for a young woman that age, just out of school, even with a new baby . . . for a young woman like that to not have any friends at all would be so unusual that it would just leap out at you. It would be so rare—I don't mean it's rare. It's probably not that rare, but it's the kind of thing you would see in a minute. You'd have to."

"What if she was just close to her family?"

"Especially if she was close to her family. You're the psychologist here."

Tim seemed to think that over. A slow, embarrassed grin started to turn up his mouth. "Okay, you're right. You got me. I must not have thought that through." He looked away from her, stared out the window a minute, and then looked back at her. His voice was almost casual. "So she probably had friends, but her parents and her husband didn't know them. Maybe they didn't want to know them. Maybe they did know but didn't want to admit who they were."

Vicki thought about what he was saying. "Not really likely, but possible."

"Yes, possible. Especially if they didn't approve, huh? A heroin addict?"

Vicki stared. She wondered for a moment if maybe he had thought this through, if he had been prodding her, poking at her, pretending ignorance to get her reaction, to see if she would confirm what he was already thinking. It was just the beginning of a thought, a suspicion, and then she lost it, dismissed it in the course of the discussion to be brought out later, puzzled over. She brought her attention back to the subject that had started this line of thinking. It was falling into a pattern. She watched his face closely as she spoke.

"So, if she had friends they didn't want to talk about . . . what?" She had the eerie feeling that he had actually been leading her somewhere with this.

"Look at it like this, okay? Bear with me, Vicki, see if this doesn't make as much sense as a suicide. There's a boyfriend or a heroin dealer at her house, somebody that even she doesn't want to admit to. He's the one that loses control when the baby's crying and commits the assault. He's afraid she'll lose her nerve and identify him so he kills her. He uses her husband's gun, shoots her at close range while she's high, right after he's helped her to shoot up . . ."

"Her husband's gun?"

"Yeah. Got it for her protection because he's gone all the time. Another one with that brilliant idea."

"Okay, go on."

"He comes up with the gun, surprises her. She's just in the act of throwing her hands up instinctively to shield her face when he pulls the trigger, shoots her in the face, spraying powder on her face and the palms of her hands only. He wipes the gun down thoroughly, then puts it in her hand to get her fingerprints on it and leaves it on the bed where it would have fallen if she'd done it herself."

"How was she dressed?"

"She wasn't."

"She was naked?"

"Right."

Vicki had not expected that answer. She had to think about it for a moment. "Had she had sex?"

"Not recently."

"That's . . . don't you think that's odd?"

He looked away and shook his head. "I'm afraid the experts on suicide say it's typical."

"Oh. People get naked to kill themselves?"

"Women do. It's not unusual, anyway. I don't think it definitely proves anything one way or the other."

"But there was a note."

"I don't know about the note. Somebody could have made her write that. Maybe she was just starting to write a note . . . I don't know. But see? Murder still fits all the physical evidence, and fits it better than a suicide."

"What about the note?"

"Yeah, well, I guess I'd be more convinced about the note if she'd said more or signed it or something."

"Did you explain this to the coroner?"

"Sure."

"And?"

"You got the weapon, a note, lots of motive. What's to investigate?"

"He's got a point."

"Do you think he has?"

Vicki sat back and stared, trying to make herself believe it. But, of course, that was not what this man wanted to hear. He was a psychologist, and in a sense, he had released this "patient" and she had gone home to commit suicide. Of course he didn't want to believe it if there was any possibility of another explanation. And there was room for doubt with the powder residue, the odd way that she did it.

"I don't know. I think so." She focused on Tim's face. When she was a prosecutor she was used to inspectors telling her the way it was, whether she agreed or not. This guy honestly wanted to know what she thought. He was staring at her hard, forcing her to ask herself what she deep down believed was true about all of this. She realized that she hadn't really wanted to think that hard about it, and that she didn't want to think that hard about it now. "I really don't know."

He looked away, seemed to relax a little, almost as though he were letting her off the hook. His next question was transparently casual.

"The Wilkinses say anything?"

Vicki shook her head. She'd expected him to ask about that and she'd already given it some thought. "Not a thing. We're getting along much better but they still seem very private. They don't talk about themselves or their situation. I had to ask about the father."

"What did they say?"

"Just that it was important to their business to have him in Europe and that he agreed that the baby would live with them."

"Nothing else?"

"No, they didn't volunteer anything and, frankly, I didn't really quiz them about it."

"What do you mean, they seem private?"

"Oh, nothing that unusual. They just seem to keep their business to themselves, don't seem to want to talk about their own situation. For instance, they've never said a thing to me about how the baby's injury occurred or why I turned in their daughter to the police. Mrs. Wilkins was really pissed about it at first, but she never asked me a thing about it."

"Maybe she didn't have to."

Vicki looked at him across the table. "What does that mean?"

"She didn't ask because she already knew the answer."

"You mean she might have had a reason to believe that her daughter might batter her own baby?"

"I'm not sure what I mean, but, yeah, something like that—her daughter or somebody else. Mrs. Wilkins might have already known who did it and she wasn't particularly surprised."

"They were so distraught, though. You should have seen how upset they were!"

"Doesn't mean they didn't see it coming."

"Tim, that doesn't make any sense. Why would they hide it if they knew who did it and it wasn't their own daughter?"

"I don't know. I'm probably wrong about that. I upset you, I'm sorry."

"I'm not upset."

"Okay." He gave it about a beat. "Can we talk about something else?"

She realized that he was right, she had been getting defensive on behalf of her patient's grandparents, whom she had just been feeling more comfortable with. She *had* been upset. She smiled, a little embarrassed at getting caught. "Okay, let's talk about something else."

"Is there any chance that you . . . ? Are you originally from San Francisco?"

"Los Angeles."

"Well . . . Shea isn't that unusual a name but it's not as common as Murphy. Any chance you know somebody named Cody Shea?"

Vicki could feel her jaw drop in surprise. "You know Cody? That's my brother's name!"

"Used to know him, if it's the same guy. Long time ago. Seventeen, eighteen years ago, maybe."

"How in the world . . . ?"

"The Cody Shea I knew was a rodeo bronc rider. Damn good one."

"That's him! You were in the rodeo?"

"I said it was a long time ago. What's he doing now?"

"He's a cop, too. In Ventura."

"No kidding!" Murphy laughed out loud, an easy, fond laugh. "I guess that makes sense. Wasn't your dad a—?"

"LAPD, yes."

"Oh, yeah, I remember."

"Cody is married and has . . ." She held up one hand, all fingers extended. "Five kids. Five!"

Murphy laughed again, grinning ear to ear, blushing as though maybe a little embarrassed. What was there to be embarrassed about? "That doesn't surprise me. He used to hang around with this big girl . . . I want to say Elizabeth or something?"

"That's her, Beth. He married her and had four boys and a girl."

Murphy kept grinning. "That's good to hear."

"So, you were in the rodeo? I'll tell him I met you."

Murphy waved a hand as though to dismiss the idea. "He probably wouldn't even remember me. I just followed the circuit a couple of years. He was a real pro, a real cowboy. I was just a wanna-be kid."

Vicki sat back, relaxed for the first time at this lunch. She could picture him as a wanna-be kid at a rodeo, like so many of the contestants, wide blue eyes, open grin under a new cowboy hat, wearing a new shirt he couldn't afford. It was an endearing picture. Okay, she decided. She liked him.

"Five?"

"Five. His oldest is in high school. Straight As. He scored 1600 on the SATs."

"Proud aunt talking here?"

Vicki laughed. "You betcha!"

"You have kids?"

Vicki hesitated. "No, I don't have any of my own. You?" She wondered if she would get around to telling him about Mary.

"No. Never married. You?"

"Divorced a long time ago." She thought about it but she was so relaxed she went ahead and kept talking as though she had known this man for years. "I guess that's one of the reasons I got so attached to Charlotte. If I was married and had children of my own, I probably wouldn't keep doing that."

"I thought you spent a lot of time up there with her."

"Yeah, I know. One of the other doctors even commented on it. I should have better professional detachment, but it's hard. It's been really hard to give it up, too. She'll be going home and I'll probably see her twice a year or something." She looked up, saw him watching her thoughtfully, discreetly not saying anything. "I'm being silly."

He smiled, shook his head, and looked away. Then he looked at her again. "You're being very decent."

She smiled at him and slumped back in her chair. "That a psychological diagnosis?"

"You're being perfect."

Eleven

"What's the name? Tim Murphy?" Cody's voice sounded distant on the telephone. She could tell from the sound of it no bells were ringing right away.

"Blond, blue eyes? He asked about you, said he knew you from the rodeo?"

Bong. She could hear the change in her brother's intake of breath. "Oh, shit! That Tim Murphy! How'd you meet that crazy son of a bitch!"

"He's a cop in San Francisco."

"Tim Murphy?"

"Yeah—"

"He became a cop? Lord help us! The man's totally crazy!"

Vicki could feel herself becoming disappointed. She'd hoped they had been friends. "Why do you say that?"

"Bull rider. They're all crazy."

"Oh, is that all?"

"No, he was crazy, even for a bull rider."

"Well, Cody, people do grow up." She realized she had hoped for a much better recommendation than what she was hearing.

"That's true, most people do, but it'd surprise the hell out of me if you said he grew up. He was one wild son of a bitch. What's he in, Narcotics? S.W.A.T. team?"

"He was in Narcotics. He's working Homicide now."

"He won't stay there. Too much of a desk job."

Vicki felt herself growing irritated. "How can you say that? Hasn't it been seventeen or eighteen years since you even saw him?"

"Uh-oh." He paused and Vicki knew she'd given herself away. When he spoke again his voice was quieter. "You seeing this guy?"

Too quick, she answered, "No. I just met him a couple of weeks ago."

"Oh, okay." He seemed to take her at her word. He sounded relieved.

"All right, Cody, you can't leave it at that. What's the story?"

"You remember when I lost my front teeth and got my nose broke?"

"Yeah, the horse kicked you?"

"He was the horse."

Vicki sat there a moment, staring into space, completely silenced. Her opinion of Tim Murphy had just plummeted about a mile. "He hit you?"

"Well, to be fair, I hit him first."

Involuntarily, Vicki rolled her eyes, remembering those days. "You hit him? You beat him up?"

"You kidding? He knocked out my teeth and broke my nose. That was the end of that fight."

Vicki was shaking her head. Instinctively, she was on her brother's side, angry at Tim Murphy in retrospect for whatever he had done to set Cody off in the first place. He must have said something crude about Beth or done something equally terrible. She was a little angry with herself, too, for actually liking the thug just a few minutes ago. "I had no idea he was like that. Why did you hit him?"

"He took my hat. Lifted it off my head in a bar. Just clowning around, but he was a bull rider and it irritated me, so I decked him. He sure got up quick, though."

"Oh, good lord, Cody!"

"Jesus, Vicki, that was . . . I must have been about twenty-two or

-three years old. He couldn't have been much older than nineteen or twenty. But he was considerably bigger than me."

"Cody, that is about the silliest—"

"Now, big sister. That was a helluva long time ago. Did he really ask about me?"

"That is one of the stupidest things I've ever heard!"

"Well, don't get mad, now. It's a little late, don't you think? What's all the fuss about? Did he ask you out or something?"

Vicki heard herself trying to backtrack. "No, nothing like that. He was asking me some questions about the mother of one of my patients and asked if I might know you. He said he didn't think you'd remember him."

"Hah! That's a good one. I saw that son of a bitch whip three guys all at once in Tuscon. That one wasn't his fault, though."

"That's all, Cody. I just asked because I thought you'd been friends."

"Well, we were, kinda. After that thing in Tuscon everybody liked him better."

"Great. Because he beat up three guys at once?"

"No, because he was standing up for somebody else that—"

"Okay, that's all."

"You think it's all a lot of macho bullshit." She could hear a familiar, gentle laughter in his voice. Patronizing.

"It *is* a lot of macho bullshit."

"Vicki, it was nearly twenty years ago. He might have turned out all right. I did, don't you think?"

"Cody . . . yes, Cody, you turned out great." She thought of his swarm of children, Beth with the huge generous heart. Both of them so patient, and the way they would reach out unconsciously to touch each other amid the noise and the turmoil that would drive other people crazy in a minute. "You really did."

"So, when you coming home?"

"I don't know. How's Dad? Seen him lately?"

"Oh, we get over to the ranch about once a month. Kids bug me to go all the time, except Wes. He's old enough that he just wants to hang out with his friends when he's not studying."

"How's Dad?"

"Well . . ." Vicki felt a tightening in her chest at the hesitation. She knew the answer but she'd hoped for something better. "He's doing all right."

"Just all right?"

"He's slowing down some. I wish I could get him to stay off the three-year-olds."

"He get thrown again?"

"A couple of months ago. Didn't break anything, but you could see he was stiff and sore a long time afterward."

"Did he see a doctor?"

"You kidding?"

"Well, how does he know he didn't break something? Oh, never mind, I'm coming down."

"Oh, Vicki, it's not exactly an emergency. He seems all right now."

"Why didn't you call me?"

"I didn't know it myself until a week after he fell. He was getting around okay then."

"Cody, what you and Dad call 'getting around okay' would mean a stay in the ICU for a sane person."

"You know what the problem with doctors is?"

"I've heard it, Cody."

"You're all like a guy walking around with a hammer. Everything looks like a nail."

"Well, I can't help it. He's staying out there all by himself . . . I'm going to call him."

"Uh, call him in the morning. He's up early."

Vicki glanced at her watch. Eight o'clock. "It's not that late."

"Well . . ." Obviously, Cody was holding something back, something he didn't want to say; but he was ambivalent enough about it that he let her know with his hesitation.

"What's going on, Cody? Is he drinking more?"

"Not any more than usual, that I know of."

"Then what?"

"Well . . ." Vicki heard an embarrassed chuckle. "Beth's laughing at me. He's got a girlfriend."

"Who?"

"Who we talking about?"

"Dad?"

"Don't be so surprised. Nothing wrong with it, Vicki."

"Oh. No, of course not. How old is she?" She thought she sounded judgmental even to herself.

"About the same age as him. Seventy or so, I'd guess."

"A widow?"

"No, she's got a string of husbands spread out in different towns all the way to Albuquerque. She dances topless in L.A."

"Oh, Cody!"

"Well, how would I know? I suppose she's a widow. Has her own house about ten miles away. Really, Vicki, you'd like her. She's good for him."

"What's Beth think?"

There was a pause while she could hear the phone being fumbled, then the familiar country twang, the warmth. "Hi, Vicki!"

"Hi, Beth."

"Vicki, you're gonna love her. She is sooo sweet!"

"You think so?" Beth liked everybody.

"She is sooo good with the kids. They love her!"

"Well . . . that's good." Vicki was getting irritated with herself for being so skeptical, so damn cynical.

"You remember Roger? The old guy?"

"How could I forget?" Roger Dorr was the old man who had saved her life once. She certainly would not forget him.

"Well, he's not driving these days. Sometimes when she comes over to your dad's place she goes and picks up Roger on the way. They're all three great friends."

Vicki could feel herself relax for the first time since Cody had started this. She grinned and sat back in her stuffed chair, rolled her eyes, and grinned.

"Well, okay, then. If Mr. Dorr likes her, she's probably okay, huh?"

"Sure."

"Tell me, Beth. You remember this guy, Tim Murphy, that I was asking Cody about?"

"Well, yeah."

She wasn't going to volunteer her opinion. That told Vicki something already, but she had to ask. "What do you think?"

She heard Beth take a breath and let it out. "Why are you . . . ? Oh, never mind, I know why. Well, it's been a long time."

"You didn't like him, huh?"

"I wouldn't say that. You really can't *not* like the guy. I just wouldn't recommend him to my sister, that's all. But it has been a long time . . . and people do change, you know."

When Vicki played the conversation back to herself later, she couldn't help but make the obvious jump to the incongruity between her brother's view of this guy eighteen years ago and the Ph.D. she sat across from at lunch. Cop or not, he had certainly changed, and rather drastically from the young irresponsible boy he must have been.

She kept telling herself that she wasn't interested. If he was three years younger than Cody then he was at least eight years younger than she was. Even if she were interested in him romantically, which she certainly was not, after she thought about it, there was no indication he was interested in her.

Except maybe he was. He called her when he really didn't need to. Her input on his investigation was minimal, if anything at all. And he didn't just call to talk to her on the phone, he kept suggesting that they get together, didn't he? She could feel herself warm up with just the thought. Maybe he would call again. Oh, she thought, that's ridiculous. Maybe not. She was wasting her time even thinking about it.

Glancing at the clock, Vicki dug out her old address book. Nine o'clock wasn't late for a phone call, right? She found Augustus Kane, and was surprised to discover that she did have a home number for him. It was old, at least, what? Ten years since she put it in her book? She tried it anyway. Now that he was a deputy chief, he probably had changed his home number to an unlisted one.

A woman answered. An African American voice, at least.

"Hi, this is Vicki Shea. I'm trying to reach Chief Kane. Have I got the right number?"

"What's your name?"

"Vicki Shea. I know Augy from way back and I wanted to ask him about some gossip." She tried to make her voice sound friendly and funny, but the woman wasn't responding.

"You said Vicki Shea?"

"Right."

"I'll check." She sounded unfriendly—maybe, actually, a little hostile.

"Vicki! That really you?"

Augy certainly sounded like his old self. She could picture the big round face, the big grin. "Hi, Augy. How you been?"

"Oh, just getting fatter. How about you?"

"Great."

"How's the doctor business? Better than the lawyer business?"

"Not much, but it's more fun. Less bickering. Was that your wife that answered? I hope I didn't get you in trouble."

"Nah. A strange woman calling me at night once in a while might raise my stock around here. Keep her on her toes. What can I do for you, Vicki?"

"I wanted to get the story on a cop I been dealing with. You might know him."

"Somebody giving you a bad time?"

"No, nothing like that. I called in a child abuse report and the mother wound up committing suicide. It's complicated."

His voice sounded serious, sympathetic. "Yeah, I guess so."

"Anyway, this homicide cop . . . well, I was just curious. He's got a Ph.D. in psychology but he's working Homicide—"

"Tim Murphy?"

Vicki had to chuckle. "Right. You know him, huh?"

"Actually, quite well. What's the question?"

"Uh-oh. Is this a friend of yours? Maybe I shouldn't have—"

"No, no, it's all right. Not exactly a friend . . . he's . . . I don't know how to put it."

"A protégé?"

"Well, kinda, I guess. I guess you could say I had him under my wing for a while a few years ago. He still calls sometimes."

"It sounds like I'm making you uncomfortable. Would you rather not talk about him?"

"Well . . . you're an old friend, Vicki. I guess it depends on why you're asking. Is it a personal question?"

"Actually . . ." Vicki wondered if she was that transparent to *everybody*, or only to her family and old friends like Augy. Might as well be honest. "Yes, there's no reason to ask except I've been getting to know him and I got real curious."

"I see." Vicki heard the hesitation in his voice and wished she hadn't called. She was making him uncomfortable and she hadn't meant to do that. Then his voice seemed to indicate he had decided something. "I'll tell you the story, but you just forget you heard it from me, okay? He might not like it if he knew I talked to you about him. It's not exactly a state secret, so he might not mind, but I'm not sure."

"Okay. I won't say anything."

"He was involved in a bad accident, killed a couple of people. Innocent people. Actually a couple of children, if I remember it right. Yes, two children under five years old."

"Traffic accident?"

"Right. This was eight or nine years ago. He was always very ambitious, a real hard-ass, very aggressive on the street, placed first in every promotion test he ever took. He got into Narcotics young. Probably still too young for his own good to get in with that bunch. Anyway, he was on duty, heading across the bridge to Marin to pick up a prisoner or some damn thing. He recognized a suspect that he'd been looking for going the other way, headed back toward the City, and he did a U-turn right in the middle of the goddamn Golden Gate Bridge. These people—a mother with her kids in an old Chevy station wagon—the mother lost control and hit a SamTrans bus head-on. Mother survived but the two kids were killed."

"That's . . . that's awful!" She couldn't think of anything else to say.

"Worse than that. Just about the worst mess I ever saw where the officer didn't just resign or get fired."

"What did they do to him?"

"Oh, I think he had a six-month suspension, lost some rank. Lots of people wanted to fire him but his boss really went to bat for him.

Managed to salvage him but just barely. I got to say, he wasn't much help. He was a total mess."

"I'll bet. Were you the boss that went to bat for him?"

"Yeah, I got right in the middle of it. I was ambivalent as hell about it, but I couldn't let him get fired. I thought he would just quit. I even told him he should. He'll never make lieutenant with that on his record."

"So why didn't he?"

"I'm not sure. His car wasn't hit, but he stayed at the scene and took responsibility for the whole thing, didn't try to wiggle out of it at all—but then he didn't resign. It was like he didn't have anything else to do. It was like the police department was the only family he had and he just couldn't quit, no matter what they did to him."

"He doesn't have a family?"

"That's another story. I guess he has one, but they haven't spoken to him since he left high school. I never did know what that was about, but somebody told me they were trailer trash or something. I shouldn't say that because I don't know, but he doesn't have anything to do with them, I know that."

"Hmm."

"You know, Vicki, I hate to even be telling you all this. I really like the guy."

"You do?"

"Yeah, I guess. This accident thing really . . . I don't know, I guess it made a pretty big impression. He's completely, completely different now."

"I'll bet."

"Even more than you might think. He was . . . I don't know, but I believe he was suicidal. I do know he cracked up, sort of. The shrinks got ahold of him and he was hospitalized for a few days, involuntarily, then somehow he managed to get himself out. After that he was on suspension, had time on his hands. I thought for a while there he was going to get religion, but then it seemed like he was just reading everything he could get his hands on. When he came back on duty they stuck him out in Potrero. He was working a regular beat and going to school full-time. Like there wasn't enough time to do everything he wanted to do, or like he was just keeping himself so busy he couldn't think, you know?"

"Probably the best thing for him, huh?"

"Well, maybe. I don't think he's over it yet, though. He'll probably never get over it."

Vicki thought about it for a moment but then asked, "Were these children by any chance Hispanic?"

"Yeah, I think they were. What made you ask that?"

"Nothing, really. I was talking to him once and there was this little girl he kept staring at. He seemed a little upset by seeing her."

"Hispanic?"

"Yes."

"Well, I'm not surprised. He'll never get over it."

Twelve

"Dr. Shea? Can I ask you something?" Jenny, the clinic receptionist, was standing outside the examining room, the toggle for her headset dangling over her shoulder like a new accessory. Jenny would not have abandoned her post to bother her without a reason, so Vicki stepped into the hall.

"Can I squeeze in a new patient for you this afternoon? It's a Mrs. Wilkins. She says she knows you."

"Of course, but Charlotte's not a new—"

"She said to tell you it's not Charlotte. It's a neighbor's kid or something with bad stomach pains. Mrs. Wilkins wants to bring him in if you can see him. She didn't want to take him to the Emergency Room."

Vicki shrugged her shoulders, smiling at the implied compliment. She was already running behind, but she thought Cynthia Wilkins would not be asking if the child didn't need attention. "Sure, okay. Tell her to bring him on down at the end of the day and I'll take a look."

It had been very hard to send Charlotte home, to break the connection that having her in the hospital provided. Vicki had allowed herself to feel a little sad that she was giving up her daily contact with the child, even though she thought the feeling was silly. She would not let anyone know she was having difficulty with it, ever. Still, even three weeks later, she was delighted to hear that Cynthia Wilkins was coming to the clinic, even if she was bringing another child. She would get firsthand news on how well Charlotte was doing and that would make her day a good one.

Shortly after five Vicki headed toward the examining room where the staff had put Mrs. Wilkins and the new patient. She had been hearing the child ever since they had arrived at the clinic a few minutes earlier.

There was no time for a greeting. The kid was howling. A skinny five-year-old was sitting on the examining table in his underwear, doubled over and bellowing agony as he gripped his middle with his wrapped arms.

Vicki leaned over and tried to look in his face. "Where does it hurt? Can you point to where it hurts for me?"

The kid subdued the bellowing and stared at her, his face pale and anguished, clearly bewildered and frightened.

"Can you point—?"

"He doesn't speak English."

"Oh." Vicki looked at the blond child. "He's so thin! What does he speak?"

"I'm not sure. Maybe Albanian."

"You don't know?"

"No, I—"

The child's renewed cries swamped whatever else Cynthia was trying to say.

Making shushing noises, Vicki had to work with sign language and brute force to try to get him to lie back on the examining table. His skin was hot and dry to the touch. Finally, she had to get some assistance from the late afternoon nurse to draw blood and get his temperature. It was 104. When he controlled his lamentation for a minute, Vicki probed gently on the tense, protuberant abdomen. With the flat of her hand, she pressed on the right side and then abruptly lifted it to check the rebound. The boy screamed. The nurse did her best to comfort him, as though protecting him from the mean doctor.

Vicki dragged Cynthia into the hallway to be able to be heard. "How long has he been like this?"

"Since last night about seven. He's been steadily getting worse."

"This kid has to be hospitalized. He needs surgery."

"Appendix?"

"I'm ninety percent sure."

"All right."

"I need you to get the parents down here to sign consents and so forth, all right?"

"I can't."

"Can't what?"

"I won't be able to get the parents. I mean, I think they're out of the country."

"Out of the country? How about a relative?"

"It's all right, I'll take responsibility for him."

Vicki thought about it, but not for very long, with the wailing continuing from the examining room. "Well, we really don't have any choice. Take him across the street to Gunnison. Go through the Emergency Room. I'll call and let them know you're coming. I have to locate a surgeon and then I'll meet you over there, okay?"

It took longer than Vicki had thought—first, finding someone available, and then someone willing to take on a case without a parent to consent. By the time Vicki arrived, the ER doctor on duty, James Nelson, had the labs back. The boy had already gone to Radiology for a flat plate of the abdomen. The doctor was adjusting a Fiberglas ankle cast for a dark-haired college student. He handed Vicki his notes on the lab reports.

"Judging by the white count, it might have already burst."

"Did you give him some Demerol?"

"You bet. It was that or go deaf." Dr. Nelson had thin, wiry arms sticking out of the short sleeves he habitually wore in the Emergency Room. He was a slight man, his age indeterminate, but he looked as though he had been battered by a rough sea and left to dry out on the beach. He looked at Vicki quizzically. "The lady that brought him in doesn't speak the same language he does. Any ideas on how to communicate with him?"

"Anybody in the hospital speak Albanian?"

"Not that I know of. We can try an announcement on the intercom."

"Excuse me, please. You ask about Albanian?"

Vicki and Dr. Nelson looked at the patient with the ankle sprain. He was looking helpfully from one to the other. "I have Albanian."

Vicki recovered from her surprise first. "Are you Albanian?"

The student grinned and shook his head. "Palestinian. But I have a little."

Just then the little boy returned to the emergency room on a gurney, no longer crying. Cynthia Wilkins was marching next to him, a protective hand on his shoulder. Vicki pointed to her patient. "Can you translate for us?"

"Sure. I try." The student raised his voice and said something that Vicki assumed must be Albanian. The little boy ignored him. The student spoke to him twice more and then shook his head. "Not Albanian."

He tried German, which Vicki could at least recognize. That got the boy's attention, but he still looked puzzled and didn't reply. The student said something else in German, a long sentence. The little boy stared at him, then at the doctors, then back at the student.

The student licked his lips in concentration. "Not German or Swiss." In quick succession he tried phrases in French, Spanish, and then something that only sounded guttural to Vicki.

The boy shouted something back. They were the first words Vicki had heard from him, but they were not only in a language she couldn't even identify, he was beginning to cry again. He only got out a few tuning notes.

The young Palestinian linguist said something else in the language that had drawn a response. The boy got quiet and looked at the student, still puzzled but intrigued. Sobbing a little, he hiccoughed. He said something again, this time a longer sentence.

The student glanced up. "A little Russian, but not his language. Might be Latvian." He said something else to the boy, who answered promptly this time. "Yes, he's Latvian. Sorry. I don't have Latvian. My Russian worse than my English. Sorry."

"That's okay, you did great." Vicki looked around at two nurses who had stopped what they were doing to watch. "Can we find someone who speaks Latvian?"

One of the nurses nodded, already turning and heading for the phone. "Latvian? No problemo."

Vicki looked at Cynthia Wilkins. "Albanian?"

Cynthia shrugged, her voice a little cool. "I guess I get them mixed up."

"When will the mother be back?"

Cynthia nodded as though she had been waiting for that question. "Her mother was very ill so she went to be with her. I don't know when she expects to return, exactly."

"The father?"

"I've never met the father. He's not around."

"Have you got a phone number or something?"

"No, sorry. She'll probably call in the next few days to check up on . . . Peter."

Vicki noticed the hesitation. "Peter? That's his name?"

"Well, that's what we call him." She made a fast shift of topics. "I told them at the check-in desk that I was his aunt, so it'll be all right." Suddenly, she brightened. "Frank will be home tomorrow. He can translate for us."

Vicki glanced over to see the surgeon, Bond Yee, walking in, holding the X-ray films in his hand, heading for the view box. Vicki looked back at Cynthia and frowned. "In the meantime, he's going to go to sleep and then wake up with staples holding him together."

They waited in the Emergency Room until the child had been sedated and prepped, then walked down the hallway together. Vicki sensed that the older woman was concentrating, filled with nervous tension.

"Don't worry. A burst appendix is kind of a big deal but not anything like as dangerous as it was a few years ago. Bond looks young but he's handled quite a few cases that were a lot worse than this. He'll be fine."

Vicki heard Cynthia's sharp intake of breath, as though she were about to say something, but then she didn't say it. When Vicki glanced at her, she was looking at the floor, apparently lost in thought as they walked slowly up the corridor.

"What happened? You get stuck babysitting for a neighbor when this thing came up with her mother?"

Cynthia hesitated, then nodded. Again the sharp intake of breath, but again she seemed to change her mind about what to say. Then, finally, she spoke.

"'Got stuck babysitting.' That's a good way to put it. Listen, Vicki . . ."

She didn't go on. Obviously something was on her mind. Vicki thought there might be a problem with Charlotte now that she was home from the hospital. She'd seemed to be doing well when Vicki saw her last.

"Is Charlotte okay?"

"Oh, Charlotte." Cynthia smiled fondly; apparently it was a more pleasant thought than what she'd been working on. "Yes, she's doing beautifully, thanks to you."

"But there's a problem? Something with the exercises?"

"No, not about that."

"Something else?"

"Well . . ." Finally, Cynthia seemed to make up her mind. "I wonder if you could come over tomorrow morning. There's a problem, but you have to see it for yourself. I don't know how to describe it."

Vicki's eyebrows went up. These people who seemed to be so sensitive about their privacy were going to invite her over to their house? "I have clinic in the morning. I could come over now, though, if you'd like. He won't be back from surgery for at least three hours."

"Well . . ." Cynthia was hesitating again. She stopped walking and stood perfectly still in the hallway, looking out the nearest window. It was dusk outside, and a San Francisco, wind-driven fog was churning the one tree that interrupted the pavement of the parking lot.

Her voice was soft, thoughtful, or maybe a little afraid. Vicki realized she had never seen this woman look frightened but she might be now, from the sound of her voice. "I'm not sure about the doctor-patient thing. The confidentiality thing. Are you still a lawyer?"

"A lawyer? Yes, but—"

"Could I retain you as a lawyer?"

"I really don't practice law anymore. I couldn't handle anything for you myself, but I could suggest somebody if—"

"I don't need you to do anything. I need advice."

"Cynthia, I couldn't do that, if it involved Charlotte—"

"No, nothing to do with Charlotte." She seemed to have made up her mind now. She was more like the Cynthia Wilkins that Vicki was used to seeing. She pulled out her checkbook with a decisive gesture. "How much for a retainer?"

Vicki shrugged. "Well, if you make it a hundred dollars then if the issue ever comes up later, it won't look so much like a sham."

"Okay, it's a deal." Cynthia was writing furiously. "Can I make it a thousand, just to be sure?"

"Maybe you should just tell me what this is about."

"The address is on the check. I'll go home a little ahead of you so I can make sure . . . I really can't explain it, I have to show you."

The house was huge, planted sedately among its peers in Pacific Heights. Vicki looked at the address on the check to make sure, but she wasn't really surprised at the opulence. She already knew they were rich. She just hadn't realized how rich. This house was worth an easy five million or more. Vicki realized that, for all she knew, the lot alone might be worth that much. She was so far out of her depth that she didn't even know how to make an estimate of the kind of wealth that lived in this neighborhood. She looked down at the jeans, cotton blouse, and old jacket she had changed into at the hospital and wondered if the neighbors would be offended at seeing her and her five-year-old Volvo parked on the curb. Well, she thought, they'll probably just assume it's a delivery person of some kind. She expected a liveried maid or even a butler to answer the door.

It was Jack, without the sport coat and tie. His welcoming smile was polite enough, but strained, as though he would not have agreed with his wife's decision to have Vicki visit their house. His greeting had little of the formal grace that Vicki realized she had come to expect from him.

"Come in. Quickly, please." He peered past her at the street before he firmly closed the door and then tested it to make sure it locked.

"Hello, Jack."

"Oh." He seemed to realize, suddenly, what his greeting looked and sounded like. His face reddened with chagrin. "I do apologize. I'm a little flustered, I guess."

Vicki was immediately sorry she'd embarrassed him. He shifted uncomfortably from one foot to the other, as if he didn't know what to do for a moment. "Can I get you something?"

"No, thanks."

"Well . . ." He seemed to give up on the amenities. "Cynthia's in the basement."

She followed his back as he led her down a formal set of carpeted stairs. Not exactly a root cellar. The stairs ended in a corridor, and Vicki thought she heard children's voices. The carpeting in the hallway was deep, patterned, more like the carpeting in an expensive hotel than in a basement fitted out with a recreation room. The baseboards were wooden and the wallpaper textured. Yes, she was hearing children, laughing.

"Somebody having a party?"

Jack looked around at her, a quick glance as if he wanted to see her reaction before he plunged ahead down the hallway. "Well . . . kind of, anyway. Kind of a children's party."

She followed Jack into a large room at the end of the hallway, a lounge with indirect lighting, a wet bar, and the biggest television screen Vicki had ever seen. The bar held multiple gallon jugs of milk, boxes of crackers, a large aluminum pot with the handle to a ladle sticking out, stacks of bowls.

Vicki froze in the doorway. She stared, unable to move until Jack took her elbow, brought her into the room, and closed the door behind her.

At first, children seemed to be everywhere, moiling like minnows in a bucket. A Mexican woman in her fifties was carrying a washcloth and pursuing a naked toddler who was wriggling away between other children every time she got close. No, it wasn't that many children. A dozen or so, but . . .

The sound was muted on the television, which was showing an animated movie having something to do with a cartoon lobster. A few of the children stood in front of it, rapt. The other children ignored it. Several boys were tumbling and wrestling on a king-sized mattress on the floor, one of several in the large room. Closer to her, Vicki saw a girl of about five or six lecturing and shaking her finger at a younger child in a diaper. Vicki wasn't even sure it was the same language that the little boy with the burst appendix had used. Then she realized why she had frozen in the doorway.

They were all skinny. Every single one of these children was malnourished—no, emaciated. They were wearing cotton T-shirts and shorts or sweat pants, all apparently bought at the same time. Recently. The children's necks looked pencil-thin, supporting heads that were too big for the necks to hold. Arms had prominent elbows and hands. Some of the wrestling boys had shucked off their tops and where she could see their bare backs, the shoulder blades stood out, ribs cleanly defined through parchment-like skin. The little girl who had been scolding the toddler looked up at Vicki with hollow, adult eyes, wide with misgiving and suspicion, but fascinated, too, with this strange new lady. She wrapped her stick-like arms around the toddler and turned him away from the adult while she stared over his head.

Vicki wasn't aware she was kneeling until she felt the carpet under her knees. She held out her hands to the little girl, palms up.

"It's okay. I won't hurt you. I want to look at both of you up close." She tried to smile, but her mouth felt wrong and she could already feel the heat of tears behind her eyes. She took a firm grip on herself. She could not cry, for Christ's sake. Her voice sounded firmer. "It's okay. Come here so I can get a look at you."

The little girl maintained her hold on the other child and backed away, dragging one leg awkwardly.

"Oh, the poor thing! She seems so frightened."

"Should have seen them a couple of days ago. They were all terrified, just absolutely terrified, when they arrived."

When Vicki could tear her gaze away from the children, she saw that all three adults were watching her, waiting for a reaction from her.

"Whose children are these? Where are the parents?"

Jack shook his head. "Probably dead. We don't really know. They're from Eastern Europe somewhere." He looked at his wife, a long look, then back at Vicki. "They're not here in this country legally."

Vicki nodded, beginning to take in the situation. Then she had another thought. "Where's Charlotte?"

Cynthia spoke up. "Upstairs with a nurse. We were afraid . . . see, those open sores. . . . We don't know what these kids might have been exposed to."

"Oh, you are absolutely right about that."

"Can you tell? I mean, obviously they need food, and the skin sores, and several of them have diarrhea, but can you tell if any of them is really sick?"

"I need labs, screening tests, sputum, blood, urine and stool samples. . . . Oh, my lord. I don't know how I'm going to do this. I'll have to get together an old-fashioned black bag." She laughed at the thought and looked at the Mexican woman, who up to this point had been looking worried but now was smiling with evident satisfaction.

"San Juana, this is Dr. Shea. San Juana has been absolutely crucial to us."

Vicki nodded, trying to smile back. "But how do you communicate with them?"

San Juana shrugged and continued to smile, maybe a little proud, a little surprised at the question. "They're only children."

"Yes, I see." Vicki looked back at the little girl. She had at least quit retreating. She stared at the new adult, obviously fascinated, but nervous about her intentions. "Hi, little one." The little girl stared. "I'm Aunt Vicki." She pointed to her own chest then glanced at the adults, grinning quickly. "My brother had all the children." She looked back at the child. "Can you say Aunt Vicki?" The child stared at her out of sober eyes.

Vicki looked back at Cynthia. "But how did they get to you? How long have you had them? Are they actually staying here?"

Jack removed a small child from a straight-backed chair and sat down. "It's kind of a long story."

Vicki sat cross-legged on the carpet. "I'll bet." The little girl was closer now, obviously very curious. Vicki continued to hold an inviting hand out in her direction as she listened to Jack Wilkins.

"Well, you know our business is mostly in Europe . . ."

Cynthia put a restraining hand on his shoulder. Her face wore a look of wary concern. "Maybe . . . I'm not sure . . . Maybe you shouldn't know too much about it."

"Something illegal?"

"Well, yes."

The child, without Vicki realizing that she'd come closer, sat in the cradle of her spread knees and crossed ankles, folded her own hands in her lap, and sighed, a huge and audible sound of relief. Vicki folded her arms around the child and thought, involuntarily, of the plastic skeleton hanging in one of the examining rooms at the clinic.

"Can you say Aunt Vicki?" She pointed at her own chest again as she said it.

The child's voice was soft, almost as though she were afraid to speak up. "Ant Vicki."

"Good!" She hugged her and laughed. "I'll be your Aunt Vicki."

"Ant Vicki."

Still laughing, Vicki looked back at the adults. "These kids are illegal aliens. So what?" She glanced at San Juana, but she had resumed her dogged pursuit with the washcloth, swiping at children indiscriminately as she caught them. "Illegal aliens are all over the place, right?"

Cynthia nodded emphatically. "Well, yes, that's what we thought, too. I mean, they are, but they usually have family or somebody with them."

"So these kids are orphans? How did they wind up here?" She saw the Wilkinses as look at each other for a long time. "Look, if I'm wearing my doctor hat I need to know whatever you can tell me about their background so I can guess what kinds of parasites they might be carrying and so forth. As your attorney, I need to know what your involvement is so I can decide if you really need a lawyer and, if you do, what kind of a lawyer you really need. Okay? You have to tell me."

She watched the two of them think about it, looking at each other, communicating without words, hesitating.

Vicki switched into her most authoritarian lawyer voice. "No holding back here. This is a confidential conversation. You started to say something about your business in Europe. You broker sugar or something?"

Jack spoke, somewhat relieved to talk about business. "All kinds of commodities, actually. We represent American exporters, a number of very large groups, in about a dozen European and Middle Eastern countries. A few years ago we started going into Yugoslavia, the Balkans, the former Soviet Union countries. . . ."

"So that's why you thought these kids were Albanian? You thought they were from Kosovo?"

Cynthia had retrieved her own chair and sat with her elbows on her knees, her head down as she seemed to picture the places they were talking about in her mind. "It's all the same, Vicki. The adults start shooting and hacking at each other and—" She gestured at the roomful of children. "—these are the casualties. It's infinitely worse in Africa, but we don't get to Africa."

Vicki nodded, seeing a whole new side to these people. "Okay. So you saw these children on one of your trips? What did you do?"

Jack's voice was quick. "Been doing."

"What?"

"It's not what we did. It's what we've been doing. For the last couple of years, we've been smugglers."

Thirteen

Answering her cell phone on the second beep, Elaine's voice was sharp, businesslike. "Elaine Cohen."

"Hi, it's Vicki." Vicki was calling from her Volvo, pulling away from the curb in front of the Wilkinses' house.

"Yes, Dr. Shea. What can I do for you?"

"Uh-oh. You must be in a meeting, huh?"

"Yes, Doctor, I could meet with you."

"You want me to get you out of the meeting?"

"Yes, Doctor, that would be fine."

"Are you sure it's okay? It can wait. Oh, what the hell, I need some help. Can I take you to dinner?"

"Yes, Dr. Shea, I agree, it does sound urgent. I'll need to review that subpoena myself, before you testify in the morning. You're in the North Beach area? Tell me exactly where you're going to be in the next . . . oh, fifteen minutes or so."

By the time Vicki parked her car and came through the door of the restaurant in North Beach, Elaine was already enthroned on a barstool. She'd been watching the door, and when she saw Vicki she grinned behind oversized glasses and held up a glass of wine with one hand and the turned-up thumb of the other. A two-fisted gesture of triumph. As Vicki took the stool next to her, Elaine slapped the bar in giddy exhilaration.

"First time I've been out at night in six months! The au pair was ready to kick me out in the street!"

"I rescued you from a meeting?"

"A date."

"Oh, Elaine! Why didn't you just say so?"

"Believe me, 'rescue' is the operative word. The rat had already been toking weed before he came by the office to get me. I never should have accepted. I was just so flattered—what's the matter?" Elaine's grin faded as she took a closer look at Vicki's face.

Vicki took a deep breath and let it out. "You don't know anything about immigration law, do you?"

"Matter of fact, I do. We represent a couple of high-tech companies that are trying to import some people from India. If you don't do immigration now, you might as well forget it with those companies."

"But your firm doesn't handle immigration cases, does it? It's such a specialty."

"The rest of 'em don't, I do. It's too technical and too specialized to do occasionally—too much to learn—so I handle all of the immigration stuff for any of our clients that need somebody with that kind of expertise. Why? Got a doctor with a visa problem?"

"This would be more like the other end of the social spectrum."

"The other—? What, Mexican farm workers?"

"No, but more like that. These are children. Refugees from Eastern Europe."

"Oh. Patients of yours?"

"I guess they are, now."

"Okay. Have the parents call me." She made a distasteful face. "I hate to ask, but can they pay anything? The partners—"

Vicki waved off the question. "There's money for that. But the parents aren't with them. No relatives are with them at all."

"How many kids we talking here?"

"About a dozen, that I know about."

Elaine stared, her face growing serious. "A dozen? Twelve?"

"More or less."

The maître d' called out the name "Cohen" and Elaine raised one hand to wave at him without looking away from Vicki's face. "I think you better tell me more about this. But don't tell me any names until I decide if I want to be involved, okay?"

"Why?"

"Just tell me about it."

They were led to a table at a window, although Vicki thought they hardly needed to showcase two single women. The place was already full. A man at the otherwise empty bar was trying to look them over without getting caught at it. Oh. No, he was trying to get a look at Elaine. Elaine was in her mid-thirties, a thick corona of black curls, great legs in a mid-thigh skirt. Vicki suddenly felt every one of her forty-five years.

"Okay, what's the story?" If Elaine had noticed being noticed she wasn't going to show it. Vicki decided she was used to it. Ah, yes, she remembered that, too.

"Okay. The kids." She hesitated long enough to marshal her thoughts, get back to the subject at hand. "These people I know have a business that takes them into Eastern Europe."

"A business?"

"A legitimate business, I'm sure of that."

"O-kay." Elaine's eyes hooded, her brain seemed to whir and click to file that away for more questions later.

"They got into the Balkans and just by chance saw this refugee camp—"

"What country?"

"Somewhere in Yugoslavia, I think. Does it matter?"

"You bet your booties. Is this where the children are from?"

"No. I think they're Latvian, but I'm not sure."

"Never mind. We can come back to that." Click-click. Elaine filed that one, too.

"My friends saw these children . . ." She could almost see Elaine's brain whirring, filing, categorizing information, her face blank and serious. "I'm not describing this well, like they showed it to me."

"Doesn't matter, go on."

But it did matter. That's why Cynthia had insisted on showing her instead of just describing the situation. Vicki wanted Elaine to see the picture the way she had seen it.

"These children were starving, Elaine. They were little stick figures, stranded by themselves, absolutely terrorized, stuck in a crowd of orphans and lost children. They're small and helpless and scared to death, and nobody was taking charge, making sure they got fed, a warm place to lie down."

"So what did they do? They didn't just load them on a plane."

"No, they didn't. They started asking around, making enquiries, trying to find out what they could do. They have money. They wanted to do something about these children, you know?"

"Sure." Elaine seemed impatient with the details of motivation. "So how did they get them into the States?"

"They don't know."

"They don't know how they did it? You believed this?"

"Well, yes. See, eventually, after they had been asking around, off and on for a month or so, they made contact with this adoption group."

"Oh, please!"

"I'm just trying to tell you what they told me!" Vicki felt a quick and unexpected flash of temper.

Elaine stared, then held up her hands in surrender. "I'm sorry! Don't get mad. I'll keep my mouth shut, okay? Go ahead and tell me."

Vicki dabbed at her mouth with her napkin. "Sorry."

"No, that's okay. This is more important to you than I realized. Go ahead."

"Elaine, if you could see what I just saw, these cheerful little faces with these skinny little arms and legs . . ." She had to stop. She could still almost feel the little bundle of bones in her lap.

After giving it a couple of beats, Elaine's voice was softer than before. "An adoption agency. And then?"

"Yeah. There was this group, I don't know if they were like an 'agency' connected to some kind of a larger group . . . I just don't know about that. Anyway, this first group was in contact with these other people in the United States who had adoptive parents lined up, waiting for children like this, but they had to get them transported. If they did it legally, going through the international adoption procedures one at a time, it would take years. They said they could get the children—a lot of children—transported in, but they would have to pay the transportation people up front."

Elaine opened her mouth as though about to make an acerbic comment on that ploy, then changed her mind. When she spoke, her voice stayed with the softer, sympathetic tone.

"Your friends deal with these 'transportation people' directly?"

"No, they said they never met them. One of them, one of the people I know, met the woman in Los Angeles that dealt with the children after they arrived. They did as much checking as they could. She actually met a couple of adoptive parents. Anyway, finally they were convinced that it was legitimate."

"Legitimate?"

"Well, that this group was doing what they said they were doing."

"Okay. So they put some money in it?"

"Yes." She watched Elaine, thinking about what this sounded like. "Look, these people are very sophisticated. They're not young. I think it would be very difficult to scam these people."

"Your friends."

"Right. And anyway, they obviously got some children into the country because now they're hiding in these people's basement."

Elaine's back went rigidly erect. Her neck actually seemed to lengthen as she came to full attention. "In their house?"

"Yes."

"Oh dear God! Right now?"

Vicki quickly looked around, then gestured with one hand to keep her voice down. "Yes! That's what I'm trying to talk to you about."

Elaine leaned forward over the table, whispering urgently. "Your friends are courting major disaster here, Vicki. Major, magnificent legal problems! Do they realize that?"

"What do you want them to do, throw 'em in the bay?"

The waiter was suddenly just there, clearing his throat. "Have you decided? Or do you want to take a few minutes?"

Both women jumped as if they'd been hit with a cattle prod. Elaine looked down at her menu, but Vicki recovered quickly and ordered for both of them.

"Vicki—" Elaine looked at her as though she were a wayward child herself. "Vicki, you don't have any idea how serious this is?"

"Well, I know it's a technical violation of immigration law—"

"Listen a minute, okay?"

"Okay."

"Two months ago some coyotes—coyotes or snake heads, that's what they call the smugglers—they were bringing a caravan of people over the border in Texas. They got into a chase with the border patrol, crashed one of the vans in an arroyo, and killed about a half dozen people, some of them children. You didn't see this on the news? It was all over the TV."

Vicki shook her head. Having something on television would be a good way to hide it from her.

"Anyway, that's not the worst part of it. You listening?"

Vicki had been trying to say something, but when Elaine put it like that she closed her mouth and nodded quickly. "I'm listening, go ahead."

"The coyotes set up an ambush at the crash sight. When the border patrol caught up with them—four agents in two cars—they killed all four of them. Automatic weapons, the works."

Vicki was too surprised to say anything. She hadn't given the actual mechanics of smuggling much thought. Elaine let the first part of the story sink in, then went on.

"I guess it was overcast, so they couldn't get an airplane on 'em to see where they went. The rest of them got away into the canyons in another van and an SUV. I got the details because all the immigration lawyers were talking about it, the ones representing illegal aliens, how it was going to make their job really, really hard for awhile."

Vicki nodded. "Representing Mexicans?"

"These weren't Mexicans. Not even Latin American or Chinese, either. These were Europeans, they think. There was a doctored passport in the van that crashed, a crude job but it was in Italian, if I remember the story right."

Vicki had to sit back and take a deep breath while her mind raced. This wasn't the same thing, was it? No, probably not. These kids weren't Italian. And besides—

"Elaine, these people—these are good people, I'm sure. I'm positive they wouldn't have anything to do with anything like that."

Elaine picked up her wineglass, stared at it, put it down again. Finally she looked at Vicki.

"They never dealt with the smugglers, right? Didn't even know who they were?"

"That's right, they just put up the money."

"How much?"

"I didn't ask."

Elaine nodded, thoughtfully. "Okay, back up a minute. Tell me what went wrong. How did they wind up with the children?"

"They're not sure, but something obviously did. Two days ago a van pulled up in their driveway, opened up, dumped all these scared kids out, then took off."

"Twelve kids in one van?"

"They must have been packed in like sausages. They said the kids were so terrified that they just huddled together, literally shaking with fear."

"Didn't the driver say anything?"

"He said he didn't speak English."

"He said . . . ?"

"Gestured, I don't know. They didn't find out anything from him."

"What about the woman in L.A.?"

"Phone just rings. No answer, no machine, nothing."

"She's probably been arrested."

"You think so?"

Elaine made an impatient gesture. "Oh, I don't know. Yeah, seems likely, doesn't it to you?"

"I hadn't thought about it."

"Your friends—oh, hell." Elaine dove into her pocketbook and came out with a steno pad and a pen. "You might as well tell me their names. They obviously need a lawyer in the worst possible way. I can do the immigration, Jim Gonzalez can do the criminal, if it comes to that. He's a senior partner."

Vicki sat back and sighed with relief. "Thank you."

"Don't thank me. They're paying clients, right?"

"Oh, that's right." Vicki retrieved Cynthia's check and passed it across the table. Elaine focused on it a moment and then smirked.

"I see you haven't forgotten how to practice law entirely."

"She was concerned about the confidentiality."

"Smart lady." She looked up from copying the name and address. "You should be concerned about it, too." She passed the check back.

"That's all right. You can just put it in their file."

Elaine held it up in front of Vicki. "Cash it. Open a file, stick a photocopy of it in the file, and then cash the check to preserve your own legal butt."

"I don't even have a trust account."

"Who needs it? You've already spent a thousand bucks of your time on this case tonight."

"Oh, I don't know . . ."

Elaine waved the check. "Take it! I intend to eat and drink a good tenth of it right now."

Vicki laughed and took the check. When she looked back up, Elaine was regarding her thoughtfully. "Vicki, I know that the—" She had to check her notes. "—the Wilkinses are your friends. But no matter how nice and decent they are as human beings, right now they are felons."

"I was afraid it might be serious. It's a felony? Harboring illegal aliens?"

"How about conspiracy to smuggle the little hoodlums into the country? That's serious, all right, if you're a U.S. attorney." Elaine was watching Vicki's face for reaction. "How long have you known about this?"

"Just tonight. I was leaving their house when I called you."

Elaine nodded as she picked up her fork to pitch into the calamari in front of her. "That was smart. You haven't told Liz about any of this, right?"

"I haven't talked to anybody but you since I knew about it. I will have to talk to her, though."

Elaine looked up. "Why?"

"I have to get lab work done on all of these kids. You can't tell what they might have with just a physical exam. I need to run screens on all of them, and probably some follow-up labs and films on a few of them. Liz can help me figure out how to get the paperwork through San Francisco General."

Elaine stared. "What are you talking about? You're giving these kids physicals?"

"Elaine, I have to. One of them's already in surgery, probably with appendicitis. You should see what they look like!"

"Oh. Well, I suppose . . ." Elaine seemed to think it over for a minute, then shrugged her shoulders. "Can't be helped, I guess. General Hospital must handle this kind of thing all the time, huh?"

"Sure, of course."

"But don't tell Liz any more than you have to. You don't want to drag her into the middle of this. And by the way, I'm sure I don't have to tell you to do no more than your duty as a doctor, right? I don't need you or Liz as clients." She grinned. "You can't afford it."

"No. Maybe I should have her talk to you, though, huh?"

"Just don't tell her any more than you have to, to get your lab work done. She can call me if she gets nervous."

Vicki looked down at the plate of pasta in front of her and wondered when it had arrived. "What can you do? Any ideas?"

"Well . . ." Elaine was attacking her squid with good appetite. The impersonal legal puzzle appealed to her. "I suppose the first order of business is to get these kids to the proper agency. Have to figure out a way of handing them over to the INS before we do anything else."

"What happens then?"

"Probably be best if we sit tight for a while and see if the Wilkinses get busted. If they did arrest this woman in L.A., they'll have their names and numbers by now—"

"I meant, what happens to the children when they get turned over the INS?"

"Eventually, probably they'll be repatriated. Depends a lot on where they're from, but if they're Latvian, probably straight back. Well, eventually. Sometimes they move fast, sometimes it takes 'em forever to process anything. If they were from Cuba or some other place we have a dispute with, it might be different. If they're from a country we're friendly with or that we don't want to offend, forget it."

"What about in the meantime?"

"Detention. They put them in jail."

Vicki thought she hadn't heard right. Elaine couldn't have said that. Surely nobody would do that. "They put them where?"

"In jail. INS doesn't have any facilities of their own. I guess they might have something in Florida or someplace, but not around here."

"They would put children in jail? Children who didn't do anything?"

"Well, they're here."

"But they didn't—"

"I know it sounds harsh, but it's probably not that bad. They have to put them somewhere in confinement until they can deport them."

"But if they're orphans—"

Elaine was shaking her head as she speared calamari, not looking at Vicki. "Doesn't matter—"

"Why can't they just put them up for adoption?"

"Oh, right!" Elaine threw her head up and laughed. "Do something logical? Forget that! No way!"

"But if they're orphans . . . !"

"Vicki, forget it. No way." Her laughter faded as she looked at Vicki's face. "Vicki, don't make yourself crazy about this. It is absolutely hopeless. These kids came into the country illegally, they'll go back out legally. There is no possibility, not even a remote possibility, that anything else is going to happen."

Vicki's voice sounded small, even to herself. "But they're children."

"I know. And you've seen them." Elaine speared another squid but then looked at it and finally laid down her fork without eating it. She reached for her wineglass and finally looked at Vicki again. Her voice became soft as she looked at Vicki and seemed to really see her, finally.

"I'm sorry, Vicki. It is truly hopeless. It's just not possible that it will come out any other way."

Fourteen

"Okay, I'm ready!" Liz Abrams had a flash of excitement in her eye that Vicki had not anticipated. It was raining again, so Liz was wearing a yellow poncho over her nurse's uniform and the clipboard stacked with forms in her hand was wrapped in plastic. She put down the samples tray she was carrying, pushed the hood of the poncho off her head, and grinned at Vicki in one of the clinic's offices. "Are they here?"

"They're at a private residence. I'll have to take you."

"Do I get to be blindfolded?"

"Not funny."

"Come on! This is exciting, don't you think?"

Vicki stopped writing in the chart she had been working on and looked at her friend. She was about to give her a stern admonition, then thought better of it.

"Serious, too."

"Well, let's get started. I'd like to get back by four."

"I forgot to ask. You think to bring needles?"

"Plenty."

"Okay, let's go. We can take my car."

Heeding Elaine's warning, Vicki had told Liz only that there was a group of children that needed a workup and she couldn't bring them to the hospital because of immigration problems. When Liz pointed out that immigration problems were not exactly unusual at San Francisco General, Vicki told her that she couldn't tell her any more about it, but she had to have the labs done soon and they would be paid for with cash.

In the car, Liz was still grinning. "Okay, I got it figured out."

"Don't ask, Liz."

"These are the children of dope smugglers, right?"

"Too much television, Liz. No."

"Chinese spies?"

"Forget it. You don't really want to know."

"Worse than Chinese spies?"

"No, not—look, Elaine said for me not to tell you anything you didn't absolutely have to know to get the lab work, okay?"

Liz's voice rose in indignation. "Ah! Elaine knows all about this and I don't? That little—"

"Elaine's handling the legal side of it, I'm the medical."

They rode in silence until Liz looked around at the Pacific Heights neighborhood they were driving into.

"Some barrio! You sure their parents don't deal drugs?"

Vicki didn't respond. Instead of parking on the curb, she drove up the driveway, past the house, to park out of sight of the street. Jack had apparently seen them drive up; he was holding the back door open as they ran through the rain to get inside, carrying the paraphernalia they needed for the exams.

Vicki introduced them simply as Liz and Jack. Liz was no longer grinning. Vicki thought she was either impressed with Jack's somber courtesy or just with the house.

When they entered the lounge-cum-nursery, Cynthia looked up from the child in her lap and stood, hefting the two-year-old. She responded to Vicki's introduction with a warm smile.

"Thank you for helping, Liz. I know something like this must seem—"

"She doesn't know a thing, Cynthia."

"I'm just a nurse."

Vicki glanced at Liz, who had suddenly sounded very stiff and formal, for Liz. The room was changed. A blackboard leaned against one wall, and next to it was a box of colored chalk. There were four new rocking horses on springs, a small trampoline, toy cars and trucks everywhere, plus a whole cotillion of dolls. There was a three-foot stack of videos next to the television.

When Vicki looked back at her again, Liz was still standing just inside the room, poncho dripping, damp hair over eyes that were growing bigger as her mouth turned down. She stared at the children en masse and then at them individually. Vicki knew exactly how she felt.

Suddenly, Liz was all efficiency. "Have you got another room for the exams?"

"Yes, there's an adjoining room right here." Cynthia opened a door to show them. A bed had been moved in and there was a table to write on and hold the equipment. Liz strode in without another word and started setting up.

San Juana supplied new, mostly Hispanic names to put on the forms and the sample vials and slides. Together, the three of them decided by majority vote on an age for each child, all of them between 10 months and 7 years old. After they drew blood from the first patient there was a small riot, but Cynthia quelled it with cookies and another video. Vicki could hear the sound of explosions and screams from the action thriller they were watching and wondered whatever happened to cartoons.

They were on their fourth or fifth examination, name-tagging each child to keep the bloodwork straight as they went, when Vicki was mildly irritated by the battle noises coming from the next room. She looked at San Juana.

"What in the world are they watching?"

Liz's voice was matter-of-fact. "*Terminator 2.*"

"You've seen it?"

"One zillion times. If my husband ever brings home another Schwarzenegger movie . . ." She stopped what she was saying to help hold the head of a little urchin who wanted to see the instrument Vicki was trying to use to look in his ears. The boy turned his attention to the stethoscope, holding it up in front of Liz with a questioning look.

"That's a stethoscope."

"Stet . . ."

"Stethoscope."

"Stessope!"

"Good! Say stethoscope."

"Good! Say, stesscope!"

Vicki laughed. "Not going to take him long."

When she spoke again, Liz's voice sounded confidential. "Are you going to need to get some prescriptions?"

"Yes, I sure will."

"We can go through the hospital pharmacy."

"Thank you, Liz. I really mean that."

"It's okay."

"Tsokay!"

"Okay."

"Okydoky!"

"Hey, you already got a head start!" Liz picked him up and took him to the other room to trade San Juana for another one.

Vicki glanced at her watch. "We're not going to get through before you have to leave."

"No, it's not anything important. Let's finish up here." Liz flipped open a cell phone, held a finger in the other ear while she talked. Even after she hung up, she stood for a moment and stared at the wretched-looking children.

Except they weren't wretched. Their immediate hunger satisfied continuously from vats of macaroni and cheese, crackers and peanut butter, gallons of milk, and now bags of cookies, even the skinny arms and legs seemed charged with energy. With the sores cleaned and covered with patches, hair washed, they were exuberant, charged, cheerful beyond any right. If they were homesick or missed their families, they didn't show it. It was as though their pasts had dropped away, disappeared into some forgotten story as they thrilled to their new surroundings and wanted nothing more than to explore and play. Vicki realized she was surprised that they knew how to play.

Vicki purposely saved the little girl who had crawled into her lap the day before for last. Under her thick chestnut hair were a pair of scars. One was surgical and the other round, most likely a bullet wound. She had been lucky to be near a good medical facility when she was shot. Vicki watched as the child walked back and forth for her, dragging her left foot, lurching it forward, using her pelvic and abdominal muscles. Vicki looked at her hand, opened the fingers one at a time, held her head between two hands and examined the face.

Cynthia came over and stood next to Vicki to watch. "Brain damage?"

"Yes."

"I thought so. Now that I know about it, I seem to see it all the time. Charlotte will come out better, don't you think?"

"Oh, definitely. She already is."

Impulsively, Vicki picked up the little girl and held her on her hip. The child grinned and then shyly turned her face into Vicki's shoulder. Then Vicki could hear her whispering. She turned her head to hear better.

"Aunt Vicki."

Vicki burst out laughing. "Yes! Aunt Vicki! You got it right." She involuntarily squeezed her and then stared back into the child's smiling face.

Liz had assembled her sample tray, stacks of paperwork on top, next to the door. She walked over to the bar and absently munched on a cracker as she stared at a framed photograph behind the bar. Vicki realized with a shock that it was a picture of Julia in what looked like a party dress, standing under some trees in a park. The photograph was so big that Vicki realized it could not have been there before she started the exams of all these kids. She would have noticed it, she was sure. Jack must have hung it there sometime this afternoon.

Vicki realized that she was putting off leaving, hardly fair after Liz had given her all this help. "Okay, I guess we're ready, huh?"

Liz nodded. "Look, if you want to stay, why don't I just take a cab?"

"No, I wouldn't make you—"

"I'm serious. You want to stay and talk a little and it's really no big deal to me."

Vicki hesitated. "Well, maybe you could take my car to Gunnison and leave my keys at the ER nurse's station."

Liz held out her hand and grinned. "A deal. I always wanted to park in a physician's slot." She looked at the stack of things she had to carry and then looked back at Vicki, her face bright. "Want to help me load up?"

The rain had stopped, leaving a gray sky that seemed to be about ten feet over their heads. As Vicki braced the tray of vials in the front seat of her car, Liz hovered near her shoulder.

"Vicki, what are you getting yourself into?"

"I'm not. Not really."

"I don't want to know any more what this is about but . . . well, really, Vicki, anybody can see these kids don't belong here."

"Oh, I know . . ."

Liz touched Vicki's arm to make her look her in the eye. "Look, I'm not doing any more than I would for any kid that came to the hospital. I'm not worried about that, okay? But you! Vicki, you better talk to Elaine some more or something."

"I have."

"Well, then you better listen to her." Liz frowned into her face but then couldn't help it. She looked down as a small smile stole into the corners of her mouth. The humor was back in her eyes as she peered at Vicki through her bangs. "I know. You just want to hug 'em all, don't you?"

Vicki smiled and didn't answer.

"Okay, see you back at the ranch."

"Thanks, Liz."

Vicki watched her back the Volvo out of the long driveway, all the way past the house to the street. Vicki's pager went off. She punched in the number from the readout, still standing in the driveway.

"Hi." A man's voice.

"Who's this? This is Dr. Shea. I just got a page for this number."

"Oh, sorry. It's Tim. I left you my home number."

"Hello, Tim. What can I do for you?" She realized how lilting and playful her voice sounded, and that she'd been wanting him to call.

Then she remembered. He was a cop and she was doing something vaguely illegal, or might be. All these ideas ran by very fast while she went hot and cold all at once, standing in the open, in the driveway. She ran the fingers of her free hand through her hair and realized she was pacing. She tried to focus on his voice, what he was saying.

"Listen, you like music? I mean, I just stumbled onto two tickets for the symphony, if you're interested. I know it's short notice, but I just this minute got them from a guy that couldn't go. His wife is pissed." He chuckled irrelevantly.

Vicki realized he was nervous. "You don't mean tonight?"

"Yeah. Actually doesn't start until eight-thirty. I know it's short— I mean, I just thought you might like to—"

"No, that's all right. Uh, sure! Can . . . ah . . . can I meet you there? Time's going to be tight. Would that be all right?"

"You bet. I'll wait outside in front. It's at Davies." His voice sounded relieved as much as anything else. Then Vicki remembered, pictured the Volvo backing out of the driveway.

"Oh, God! I just sent somebody off in my car."

"Well, I can come give you a ride. Where are you?"

She had a flash of him coming to the Wilkinses' house, all the questions.

"No! No, that's okay. I can get a lift. I'll meet you there at eight-twenty."

"Great! Well . . ."

" 'Bye, Tim. I got to rush."

"See you there."

The phone went dead and Vicki stared at it, wondering what she had just done to herself. "Oh, shit." She looked at her watch. 6:10. "Oh, shit!"

She went back downstairs, almost running. She wanted to ask a few more questions, but she wasn't sure she should. She should leave that to Elaine, shouldn't she?

The movie was finally over and the television dark. The little girl with the hemiparesis, the left-sided paralysis that made her limp, was waiting for Vicki just inside the door. Vicki picked her up and put her on one hip again. She stared at Julia's picture, trying to think what she could ask that would be all right.

Jack chuckled self-consciously. "Oh, you saw Julia's picture."

"It's beautiful."

"We wanted her to be here, sort of. She's . . . she was responsible for this, you know."

"She was?"

"She was the one that wouldn't let up. Once she saw those children—it was before she had her own—she just wouldn't stop for anything."

Cynthia's voice was quiet, reflective. "She's the one that located Mrs. Fairchild in Los Angeles. Dragged me down there to meet her and talk to those parents. She met a lot of people involved that we never even had contact with. Just kept pushing, pushing. Just had to get those kids out of there or die trying." Her voice faded, realizing what she'd said. She sighed.

Jack smiled at his wife. "Didn't take that much to get you into it."

"Or you and Frank either, Jack."

They pointed at each other simultaneously and said almost in chorus, "This is all your fault!" They both laughed, an old joke, apparently, while Vicki looked on and smiled, enjoying the intimacy. She caught herself.

"You call Elaine?"

Jack nodded. "Appointment tomorrow at nine o'clock in the morning."

"Good. You'll be in good hands there." But she was feeling uneasy about it. Elaine was going to immediately convince them to let all this go. Immediately, before anything else.

She frowned and glanced at her watch. "I'm awfully sorry, but something has just come up." They looked at her attentively, full of concern. She had to smile, let them know she wasn't just ducking out. "I just got an invitation to the symphony."

A man's voice outside in the corridor startled her. "All right, where's everybody hiding!"

Jack shouted, leaping for the door, "In here, Frank!"

"Waiting in the bar, hey? Great idea."

A large man, gray-haired and rotund, filled the doorway and stared. His voice dropped to *sotto voce*. "Uh-oh."

He looked around the room until he saw Vicki. "These are all yours, I hope?"

Vicki had to laugh out loud. "No, not mine."

"Uh-oh."

Jack was grinning at him. "How's your Latvian?"

"Latvian? So-so."

He leaned toward Vicki, bracing his hands on his knees so that he was eye to eye with the little girl she held. He said something to her and she grinned back at him and answered, a few words ending in "Nadya."

"She's Russian." Then, to the little girl, "Ah, Nadya. A pretty name." He repeated his compliment in Russian, and Nadya, thrilled with the attention, hid her face against Vicki's shoulder again.

Cynthia stood and touched her husband's arm. "Jack, Vicki has to hurry. She needs a ride."

"Oh, I can take a cab."

Jack shook his head. "Wouldn't think of it. Come on, Frank, you can ride with us, and I'll fill you in."

"No drink, huh?" He looked at Vicki. "Just kidding. You Vicki?" He stuck out a catcher's mitt for a hand. "Frank Sanderson."

"I guessed."

He looked her up and down, holding on to her hand. "But you have to ride in the backseat. I can't get into it."

Vicki laughed again, liking this Falstaffian character immediately. "It's a deal."

She set Nadya on her feet, but the little girl clung to her neck. Vicki kissed her cheek and told her she would be back. Frank translated before Vicki remembered that he could. The child let go and looked up at Vicki with shining eyes, her face fixed in a rigid, anxious grin. In spite of the grin she was electric with tension, clasping her hands in front of her for something to grab onto. One of her front teeth was missing, its partner crooked and loose. Her eyes were filled with radiating, absolute adoration. Quickly Vicki backed out of the room and turned away, walking fast.

Vicki sat behind the driver's side in the back of the Jaguar. By twisting a little, his hand on the back of Jack's seat, Frank could look at her as they talked.

"You're the doctor, huh?"

"Oh, so you did already know. I wasn't sure."

Frank rolled his eyes, indicating he knew about the children. "Oh, yeah. So how's the one in the hospital?"

"Doing great. Got a volunteer to come in and talk to him so he doesn't feel quite so isolated. He'll be back home—well, out of the hospital—in a couple of days."

Jack looked at Vicki in the mirror and then at Frank. "Vicki got us a lawyer. Going to see her in the morning, so you probably better come along."

"A lawyer?" Frank rolled his eyes again. "Wouldn't miss it." He yawned and Vicki thought of a lion, sleepy in the sun. He looked back at her again. "Sorry. Jet lag."

"You just got in?"

"From Budapest, by way of New York and Chicago. So what do you know about Fairchild?" The eye he fixed on her was no longer full of humor. It had gone serious and wide awake in a second.

Jack held up a hand. "She's not . . . she doesn't know anything about that, Frank. She's a pediatrician, helping us out, that's all."

Frank continued to stare at her. The look was not hostile, but definitely serious. He glanced at Jack and then looked back at Vicki. "That's best."

Vicki nodded, readily agreeing. "Okay."

Frank's voice was still directed to the backseat. "I saw Charlotte before I came downstairs. I honestly can't see anything wrong with her. I mean, I guess the way she holds that one hand, but it doesn't seem bad to me." He was asking her and there was real concern in his voice.

Vicki smiled back at him. "She's doing much better. I'm very pleased with her."

"But still too early to tell, huh?"

"Afraid so."

Frank twisted his bulk to look at Vicki more directly. This time, his eyes were deadly serious, skewering her in a second. His voice, a quiet low rumble, drilled into her.

"Julia did not hurt that child."

Jack's voice broke in immediately. "Frank, let it go! Just don't, okay?" His voice sounded angry, as though he were calling off a large, unruly dog.

Frank's voice dropped the edge. "Sorry."

He glanced at Vicki, back at Jack, back at Vicki.

"Okay, but there's things that you don't—"

"Frank!" Real anger this time.

Frank looked at his friend and partner, a little frustrated, a little sheepish. "Oh, never mind. I apologize. I must be tired."

"Just let it go."

"Okay." Frank lifted his big hand off the seat and gently patted the back of Jack's head. He fixed Vicki once more with his eyes, then turned in his seat to face front. "Okay, I'll drop it."

Vicki looked down at her lap, then out the window. She thought that the reason Frank hadn't talked to her when he came back for the funeral was that he didn't trust himself, or the Wilkinses didn't trust him and had kept him away from her. He'd been that angry. He was angry still. Vicki realized she didn't blame him.

Fifteen

Vicki miscalculated on the rain. She'd barely had time to shower and select something to wear, then left her raincoat at home because it didn't go with her evening shift. She wore a long cashmere coat instead. She held it over her head, vainly trying to protect her hair as she ran for the front of Davies Hall in three-inch heels, splashing through a puddle next to the curb that she didn't see until too late.

Tim was standing under a sensible umbrella, tickets in hand like a scalper, grinning at her as if he thought she was trying to be funny. He was dressed in black, down to a small black bow tie. She thought he looked elegant. What happened to the cowboy? She didn't care.

In the past six weeks he had called her twice for breakfast and they'd had lunch three times. Vicki had about decided that if she was going to see him in the evening she was going to have to be the aggressor. She had been going up and down on the subject, wondering if he was interested in her as a friend, not a romantic interest.

For that matter, she wasn't at all sure what her own intentions were. She'd wondered if she wasn't the one keeping it at a distance, keeping their conversations to safe topics, like work, her days as a prosecutor so long ago, how the business had changed. Safe topics, not particularly personal, and yet she'd still been attracted. In her younger days, maybe when she had more confidence, fewer qualms and second thoughts—or maybe just fewer thoughts at all—she would have just dragged him off to bed. Still, she'd called Cody and Augy about him because she was interested, whether she wanted to admit it or not.

Losing her embarrassment in a burst of laughter at what she knew she must look like, she realized she really didn't care. The look in his eye told her she couldn't look all that bad. She was happy to see him. Seeing somebody in the evening was a lot different from lunch, and now, by God, he'd finally been the one to nerve himself to make the leap. Wet feet, she decided, were not that big a deal.

She lowered the coat and gripped his arm to get under the umbrella as they headed inside. They got to their seats just as the lights were dimming. Vicki took a deep breath and let it out. It was too late to read the program.

"What are they doing?"

Tim looked at her blankly. The detective didn't have a clue, eyes innocently wide. She had a sudden sharp urge, completely unexpected, to reach over and grab a handful of that blond hair. Can't do that in public.

She faced front, made herself think about the unreadable program, wondering what the name of the composer would be. She hoped it wasn't anyone born after 1900. It wasn't. Within the first two bars she recognized Mozart and had to try not to grin in triumphant satisfaction. She looked at Tim, wanting to see his reaction. He looked like a schoolboy—polite attention, expecting to be bored. He had no idea what was coming.

His elbow was on the armrest between them, his sleeve touching her upper arm. She wanted to put her hand on his forearm, but she didn't. Couldn't do that, could she? No, of course not.

With a small jolt, she realized that she couldn't tell him what was most on her mind.

She looked front. She was suddenly intensely disappointed. She tried to concentrate on the music, to lose herself in it and relax, but her mind kept nagging at her. She couldn't talk to him about the Wilkinses' problems, even hypothetically, without the names. He knew too much about them, so he would see through it sooner or later and figure out who she was talking about. It wouldn't be fair. She had to leave him out of it.

Well, that was okay, wasn't it? She wouldn't be telling anybody about it, right? So why had she thought about talking to him about it at all?

The precise intricacies of Mozart were executed flawlessly, with a touch of the conductor's own take on the score. The motif seemed to almost intrude on the running strings of thought surrounding it, a surge like a first thought, a primary idea, forging through to the surface, heard between and above the rippling of the lesser thoughts, the second guesses, the afterthoughts, the details of trivia that were all still important individually and in their accumulation—and through it all the master of harmony, the unity of the piece, was perfect. Hearing Mozart, Vicki felt she was directly in touch with a distinctly human mind, busily at work, pouring forth in detailed precision, mathematically clean and yet pure emotion. Just when she thought she was concentrating on listening, on hearing the notes, the details of the polyphony, the technical performance, she found that the mind had caught her and taken hold. She had to hold herself back and then her own mind merged with it and pulled her in.

She only allowed herself the barest glance at Tim, trying to keep her eyes and thoughts on the front, on the music, so as not to spoil the trance.

She had the impression that his face, his expression as he sat, absorbed in the music, was not at peace. He seemed more than just a little disturbed, unsettled. He looked, in that unguarded moment, truly anguished. She had to look again. This time he caught her and smiled back. Just what she hadn't wanted him to do. Not the smile— that was pleasant. She hadn't wanted him to catch her looking.

The program got out at nearly eleven. Vicki realized that she had skipped dinner and wondered what she had in her refrigerator at home, wondering if Tim would want to go somewhere this late.

The rain had stopped, at least. Murphy looked up at the low fog as they stood on the sidewalk in front of Davies Hall. He looked down at her, grinning again. "I'm starved."

"You read minds?"

"You hungry, too? Stars?"

She thought about the expense. He couldn't afford it and she didn't really want to argue with him about it. "The kitchen's bound to be closed, don't you think?"

Tim shrugged. "Who knows? My last nighttime assignment was Potrero and we don't want to go there."

"Would you settle for a hamburger?"

He laughed. "I was afraid to suggest it to a doctor."

They went in his car after she got hers out of the garage and parked on the street in front of City Hall so it wouldn't get locked up overnight.

The diner was a practical-looking place, a chain with overworked staff and generally hardworking customers. They were decidedly over-dressed, but at least one other couple looked like they had come from the symphony. Vicki and Tim ordered immediately. Tim said he wanted the fat-free bacon-burger and fries.

The waitress, no novice, gave him a wry look. "Right. We can follow that up with the low-cal pie and ice cream if you want."

They watched her detour to another table. Vicki suddenly remembered talking to her brother.

"Cody said to tell you hi."

"Cody? He did?"

"Beth, too."

He grinned again, a bigger, more satisfied expression than she would have expected after what they said. It seemed important to him.

"Okay, Tim, you got to tell me something I've wanted to know for a long, long time."

"What?"

"Why would any sane person get on the back of a Brahma bull?"

"They wouldn't."

"Oh." She thought about it. "But you did."

"Who said I was sane? The first time I rode a bull I was sixteen years old. All those hormones—by definition, a sixteen-year-old boy is not a sane person."

"Yeah, but you kept doing it. Why would anybody keep doing it?"

"Some people are real slow learners. You will note, please, that I have stopped riding bulls—trying to ride bulls."

"It's a halfway serious question. You're a psychologist now, haven't you ever thought about it? I just can't imagine what would motivate anybody to get on the back of one of those things, knowing the bull's not going to like it and knowing he's going to try to throw you off and turn around and stomp all over you."

"Actually, I have avoided trying to figure out that particular syndrome. Don't want to think about it too much."

"Why? Because it's not too bright?"

He chuckled and looked around in mock guilt. "Look, Vicki, would you want the things you did when you were seventeen, eighteen, nineteen years old to haunt you the rest of your life?"

Vicki couldn't answer. She tried to keep her face pleasant, tried not to show her sudden mortification.

He saw it anyway. "What did I say?"

"Huh?"

"What upset you?"

"Oh, I'm sorry. I walked into that one. It's not your fault. I had a baby when I was nineteen. I got married when I was still in school and the baby had cerebral palsy. Died when she was four. I . . . ." She shook her head in confusion. "I'm sorry, I . . . ." She couldn't think why she was suddenly apologizing.

"It's okay."

"No, I don't know why I blurted that out."

"It's okay."

"I thought I was over all that. I don't know why—"

"Because it's important. You just wanted to say what was important, that's all. Nothing wrong with that, right?"

She took a deep breath and let it out. He was watching her with that kindly smile, the psychologist's smile. "You know what, Tim?" She didn't wait for a response. "You don't act like a cop *at all*. Not in the least little bit."

"Good or bad?"

"It's good. You're more like Cody than you know."

"I am?"

"Oh, never mind. I'll tell you about it when I figure out what I mean."

He sat back in the booth and relaxed, watching her, ready to change the subject. "You still see the Wilkins family sometimes?"

She went cold. She had thought he might ask about them but then she had forgotten. He didn't always bring them up.

"Charlotte's still my patient."

"Oh, yeah. No new information, though, huh?"

"We talk about Charlotte." Her stomach went tight. She hadn't exactly lied, but . . .

"I should probably just give that one up. It would not be the only file I have with an unsatisfactory explanation." His eyes wandered around the restaurant as though he knew she didn't want him to look at her. His voice sounded too casual. "Have you gotten to be friends? I mean, with the Wilkinses?"

Vicki felt the blush start in her neck and rapidly flood her face. He'd seen right through it, the half-assed answer she'd tried to slip by him. She felt a quick surge of irritation at him. "Is this a social occasion or business?"

"Ooh!" He looked and sounded wounded, but kept smiling, trying to brush it off but genuinely embarrassed.

Vicki wished she could take back the sharp words. "Sorry."

"Actually, when I got the chance to grab those tickets all I thought about was an excuse to see you." He let that sink in. "You seem to have something on your mind, though. I just wondered . . ."

"Tim, I'm sorry. I guess I am tense about that, about them."

"It's just that not everything that goes into my head has to go directly down on some report. I thought . . . I guess I thought you might want to talk about them, but . . ."

"No, please. I just . . . is it even possible to talk to you 'off the record' about them?"

"Sure."

"Don't just say that. It puts you in a bad situation, doesn't it?"

"I have been known to have friends, Vicki. And I'm good at confidences with friends as long as they're not confessing to a recent murder."

Vicki smiled and let up a little. "I trust that hasn't happened."

"Well . . ."

"It has?"

His face was serious. He looked down. "That's the bad thing about Narcotics, about the undercover business. You make friends with these people. They think . . . if you do it the way you're supposed to, they think of you as a buddy and then . . . They don't show that part on television." He suddenly looked up. "But this is different. I'm not working now. I'm out with a very attractive lady with whom I am interested in getting better acquainted. Believe me, this is different."

"Tim." She was relaxing again, laughing at him now. "Do you have any idea how old I am?"

"I have an idea."

"I am forty-five years old. I think I'm at least eight years older than you are. Did you realize that?"

"I figured it out. Had to be seven or eight years."

"How did you—?"

"Well, law school takes three years, med school four years, then residency, two years for pediatrics. You practiced law for about ten years or so. Had to be something in that neighborhood, seven or eight years at least. I'm thirty-six."

"Oh, lord! That's nine years' difference."

"Is there a limit?"

She continued to smile at him, watching his face for any kind of clue. Finally, she quit smiling and answered. "I don't know."

He shrugged. "Look, Vicki, I think about it like this. There are so many things that people can do to each other. I mean there are so many godawful things to worry about, that's just not one of them."

She looked at him for a long moment and realized she didn't have any idea how she really felt about it. Nine years—well, that was just too much, wasn't it? She realized he was still watching her, waiting for something.

"Sure you wouldn't rather talk about bulls?"

He laughed easily. "I could tell you a lot about what they look like from the ground. They look pretty ugly when you're upside down in the sand."

"How do you keep from getting hurt?"

"You don't. Those animals are truly big and outrageously evil-tempered. You always get hurt."

"But people keep on doing it."

"No, they don't." He shook his head, watching the hamburger being placed in front of him. "There's good scientific authority that ninety-nine-point-nine percent of the population has never tried to ride a bull." He picked up the hamburger and held it out for her to see. "Most people just eat them." He demonstrated.

She laughed out loud. "No, I mean some people keep doing it."

He chewed thoughtfully a moment. "Well, I guess it's a way to demonstrate to yourself that you are willing and somewhat able to overcome fear. Plus, when you look at it, just stand there and look at a bull, you know it isn't possible to ride him. The first time you stand next to one and really look, even when you've seen other people do it, you think it must have been some kind of trick because every single one of your brain cells is telling you it can't be done. It seems impossible, so you absolutely got to do it. Just about any bull-rider would tell you he's trying to win the money, but although he's quite ignorant about most things, he really does know how unlikely it is that he will win any money. It's like how some people break the law when they could never in their most lucid, sober moment tell you why they did it."

Vicki nodded, remembering some of the cases she'd handled as an assistant district attorney. "I thought they were just that dumb."

"Well, yes, some of them are." He looked at his water glass thoughtfully.

Vicki chewed her own hamburger, watching him watch his water glass.

"How about this?"

He looked up abruptly. "Yes?"

"Can we agree that any conversation we have about the Wilkinses is off limits? I mean you can't use it in your investigation? If they've broken any laws, you can't use it against them."

"Sure." The way he said it, he didn't believe Mr. and especially Mrs. Wilkins would break the law in any important way.

"Don't just say 'sure.' Can you really do that?"

"Yes, ma'am."

"I'm serious."

"What are we talking about?"

"Well . . ." She took a deep breath, let it out, decided to tell him.

Tim ate in silence while she went through the whole thing. Once she started talking about it, she felt as though she were talking to a friend, maybe even a kind of, maybe, possibly potential boyfriend, but that part wasn't important. He was eating, but clearly attentive to what she was saying, watching her hands, her gestures, absorbing everything that she said. She didn't sense any disapproval, any judgment at all about what she told him. He seemed sympathetic. It was the eyes again. She would have to think about those eyes, what it was about them.

"So what do you think?" She said it as though she were dumping it all in his lap.

"I thought that about Frank, too. When I talked to him he was righteously pissed, but what's new? I arrested his wife." He thought about it. "I also thought there was something else he wanted to tell me but he never would. It was more his attitude, like if I knew the whole story I would never have arrested her."

"You've heard that before."

"Sure, all the time. Now I see why he wouldn't tell me, though."

"Are they in a lot of trouble?"

He looked surprised that she would ask. "Yeah, I suppose so, with the Feds and smuggling. That's big-time business. The rest of it, I have no idea. We stay clear of anything that looks like an immigration problem. If we charge somebody that turns out to be illegal, the INS comes in and does their thing, but we don't have anything to do with that part of it. That's what the DA is for, to figure out things like that."

"Do they really put children in jail?"

"The undocumented ones that aren't charged with anything else? I've heard that, yeah. In Juvy, I guess."

"Juvenile Hall?"

"I guess so. Maybe the Feds keep them. They wouldn't put them in the city jail. Want me to find out?"

"Could you?"

"Sure, no problem. What about the Fairchild woman?"

"What about her?"

"Want me to find out if she's been arrested?"

"I don't even have a first name."

He shrugged. "Woman named Fairchild in Los Angeles, arrested on an immigration matter. I could probably find that out on-line."

"It might make some difference to Elaine."

"Make a lot of difference. If she's been arrested she's probably already told the Feds all about the Wilkinses' involvement. Your friend Elaine is right about that."

"Don't do anything that might get you involved. I wasn't asking you to do anything."

"I won't. That information is not exactly secret. It was probably in the paper down south." He picked up his coffee mug, started to take a sip, but stopped before it got to his mouth. "That goes for you, too, right?"

"What does?"

"Well, you're just giving these kids whatever medical attention they might need. That's all you're doing, right?"

"Yes. Right." But her voice held no conviction. She sat back in the booth with her hands in her lap and felt helpless. She couldn't stop thinking about that missing front tooth, the anxiety in those eyes, the face grinning hard in such an anguished, desperate effort to please. Vicki had a sudden mental picture of little Nadya, dragging her left foot among uniformed legs, heading into the jail.

Tim leaned forward to catch her eye. "What is it?"

"Oh, Tim. If you could just see them. They're so young—" Oh.

Vicki stopped her voice and stared hard at Tim's face. Oh, yeah, wait a minute. He would know what small children looked like. He had seen those dead children on the bridge. But she could see little of that in his face now as he looked at her. The sudden, troubled cast of his eye that had stopped her voice gave way to the kindly crinkles at the corners of his eyes. It was a professional face. That had to be what it was, masking what he had thought of when she talked about seeing the children. She remembered the way he had looked in the Moffett cafeteria when those children close to them were making noise, the deep discomfort until she had suggested they take a walk. Yes, he knew what small children looked like.

He assumed that she knew nothing about his accident and he was trying not to show anything, but he had thought of it, listening to her talk about those children's little bodies, seeing her word picture of children in trouble.

And now she couldn't say anything about his accident, either. If he wanted to tell her about it sometime, she had to let him do it in his own time. Even without the consideration for Augy, she would have let him do that.

Tim was still leaning forward, watching her. "You want to talk about something else?"

She laughed. It was a burst of relief more than mirth. He had seen her tension and let her off. Just that easy.

"I want to know your deepest secret."

"My deepest—?"

"Why did you take up psychology?"

Now Tim laughed, caught by surprise. "At the time I started it, I was thinking a lot about it. I thought they really knew something. I didn't realize the difference between science based on empirical data and a belief system based on hunches and labels. It's not as bad as that, but I think psychiatrists have a better shot at dealing with mental problems using pharmacology than any psychologist has."

"Did you get psychoanalyzed?"

"Of course. It's required."

"Ask you about your mother?"

He laughed again. "Yes, lots of questions about my mother."

"Well?"

"What, my mother?"

137

"Yeah, was that a big deal?"

"Not to me. My mother was fine. She had too many things, but she was fine."

"Too many things?"

"My father was a successful businessman. He had a string of furniture stores scattered all over the East Bay, one in San Francisco."

"I thought you were supposed to be a farm boy."

"We lived outside of Walnut Creek. Dad ran a few cows when that was a good tax dodge, had a bunch of horses. My folks were from Oklahoma, thought people were supposed to live like that, I guess, even if they didn't have to."

This is what Augy thought was white trash? Some detective. "Is your father retired?"

"Yeah, he sold it all when I was in high school. Moved to Florida with his secretary."

"Oh." Vicki suddenly sat up straight and stared. No wonder he didn't talk to the other cops about it. She had already found out more than they had in years of knowing him.

He looked up at her suddenly. "How about you?"

"Pardon?"

"I bet you and your mother were close."

"Actually, I hardly knew her. She left when I was nine. Took off with a real estate developer. He didn't like kids."

"Oh."

"Dad moved us to the ranch to get us out of the city. I think he saw enough as a cop that he didn't want us anywhere near it."

Now she was aware that he was watching her and she didn't want to meet his eyes. Finally she did. He was smiling.

"Sure you never rode a bull?"

That fast, she started to make a ribald, smart-ass remark about riding an occasional bull, then realized what she was about to say and stifled it. "I'm sure." She grinned and watched him grinning back.

"It's late."

He nodded but didn't look at his watch. "Yes, it is."

"I guess you better take me back to my car."

"Okay."

On the ride to City Hall, Vicki was quiet, thinking about the children, Tim, all mixed up together now. Maybe she shouldn't have told him about it. But she was glad she had. Somehow, though, it didn't seem right to just tackle him and drag him over to her apartment. She had to work tomorrow. She had to be seeing patients, so she needed to get some real, actual sleep, if she could. Why was she being so damned inhibited? Why the hell was he so damned understanding about it? But she knew she wasn't going to do it.

He stopped his car in the street behind her parked Volvo, threw open the door, and rushed around to open hers before she could do it herself. She had to smile. The young, naïve cowboy had finally come out. The smile was because she had known he was in there, the homicide detective a mere sham, a cover, probably not even convincing to him.

This moment could be awkward. A first date. Like high school kids—a pair of them, awkward as adolescents, having learned everything and then forgotten it all in the intervening decades. She knew he wasn't going to make the first move. She had a flashing thought that she would have preferred that to him just being . . . awkward. As she got out of the car, she grabbed both his hands and kissed him quickly on the mouth.

"Thank you, Tim. That was the most fun I've had in years."

He squeezed her hands then loosened his grip. "Good night, Vicki."

She quickly got into her car. Awkward—why did they both have to be awkward? What happened to the free spirit of a few years ago? Why couldn't she just let things run their course and wind up in bed if she felt like it? Was it just because it had been a long time? Oh, yeah, time. She was already regretting having used the "y" word—as in "years." Nine of them. Maybe it didn't matter. She decided she would not think about that tonight.

Sixteen

"Dr. Shea?" Jenny's voice vibrated with tension.

Vicki was in one of the clinic offices, trying to reassure the parents of a twelve-year-old with pneumonia that their son would eventually be all right. The receptionist knew she wasn't supposed to interrupt a parent conference unless a call was truly urgent. Sometimes it seemed as though anything, including bathroom breaks, that took Jenny away from the switchboard made her nervous.

"Yes?"

"I'm sorry. It seems there's an emergency. I have to ask you to take a call." She looked at the parents, embarrassed at this breach of professional etiquette. "I'm sorry."

The father, plainly irritated, gestured at the phone. "No, go ahead. Please!" His gesture and voice implied that the interruption was no more than he had expected.

Vicki reached for the phone on the desk, trying to convey that this would only take a moment.

"Dr. Shea." Jenny's voice rose, her anxiety level rising even more. "Could you take it out here? You need to take it in the front." Again a nod to the parents. "Sorry."

The father threw up his hands in exasperation. "Take your time. Looks like we got all day."

In the hallway, Vicki looked at the receptionist, the question in her face without her having to ask.

Jenny whispered, "It's the police."

Vicki visibly relaxed. "Inspector Murphy?"

Surprised at the response, Jenny nodded. "Yes."

Vicki shook her head and grinned. "Don't worry about it. Did he say it was an emergency?"

"Very emphatic about it."

"Really?" Vicki rolled her eyes and shrugged as she went into an empty examining room and picked up the phone.

"This is Dr. Shea." Emphasis on the "doctor," but her voice had a smile in it.

"Fairchild isn't telling anybody anything."

"What?"

"She's a 187."

For a very brief second Vicki had the completely irrelevant thought that now Tim sounded like a policeman. This was a cop on the phone, not the innocent-looking young man in the seat next to her at the concert. Then she realized what he'd said. She knew what it was, the code for a homicide instantly clicking, but she didn't want to accept it that fast.

"She's what?"

"She's dead. Murdered. I think it's very important that we get together and talk. I'm coming over to the clinic right now, okay?" He was not really asking.

"Yes. Sure, okay. Right now?"

"I'm headed out the door."

"But Tim . . . how . . . ?"

"All I know is what I was told on the phone, but I got an earful. I'll be there in twenty minutes." He hung up.

When Murphy arrived, Vicki turned him around and steered him outside to the sidewalk. She was in fairly good standing with her group, but she thought she wouldn't be if she had cops visiting her at the office very often. Today Murphy even looked like a cop.

The two of them walked slowly up the sidewalk as they talked. The weather had turned nice, and for a change the wind was not threatening to rip her hair out if she was outdoors for more than five minutes. It was pleasant.

Tim Murphy's face, however, was not. He looked grim.

"They sure it was a homicide?"

"Unless somebody can—" He stopped the cop's sarcastic comeback. He seemed to be all cop, suddenly. So that was in there, too. Vicki realized she was disappointed. She was irritated at herself for giving it any thought under the circumstances, but she missed the other Tim Murphy. She glanced at him but he was gone, this scowling cop in his place instead. He didn't look at her as he continued, trying to explain gently to a non-cop.

"She was cut up. Quite a bit."

Vicki felt a chill run down her back. His attitude, his grim face had told her to expect something like that, but hearing it was another matter. He had quit talking, so she glanced up at him, finally giving her full attention to what he was saying.

"Torture?"

"Maybe. They're faxing me the autopsy." He suddenly seemed to make up his mind about something. He stopped in the middle of the sidewalk and turned her by the shoulders to face him.

"Here's the important part, to you. She had just taken a big hit of heroin, just a short time before she died. I don't know how they know that—"

"It metabolizes."

"What?"

"Heroin metabolizes into morphine and they can get an idea how long it's been in the system by the amount that has metabolized."

He brushed the information aside. "Okay, but here's the thing. She had no tracks. There was only one very recent venipuncture. There's no real evidence that she was an IV user except what was in her system and two dime bags in her purse that had no fingerprints on them."

Vicki blinked, looking at his face.

"Well, that's evidence—"

"No, listen to me. Here's somebody with no known involvement in drugs—a widow with two grown sons—gets murdered with a load of dope on board. Here in San Francisco we got a young woman whose drug history is not consistent with heroin, and that history is several years in her past—she dies under equivocal circumstances with a big dose of the same stuff in her system."

"Oh." She took another step, thinking. "You think . . . ?"

"Well, Vicki, you and I happen to know that they knew each other and that they were working together on something illegal."

The chill in Vicki's spine deepened. "But that was just children—"

Tim brushed that objection aside, too, boring in on the point. "It's called smuggling." He took a deep breath to calm down his impatience. "Think about this. The children were out of the country, foreign nationals. Now they are in the country without benefit of customs or immigration or anything else. They had to make that transition somehow. Why not send along something financially worthwhile with them? Say, like a valuable imported substance?" He watched her face and Vicki was aware of him doing it. His voice softened a little, and he managed a small smile.

"I mean as long as you're making the trip . . ."

She did not smile back, although the humor was familiar. "I take it the Los Angeles police don't have a suspect?"

"Nothing yet. The guy I talked to had only put in one full day on it, so far. Her neighbors all knew her as Aunt Rita. She was a nice, older lady that spent a lot of time in her garden. The woman next door mentioned that there seemed to be a lot of children that would come and visit for a few days and then leave. Rita Fairchild worked part-time at a school library, so they just figured that's where the kids came from."

"What did you tell him?"

"Who?"

"The cop you talked to. What did you tell him about why you were making inquiries?"

"Told him an informant suggested I contact her."

"An informant?"

"Had to tell him something, right?"

"I suppose."

"He won't ask for details about an informant."

"The informant's glad." Her voice sounded cold, even to herself, "But, believe me, he wants to know."

Vicki stared at him, at his eyes, searching out the question he was asking, knowing already what it was. "Oh, shit!"

"Have to, Vicki." He stared at her hard.

"Have to? What did you tell him?" She stared back; her own eyes, she knew, were just as hard as his.

His look softened immediately. "Not a thing. I wouldn't do that without talking to you first."

She had to look away. She couldn't look at him. "But now you're saying I don't have a choice."

"You can take the Fifth, but you didn't do anything wrong yourself."

She still wouldn't look at him. "You going to drag me down there?"

"No, no, no!" He sounded genuinely upset. She wouldn't look at him. "Vicki, think about it. Two people are dead. Everybody thought the first one was a suicide, but you didn't believe it—"

"I didn't?" Now she was angry.

"Okay, I'm the one who didn't. But now you've got to see it, too, right? Isn't there just too much here to kiss it off?" He paused and ducked his head, trying to intercept her stare at the sidewalk, trying to get her to meet his eyes. "Vicki, you see it, right?"

She had to look the other way to keep from looking at his eyes. Now he didn't sound like a cop and she was afraid to meet his eyes.

"Vicki?"

"Tim . . . Tim, I violated a confidence. I should never have said anything at all. I had no right."

"Vicki—"

"I had no right to violate the patient's confidence. The parent or guardian is in the same position here as if they were my patients. I had an ethical duty. I never should have opened my big mouth."

"Vicki, I know that you . . . I know it's upsetting, but you do see it, don't you? It's different now."

Finally, Vicki looked at him. "Damn right it is." She turned and started back toward the clinic. "I have to talk to Elaine."

With a couple of fast steps he was walking next to her. "Vicki, think about this. Just think about it for a moment, okay?"

"You said I don't have a choice."

"I didn't say that, but think about it. Your friends could be in danger themselves."

That stopped her. She wanted to believe that it was a ploy, too easy to give her an excuse to talk to the cops, but then . . . What if he was right? What if Julia was murdered, and the reason had something to do with her knowledge of smuggling, whatever that was? Tim was still watching her. She knew he could see her hesitation.

His voice was soft. "You want to take a look at the autopsy? He's mailing me a copy of the pictures."

Vicki closed her eyes, trying to block out the mental image of a corpse with gaping knife wounds. She had seen that kind of autopsy before and he knew it.

"No. I have to talk to Elaine."

Tim walked next to her, still trying to catch her eye. "Call me as soon as you've talked to her, okay?"

She kept walking, pointing her nose at the clinic door and not slowing down, even when Tim stopped on the sidewalk outside.

As she opened the door and went in, she still didn't look at him, but over her shoulder she said, "Okay." She closed the door behind her, leaving him standing there.

Inside, the clinic looked normal. Two mothers, both of them familiar, were chatting in the waiting room amid the clutter of dog-eared children's books, plastic blocks, and stuffed animals. They stopped talking as soon as she came in, and smiled at her, probably hoping to be called in next. Vicki automatically smiled back as she headed past them to a telephone. Wasn't there something else in their faces? Why did they stop talking? Something, but she didn't have time for it.

She got Elaine on the line in a minute. She must have been expecting the call.

"You meet your new clients?"

"Damn straight. I need to talk to you."

"I need to talk to you, too. Something else has come up, having to do with the same case."

"Oh, they told me all about it." Elaine's voice, a touch of exasperation, told Vicki she thought it was a bad situation.

"There's some more they don't know about. I just found out from the police."

"Oh, really?" Elaine hesitated and Vicki could picture her face, her brain whirring, putting facts together. Her voice, though, sounded more personal.

"Look, I have to go home at five. Come to my house, okay? I need a glass of wine, anyway."

"Best offer I've had all day. I might be later, like seven or so." Vicki looked out the window. She couldn't see the front of the clinic from where she was and Tim wouldn't be just standing out there, anyway. What was she thinking?

If Elaine heard anything in her voice, she was too busy to ask about it. "Okay, babe. See you whenever you get there."

When Vicki turned around, a nurse, the shy one in the clinic, was standing in the doorway holding her next chart. The smile on her face was funny— expectant? Vicki couldn't figure it out. She thanked the nurse and headed for the examining room. She saw the receptionist with a cup of coffee. When Jenny saw her, she grinned, too. The same funny, expectant look. Oh, Christ! Vicki knew what it was. A *man* had called her and come to see her, and now everybody was going weird. Somehow, the way she had steered him outside, maybe her body language while she was waiting for him, had told them it was a social call and special, too. She really, really was that transparent.

She smiled to herself, then remembered the conversation with Tim and quit smiling. Why did everything else still seem normal? She was about to become a witness in a goddamn homicide investigation and it was all because she had shot her mouth off to a good-looking hunk, just because he was being nice to her. She suddenly felt pathetic, an old spinster, making an absolute fool out of herself.

After Vicki finished with her last clinic patient, she picked up a message and a package of medications, sent by Liz, by courier from General. There were a couple of different topical salves for the sores, some pills for the diarrhea, an antifungal cream.

Vicki glanced at her watch and dialed Liz's number at home. Her husband, Arnie, answered in the midst of a background clamor of children's voices, arguing with each other.

"Hi, Arnie, it's Vicki!"

"Well, hello, Vicki, how's it going?"

"Fine. I need to talk to Liz real quick, is she around?"

"It's Friday night, my turn for combat duty. She might have gone out with her buddies at work for a Friday night toot. Shall I tell her to call you?" The background noise was getting louder and Vicki pictured the orthopedic surgeon in an apron with a spatula in his hand.

"It's not that important. I just wanted to thank her for something. Tell her I'm heading over to Elaine's. I'll call her later."

"She's usually home by nine on Fridays. Rebellion's getting out of hand. I better go."

"Okay, thanks, Arnie."

She still had to do rounds before she went to Elaine's.

The little boy they had been calling Peter was sitting up in bed, a pile of picture books around him and the TV blaring. There were two other children in the same room. When Peter saw her, he waved.

"Hallo!"

"Hi, Peter. How you feel?"

"You feel!" He didn't know what the words meant but he was game.

When she lifted the bandage to look at the surgical wound, he pointed to it. "Staples!"

"Yes, staples."

He held up his hands as though working an office stapler, making a vaguely machine-like noise. "Staples!"

The other children laughed. A little girl of about eight or nine spoke up. "We're teaching him English."

Peter affirmed, "Teachy English!" He pointed to the wound. "Staples! Cool!" The other children laughed and he turned to them and grinned.

The little girl encouraged him. "That's right, Peter. Cool!"

"Tha's right! Cool!" He seemed to love the idea that he was stapled together.

Next stop was the Wilkenses' house.

Vicki drove up the long driveway to the back of the house. No one answered the back door when she knocked, and there was no doorbell at the back door. After about five minutes of fruitless rapping, she decided to try the front. She caught sight of a movement in the corner of her eye and saw San Juana watching her out of an upstairs window and waving at her. San Juana gestured at the back door and so Vicki went back to wait for her.

When she opened the door she blocked it with her body, but she didn't look exactly unfriendly. She seemed unsure what to do.

"The Wilkinses had to go out."

Vicki tried her friendliest smile, holding up her package. "I brought medicine. Can I show you what to do?"

That seemed to be enough for a passport. San Juana relaxed and smiled. "Oh. Oh, sure, come on in." She securely double-locked the door behind Vicki.

As they headed down the stairs, Vicki had to ask. "They leave you alone with all of those kids?"

San Juana's voice was matter-of-fact. "My sisters are helping out."

"Sisters? How many do you have?"

"I've got eight, but only three of them are here now."

"Nice to have reinforcements."

"The only way."

Vicki sat on the floor to examine skin lesions and apply ointments. She explained the different medications to San Juana, who put it all down on a list she had made up. The woman was organized.

Nadya stood next to Vicki, her little hand on Vicki's shoulder, waiting her turn. Vicki checked her over quickly, but she didn't need any medications. There was an asymmetry in Nadya's face, a slightly relaxed left side that showed in a very small droop of the left eye, a slightly off-center look to the mouth. To most people it would simply be endearing; to Vicki it was evidence of central nervous system pathology. But it was endearing, too.

Vicki talked to her as she checked her. "You seem to be doing pretty well, huh? Getting enough to eat? You helping out with the babies?"

"Bebe." Nadya looked at her for confirmation that she'd said it right.

Vicki pointed at a diapered urchin reeling past them on unsteady legs. "Baby."

Nadya frowned and pointed at the same toddler. He had a large sticky scab across the back of his head. "Pobrecito!"

Vicki laughed out loud and hugged the little girl to her. "Yes, poor little thing. Poor baby."

Nadya squirmed around until she could lock her arms around Vicki's neck and then squeezed so hard that it hurt.

Vicki had to work to pry her off as she stood up. She kissed the child's cheek. "I'll come see you again, okay?"

Nadya's eyes filled with tears and her mouth turned down in desperate disappointment. She started to sob until Vicki kissed her again quickly.

"I'll be back. I'll see you again, soon, okay?"

The little face struggled, then produced the grin, the painful, strained, completely absorbed grin with a gap in the middle, the eyes tearfully pleading, wordlessly hoping.

Vicki almost ran up the stairs, trying to think about Elaine, trying to only think about going to Elaine's.

She accelerated backwards out of the driveway, jumped over the curb as she cut it too sharply, came out onto the street, then slammed into drive and sped away. The child's face, though, stayed right with her.

Seventeen

Karen, Elaine's young British au pair, met Vicki at the door and led her toward the back of the house. As she passed the dining room, Vicki could see a file folder open on the table, the draft of a thick pleading, probably interrogatories, with red ink changes all over it. Vicki did not miss interrogatories. In fact, now that she thought about it, she was surprised at how little she missed any part of practicing law. She remembered other parts of it, too—what a huge kick it had been, at the time, to be the center of attention in a courtroom—but now that seemed to have been a long time ago. So much had changed.

Elaine was in the nursery, sitting on the carpet with throw pillows all around her on the floor. Justin navigated his way among pillows, toys, and discarded laundry while holding a juice bottle tipped up at the best angle for gravity feed. Elaine tried to grab him as he ambled near her, but missed. Her face glowed with animation.

"Hi, Vicki! Pull up a pillow, I want you to see this." She beamed at her child. "Justin?"

The boy ignored her. Spotting the doctor, his face grew somber. This was the lady who gave him shots. Vicki knew the reaction too well. She sat down and smiled, trying to look harmless. "Hi, Justin."

Justin lowered the bottle, then raised it and waggled it at her. "Hi." His expression of sober caution did not change.

Elaine was gushing. "Justin! Show Dr. Shea how you can dance! Come on, dance!"

Instead, he retreated to his mother's lap and tucked in his arms, warily keeping a close monitor on what this doctor might be up to this time.

"Oh, now he won't do it! You should see him dance!"

Vicki had to smile at her. Elaine, the bull-bitch lawyer, was just like every other mother when she got home. Every little antic was further proof positive of her child's exceptional talent and probable—no, unequivocal—potential for true genius. No other kid had ever learned to say "hi" or to wave quite like that, or to squat on a toilet or to grow a tooth. Absolutely everything was new and fabulous.

This time, though, Justin did seem to look exceptionally good to Vicki, too. It took her a moment to realize that she was admiring the roundness of his limbs, the fullness of his face. No refugee here.

Karen was leaning in the doorway, bored. "Shall I take him?"

Elaine seemed disappointed, a child herself. "Oh, I suppose. It's bathtime, anyway, huh?" She looked down at her son, ensconced in her lap. "Ready for bath?"

Justin unplugged the bottle and squirmed. "No!"

"But you love the bath!"

"No! No bath!"

"Now, none of that, buster." Karen snatched him up without hesitation. "Time to make a mess out of another room. Would you like that? Want to make a mess? Want to splash?"

"Splash!"

"That's the ticket. Big splash."

Vicki heard their voices trailing down the hall. "Big, biiiiig splash!"

"Well . . . maybe a medium-sized splash, huh?"

Elaine, still sitting, her lap empty now, sighed. "I am so lucky."

"Yes, you are."

"She's only seventeen years old, can you believe it? She'll probably announce any day that she's pregnant and getting married."

"Really?"

"Oh, not really. I just figure it can't last." She looked around the room, but Vicki could see her mind working. "I talked to your friends." Finally, she turned back and looked at Vicki directly, a look that was definitely loaded.

Vicki nodded and waited for her to go on, watching Elaine's mind whir behind the glasses.

Finally, Elaine pushed herself off the floor and began picking up toys, tossing them into an open chest as though distracted, not sure what to say about the "friends." Vicki started to help. Elaine saw her, looked down at the truck in her hand, and then dropped it. "Oh, don't bother, Vicki. Let's talk in the dining room and I won't have to look at it."

As she followed her down the hall, Vicki saw Elaine push her fingers up under her dark curls, lift the mane, and shake it out, as though lifting one load to make way for another in her head, making a transition. She took a turn into the kitchen before she reached the dining room. As she opened the cupboard and reached for glasses, she asked, "Wine?"

Vicki shook her head. "Not for me."

"Really?" She glanced at Vicki as she reached in the refrigerator for an open bottle. "I'll bring an extra glass in case you change your mind. You might want to change your mind."

Vicki frowned. "Was it that bad?"

"Well . . ." Elaine's voice rose high on the register as she shrugged and headed into the dining room. "Yes and no. Some good, some bad. Like everything else, right?"

"Sure."

Elaine closed up the file on the table, then pulled a yellow pad filled with notes out of her briefcase. She crossed her legs and made herself comfortable in a chair as she poured.

"The good news is that they gave me fifty thou as a retainer. A part of that is going to be yours for the referral, by the way. I forget if it's twenty-five percent or a third. I'll ask a partner."

"I don't want a legal fee, Elaine. I don't know one thing about immigration law. I was a specialist in medical malpractice."

"Nobody knows anything about immigration unless you deal with it all the time. It's too technical for other people to keep up. That doesn't matter, that's why you got me to consult with." She shook her head as though to get her mind back on the topic. "You need to accept a fee unless you want to be answering questions sometime down the road. Attorney-client works better than the doctor-patient privilege these days." She saw Vicki's face. "Oh, don't worry about it. We can talk about that later. Besides, it may be academic if I have to just give most of it back."

"Give it back? Why?"

"They may not be willing to cooperate at all. There's a lot they're not saying, you know? Stuff they leave out."

"Well, it was only a first interview."

"True. You never get all of it the first visit, but—oh, never mind. Maybe they're okay, but they're probably going to refuse to take my advice. I know for sure what my next step is going to be. I'm going to write them a nice detailed letter, certified, giving them my best legal opinion. I haven't done all the research yet, but I know enough to tell them the direction it's probably going to go. They don't like it one bit, I can tell you that."

"So, you're sending them a CYA?"

Elaine nodded. "I *always* cover my ass, especially with people I'm not sure about." She gave Vicki another meaningful look. She sipped her wine and then looked at her notes, shifting gears.

"Okay, here's what I can piece together. This is co-counsel talking here, okay?"

Vicki nodded. "Yes, I understand."

"Okay. These folks have been financing a fairly extensive people-smuggling outfit. Maybe more than one, they don't know all the details. In fact, according to them, they know hardly any of the details. Their daughter, the one who died . . ."

"Julia."

"Right, Julia. She's the one who got the deepest into it, actually carrying around bags of currency, I suppose, to pay off these guys. Cynthia thought they were Turkish, but then she thought they might not be. To tell you the truth, Vicki, it's just as well she keeps saying she doesn't know. Anyway, Cynthia says they thought they were just doing a one-time operation, the kids that they had seen—I guess they got attached to them or some damn thing. But when it worked the first time, after they saw these kids in L.A. headed out to adoptive parents, Julia turned right around and went back for more. Cynthia and Jack didn't want to tell Frank what they were doing, but it is a partnership, so of course they finally had to tell him where the money went. He apparently warmed up quick, got as feloniously enthusiastic as the rest, once he knew what was going on. They probably transported a hundred kids, maybe a few more than that before something—" Elaine's face lit up with humor, shifted gears again in mid-sentence. "You know, I don't think these people are your average American business people."

Vicki shrugged, taking the remark seriously. "I don't know. I really don't."

"You think your average American businessman smuggles kids into the States?"

"No, but they might want to. I don't know anything about any of it." She waved off the distraction. "Keep going. They paid for smuggling in about a hundred children and then something happened? Something went wrong?"

"Right. The first thing that went wrong was that Julia comes back from one of these clandestine meetings with more than change from the transaction."

"She got pregnant."

"Right. Her boyfriend was . . . well, it sounds like he was already married, although the Wilkinses weren't too sure about that, and I believed them. Maybe he just didn't want to be bothered. Anyway, there was obviously some impediment, so Frank stepped in at the last minute. I guess she really, really wanted this kid and wanted to provide as normal a family as she could come up with." Elaine rolled her eyes at the reasoning.

"So Julia and Frank . . . ?"

"I don't think they ever lived together. I didn't ask, but that was my impression. They had a civil ceremony and Frank's name is all over the child's records and pedigree, but I think that's all. Nobody has ever met the father."

"Nobody?"

"Well, nobody who can tell us about it. Our clients say they have no idea what he looks like, even what nationality he is. They can only surmise that he's Caucasian because the baby seems to be."

"But why wouldn't she tell them? They're not that old-fashioned, are they?"

"No, they are not."

"Then . . . ?" Vicki watched Elaine's face. Elaine was watching her, anticipating something. Then Vicki realized what it was. "Oh! She was still seeing him?"

"Ta-dah! Congratulations, you have just hit on a most important issue, that I, for one, would rather not know any more about."

"She was?"

"You asked the right question. Nobody admits they have the answer to it for sure. All right, they have me convinced me that they don't know. But if she was still seeing him, it means he was here in the States because she hadn't been out of the country for a year."

Vicki studied Elaine's face, trying to see if she saw the significance of what she was saying. "But how did she pay for this last . . . this group of children that just showed up?"

"Their story is that she told them she knew how to get the money to the smugglers, just give her the cash and she would take care of it, don't ask questions. They thought she was sending it through the mail or something."

"Through the mail? How much cash?"

"Two hundred thousand."

"Through the mail?"

"They claim Julia just took care of it and wouldn't tell them. At least in retrospect, even the Wilkinses admitted he had to be here. Probably right here in San Francisco."

Vicki leaned her elbows on the table, her hands over her mouth as she stared into space, thinking hard. Her voice was barely audible. "Oh, my God."

Elaine nodded. "Right. I know just what you're thinking. Cynthia, Jack, and Frank Sanderson, all three are sure there was somebody else there at Julia's house when the baby got hurt. I think they're probably right."

Only Vicki's eyes moved, shifting to look at Elaine. Then she lowered her hands to the table. "They told you about that?"

"Yes. But they don't blame you anymore. They can see how it looked and Julia would never openly admit, even to them, that anybody else was there. She didn't completely deny it, either. Just said she couldn't tell them. They didn't say this, but I know why she wouldn't tell them. Her father and Frank, both are at least that old-fashioned. They were ready to kill whoever had hurt that child. Not literally."

"Did I tell you she was murdered?"

For once, Elaine looked startled. "Who? Julia?"

Vicki nodded and looked down at the table.

Elaine pushed the bottle and an empty glass across the table, her face serious, concerned. "I thought it was a suicide."

Vicki poured for herself. "I did, too."

"But now you think it was murder?"

"I told you, there was something else I found out."

Elaine's face changed as she remembered their brief telephone conversation. "Oh, yeah. What's this new information and what are you doing talking to the police about it, anyway?"

Vicki shook her head and looked away. "Oh, this is embarrassing. This is a friend."

"Oh." Elaine gave her a quizzical look. "A police officer kind of friend?"

"Yes. I wanted to see if I could find out about this contact they had in Southern California."

"Oh, right." Elaine looked down at her notes on the yellow pad. "Somebody named Mrs. Fairchild?"

"Yes."

"Yeah, I wrote it down to follow that up, too." She paused, looked up at Vicki. "Why is it embarrassing?" Her brain whirred, then her face broke into a huge, mischievously delighted grin.

"Oh! I get it!" She laughed out loud. "Vicki! You're shtupping a cop? Christ almighty! I was ready to give up on you!"

"I'm not sleeping with anybody." Vicki could feel her face glow with the rising flush.

"Hah! Don't try to kid me! Well, okay, maybe not shtupping him, but I bet it's not your fault if you're not."

"I'm going to leave."

Elaine howled with laughter. "Don't even think it! Have some more wine. You're going to tell me all about it."

"Really, Elaine, there's nothing to tell. I mean it. Nothing."

Elaine quit laughing but kept the grin, watching Vicki for signs of what she was thinking. "Okay, if you don't want to tell me, don't." She kept grinning. "We can get back to it later. What's the information?"

Vicki filled her in on her last conversation with Tim, including the fact that he wanted her to talk to the detectives openly and that she had told him she would call him back with an answer.

Elaine took more notes on the yellow pad, watched Vicki's face intently, and read between the lines.

"So Fairchild was murdered, some of the circumstances are similar to the circumstances of Julia's death. Sounds bad to me."

"Me, too."

"And on top of it, Fairchild was mutilated?"

Vicki's voice was barely more than a whisper. "Yes, or tortured. Might be able to tell from the autopsy, but maybe not."

Elaine nodded, thinking, watching Vicki for a long time. "The most obvious reason somebody might do that—well, two obvious possibilities—either to get her to tell them something she doesn't want to tell, or to send a warning to someone else, right?"

"Yes, I thought of that." Vicki looked up. She hadn't realized it, but she had made that connection before Elaine said it. Elaine was staring at her, still waiting.

"So, you going to call him back? This cop?"

"I told him I had to talk to you first."

"And what's my advice gonna be?"

"Don't talk to him."

"Of course." She thought about it. "Except now we do have to let the police know something, don't we? I got to get Jim Gonzalez into this to see how to handle it." Elaine gave it a couple of beats. "So, you going to call him?"

"Oh, Elaine, I don't know."

"Look, Vicki, what's to be gained by talking to him besides . . . well . . ." She shrugged, her palms up. "Answered my own question."

"No, Elaine. Let's don't get into that, okay?"

Elaine shrugged again. "We can get back to it."

"You said the Wilkinses wouldn't follow your advice."

"Oh, yeah. Well, they didn't exactly refuse yet. To me, it's real obvious. They got this house full of kids that they shouldn't have there. They can't just keep them, right?"

"Why not?"

"Twelve kids?"

"Okay, but what did they want to do?"

"Obviously, they don't know about Fairchild. They were holding out hope that she'd get in touch with them and then everything would be back to normal. Sort of. Whatever normal is for this particular scenario."

"Well, Fairchild's out of the picture now."

"Clearly. The INS has to be notified somehow. I'd have to work out something with the U.S. Attorney's office, make some kind of arrangement to turn them over—"

"Just put them in jail? Just like that?"

"You sound like the Wilkinses did this morning."

Vicki heard the sound of the doorbell and looked at Elaine. "You expecting someone?"

Elaine nodded, looking back at Vicki. "The cavalry. Reinforcements."

"Well, I won't stay, you've got—"

"Don't you move, young lady." Elaine rose from her chair and headed for the front door. She tossed her voice over her shoulder. "Well, you could get another glass down."

Vicki found another wineglass. She was thinking about how to gracefully get away. She needed time to think by herself. She didn't

think she needed to listen to lectures from another lawyer, no matter—
She recognized the voice in the front hall. Liz Abrams. They were
ganging up.

As Liz came into the dining room she didn't even pause for a greeting. "I found you a pediatrician."

"What for?"

Liz looked at the table, the bottle of wine, the pad of notes, anything but at Vicki. "To take over the workup on these kids, get you out of it."

"Why?"

"It's Stephani Swenson, know her?"

"No. Why—?"

"She spent three years in Guatemala." Liz finally looked at Vicki and Vicki could tell she was trying to be enthusiastic, a selling job. "She knows all about parasites, foreign bugs, malnutrition, all of that."

"Guatemala is not in Eastern Europe."

"Closer than San Francisco. Well, at least in conditions."

"Liz, I'm just fine, thank you. I don't need for you to get me out of anything."

"I saw your face, Vicki. You need to just leave that whole bunch alone, understand?"

Elaine pulled a chair back, indicated for the other two to sit down, but directed her remark to Vicki. "And she doesn't even know about the murders."

Liz stayed on her feet. "What murders?"

"See? And we're not going to tell her, either."

Vicki sat down and put her head in her hands. "Oh, Elaine!"

"No, don't tell her. Leave her out of that."

"What murders? Jesus Christ! Elaine!"

Vicki shook her head, still holding it between two hands. "Will you two please—"

"What murders? Who got murdered?"

Elaine's voice was matter-of-fact, firmly in control. "Nobody you know or met. You saw the kids, the whole operation looks funny, right?"

"Yes."

"That's all you need to know. Think of the murders as part of the funniness."

Vicki still wouldn't look at her. "Liz, sit down. The Wilkinses' daughter was killed a month or six weeks ago, and now we found out that somebody else that had something to do with the kids was killed in Los Angeles. Honestly, that's just about all we know."

Liz remained standing. "Isn't that enough?" She looked at Elaine. "Is this my glass?"

"Help yourself."

"Listen to me, Vicki." Obviously, Liz had been rehearsing this on the way over from Mill Valley. Vicki at last looked at her as she went on. "You may be experienced in a lot of things, but you are just a new doctor. You get yourself mixed up in something shady, and the medical community will *not* rally to your support. Your own practice group won't even do that, understand?"

"I'm not mixed up in anything. I'm just a doctor, doing what a doctor ought to do."

"Fine. Then step aside and let Stephani finish up."

"Liz, it's not—" She had started to say it was not that simple, but then realized she would have to explain why and she realized she had no idea how to put it. *Why* was a tough question. She found herself gaping, not able to finish her thought.

Liz dropped the sales-pitch tone. "Vicki, this is a couple of your best friends, here right?"

"Yes, of course."

"I know how these kids affect you, but it's not . . . it's just not good."

Elaine's voice had become quiet, too. "What she's saying is that it's absolutely hopeless. What you want to do is impossible. There are millions of children all over the world that need help but you're just a single pediatrician in San Francisco. There are agencies you could work with if you want to do that. I mean legal agencies, United Nations Children's Fund, people like that, people that are not outside the law."

"I know." Vicki took a deep breath but let it out without saying anything. There was no point in arguing.

Liz leaned toward her. "Vicki, I saw you with these children, but there isn't anything you can do about them." She looked at Elaine. "Right?"

"That's right. It is completely impossible that you could do anything other than turn them over to the proper agency that deals with people like this."

"Put them in jail."

"Well, they don't have any other place to keep them. It's not like they're—"

"Then send them back to the camps they came from."

"Vicki, you can't do anything about that. It's beyond your power to control that, understand? You do understand, right?"

Vicki's pager went off. She automatically fished it out of her pocketbook and looked. Tim's home number. She kept her expression unchanged and put the pager back. When she looked up, both Liz and Elaine were watching her.

"It's okay. I can return it later."

Elaine stared hard at her. "It's him!"

Liz looked from one to the other. "Who?"

"Him. Look."

Vicki could feel the flush start all over again, absolutely transparent to the world. "Oh, Elaine!"

Liz's eyes widened as she started an open-mouthed grin, the light dawning. "A beau?"

"She's shtupping a cop."

"Elaine!" Vicki was beginning to get angry but amused at the same time. "I'm not shtupping—can't I have a private life?"

Liz's face became mock serious. "I can't imagine why. You're single."

"Yeah, Vicki. Look at it this way," Elaine said. "You and I don't have an obligation to be irresponsible and reckless. We're divorced already."

"Who's irresponsible and reckless?"

"How many kids you got, Liz?"

"Oh. Not the same thing."

"You're right." Elaine shifted her focus back to Vicki. "Okay, you going to tell us about this guy?"

"There is really, really, really nothing to tell. You would be bored to death. I just got a call from a friend who's a police officer who was investigating Julia's death, and now he wants to know all about the Wilkinses."

Liz's expression was deadpan. "Not the first time he's called. Or the second."

"He's called a few times."

Liz smirked. "Bet he's cute."

"Liz, he's nine years younger than I am."

Both of them howled with delight, Liz clapping and Elaine tipping so far back in her chair she was in danger of going over. Elaine held her hands up and shook them as though her fingers had been burned. "I bet he's been sniffing along behind you like a homesick bloodhound! Maybe you better just slow down."

"Oh, please!"

"Let me guess. Blond?"

"Yes."

"Beach boy? Surfer?"

"No, and I am not answering any more questions. I haven't even so much as kissed the man—Well, I mean, just . . ."

"I knew it!" They both howled again, a raucous, raunchy chorus.

Eighteen

Vicki almost felt battered by the time she got home. The empty apartment seemed to welcome her. It was her private place, her lair, full of familiar objects, and quiet even on a Friday night. It was her refuge. It was the best place to hide and give herself time to think.

Maybe they were right. Well, no question, if she let herself think about it. Liz and Elaine were correct, that she should not go any further down that road, on some hopeless, doomed effort to rescue a few children—just patients, really—that honestly, realistically, could not be rescued. Nobody could save them from the circumstances of their birth, and the death or disappearance of their parents. At least, not this way, not instantaneously, by paying some money and bringing them to this country.

Vicki knew that there were legal adoptions, that American couples went to Eastern Europe and somehow came back with children who had papers, legal immigrants. Vicki wasn't sure how it worked, but she knew it was terribly expensive and it took a long time. But these children? All of them were malnourished, some had skin diseases that needed treatment, one, at least, with visible brain damage, and the others, possibly damaged just from the lack of an adequate diet. Who would adopt that little girl with the gap in her grin, but with a leg that dragged her down as much as it bore her along? Send her back? To what? Another bullet?

Vicki did not doubt Elaine's judgment. Immigration law was so specialized that only someone as up on it as Elaine would be able to give her decent advice about it. Vicki knew, deep down, that Elaine was saying what she herself might have told someone if she had known more about the issue, if she had known what the correct answer was before she saw that child. But she wasn't convinced that it was right. It didn't feel right. But what else? They were supposed to just turn everybody in to the cops and say, "Oh, well"?

Vicki still had not called Tim back, because she didn't know what to say to him.

At least he was principled, thank God. He hadn't just jumped over her and used the information that she had gratuitously handed to him. He was waiting for her to release him from his personal promise of confidentiality. He knew that she would have to let him use the information unless she could think of some rational, legal alternative. But what? That was the problem. There wasn't any legal alternative. That's what Elaine kept trying to tell her.

But the only way that Tim knew about the children, the smuggling, the connection with Rita Fairchild, was because Vicki had told him about it in the strictest personal confidence. If the information had not involved a police investigation, then what she had told him probably wouldn't have mattered at all. He didn't have a direct obligation to go after suspects on federal offenses as long as they didn't involve a simultaneous violation of state laws. Probably he wouldn't even care. No, certainly, he wouldn't care about somebody's problems with immigration.

But now it was no longer a matter of a purely personal confidence, a private confession of relatively minor wrongdoing by her patient's guardians. Now, with Fairchild's murder and its similarity to Julia's death, it was a matter that he had specific, significant reasons for pursuing. Now he couldn't just ignore it, even if that's what he wanted to do. He had an obligation to follow the rules, and the bare rules would tell him he had to report this to the feds, to the INS.

If it hadn't been a matter of a personal confidence, he would probably have done that already or at least put it in motion through the DA. A lot of cops would have just taken the information and skipped right past her, personal confidence or not. It was what they were supposed to do, wasn't it? The very last thing he was supposed to do was to be concerned about personal matters, personal obligations to friends.

She could just ask him directly. No, that was silly. She knew the answer to that question. He didn't really have any choice, once the immigration violations became part of his official investigation. If she asked him he would have to tell her that he was going to turn them in. The Wilkinses would be on the way to jail and the children would be on the way back to Eastern Europe. But he hadn't done it yet. He was waiting for her, letting her feel like she had some say.

That thought led her to the other, more personal aspect of the conversation. Liz and Elaine had seen through her so quickly that it had seemed funny. But now, in her own apartment, thinking rationally without the ribald jokes, her personal interest in Tim Murphy seemed almost trivial next to the other problems. It wasn't as if she had an ongoing relationship with the man. It wasn't even a sexual liaison, something that in her past would not have been unusual at all. This relationship was nothing, wasn't it? Now that she thought about it coolly?

Except it wasn't "nothing" entirely. Vicki shook her head, not making sense to herself, even.

Well, okay, but this was a more serious situation now. She had better put that part, the personal part, the part about her personal wishes out of her mind. She just had to, that's all. Forget it. Too much of an age difference anyway, right? She already knew that, right? Right.

She was not convinced, but she thought she was on the way. Nothing truly intimate had even been said between them, nothing had been spoken and nothing had happened. If she broke off thinking of him like that now, there was nothing to get over. Like what? Good time to cut it off. There. Okay.

She did not feel appreciably better.

She ran the water in the tub, full hot. Relax. Go to bed. Almost midnight. Too late to call him now anyway.

She knew the phone was going to ring before it did. When it actually sounded, she stared at it, then picked it up with a decisive sweep of her hand, punched the button with authority.

"Dr. Shea."

"It's Murphy. Thought you'd be home by now."

"Hold on." She turned off the water in the bath, walked into her dining room, and sat down at the table as if he were there, sitting across from her, waiting to talk.

"Tim?" There was almost a whine in her voice. Damn it!

"Yeah, I'm here."

"Tim, how am I going to admit to Cynthia Wilkins that I ratted on her?" There, that was it. The question crystallized as she spoke it. That was the real problem. Trivial, but vitally important to her at the same time.

"Let me tell her."

"Oh, Tim. I could never do that. I have to tell her."

"You can be there. Take me over to the house with you. Get me in the door and let me handle it from there."

When she didn't answer for a moment, he spoke again, his voice a little lower, less insistent. "Unless you can think of something better, I think that's the best way. Just think about it, okay?"

"Okay." She heard herself answer before she was ready, agreeing to something she did not agree to. She shook her head silently and rubbed her eyes with her free hand. Her decisiveness had deserted her instantly at the sound of his voice.

His voice remained quiet. "I talked to L.A. again this afternoon."

Vicki opened her eyes. "And?"

"Rita's house was ransacked when she was killed. Either somebody was looking for something or they wanted it to look like a robbery. The cops inventoried what was left pretty thoroughly. There's no black book, no records of contacts or children or adopting parents. Nothing. If she had records, she kept them somewhere else or they're gone."

"You've seen the inventory?"

"They faxed me the whole report."

"What did you tell them?"

"Nothing yet, but they're expecting some help from me. That's the protocol."

"Oh. I guess it would be, huh?"

"Listen, Vicki . . . it's late and you're tired. Think about it overnight, okay? But think about this. The lady had to have records of some kind. She almost certainly had the Wilkinses' name and numbers, right?"

"Maybe just Julia's. We already knew they had that."

"Right, but even if they didn't before, whoever did this to Rita Fairchild has Julia's address now. How long would it take somebody to track the Wilkinses down from Julia's, huh?"

"I . . . I don't know . . ."

"Okay. Just don't think it over too long, okay?"

"No. I mean, okay."

"Vicki?"

"Yes."

"You know what I'm concerned about, right? We don't know what went wrong with this situation. Heroin is involved somehow, and we already know they were smugglers, whoever they are. Suppose what we're seeing is some very serious people trying to cover their tracks? Know what I'm talking about?"

"Yes, sure. I've thought of that, too. But the Wilkinses really don't know anything that would lead you to . . . whoever this is that killed Mrs. Fairchild."

"Well, maybe they don't. The more important question is whether the bad guys know that they don't know. All they have to do is think that the Wilkinses know something and they could be in some serious trouble without help."

"Even with help." Vicki had to agree with what he said. She was getting more alarmed about the Wilkinses' safety, the more she thought about it.

Vicki rubbed her eyes again, trying to think. "Doesn't it seem more likely, though, that whoever killed Julia knew that they had only dealt with her? I mean, it's been more than a month. If the Wilkinses were in danger, wouldn't something have happened before now?"

"How do we know for sure?" Tim's voice was patient, reasonable. She could picture the reasonableness in his eyes.

"I guess . . . I guess we don't know that for sure, huh?"

"Exactly." His voice sounded firm, but there was understanding there, too. He wasn't pushing her that hard. She heard a further softening in his voice. "I'll talk to you tomorrow." He hesitated. "Goodnight, Vicki."

"Goodnight, Tim." She pushed the off button on the phone and then sat and looked at it for a full minute.

Afterwards Vicki soaked in the tub, trying to make her mind a blank. She thought she'd been in there an hour but when she got out of the bath and went to the bedroom, it had only been about twenty minutes. Getting into bed, she felt drained, as exhausted as if she had been up for a couple of days running.

When she opened her eyes again and looked, the clock said 2:30. She must have been sleeping, but she felt as though she had just put her head down. Except now there was an idea forming.

Tim Murphy would not be able to look at those kids, to actually see those children and then send them off to jail. He wouldn't! He would see those small faces and think of his accident.

She didn't have to talk to him about it, she didn't have to see the memory in his face, she felt certain that she knew him that well already. She thought of what he had looked like, his reaction to the children in the cafeteria at Moffett. Just seeing small children did that to him.

She could almost picture the scene of his accident in her mind. It took little imagination for her to see what they would have looked like before the emergency crews arrived. The children could have been ejected from the wreckage, or maybe trapped inside. He would have looked at them first, tried to see what he could do for them before he did anything else. He had seen them, looked at them. Knowing his responsibility for the accident, he would have been in terrible turmoil. He must have wanted to run. It must have occurred to him to deny the responsibility, but he hadn't. He'd stayed. He didn't leave those dead children he was responsible for, that he must have looked at close-up, and must have seen the injuries, seen the death, either there or fast approaching. Vicki knew that even for police officers, seeing fatally injured children was something they never got used to, that even the hardest were never quite that hard that it didn't bother them. It would have been doubly or triply hard for this man, not just because of who he was but because he knew that he had caused it.

Afterwards, according to Augy, he had been hospitalized, probably suicidal. Of course, he had seen it. He'd seen death in those children's faces and probably seen the potential, the wish for his own death there, too.

Vicki sat up, swung her feet to the floor, and then sat there, staring into the dark. Tim was not just a cop. She remembered that she had thought that about him right from the beginning, that he didn't look or act like a policeman, even to someone who had known lots of different cops. He was different. Augy had helped fill that in—what made him different—the accident. The potential may have been there before, but it was the accident that did it. Augy said that he'd changed, that he was completely different from what he'd been like before. Augy had said that he would never get over it. She knew instinctively that Augy was right.

The image in his mind of those children on the bridge would be so strong that when he saw these other children, live ones who desperately needed his help, he would—

Oh, wait.

My God, what was she thinking? She was going to manipulate him by showing him children that needed help? How could she do that to him?

She tried to block out the thoughts but the arguments kept coming to her unbidden.

Do what? He's the one that had wanted her to take him over to the Wilkinses' house. He knew those children were there.

Of course, that didn't mean he had to go down the stairs to the basement.

Well, but if she was taking him over there to introduce him and that's where the Wilkinses happened to be, as they seemed to be most of the time. . . . But it wouldn't be as though she were deliberately showing him the children, knowing the effect it would have on him, in order to get him to do something. Would it?

No. Forget it. It would be unspeakably cruel and she wouldn't do it. Go back to sleep, think of something else. She tried to lie back down. What was the point of showing him the children, knowing he wouldn't just look at them and see contraband? The point, of course, would be to get him to help.

Help what? How?

Well, to help her figure out how to avoid Elaine's jail sentence. To try to figure out how to avoid letting the INS ship them right back to the squalid refugee camps they came from.

Nadya's face grinned at her, that painful, hopeful grin with the missing tooth, the little droop in her eye. The face had been there all along. It wouldn't go away, wouldn't be dismissed. What would happen to a child like that, one with handicaps, visible physical impairments? She would never be adopted legally by people who could see her. With all the other, relatively undamaged children available to anybody who went there to look, she wouldn't have a chance. How would she grow up? What could she look forward to? Vicki realized she had no idea, but she knew it would not be much.

But if she were here, where thousands more prospective parents were available—people who wanted children in any event, who didn't have the tens of thousands of dollars it would cost to go to Europe and pursue a legal adoption—with all those people to choose from, somebody would want her, somebody would see that smile the way Vicki saw it, somebody would appreciate that affectionate, generous nature. Maybe somebody like a single doctor who really needed somebody to mother. No, can't think about that. But there would be somebody, wouldn't there?

Not if Nadya had to go back.

Jesus! What was she thinking? What in the hell was Tim supposed to do about that? A city policeman was not the person to go to in order to circumvent federal immigration law. There wasn't anything he could do about that, right? Of course not. Nothing he could do.

Except this wasn't just any city policeman. This was Tim Murphy. He would try to come up with something more creative than calling the goddamn INS. Wouldn't he? Vicki knew she was fast running out of ideas, places to turn. Maybe Tim would be able to think of something.

Vicki knew he would try. Even if he didn't see the children. He would try to come up with something for her. He was at least interested in her, maybe more than that. From the sound of his voice on the phone, maybe he was already trying to tell her that he was more than a little interested. He knew, she was certain, that she was interested in him. He would try to come up with something for her, just to help her, and then seeing the children on top of that. . . .

When the phone sounded, Vicki grabbed it automatically, looking at the clock as she swung her feet to the floor. 4:35 A.M. She must have fallen asleep again after all. She switched on the light as she tried to focus.

"Dr. Shea."

She heard the nurse's voice, yelling away from the receiver on the other end. "I got her! I got Dr. Shea on the line!" Then, into the receiver, "Just a minute."

A man's voice. "Dr. Shea?"

"Yes, who is this?"

"This is Mark Tanner, head of Security?"

"Hospital security?"

"Yes. It looks like one of your patients may have been taken from the hospital. The police are already here, but I wondered if there might have just been a misunderstanding—"

"What do you mean? My patient was taken where?"

"We don't know. There was a man, or maybe two of them, the nurse isn't sure—"

"Which patient?" But she knew. Wildly, she hoped she was wrong.

"See, that's what I'm trying to find out. He didn't speak English, so we're not sure if it might have even been family."

"Who didn't speak English?"

"Your patient. Peter something? Had an operation a few days ago?"

"Peter! He's gone? He's not at the hospital?" With her free hand, Vicki rubbed hard on her forehead, trying to make sure she was fully awake.

"Right, that's what I'm trying to tell you. The nurse said the other kids in the room started yelling, and when she went in they said this man had come in the room. Their story's pretty confused. You know kids."

"Jesus Christ! Did you say you called the police?"

"Well, the nurses called the cops and the FBI before they notified me. Should've called me first, instead of everybody getting so excited. Everybody needs to just calm down here."

"Just tell me what happened."

"See, I'm thinking it's probably not really anything to worry about. I called the boy's aunt and she's coming down—she's American, you know. She says she doesn't know anything about it, but she seemed kind of vague about the parents. Understand what I'm saying?"

"No. What are you talking about?"

"Well, I'm thinking, you know how foreigners are. Don't you think his parents got back in town and probably took him without knowing they had to check him out?" He seemed pleased with his reasoning. "I mean, they probably didn't even know he had to be discharged."

Vicki took a second to control her voice. All business.

"I'll be right there."

Nineteen

Driving with one hand, Vicki jerked a brush through her hair and scowled through the windshield. She'd tried the Wilkinses' number before she left, and San Juana's sister, Consuela, had told her that Cynthia and Jack had already left for the hospital. She said they were very upset. Obviously, they hadn't known Peter was going anywhere. That wouldn't have made much sense, anyway. He was going to be discharged in just a couple of days.

Okay, she couldn't put this off any longer. She had to bring Tim into it, just had to. She didn't have any idea how to deal with the FBI. No, that was wrong. She'd dealt with them a long time ago on a couple of her prosecutions— it was Cynthia she was worried about. She couldn't let the woman lie to the FBI, or to the police either, for that matter. That was a crime all by itself. Vicki could picture Cynthia getting herself in deeper and deeper, and she couldn't imagine her just coming clean. But she had to, right? Of course she did, now.

Vicki fumbled in her pocketbook until she came up with her phone. Steering with the back of her hand braced on the wheel, she started to punch in Tim's number and then stopped. She would be at the hospital in another few minutes anyway. Maybe she should just wait and see how Cynthia was handling it. Let her deal with it however she was going to do it, as long as she didn't ask Vicki to lie about something. Vicki knew that she, herself, was a terrible liar; that she would never get away with it, even to buy time. So what the hell was she doing coming down here?

She parked in the garage across the street from the hospital; the physician's slots were mostly open this early in the morning. She switched off the engine and sat still for a moment. What was she going to do? She didn't want to go up there and just blow the whistle. Well, she couldn't sit in the car all morning, either. She shook her head, opened the door, and got out. She started off walking, then trotted up the stairs to the hospital's main entrance. She didn't know what she was going to do but she had to be there, that's all. It was her patient.

She took the elevator to Pediatrics, telling herself to calm down, to keep her mouth shut as much as possible.

The Wilkinses were at the nurse's station, sitting and talking to a young man who had to be FBI. He was smiling, chewing gum, trying to be reassuring. As Vicki walked up, she saw Cynthia's eye, a hard look, giving her a warning, a quick glare of caution that turned benign as she looked back at the agent.

Her voice sounded as earnest as Vicki had ever heard her. "So you think this is just a misunderstanding?"

The agent was smiling, bored. "Sure. See it all the time." He glanced up at Vicki.

Jack smiled beatifically. "Good morning, Dr. Shea. Looks like Peter took a trip with his uncle or something. We didn't know anything about it." Vicki thought that if anyone bothered to look they would see that Jack's smile didn't involve his eyes at all. His mouth was turned up, but his eyes were round and frightened. He looked back at the agent. "This is Peter's pediatrician, Dr. Shea."

The agent nodded politely, only modestly irritated at being interrupted. "Good morning. Nobody said anything to you about taking the child out of the hospital, did they?"

"No." She shook her head. "No." She pressed her lips together.

"Well, it's probably nothing to worry about. They'll probably bring him back here or call the Wilkinses about his clothes or something."

"Oh." Vicki knew she would be incapable of saying any more than that without giving herself away to anybody who was really listening and watching her. "Well, I have to see a couple of patients." She nodded to the Wilkinses and headed down the hall to the room Peter had been in before he was taken.

As she came in the door the other children looked at her. Two of them she had seen a couple of days earlier, one was new. They were not playing, but talking earnestly with each other. Their talk stopped when she came in the room. She noted that, for once, the TV was off. She sat on the edge of one of the beds.

"So, what happened?"

"Peter got kidnapped!" It was the little girl. Vicki wasn't sure why she was in the hospital, but thought it was for a persistent kidney infection. She did not look particularly sick now. She was, however, indignant.

Vicki tried to sound reassuring. "How do you know he wasn't taken out by a relative?"

"Dr. Shea, he did not know this guy. Even though the guy spoke to him in his language, he didn't know him. He was scared."

"You heard them speak to each other?"

"Yeah!" It was one of the little boys, an eight- or nine-year-old. "It was like 'jibber jibber jibber' and then Peter got scared."

"How do you know he was scared?"

"He started to cry!" It was the little girl again, frustrated at having to explain the obvious.

"He was crying? Didn't anybody hear him? The nurses?"

"No! We tried to tell them! As soon as he started to cry, the guy just crammed his hand over his mouth and took off with him!"

"Did you tell this to the police?"

"They won't listen!"

The other little boy sounded dubious. "Well, the cop listened, that first guy that came in."

The little girl overrode him. "The FBI guy wouldn't, though! He didn't hear anything we said!"

"Did the policeman ask you what the guy looked like?"

"It was one of the cleaning guys!"

"Who?"

"The guy that grabbed Peter! He had on that green uniform, and look!" He pointed into the hallway just outside their door. "He had that mop and roller bucket thingy."

"You told that to the cop, right?"

The little girl shook her head. "He wasn't here long enough. He said the FBI would talk to us, but that guy didn't listen to anything."

Vicki nodded, her face serious. "Well . . . well, they probably know what they're doing."

"But what's going to happen to Peter?" The three of them stared at her, at the all-knowing doctor, waiting for an answer.

Vicki had to turn her face away, then she looked back at them, trying to appear calm. If she tried to lie to them they would see it in a second. "I don't really know. I hope he'll just bring him back."

Vicki went into the hallway and looked down the corridor at the nurse's station. The FBI agent was on his feet, smiling, talking instead of listening while a nurse smiled back at him. Vicki could see Cynthia's head, her face smiling, looking exactly like what a kindly, harmless, somewhat dense older woman was supposed to look.

Vicki started to walk down there, to make sure they got the description of the man from the children but then she stopped. What if they started asking her questions? She wasn't going to hold anything back if they asked. Shit! Call Tim.

She punched in his number on her phone and listened for him to wake up.

His voice was husky. "Murphy."

"Tim, I'm at Gunnison. You got to get down here. Peter's been snatched out of the hospital and the Wilkinses are not telling the FBI—"

"Wait, stop. What are you talking about? Is this Vicki?"

"Yes! Just get down here. That kid that had the surgery?"

"Oh, yeah. Okay." She could hear the beginnings of a yawn. "I didn't know who you were—"

"You hear what I said? Somebody kidnapped him out of the hospital!"

The yawn stopped. "You sure?"

"Tim! *Get your ass—*!"

"Okay, okay. I'm on the way."

Vicki punched the off button on her phone with enough force to push Tim out of bed. She looked down the corridor toward the nurse's station for a moment, then turned and went the other way.

She knew where the Housekeeping office was in the basement near the furnace. If the night shift supervisor was where she was supposed to be, Vicki thought she could at least find out if they had hired any Latvians lately. It was somewhere to start anyway.

Her mind was whirling with the possibilities, none of them making a lot of sense, as she took the service elevator to the basement. It wasn't until the doors opened that she remembered what time it was. It was still night down here, below ground level and an area that didn't normally see a lot of traffic. The lights were out for the most part. A work light was on far down the corridor to her left, but if a light was supposed to be on in front of the elevator, it was burned out.

Vicki hesitated, her hand on the door of the elevator to hold it open with its interior light illuminating the area in front of her. She couldn't see anyone. She listened for voices, a radio, anything that might tell her where people were. Nothing.

Wheeled canvas laundry hampers were lined up like a wagon train along the wall opposite the elevator doors. Off to the right, just at the edge of where the light reached, she could see a row of gray lockers, but the light did not reach more than the first two or three metal doors. She could see nothing down at the end of that hallway, not even an electric exit sign that should have been there pointing the way to the elevator where Vicki was standing.

Still holding the door, Vicki looked for a light switch but couldn't see one. Listening to the silence she could feel the tension mounting in her neck. Stupid. She was spooking herself.

"Hello!" Her voice sounded firm—stronger than she felt. She listened. She put an extra tone of authority in her voice. "Anybody down here?"

No reply. No sound of any person moving around. Anybody in this section of the basement should have heard her and she realized it was so quiet that she would be able to hear somebody if they were doing anything other than standing still. Nobody down here at all?

She knew the Housekeeping office was down the other corridor, away from the lockers, near where she could see the glow from a work light. That's where the hospital's fifty-year-old furnace was. Maybe the night supervisor had just gone to the bathroom or gone up to one of the wards for a moment to deal with some mess. She would, no doubt, be back in a moment. She was supposed to be down here, ready to respond to a call, to dispatch one of the night crew when the inevitable dropped glass or sudden vomiting spell occurred somewhere in the building. If she wasn't here, she would be right back.

Vicki released the elevator door and started for the office. She hadn't gone more than three steps when the doors shut and the light extinguished with the closing of the doors. She was standing in what would have been, except for the distant work light, total darkness. This couldn't be right, could it? Did people sit down here in the dark? She stood still and listened. Nothing.

As her eyes adjusted to the dark she could see, faintly, the canvas of the laundry hampers, where the line stopped. There was another corridor that went off from there, leading to the old laundry room, not used much at night because everything was sent out now. But the junction of the corridors . . . that's where the light switch would probably be, right?

Vicki had to grope for the opening, the marble corner where the corridor began. Why wasn't there a work light on down that way? She slid her hands along the wall but couldn't locate a switch. She tried the wall on the other side, but couldn't find it there either. Jesus! Vicki felt herself growing irritated. The switches were illuminated in other parts of the hospital. Why not down here where there was never any daylight?

She stopped moving her hands and stood absolutely still in the darkness. Of course they would be. There would also be lights on, at least some kind of nightlights in all of the corridors. Was a circuit breaker out?

Vicki eased backward until she could see the glow from the work light again. Okay, she was wasting time. She stepped off sharply enough but then slowed when she heard the noise that her shoes made on the linoleum floor, and proceeded, to her own irritation, on tiptoe.

The work light wasn't in the office. The office was dark, the door standing open, a dark hole in the wall, the faint gleam of the light off metallic furniture inside. The only light was in the room across the hall, on the ceiling over the furnace, a single dim bulb inside a wire cage. It was an emergency light, no doubt on a different circuit from the rest of the power in the basement, connected to several other emergency lights around the hospital that always stayed on.

Vicki felt in her pocketbook but she knew it was futile. She didn't carry a small flashlight like any sensible person would, like her father kept telling her she should. She stopped her hand and listened. Had she heard something? Back toward the elevator?

She stared hard into the blackness of the corridor. She realized she was holding her breath to hear better and finally let it out. Nobody was there, surely. Anybody in the dark down there would be calling to her, asking about the lights, right? She moved her hand slowly in her pocketbook, trying not to make noise, even though she knew if there were anybody around they could see her.

She came up with the phone, stepped closer to the furnace room door where the light was so she could see the keypad, and called Pediatrics. She knew that number without having to think about it.

"This is Dr. Shea. I'm down at Housekeeping in the basement. This place is totally dark down here. A circuit's out or something. Can you call—"

"Want me to call Maintenance?"

"Yes, would you? Tell 'em to get some lights on down here?"

"Sure. I'll do it right now."

"Thank you."

Vicki pushed the off button and felt a little better. She went into the hallway and stood still, listening. There couldn't be anybody down there at that end of the hall, could there? The corridor back toward the elevator was pitch black. She stepped into the furnace room, because that was where the only light was, then realized what she was doing. She was frightening herself because a damn circuit breaker was out. She went across the hall to the doorway to the House-keeping office and peered in, trying to see.

It was a tiny office, probably a utility room before Housekeeping took it over. There was only room for a small desk right in front of the door and a cabinet to one side. As her eyes adjusted again to the dark she could just make out the outline of the desk, a faint gleam along the worn metallic edges.

There was a dim, pinpoint reflection from above the surface of the desk and Vicki tried to remember what was there. A desk lamp? No, this was on the other side of the desk, wasn't it? She stared hard into the darkness of the office, beginning to make out something on the other side of the desk. She moved to one side so that a little more light would penetrate the room from across the hall.

Gradually, very slowly, Vicki realized she was seeing a face. A scowl. Somebody was sitting at the desk! Her heart almost stopped as she leaped backwards with a cry.

"Jesus! Who is it? Who's in there?"

Nothing. There was no movement in the office, no sound of breathing. Vicki's heart was pounding, thudding in her chest, almost audible. Where was Maintenance with the fucking lights?

Her knees wobbling to the point that she was stumbling, Vicki moved back into the furnace room, never taking her eyes away from the darkness in the office across the hall. She got her phone out, but her hands were shaking so badly she could hardly hold it. Calm down! She tried taking a deep breath but it did no good. When she tried to punch in numbers on the phone, it slipped from her hand and clattered away from her on the floor. Shit!

She stood still and stared hard at the dark in the office across the hall. No movement. Nothing. She could see, more with her memory than with her eyes, the face across the desk, eyes open, staring straight ahead, scowling, she thought, right at her but maybe not. Dead? Where were the fucking lights?

Quickly, Vicki got to her hands and knees, looking for her phone in the weak light from the overhead bulb. It had skidded into shadow under the edge of the furnace. She thought she could see it and crawled toward it. As she moved she caught sight of a lighter object out of her peripheral vision and looked.

What the hell was that? The small object was familiar and alien at once.

No!

The yelling was in her head. The object was at the back of the furnace, visible just behind the corner.

No! No! No! No!

It was a child's foot.

Fighting to overcome the horror of recognition, Vicki made herself crawl toward it until she was sure. She could see the little toes, the nail beds dark gray in the dim light. She forced herself to reach forward and make contact. Cold. Ice cold.

Forcing herself to act, Vicki struggled to get her hand on the child's leg, grab hold, and work him out from the tiny space behind the furnace, grease and dust balls stuck to his bare leg. Limp, cold. As she pulled the body free, the shirt rode up and she saw the staples.

Vicki was hearing squeaking noises, realized she was making them, and stopped. She lay Peter on the floor, tipped back his head, covered his mouth and nose with her mouth, and blew. The head between her hands wobbled unnaturally, rolled loosely to the side as though not fully attached to the rest of the body. Shit! His neck was . . .

She heard the elevator door open, men's voices in the distance.

Vicki erupted. "Code! Code blue!"

As she vainly tried to blow air into the resisting lungs, she realized she had been screaming. She could hear the male voices in the corridor near the elevator and she blew again.

One voice, nearer, was calling to her. "What? What's that?"

The sound of her breath in the child's chest was like a broken balloon.

The lights came on. Footsteps, running toward her.

"Code! Hit the fucking alarm now!"

She was doing chest compressions with one hand, blowing into him again and again, but she could tell it was hopeless. Peter had been dead for some time.

But she wouldn't stop, couldn't make herself stop even though her mind was after a few moments functioning rationally. She kept going.

She couldn't tell how long it had been. Then the code team was there—shouting voices excited coming down the corridor, then silent and staring as they took over the small body. The ER doctor was injecting Lidocaine directly into the heart as a nurse stuck on the leads for the EKG, then they all stopped. The ER doc glanced at the flat-line screen, then bent over the small body. He peered into the eyes a long time and then sat back on his ankles.

"Call it. Time." He looked at Vicki. "This is hopeless. He's cold. Right?"

Vicki was still sitting on the floor next to him. She nodded and looked down.

"Yes. Okay."

It was quiet in the furnace room, the quiet filling the hallway, then a whispered voice in the hall, "Jesus . . ."

Vicki couldn't move for a moment, staring at the remains of her small patient. He'd been through so much, come so far. She had to stop. She knew it. She had to deal with what was in front of her. She couldn't do anything for Peter.

She looked up until her eyes met those of a nurse, staring, round-eyed and pale. Vicki had to clear her voice to speak. "The cops are on the way." The nurse stared, lips parted, listening to some inner voice, not hearing Vicki at all.

"Would you please call Pediatrics and see if an Inspector Murphy has arrived yet?"

The nurse's lips closed. She nodded, then turned away.

Vicki looked around at all the people, now stopped, staring. Her voice grew stronger. "Nobody touch anything. Not one thing."

Twenty

Tim was trying to get and hold the attention of the on-call Homicide inspector who had entered the crime scene looking as if it were still evening. An African-American, he was slender and imperial in a perfectly tailored black suit, with a cream yellow tie on a gray shirt. His razor cut looked as though it had just been finished and wiped clean. He moved with easy grace and a confident sense of his own importance as he passed the other witnesses, looked over the shoulders of the crime scene technicians, and then seemed to be homing in on Vicki. Not looking at his face, she could see his long fingers holding a leather-bound notebook. He seemed to be trying to ignore Tim, the new guy, the one who was not on call and who was, therefore, butting in.

Finally, a little exasperated, Tim raised his voice so that Vicki heard what he said.

"She's a friend of mine."

The inspector stopped and looked at Tim.

"A friend of yours." It was a statement, a repetition of what Tim had just said—not so much to help himself understand it better as to let Tim hear what it sounded like, under the circumstances. The Homicide inspector turned his head back and looked at Vicki again. He was in his forties, more Vicki's age than Tim's, and he didn't seem inclined to give Tim the benefit of any doubts he might have. His eyes were flat, blank, and a little cold. This guy looked like a cop.

Tim reached across the man, took him by the elbow, and turned him. The flat stare turned back to Tim as they slowly walked a few steps away from Vicki, the inspector nodding impatiently at what Tim was saying in a voice too low for Vicki to hear. The flat look dissolved, the eyebrows raised in sudden interest. He stopped and looked back at Vicki again. He turned back and said something to Tim, and Tim answered, nodding. This time, when the inspector came toward her, he did not seem so unfriendly.

"Dr. Shea?" He put out his hand in formal self-introduction. "I'm Don Morrison. How you feeling?"

"Little shaky."

"Yeah, not surprised." He looked her over, a different kind of once-over than he had given her before. "Listen, I'm gonna let Inspector Murphy—you know Tim, right?"

"Yes, we're friends."

"Okay, I'm going to let you go with him. He's going to get a detailed statement from you on tape about what you found, okay? I just need a couple of quick questions and you're outta here, okay?"

"Yes, of course." Vicki hugged her elbows and looked down at the floor. They were standing in the corridor in the basement, the crime scene technicians working behind them. Her knees were, in fact, shaking, but she knew she had to brave it out a little longer.

"Any indication that this child had been abused before he came into the hospital?"

She shook her head without looking up. "No. He had appendicitis, a little thin, but nothing else was wrong with him."

"Know anything about his family?"

"No, sorry. I just met the aunt." She kept looking down, afraid to meet his eyes.

"Okay." Morrison hesitated, then seemed to make up his mind. "Well, I can reach you through your pager or through your office, right?"

"Yes, any time."

"All right." He passed her a business card. "Let me know if you're going to be going out of town, okay? I'm sure Tim will get everything, but I might need a detail or two, okay?"

"Of course." She nodded without ever looking him in the face again. When she looked up at Tim, Morrison had gone back to oversee the techs dusting for fingerprints.

Then Tim had her by the upper arm and they were heading into the elevator. It seemed as though there were twenty cops and nurses in there with them, so they got out on the main floor of the hospital, Tim still holding her arm, steering her toward the main entrance until they were outside.

When Vicki finally looked up again, Tim was staring at her, his eyes full of concern and consternation mixed.

"Are you all right?"

"Jesus! No, I'm not all right. Did you see—?"

"Okay, yeah, I saw." Reflexively, he reached for her with both hands, as though about to draw her into his chest, but then he didn't touch her. His hands hovered near her shoulders and then dropped to his sides as he glanced quickly around to see who was watching.

Vicki stared at the doors, trying to see into the lobby of the hospital. "Where's Cynthia?"

"They were gone when I got here. What happened?"

"Tim, I swear to God I have no idea. I got a call that my patient was missing, that somebody took him off the ward. I got here, Cynthia was talking to the FBI, not telling them a damned thing, just letting them think it was all a mistake of some kind. The other children in his room thought he was grabbed by somebody from Housekeeping, so I went down there after I called you and that's what I found. Just what did you tell that guy?"

"Who?"

"Who? That Morrison guy, that just let his prime witness walk out."

"Oh, that." He started to grin, then caught himself. "I told him you were an ex-DA, a good friend of the chief's."

"Well, thanks."

Tim was serious again. "Won't do you much good. I got absolutely no choice. I got to bring the Wilkinses into this, get it all out in the open. That's obvious now, right?"

"Yes, all right." She knew she didn't sound convinced. What the hell else could they do? She looked up at Tim, her voice firmer, more decided. "I agree. They just have to know more than they've told me, right?"

Tim's head tilted to one side, a slightly ironic smile. "What do you think?"

"Let's go over there right now."

Tim came with her in her car so that when she pulled up the driveway and parked in back, it would not be as alarming as if they had arrived in Tim's car. The people inside would be plenty alarmed, soon enough, as soon as they saw him with her. He's the one that arrested Julia, then came around with all kinds of questions after her death. They would remember him, that he was a cop, *and* that he was already involved in this case. They would know instantly that she had betrayed them.

As soon as she had that thought, Vicki felt herself growing angry. What the hell did they expect? Did they expect her to lie to the cops and the FBI, too?

She got out of her car and stood there, staring at the back of the house as Tim got out and watched her, waiting for her to be ready. She glanced at him and looked back at the house. Nobody watching from the windows, nobody opening the door. They must be downstairs.

She looked back at Tim, patiently waiting for her. "Are we about two steps ahead of the cops, getting here?"

"It'll take 'em a while with the crime scene."

"What, about an hour?"

"Little more. Then they'll probably come over here."

Consuela, one of San Juana's sisters that Vicki had seen the last time she was here, answered the back door. She gave Vicki a tentative, worried smile and glanced shyly at Tim.

"Consuela, this is Tim Murphy. He's here with me to try to help out. Can we go on down?"

Consuela smiled genuinely then, the soul of innocent complicity. "Sure, go ahead. You know the way."

As Vicki went through the door to the nursery she saw Frank first. He was standing with his back to the door, talking earnestly to the Wilkinses. The Wilkinses, too, were on their feet facing him, frowning and anxious. Cynthia glanced over at Vicki as she came through the door. Then she saw Tim and stared. Frank saw her expression and turned his head to look.

His face went blank, then cold with recognition. He turned slowly, the big body rotating until he was facing this new menace, his expression grim. All three adults were watching Tim, waiting for something to happen. They did not look at Vicki, but stayed focused entirely on the policeman. Even the children grew quiet, sensing the tension, the fear that this strange man added to just by coming in the door.

Tim spoke before Vicki could gather her thoughts. "You heard about Peter?"

Cynthia dropped her head, then looked up. For a moment her control seemed to waver. "I just talked to the nurse at the hospital." She kept looking at Tim, pain in her eyes, as though waiting for him to explain it all to her.

Tim looked steadily back at her. "You have any idea who did it?"

Quickly, decisively, Cynthia shook her head. "No." She looked to her husband as if for help. Jack stood there with a stricken expression on his face, virtually helpless.

Frank looked down and then turned away, as if looking for his coffee mug. "Well, not for sure, but—"

"Are you here to arrest us?" Cynthia had drawn herself up. Recovering quickly from the surprise of seeing Tim, her spine stiffened until she looked regal, as in charge as ever. Her voice was firm and calm, pushing through her pain, almost a challenge, as she looked at Tim squarely, her eyes steady.

"I asked you, are you—?"

"I'm just here to try to help." Tim paused. "But you got to help me, too."

When no one said anything, he continued, his voice soothing, quiet. "I don't normally get involved in immigration matters. That's up to the feds. Believe me, Vicki would not have allowed me to come with her if I was looking at any of you as a suspect for anything I was investigating. Try to think of me as a friend of Vicki's, just here to help."

Cynthia watched him, thinking about what he had said. Tim kept speaking directly to her. "I think you would agree this has turned out to involve more than you thought it would, right?"

Cynthia let out the breath she had been holding. Her voice sounded almost matter-of-fact. "Yes. Well . . . we do seem to need some help." She glanced at Jack and Frank, but they didn't offer to add anything. Vicki thought Cynthia wasn't really expecting them to. She spoke directly to Tim, looking him in the eye, explaining except that she seemed unsure what to explain.

"We never expected anything like this. I don't know . . . we really have no idea why this would happen to a little boy. We were trying to figure it out. Frank was just now telling us—"

"Start with the kids," Frank broke in. He turned to Tim. "It turns out that some of them—not the Russians, but a few of the others—think they have relatives here in the States. That's where they thought they were going."

Cynthia picked it up, nodding her head in agreement. "Before that nurse . . . when Peter was just *missing*, we really did think a relative could have found him somehow. So then we were thinking that probably Mrs. Fairchild knows these families, or at least knows how to contact them. We were thinking that if we can just talk to her and move quickly to get the rest of them into the adoption pipeline—" She stopped herself. She sighed, thinking about it. "Well, now though . . ." Cynthia gave her husband a kind, compassionate look, as though he were the one to be protected. Jack wiped a hand over his face and waited for his wife to go on. He seemed resigned to whatever she said.

Cynthia turned her eyes back to Tim and her expression changed to one of determination. "Look, I know the police have to be brought into it now. We're going to be charged for what we've done. Okay, that's our problem, the adults' problem. But still, if we can get some help locating Mrs. Fairchild quickly, the rest of the kids—"

"That's something else you don't know about." Vicki's voice was quiet, but there was no way to break this easily. "Mrs. Fairchild has been murdered."

Cynthia stared at Vicki, then shifted her gaze back to Tim. Her mouth hung open for a moment. Clearly, this was something she hadn't even considered.

"Rita's dead? Rita Fairchild?"

Tim's eyes were the psychologist's eyes, clear and sympathetic. He spoke slowly. "Rita Fairchild was murdered. Also . . . the circumstances were a little bit similar to how your daughter died." He waited to let it sink in.

Cynthia was suddenly full of urgency, seeing the significance in this news. "You're sure it was murder? You have to tell me."

Tim watched her carefully. "Yes. It was definitely homicide and the autopsy found heroin in her system. No one can be absolutely sure, of course, but the police in Los Angeles believe she was not a heroin user."

Cynthia seemed offended, as though she needed to protect the dead woman's reputation. "Rita was a good, decent woman."

"That's what they're telling me. Not that decent people don't get caught up, but with her it seems very unlikely. They think somebody used the heroin to try to make it look like a drug killing. Somebody injected her, then killed her for some other reason. Think about it. That's the similarity to your daughter's death."

He looked back at Frank who was standing there his mouth pursed, listening. Tim spoke to him. "Frank, who was it that contacted—?"

"Because of the drug?" Cynthia's voice cut in, rising in pitch. She was very tense, staring at the policeman, fully attentive to what he had to say. Vicki thought the tension, visible throughout her whole body now, was of a different kind than fear. "The heroin, that's what you're telling me . . . that's what was similar to Julia?"

Tim Murphy could see it, too. He nodded to her. "Yes, because of the heroin."

"Was Rita . . . did Rita have a history?"

"It doesn't look like it. Just the opposite, from what the people who knew her say."

"Wait a minute, this is too much." Cynthia had to find a chair and sit down. "What you're saying is . . . then Julia . . . now you think . . . maybe Julia hadn't gone back?"

"I might be the only one, but I'm almost certain she had not gone back to any drugs. Before, I thought she might have, but I don't think so now."

Jack looked from his wife to Tim, the information just now beginning to hit home. "Really? You think somebody forced Julia to take the heroin and then murdered her?" He glanced at his wife, back to Tim. "That's what you're saying, right?"

"That's what I think happened, yes."

Frank sat down hard, the chair groaning. His face was even paler than it had been. "Well, Jesus H. Christ!" He turned his head to look at Cynthia. "You all right?"

Vicki saw Cynthia leaning forward in the chair, her hands over her mouth, her eyes filling with tears. Vicki had never seen her cry or even come close to actually breaking down, except for that one time when Charlotte first came out of the coma. Jack came up behind her and put his hands on her shoulders, but she continued to stare at Tim.

She could barely speak. "Then Julia didn't . . . she didn't kill herself?"

"No, she didn't."

"Oh, God!" She looked up at her husband. She quickly covered one of his hands with hers. "Jack?"

"Yes, I heard."

"I knew it! I knew it, didn't I?"

"Yes, you did."

"I knew it! I never doubted her. Not for one second."

"No, you didn't." Jack was struggling to talk. "I'm so sorry I did doubt her. I just—"

"That doesn't matter now." Cynthia's grip on his hand tightened until her knuckles went white. "It's okay, Jack, for you. But I always knew, didn't I?"

"Yes, you did."

"Frank?" She glanced at the other man, then turned back to keep her gaze rigidly on her husband's face.

Frank sighed. "Yeah, Cynthia, you were right."

Cynthia seemed to absorb the words, gave herself a moment to let them sink in, staring into her husband's face, getting the confirmation that she needed.

Suddenly, she released her grip on her husband's hand and swiveled her gaze back to lock on Frank. Vicki had the impression of a cannon swinging on a turret, finding the target. Cynthia's voice was deep with anger.

"Damn it, Frank. Tell him the rest." Before Frank could say anything she looked back at Tim. "You're telling us this because you think it's all connected, right? That's why you're telling us?"

Tim nodded. "I think it probably is."

She nodded emphatically. "Okay, Frank. Obviously, it's got to be connected. Tell him what you were starting to tell us."

Frank had found the coffee mug and was filling it, his back to the rest of them. "Yes, I hear that."

Jack's voice sounded more than a little angry. "Just tell him, Frank."

Frank, refusing to be hurried, carefully stirred his coffee. He glanced up at Vicki. "You told him all about the kids, right? The smuggling?"

"I told him what I know."

Frank nodded, then looked at Tim. "You won't be surprised to know that there's more."

"Not at this point, no."

He glanced at Jack, then Cynthia. "They don't know. I was just starting to tell them when you got here." He looked back at Tim and sighed as if he were just now realizing that he had to tell it. "It looks like we're being shaken down. It's a money thing, an extortion deal."

As the words hung there, Jack stared at his partner. "That's about as far as you got before. How much do they want?"

"They want four million dollars."

Tim nodded. "All right. Who is it?"

Frank shook his head, looking down at his coffee. "Not sure, exactly. Probably the smugglers, those same people. Saw how easy we could come up with a couple a hundred thousand at a time, must have decided to cut out the hard part and just go for the money."

"Four million." Jack looked relieved. He was suddenly so relieved that he almost smiled, looking from Frank to Cynthia, then, finally, at Tim.

"Well . . ." That's all he could get out.

Vicki's voice was cold. "Could we get some details, please?"

Tim's tone matched hers. "Yes. All of them would be nice."

Frank nodded. "Yeah, okay." He looked at Cynthia. "Should have told all of you."

"Obviously."

He took a deep breath and let it out. "Okay. A couple of months ago, I was contacted in Belgium. It was a few days before we signed a big contract there, so people were coming and going all the time. The guy said—"

"Who? What guy?" Tim was trying to temper his impatience, but it was getting hard.

"A Serb, I think, but he might have been Greek. I don't know his name. I just met with him once, face-to-face, and he wasn't too anxious to identify himself."

"How did he get in touch with you?"

"Just walked into my office. He used somebody else's business card. It was a legitimate card, but it wasn't his. My secretary thought he was a buyer and let him in. We're brokers, we don't discourage drop-ins."

"You checked out the name on the business card?"

"I knew the guy on the business card and believe me, this wasn't him. This guy—this Serb or Greek or whatever—he said he wanted four million bucks, just like that. I kept waiting for the punch line but he wasn't kidding. He said he—no, it was his people. He said 'my people' have contacts with U.S. Customs and Immigration. If we didn't pay up, they were going to turn us in. He spoke to me in English and I couldn't get a clear idea about his accent. I couldn't quite place it."

"That was the first thing he said?"

"Yeah, just like that. He shook my hand and then said, 'From you, I want money.' That's not an unusual sentiment, but it was a strange language construction—not one that I recognized. If he were Russian, he might have said something like, 'Money, I want,' or something like—"

"Okay, you couldn't place the accent or the syntax, but you understood him all right?"

"Oh, I got the gist of it right away. Sure, four million dollars was very clear."

"What did you say?"

"I told him to kiss my ass."

"You lost your temper?"

"Of course I did. Little snot comes into my office and demands blackmail like he had a right—"

"A small man?"

"Yeah, maybe five-five or -six. Dark hair, dark eyes. Just like about a zillion other guys over there. Brass balls, though, coming right into my office like—"

"What else did he say?"

"Okay, that's the thing I been trying to remember—exactly how he said it. He said he could make . . . it was a funny expression."

"He could make trouble for you?"

"I thought that's what he meant—that's the way I took it. But what he said was something like they would 'make miserable' for us if we didn't pay up. It was like he knew enough English to communicate all right, but he didn't understand the idiom, hadn't practiced it."

"What did you tell him?"

"I told him I was going to put him through the window. I was pissed."

"You didn't think he was serious?"

"What, about turning us in?"

"Sure. Didn't that worry you?"

He looked at Jack and shrugged. "Not really. What were they going to say? We'd only dealt in cash and Julia had said she was careful, that she could trust the people she dealt with. I thought he was an opportunist with a hell of a lot of nerve, that's all. Besides—I guess this is why I couldn't take it too seriously—this guy looked to be about seventeen years old."

"A teenager?"

"Yeah. Why would I take him seriously? I thought he was just inept, not very bright, you know?"

"Maybe he was just stupid. Did he contact you again, after that?"

"Well . . . not exactly. I mean, not him, but another man called me a couple of weeks after that. It was right after Julia died, the next day after I found out. I was terribly upset. The secretary was trying to make airline connections, I was trying to put everything I was doing on hold just to get back here to be with Cynthia and Jack. Anyway, in the middle of all this, this guy calls. I've been trying to remember exactly what he said, too, but it was something like he was the kid's uncle—that I had insulted his nephew when I told him to kiss my ass. Well, I'd only said that to one guy lately, so—"

"This was the first guy's uncle?"

"That's what he said."

"What did he want?"

"He wanted . . . I damn near hung up on him, come to think of it, when I figured out who he was talking about. Here I was, getting ready to go to the funeral of somebody who was very close to me—it was just ridiculous, you know? Except this guy—he was careful to be very courteous, very diplomatic. But then he said something like it was my fault, that I should have taken his nephew seriously."

"This was in English?"

"No, German this time."

"He was German?"

"I don't think so. He didn't sound like a native speaker, but I can't be sure about that. A lot of people in the Balkans speak German. All the time he was being so courteous, he kept saying that it was my fault, but I thought he was talking about the argument, the insult. I wasn't mad this time. I don't know why. Maybe because of the courtesy, but also I was still in shock from hearing about Julia. Anyway, I told him I didn't have time for this conversation, that I was on the way back to the States. He said he would be back in touch with me later, and then the last thing he said, again, was that I should have taken it seriously. I just blew it off. Some crazy Slav, I thought."

Jack had been listening intently. "Why didn't you tell us?"

"Jack, think about what that time was like. I don't even want to remember it. We were all so upset about Julia, the memorial service." He looked at Tim, then back at Jack. "The cops told us it was a suicide, remember?"

Cynthia's voice was conciliatory, maybe an attempt at being the peacemaker. "Never mind that, Frank. But didn't you make any kind of connection?"

Finally, Frank turned toward Tim, trying to put the thing to him, to explain what might look like a deception. "I didn't understand. I didn't know what he meant by 'make miserable' . . . I thought he meant legal trouble. It wasn't until the little kid got murdered in the hospital . . . I thought, Jesus Christ! That's what he meant! That's what they're doing, trying to scare money out of us."

Tim was watching him, his face almost expressionless now. Vicki thought she could see temper behind his eyes, but he was hiding it well. "Frank, before they did anything to Peter, why wouldn't they have tried to contact you again?"

"Oh, they did. They tried. They just didn't get through. I came back here on Thursday. I gave the secretary the rest of the week off so she could go out of town for a wedding or some damn thing. She didn't check for messages until this morning."

"They called your office?"

"About fifty times. The guy wouldn't leave his name or number, of course, but she said he left his messages in German, told her I would know what it was about. It has to be the same people. Jesus, these people have got to be really stupid."

Tim's eyes flashed but he controlled it immediately. "Stupid isn't the point. They are dangerous and very determined."

"Well . . ." The mild tone of Jack's voice seemed to surprise everyone. He stroked his neck and stared into the distance for a moment, as if he could see right through the walls of the basement. "Maybe not that stupid." He glanced at his wife then turned his gaze toward Tim. It was almost as if he didn't understand what they had been talking about. "We could have come up with that kind of money. It would have taken a couple of weeks, but . . ." He turned his face away, as though staring out over space and time. There were tears in his eyes.

Frank moved a step toward him and put his hand out, but then didn't touch him. "Jack, I swear to God. I didn't have any idea he was talking about hurting anybody. Just knowing a language isn't enough sometimes. A lot of times you miss the nuances and—"

"If you'd just listened!" Cynthia's voice almost cracked. She didn't trust herself to go on with it. She leveled a glare at Frank that could have knocked him down. She had to look away.

Frank's voice was now shaky, directed at Cynthia's back. "I am so sorry. You're right, I—"

"Okay, you can hash that out later." Tim was back to business. "Whoever was transporting the children decided to shake you down, plus they seem to be trying to cover up tracks, eliminate witnesses. I don't know why, exactly—what went wrong with the plan—but that's the most logical explanation I have for now. So who did the smuggling?"

Cynthia looked quickly at Frank, up at her husband, back at Tim. "We don't know." She looked at Frank. "We don't, do we?"

"I sure don't, and those two don't even speak the language." Frank was scowling, deep in thought. "Julia knew."

Jack's voice cut in. "She insisted she was safe. She said she didn't want us to know who she was paying the money to, but she kept saying it was okay, she could trust them, that she could handle it." His face changed and he looked at his wife.

"Wait a minute. I just thought of something." He lowered his voice, speaking only to Cynthia. "We have a lawyer, remember? We're not supposed to talk to anybody, are we?" He was hesitant, asking, not sure what he wanted to do.

Cynthia looked at him and nearly smiled. It was almost as though she were talking to one of the children. "Oh, Jack. We can't keep this up anymore. Julia, Rita, and now poor little Peter—it's time to admit it now. We took our chances and now it's time. We're going to have to pay the—"

"Wait a minute. Hold it!" Frank's voice sounded urgent. "Jack's right, we do have a lawyer. She said she might be able to negotiate or something. And she did say not to talk to—"

"Well, she's history." Cynthia was not in doubt. She was recharged with energy and on her feet in a second. "Sorry to fire your friend, Vicki, but we've got to work with this man and help the police figure this out, no matter what happens with . . ." Her voice trailed off as she seemed to remember. She lowered her gaze and looked around the room. "What am I saying?"

As she continued to look at the children, she asked the question as though addressing everyone. "If the police got told about this, officially, how would we keep them from turning these children over to Immigration? Wouldn't you have to?"

The children were in clusters, holding together and watching the strange events going on with the adults. They had not missed a single cue of tone or inflection or tears. Maybe they couldn't understand the language but they knew when it was important.

Vicki watched Tim's face. His eyes followed Cynthia's gaze. He looked at the children, then back at Cynthia, then, involuntarily, back at the children until he forced himself to look at, to focus on Cynthia instead. Vicki thought she saw his expression change as he looked at the children, but it was so quick, the professional face so quickly back in place, that she didn't know if she'd seen a reaction or if she had just wanted to see it.

Frank cleared his throat, gestured broadly at the clumps of children. "These are your basic huddled masses."

Tim ignored him, kept watching Cynthia. He could see who was in charge here, and he didn't want to let her get away. "To be honest, I'm not sure myself. I'll do whatever I can, but—"

Jack's voice was quiet, controlled, directed to his wife. "Maybe we should talk to Elaine first. I mean . . . maybe . . ."

"You are not suspects as far as I am concerned, in anything I am investigating." Tim's voice was quiet, too. "Obviously, the feds might not feel the same way about it. If you want to call your lawyer, you can, but it's not even eight o'clock on a Saturday morning."

Cynthia shook her head. "I guess we know what she would say, huh?" She directed the question to Vicki.

"Yes, of course. But you still need a good lawyer. You need to talk to her before you just fire her, even if you go ahead and talk to Tim first."

"Well, you're a lawyer."

"Not here. Here I'm just a pediatrician. Immigration law is a highly specialized field that I have never worked with at all. Now there's a new legal question, right? Some of the children have relatives here, right? You know which ones?"

Cynthia stared at her and nodded. "Sure, Frank does."

"All right, we have to find out what kind of difference that might make for them. I don't know the answer to that, but Elaine could tell us. It wouldn't make any difference to the rest of them, but for some it might. You can't just fire her, you have to talk to her again."

They stood in silence a moment, Tim and Vicki watching Cynthia waiting for some kind of decision.

Jack spoke first, an offhand question. "What time does the bus get here?"

Cynthia answered. "Between eight and nine. We got time, he can wait."

Tim did not like this news. "What bus?"

Jack finally allowed himself to smile, more in keeping with his normal gracious manner. "We thought we really needed to get the children out of this cave, out in the sunshine. We've got all these women to help. San Juana and her sisters will be back in a few minutes. We thought we'd bundle up Charlotte, take the children out to Golden Gate Park or the zoo. Maybe both."

Vicki felt a small hand on her butt. She turned and looked down to see Nadya grinning up at her, and hear the small, high, clear voice. "Aunt Vicki?"

And all the questions, all the hard choices, were gone in an instant. They were out of mind as though they had been grossly overblown, exaggerated—those concerns were trivial next to this face, this innocent grin. That small face, always a little frightened, timid but so giving, too, with her trust, that other concerns suddenly seemed secondary. Vicki immediately lifted the child to her hip and hugged her, returning the grin. She reached up and twitched her nose playfully. "How's my little Nadya?"

She glanced over and saw Tim watching her. No, he was staring at the child, his face open and slack. He looked almost normal, but Vicki could picture what was going on in his mind, so different from her own reaction. He quickly turned his face away without looking back at Vicki.

Vicki turned to Frank. "Is Nadya . . . does she have relatives here?"

Frank looked up and shook his head. "Russian." He was examining his coffee mug, turning it in his hands, his face frowning and pensive. "I should—" He checked his watch and shook his head. "We could try to do this backwards."

Tim sat at the table across from him. "Do what backwards?"

"Identify the smugglers. Have to start asking questions in Belgrade. Maybe I should just go back there."

"Belgrade?"

"That's where Julia first made contact with them."

Jack sat next to his partner, facing Tim. "We've actually been talking about this already. We didn't know what happened to Rita, but we thought we might have to go back to these other people and get another contact. There were more people than Rita who were able to place these children in homes. There's a regular system for getting papers, setting up the adoptions. Those people are all Americans, not part of the same group that is doing the actual smuggling."

Cynthia was still standing, watching the others at the table. "Okay, that's got to be the first thing. We need to find the adoption people." Quickly, she waved Tim off with one hand. "We'll leave you out of that one."

Tim rose to his feet to stop her talking. "Wait a minute. Hold it. What are you talking about?"

Cynthia looked at him with an expression of incredulity, as if she couldn't believe he was asking the obvious. "The children. First, before we get any deeper into the rest of this mess, we've got to get them established—"

"Mrs. Wilkins . . . Cynthia, don't even think about it. Obviously, you are in much greater danger than anything you have to fear from the INS. Obviously, you can't do anything with these children except—"

"The hell with that!"

Vicki saw the sudden flash, but Tim either missed it or thought he could ride over it. "Cynthia, the danger at this point—"

"The hell with it!" Finally pushed too hard, Cynthia's face went white with rage. Her eyes turned hard as marbles as she bored into this cop, completely unafraid. Her voice shook with violence, with pure rage. "Look around! Look at them!"

Tim, momentarily struck speechless, stared back at her.

"I mean it! Did you think we were talking about bags of rice? Look!"

Finally, he had to. He was forced to. There was nothing else he could do in the face of this rock-hard determination, the white-hot rage that she was barely controlling, except to drop his eyes and look at the children. They huddled, wide-eyed, staring at him, not at her—at the object, not the source of the rage. He couldn't speak, and neither for a moment, could Vicki.

Cynthia's voice lowered, but the level of intensity stayed high, almost vibrating with a pinpoint focus of purpose. "These children have come six thousand miles and about two hundred years from where they were. They will not go back. Not you, not the Immigration Service, not the FBI, not the whole damned United States government is going to send them back to starve. Not now, not tomorrow, not ever."

For a moment, it seemed to Vicki that everyone was afraid to breathe, afraid to set her off again.

Then the soft intrusion of Jack's voice, full of gentleness. "Lover . . . I know . . ."

Cynthia did not move her gaze away from Tim's face, even though he was no longer looking back at her. She had locked onto him as she had earlier locked onto Frank, her stare boring in, even though she seemed to be talking to Jack.

"These children are Julia's. She did this. She got them this far. There was always the danger, right from the very beginning. That hasn't changed. We just see it more clearly now, that's all. Julia must have seen it all along because she was closer to it. She risked more than we did, just writing checks and passing along money. Well, damn it, okay then. We can do it, too, now that she can't."

She looked at Jack, finally. "We took the risk. We knew what we were doing and that's what we did. We made decisions, remember?"

Jack nodded, and Vicki was surprised when he almost smiled. His voice was soft, directed solely to his wife. "Yes, I remember."

Cynthia nodded back, responding to his almost smile. "But these kids never had any decisions to make. Whatever chances they might have had once were taken away until Julia found them. Then she made her own decisions and took her own risks, and kept at it until she was dead. Now that's the truth."

She looked back at Tim. "I know you're a policeman and you have rules. If rules weren't important to you, you wouldn't be a cop, I suppose."

"I told you, immigration isn't one of—"

"I know you said that. I'm just telling you the way it is. Those rules are just wrong. Just wrong, damn it. These kids are not going back, no matter what. We'll face the consequences, all right, but not these children, as long as I can draw breath."

In the silence of the room, the chirping of Frank's phone was loud. He looked at Tim as he fished it out of his pocket. "That's the Princess." He spoke into the phone. "Yeah."

Jack explained. "He means our secretary."

Frank's face grew serious, intent. "Ja, Frank Sanderson." His eyes rolled up until he met Tim's gaze. He pointed at the phone meaningfully.

"The uncle?"

Frank motioned for Tim to keep his voice down as he nodded vigorously.

Tim whispered, "Find out everything you can. Everything."

Frank kept motioning for Tim to keep quiet, his face concentrating on the voice on the phone. Suddenly he erupted in German. His voice was angry at first, then he took a deep breath and spoke more quietly. He went on for several minutes.

On Vicki's hip, Nadya suddenly threw her arms around Vicki's neck, buried her face in her hair, and hung on, her breath right in Vicki's ear. The child obviously understood German. She was reacting to what was being said. Vicki held her tight and rocked her as she watched Frank.

Vicki thought that now she knew how the children felt with all the talk going on around them in English. She concentrated on Frank's face, his tone and inflection when he interrupted the caller with questions or to make a statement. Frank was breaking out in sweat, his face flushed, his eyes bulging in concentration. Once he stammered. Even in German, Vicki could tell he had tripped over his words in his urgency.

Suddenly, his face changed. He seemed surprised, then anguished. His next burst of German seemed to be arguing, explaining, but he was cut off in mid-sentence, his voice suddenly stopping as he listened. He lowered himself into a chair, braced his elbow on the table, and leaned his head on his hand. He kept listening, occasionally offering encouragement with a quick "*Ja.*"

Gradually, his voice grew calmer and when he finally spoke at length, he seemed to be conciliatory or encouraging. He clearly was not being hostile. Vicki wondered if they had worked out some kind of deal right in front of her and Tim without them being able to tell. It was possible, but she thought he had spent most of the conversation just listening, not bargaining. But he had argued some. She gave it up. There was no way to tell without trusting him for a translation.

Finally Frank was telling him good-bye, then pressing the off button on the phone, staring at the phone. After a pause, he looked up, not at Tim but at Cynthia.

"That was Charlotte's father." He licked his lips, then raised a hand to cut off any comment from Cynthia before he could continue. "I'll tell you about it in a minute. Does anything at the hospital have this address on it?"

"What address?"

"This one. Here, where we are."

Vicki spoke up. "Of course there is. It's all over Peter's chart at the nurse's station."

Frank rotated his head to fix on Vicki, but then he wasn't looking at her. His mind was working. Vicki could see the tension rising in his face and in his posture as he thought about it. Then he shifted his stare to look at Tim.

"We got to get out of here. They're going to keep killing people until they've got the money." He licked his lips again and rose to his feet. "I mean, like right now, we got to get out of here."

The door to the room burst open with the dull thump of someone using a foot to kick it back. Jack and Cynthia leaped to their feet, instinctively recoiling away from the door. Frank's chair fell, tangling his feet as he tried to move. He fell heavily, scrabbling with his hands for balance until he took the whole table down with a crash of falling plates and coffee mugs. Tim was lunging toward the door, his hand on his gun. He stopped, froze, in mid-step, as though trying to make sense of what he saw.

From the doorway, San Juana stared back at him, wide-eyed, her arms full of groceries. They all gawked at her, forgetting for a moment to breathe.

San Juana's voice was apologetic, high-pitched. "The bus is here." Her eyes sought out Cynthia. "Sorry. I didn't mean to be so loud. Did I interrupt something?"

Twenty-one

"Okay, everybody calm down," Tim held up both hands, his phone held in one, as if to make a point. At least momentarily, there was quiet, a hesitation before the group got moving Tim looked tense. "I can have this place swarming with cops in ten minutes, fifteen at the outside."

"I am not kidding. We don't have ten minutes to wait." Frank's eyes were in dead earnest. Vicki thought he looked like a man about to run, but then he didn't. He looked around, his gaze sweeping the children, then the adults before stopping on Tim.

"These guys had a caravan coming in from Mexico. They got spotted and chased and got into some kind of a gun battle. Some of their people were killed but—and here's the thing—they killed some cops, the people that were chasing them. Probably Border Patrol, I don't know. He used the word for police. Anyway, they split up in the cars, the ones that survived. They got away, but they're red-hot fugitives. He said they're afraid to go back near the Mexican border. The money. They think if they get some big-time money together, they can get out, no problem, through Canada."

He paused and licked his lips, staring at Cynthia as though he had to convince her first. "The money isn't even our worst problem, the reason they're coming after us. I don't know why, but they've got it in their heads that we, somehow, were responsible for the border thing, but they still think we can be scared into giving them money. He said he can't call them direct, has to wait for them to call him, then he'll call me back."

He looked around at the children again. "I can tell you the rest of what he said later, but we got to get these kids out of here before they get here."

Cynthia moved first, sweeping up a toddler in each arm as she spoke. "We got a bus, that's all we need right now."

Jack grabbed two more children. The pair of them were heading for the stairs when Tim stepped in front of the door, blocking it. He still had his hands up, to soften it, and his voice was calm.

"Let's don't get into a panic, here. Just wait a minute and think about what you're doing."

Cynthia stopped in her tracks and looked at Tim. He still had his phone out but hadn't punched any numbers yet. She glanced at the phone and then looked at his eyes, a hard look, but not angry now.

"Give me two days, maybe three, to sort it out and get these children placed. Otherwise, you got to arrest me now."

Tim hesitated, staring at her, his phone ready in his hand. Vicki could see him thinking, trying to make up his mind, knowing he couldn't hesitate too long.

He closed the phone. "I better take a look at the street."

Cynthia nodded as if she had expected that answer, then pushed past him. "Good idea. Send the bus up the driveway and we can load 'em up back here while you watch the front."

Vicki was staring at Tim Murphy's back as he, in his turn, headed for the stairs. She knew that something had just happened. She had almost been expecting a kind of showdown. It had gone so quickly that she wasn't sure she was seeing it and she wasn't sure what it was that had just happened.

Tim was suddenly in the middle of this. She had already told him that Cynthia, left to herself, managed to not tell the FBI what she knew. And now—Christ, if Frank could hold back something from the Wilkinses, he would certainly mislead Tim, Vicki, the FBI, anybody, if he thought he needed to. But Tim didn't see it. He was personally involved, getting himself into the middle of it, into a position that could be hard to explain later. He was putting himself—and his job—in jeopardy for when they would finally sort it out with the INS, if that's what they had to do.

And what was she doing herself? That was different. How the hell was it different? Elaine and even Liz had repeatedly warned her about doing anything like this.

They had the children on the bus in less than five minutes, including baby Charlotte, complete with car seat, blankets, a hundred pounds or so of diapers, and a scattering of trucks and dolls in the children's hands.

Vicki walked down the driveway toward Tim. She saw him standing out there next to the curb like a smoker, banned from polite society, except he wasn't smoking. As she approached, she saw him hitch up his pants, a gesture that exposed briefly, the star on his belt and his gun. Deterrence apparently was his strategy for now.

"See anything?"

"I don't know. Lot more traffic than I would have guessed for Pacific Heights."

Vicki could see at least two gardener's trucks, small pickups piled with equipment, rakes standing up like outriggers. As they watched, two different monstrous SUVs drove by, the smoked windows dark, impenetrable. Vicki thought they were probably typical for the neighborhood.

"What are you going to do?"

"Go with 'em on the bus."

Vicki turned and looked at him directly. "What did I get you into?"

He shrugged. "Don't know yet." He hesitated, staring up the street, then looked at her. "What about you? You going? You probably shouldn't."

"I'm supposed to be at the clinic by now."

"You better go ahead and go to the clinic."

She shook her head quickly, not in negation so much as trying to clear her head. Then she stared at him, momentarily captured by his face. He was in it and not even thinking about the trouble he was going to cause himself. Well, all right. There just wasn't time right now. They needed to get out of here right this minute.

The Jaguar was backing down the driveway toward them; the bus, a short distance behind, began to move, too. "I better at least check in at the clinic and see. . . . Shit! I'm going with you."

She started punching in numbers on her cell phone as Jack backed the Jaguar into the street and then waited. The bus stopped at the end of the driveway and Cynthia got off. Vicki turned away and walked slowly up the sidewalk, trying to concentrate on the telephone conversation.

Jacobs answered the phone at the clinic immediately.

"Luke, I've got a family emergency."

"Good morning, Vicki."

"I'm sorry . . . it's really an emergency, I need to take some time off."

"Hey, no big deal. Nobody here, no messages. It's probably going to be dull all day. I can call Katie if it picks up. Want me to cover tomorrow?"

"Can you?"

"Sure, no problem."

"Thanks, Luke."

"It's okay. Really, it's perfect. Martha took the kids to her mother's for the weekend, so I can use the time in harness. I might ask you to cover for me in a couple of weeks if we can make a trade."

"Sure, absolutely."

"Somebody sick?"

"Pardon?"

"Somebody in your family sick? Your father okay?"

Vicki stopped walking. Her mouth hung open as she stared into space, the phone at her ear completely forgotten.

Of course! Oh, Jesus! Why hadn't she thought of it before? Wait a minute—this could get complicated.

"Vicki?"

Luke Jacobs was still on the phone. She'd forgotten him for a moment.

"I think he's going to be okay. Luke, I'll have to explain later."

"Yeah, you sound like you're in a hurry. Don't worry about a thing. Talk to you when you get back."

"Thank you so much, Luke, I really appreciate it."

"Hey, it's a trade-off. See you later."

It took Vicki a few seconds to realize that Luke had already hung up. Her mind was racing, trying to connect the dots, to see what she should have thought of immediately if she hadn't been so concerned about Tim's and her own involvement in some vaguely illegal activity. It was going too fast again, too many ideas were occurring to her at once to keep track of what made sense and what was just foolish.

She pushed the off button on her phone and stared at it, her mouth slack. She realized that Cynthia and Tim were on the sidewalk, Jack in the street, all watching her. She looked at Cynthia, glanced at Jack and looked back at Cynthia's face, the kind look in Cynthia's eye. She could tell Cynthia knew what Vicki was thinking about, the hesitation about getting herself any deeper. Cynthia's look was not impatience. It was a look that seemed more concerned for Vicki's welfare at that moment than all of the multiple concerns of her own. If Vicki bucked out, she would not object, she would actually sympathize.

Vicki had to look away. Then she made up her mind at the same time she was trying to convince herself not to, at the same time she was realizing that she couldn't just keep whipsawing back and forth. She would have to stay with it this time, for good.

Her own eye hardened and narrowed as she looked back at Cynthia again.

"Vicki, come on." Jack, standing in the open door to the Jaguar, was anxious, looking up the street one way, then the other, his face tense.

Tim's face looked more than worried, almost haunted, seeing all those children on the bus, but he was ready to go, ready to plunge in because she wanted him to. Was that it?

She knew she had made up her mind. "Let's go. I think I might have a good idea."

Cynthia pushed Tim toward the Jaguar. "You ride with Jack behind us. If we get split up in traffic, we'll meet you at the beach at Half Moon Bay. Driver?"

Tim stopped, turned, and looked at Vicki, the question in his face. She shrugged and went to the door of the bus. Tim followed, trying to talk to her, she knew, to try to talk her out of it.

"Vicki—"

"I'm going!" Vicki boarded the bus behind Cynthia.

Cynthia was already speaking. "Driver, can you take us to a beach down the Peninsula?"

Vicki took her by the arm, but talked to the driver. "I've got another idea. We're going down south. Can you just head down on 280 while I check out something? Can you do that?"

The African-American behind the wheel was in his fifties at least, overweight and uncomfortable with the uncertainty and the apparent disorganization of people who didn't even know where they wanted to go.

"Wherever you want to go is fine with me. You got me and the bus all day, till five o'clock—or longer than that, if you want to arrange for more than one day. I just have to call it in." He started to ease himself out of the seat.

Cynthia's face was deadpan, her manner cool. "Call it in on the way. We need to get going."

The driver gestured at his console. "Phone's not working right. It'll just take a minute if you let me use your phone."

Tim had his cell phone in one hand as he held the driver back with the other hand on the driver's shoulder. "We'll call on the way. Let's go."

The driver looked at the hand on his shoulder and did not move, either forward or back toward the seat. "Excuse me, sir."

"Sorry." Tim removed his hand from the driver's shoulder and held out the phone in the other. "Here, we're kinda in a hurry."

The driver did not move. He looked steadily at Tim, as though needing to establish something. "To get to the beach? You gonna be late for a reservation?"

Vicki put on her most cheerful face. "Look at who you're carrying. How many times you want to stop for the bathroom?"

The driver looked at the children, then back at Vicki. He finally winked. "Gotcha." He took the phone, eased himself back into his seat, and started the bus.

Twenty-two

"Daddy?" As soon as she said the word, Vickie could hear the tension in her own voice. The telephone connection crackled in her ear.

"Well, hello, sunshine! That you calling all morning?" It was nothing more than the sound of his voice, his eager greeting, but she suddenly slumped back in her seat, her shoulders dropping in relief. She grinned, apropos of nothing.

"I only called twice. You must have been outside, huh?" Vicki had to plug one ear with a finger because of the noise the children were making on the bus in spite of San Juana's efforts to shush them. Frank, Cynthia, and Consuela were staring at Vicki and listening to her end of the conversation. Vicki avoided looking at them, concentrating on the comforting sound of her father's voice.

"Sure," he said. "The youngsters like to work in the morning. Loads of energy. If I'd known it was you, I'd've stopped what I was doing. You okay?"

"Sure. How about you?"

"Mean as ever."

"I heard you had a fall."

"A what?"

"I heard you had a fall off of one of the horses."

"Cody tell you that? I don't remember having a fall."

"You didn't fall?"

"I might have dismounted awkwardly when I wasn't expecting to exactly."

Vicki had to laugh. It was as though she had been there all along, as though she had seen him that morning or the day before instead of nine or ten months ago. How long had it been since she'd called just to say hello, just to keep in touch? Time didn't matter with him. He could still calm her down, give her reassurance, without even knowing what it was about or that she needed it. All he had to do was all he could do, just to be who he was.

Except now she was going to ask him for a huge favor that she shouldn't even consider asking him for. She glanced up. Cynthia and Frank were watching her with the identical question imprinted in the identical furrow between each pair of eyes. They didn't know him. They were waiting for an answer, watching her. She would have to plunge in.

"Dad?"

"Yeah, sugar." His voice was expectant, knowing already that she was going to ask for something and agreeing to it without even knowing the request.

"I need a favor. A really, really big favor."

"Sure, kid, no problem. Something I can do? Need money?"

"Not that. I need to bring some visitors to you at the ranch."

"Some visitors?"

"Some children."

"No problem. Cody brings his kids all the time."

"Well, this is more like a whole bunch of kids. Like twelve of them."

His hesitation was brief. "Oh, I get it. Some kind of a field trip? Sure, bring as many as you want. I got a couple of green colts I wouldn't trust around kids that aren't used to 'em, but I can put those two in the stall—"

"There's more to it."

"Okay." He was so eager to please he was agreeing to whatever she asked before he knew what it was. She realized she had known that he would, that she had counted on it without even having to think about it.

"If it's all right with you, we need to stay there for a little while."

"Stay here?"

"Right."

"Like sleep over?" Vicki could picture him looking around, thinking where to put a dozen children in his house.

"They'll have their own sleeping bags." Vicki saw Cynthia nodding her head vigorously and making a note to stop and buy a bunch of sleeping bags. "I was thinking they could just sleep in the barn maybe, huh?"

"Well . . . they can if they want, but there's three bedrooms, a living room, and a big porch. We can work it out okay. When you think you might come?"

"Actually, Dad . . ." Now she was the one hesitating.

"I hear children. You at the clinic?"

"Well, no. Actually, Dad, I'm on a bus on the freeway."

There was a pause a little longer this time, and then his voice not giving anything away about how he might really feel about a full-scale invasion, but sounding thoughtful. "Are you on the way down already? I mean, right now?"

"Well, yes."

There was a long silence. Vicki was trying to think of what to say. She hadn't thought through what to tell him about suddenly showing up on his doorstep with a busload of children and—oh, yeah.

"And there's, let's see . . ." She did a quick count. "Eight adults."

The silence continued. Her father's voice, when he found it, finally, sounded wary. "I'm going to need to go to the store."

"Dad, don't worry about that. Don't do anything, okay? We're bringing everything we need—sleeping bags, groceries, towels, everything. Okay?"

His mind was already running in its own direction. "I can get some beans and hot dogs, maybe some potato salad—"

Vicki couldn't help laughing out loud. "Dad, not a thing."

"Maybe we should roast a whole pig, huh?"

"Dad—"

"Should have started that early this morning. Can you all stay a few days? I could get a half-grown shoat from Roger, take the time to dig a pit and do it right. The children wouldn't have to see that part, if you think—"

"Dad, really and truly, we've got lots of people to help. I don't want you to do anything at all."

She listened for his response. Nothing. "Dad?" There wasn't even a line noise. "Dad?"

Then his voice, still talking. "—seem to be breaking up."

"Dad, can you hear me?"

"Yeah, now . . ."

But his voice was lost again in the ether. Vicki listened for a moment without hearing anything, then tried calling back. No response from the phone. She looked at the display: NO SERVICE, in red for emphasis.

She punched the off button on the phone and looked at the others. "It's fine. At least he knows we're coming." Cynthia gave her a smile that seemed to be intended to convey gratitude. She turned and stared hard at the cars on the freeway. Frank was staring out the other side watching. The children, oblivious to any concerns about watching or even about where they might be going, shouted with delight as the bus entered the maze of freeways around San Jose, the traffic whizzing by them on both sides now as the driver aimed for the particular strand of spaghetti that would take them further south.

Vicki turned around and looked out the back window. Jack was driving the Jaguar, but she couldn't see Tim. Oh. She saw his rear move between the seats. He was in the backseat, turned around on his knees, watching out the back window for anybody following them.

Cynthia was sitting on the back bench of the bus with Vicki. There were no seatbelts in the bus, so Cynthia kept one hand on Charlotte's car seat, which had been wedged into the corner with pillows and blankets. Charlotte chewed happily on a teething ring, staring with evident fascination at all the children.

Catching Cynthia's eye, Vicki gestured toward the front where Frank was talking to the driver, sitting in the seat directly behind him. "What did you tell him?"

"A hundred and fifty a day under the table, besides what we pay the bus company, plus expenses, which will include a change of clothes and toiletries."

"He's okay with that?"

"A thousand bucks, cash in advance. He's quite happy." Cynthia sat for a while, staring thoughtfully toward the front, a worried look on her face. The children were full of joy with the outing. Toys were scattered around the bus and powdered remnants of crackers were smeared in the aisles, ground into the seats with spilled milk. The little refugees stared out of the windows, chattered and squealed to each other about what they were seeing, delighted with the routine nightmare of traffic.

Vicki took a deep breath and tried to relax. She was covered for the weekend at the clinic, and her patients to be seen at rounds would be handled by either Luke or Katie. Okay, quit worrying about that. But what was she going to tell her father? If she told him everything, he would get out his gun and sit on the roof to guard them. The man was seventy-two years old, for Christ's sake.

Cynthia looked at Vicki, her face worried. "You think this will be safe? Turning them loose at your father's ranch? What I was thinking was—how do you suppose they found Peter in the hospital?"

Vicki sat back and thought about it. They had been so busy getting the kids loaded up and out of the house that she hadn't had time to think this part through. She hadn't really given any consideration to the question of how they had found Peter, although now that question seemed obvious and important. She stared at Cynthia, thinking about it.

"I don't have any idea."

"See, that's a problem we should think about. The only people that know we're on the way to your father's place are the people at the bus company. The driver had to let them know where we're taking their bus. But how many people knew about Peter?"

"Well, just about anybody that dealt with him at the hospital. There were doctors and nurses, the Latvian volunteer that came to talk with him so he wouldn't feel so isolated."

"Who was that?"

"I don't know. I never saw her."

"That's the problem." Cynthia sighed and her frown deepened. "We're just speculating about how they found him, and we don't know why they would murder a child if they were just trying to get our attention."

She looked out the window, then raised her voice in alarm. "What are you doing? Driver?"

The driver shouted back at them. "I don't know. Your friends just signaled for me to pull off here."

Vicki stood up and saw that the Jaguar was now in front of them, leading them up an exit ramp into a rest area.

They rumbled to a stop and the driver opened the door, leaving the motor running. He rose from his seat as Tim boarded.

Tim grinned at him. "Thanks. Where you going?"

The driver gave him a barely tolerant look. "As long as we stopped, I'm going to take a leak. You mind?"

"Oh. No, go ahead." He turned away and didn't see the look the driver gave him before he exited through the doors.

Tim looked at Cynthia. "We got away clean. Nobody following us."

"You sure?"

"Yes, I would have seen 'em. There were a couple of stretches there with no traffic behind us for miles. I want to know about the rest of that conversation."

Frank seemed to flinch, then he quickly covered it, nodding his head. "Yes, of course. Soon as we get back on the road. Shouldn't we be watching out here?"

"Mrs. Wilkins?" It was San Juana. "We'll go with the girls. Maybe Mr. Sanderson or Mr. Murphy could take the boys?"

Two of the boys were already standing in the aisle, one of them trying to cross his legs as he hopped up and down, now that he had thought of the subject.

Tim nodded, his face grim. "Yes, okay. C'mon, boys."

Vicki stayed on the bus with Charlotte and Cynthia and watched. Frank stood outside the bathroom with the boys, who bounced impatiently while Tim went inside and looked around. Then both men stood in the doorway while the boys scampered inside, apparently just in time.

The bus driver emerged first as though he had been flushed out, grinning at something until he saw the two men posted like sentries outside. He stopped, then lit a cigarette and stood with them, looking around. He seemed to think they were watching out for perverts.

A van pulled into the closest parking space and two white men got out. They both looked disheveled, uncombed and dirty as if they had been on the road a long time, sleeping in the van. They were both wearing long coats and seemed to take their time, looking around before they headed side by side to the restroom.

They strolled past the bus driver and Frank without acknowledging the latter's nod. Tim eased inside behind them, moving casually, his hands at his sides, hanging loose. In a few moments the boys came boiling out in a mob and ran shouting toward the bus, having a fine time now that the pressure was off. Then Tim came out, and with Frank and the driver, casually loitered near the other restroom until the girls came out, too.

Jack came up and stood in the doorway after the last of them had boarded the bus. The driver was talking to him. "I know where there's one of those big discount stores in Bakersfield. Wal-Mart or Kmart or some kinda mart. Want me to take you there?"

Jack nodded and gave him a thumbs-up. "Perfect. I'll follow you." He went back to the Jaguar, and they were finally getting back on the freeway.

Tim motioned for Frank to come to the back of the bus where Cynthia and Vicki were waiting.

Frank had obviously been thinking about what to say. He looked at Cynthia first. "His name is Hans."

"Charlotte's father?"

"Yes."

"He's married?"

"Yes. How did you know?"

She regarded him steadily for a moment until he finally nodded his head. "Yeah, all right. I guess it had to be something like that." He nodded again. "Okay, here goes."

He took a deep breath and let it out. "Hans and his brother were in San Francisco. They were on tourist visas. Their father is the guy that runs the smuggling operation from somewhere in Russia."

"They're Russian?"

"German, but they were raised mostly in Russia. The father—whatever his name is, he wouldn't tell me—he smuggles people. That's what he does and I guess the sons are working in the family business. We didn't get into that much. Anyway, the two brothers were in San Francisco. For what it's worth, Hans said they only came there to collect the money for their father. Hans wanted to do that. He wanted to come to San Francisco himself because . . . well, because he wanted to see Julia. But then after he sent the money on to his father, they stayed, waiting to see how the crossing went, I suppose. Then that shooting happened down at the border."

Vicki's question was quick. "How did they know about it?"

Frank looked at her as if he hadn't thought about that. "I don't know . . ."

Cynthia waved the question off. "Oh, it was all over television. Frank might not have seen it if they didn't cover it in Europe, but it was a big deal here. You didn't see it?"

Tim nodded. "Okay, I saw it."

Vicki remembered that she had heard about it. Elaine had talked to her about it, hadn't she? "Was this where four border patrol agents got killed?"

Frank nodded. "I guess that's right. At least it was several, and two of the smugglers died along with several children when one of the vans crashed. Anyway, after this shooting the vehicles that were left split up and went different directions. They were afraid to go back near the border so they headed north. They called Hans from New Mexico somewhere, and said they were coming to him, that he had to hide them until they could come up with some money. That's when Hans got their other brother, this kid, to come to me." Frank scowled at the floor, then looked up at Cynthia. "That kid didn't say anything about any of this. He could have told me but—"

Cynthia didn't seem to be bothered by that. "He thought it would be easier to extort the money than to get you to help somebody who had killed some policemen." She looked at Tim and raised her eyebrows, asking for confirmation.

Tim asked, "Why didn't they just get the money from Hans's father?"

"I don't know. Maybe he didn't have that kind of money, or didn't have the right kind of contacts in the States to make a transfer or something. I don't know the answer to that."

Tim nodded and continued to look at Frank, waiting for him to go on.

"Anyway, that didn't work. So they went to Julia."

Vicki shook her head. "Wait a minute. Why so much? Why four million dollars?"

"He said it was because they were hot. They knew some other people that could get them over the border into Canada, but they were too hot. The price went through the roof because everyone was looking for them."

Tim stared at him. "They knew these other people? They were rivals in the business?"

Frank waved him off. "I don't know. It wasn't that long a conversation, I just got as much of the story as I'm telling you."

Cynthia motioned for Tim to stop interrupting. "They went to Julia . . ."

"Right. They went to her to get her to come up with the money, but she wouldn't help."

"Why didn't they come to us? We're right in the same town."

"They didn't know about you. Julia wouldn't tell them anything about you or where she got the money she had paid them before. She really was careful to keep you isolated from any of it, in both directions. Remember, she wouldn't tell you who they were either."

"Us."

"Pardon?"

"She kept you isolated from it, too, right?"

"Oh. Yes, of course. She kept all of us out of it."

"So what happened when Julia wouldn't help?"

Frank grimaced and looked away. He wouldn't look at Cynthia. "Hans says that his father ordered him to get on the next plane and come back to Russia. His father told him that if the others got caught, they might drag him into it, but he thinks the real reason was that he wanted to put more pressure on Julia than Hans would stand for. At the last minute his brother didn't go with him. He made up some excuse and said he would be on a later flight, but Hans said that later he realized what he was doing was going back to Julia."

"But what happened?"

"He's not sure. When he heard that Julia was dead, he said . . . well, he was crying on the phone when he talked about it."

Tim grunted. "Okay, so you believed him. What happened?"

"Okay, he's surmising this from what other people said. His brother hurt the baby. He doesn't think he meant to hurt her that much, but when he realized how serious it was, he was sure Julia was going to turn them all in, so . . ." He didn't go on.

Cynthia stared at him. "So they just killed her."

Frank nodded, still not looking at her.

Tim was watching him carefully. "Frank. How did they know about you? How did they know to come to you, if Julia had everybody so isolated?"

"Oh, they knew about the office in Belgium. They might have even known that we were married. Yes, I'm sure they knew that."

"They just didn't know where the Wilkinses were in San Francisco?"

Frank looked at Cynthia. "They might not have known about you at all. They probably didn't. They just knew who I was because I'm in Europe and I'm the one she married when she needed a husband."

Vicki saw Tim staring hard at Frank. He wasn't buying this, and Frank wasn't looking at him or at anybody now. Tim turned his head deliberately and looked at Cynthia, an unvoiced question.

"Oh, that's certainly possible." Cynthia wasn't nearly as skeptical as Tim. "Frank has always been the lead man in Europe, Jack took the lead in the States. I'm sure most of the people Jack deals with wouldn't know Frank or anything about him."

Frank looked up at Tim. "If other people had all the contacts, they wouldn't need our services, would they?"

Tim nodded, but Vicki didn't think he was convinced. "Okay, but what about Mrs. Fairchild?"

"Hans wasn't sure about that, either. They split up, remember? He thinks the Mexican driver that had these children took them to her. And the kids confirm that. They said they were staying with some woman before they were brought to the Wilkinses' house."

Tim stared at him. "What about the drugs? Where did the heroin come in?"

"Oh, that's—I'm just guessing, but they were probably smuggling drugs, too, huh?"

Tim continued to stare, letting him go on, not commenting one way or the other.

Frank held his hands out, palms up, in a gesture of submitting the matter to Tim. "Look, I'm just surmising here, too. I didn't talk to Hans about that. But as for Rita, seems to me if it was a Mexican driver that had done this before, then he knew where to go. He could wait there, too, and let the situation at the border cool off for a while. When the other guys showed up looking pretty damn desperate, he could have got the Wilkinses' address from Rita and pretended he didn't speak any language known to man so he could dump the kids off and head for home. Something like that." He shrugged.

Cynthia was watching Frank. She glanced around the bus at the children, then back at Frank. Was she thinking about the details of her daughter's death? She was staring hard, but abstractedly, her mind somewhere else.

Finally, she spoke. "So the deal is, we just have to come up with four million bucks? Give them the money and they leave the country?"

Vicki was surprised, but then realized that she shouldn't have been. Cynthia hadn't been thinking about her own tragedy at all. She was thinking about business, about the practical business of how to get out of this, how to find a way out.

Cynthia turned her head deliberately and looked at Tim. She waited until he looked back at her and she was sure she had his full attention. "What I need is a few days. We can give them money to keep them off our backs. In a few days we might get all of the kids taken care of, but we should have a good chance of locating the families of the ones who have relatives." She looked up at Frank. "How many have relatives here?"

"Four out of the twelve."

"All one family?"

"Two siblings from one family. The other two are separate."

She nodded and looked at the children. "Which ones? Never mind, I don't want to know." She looked at Vicki. "You can't tell us how much difference that makes, huh?"

"I have to talk to Elaine. I'm just like you, it seems like it should make a difference, but I don't know what the legal status is."

Cynthia nodded and then turned back to Tim. "Okay, I really need that few days. I have to ask you. Are you still here as Vicki's friend? Or have you become official yet?"

Tim let out the breath he was holding and looked down at the floor. He shook his head and stared out the window of the bus, thinking. He glanced at Vicki and then looked back at Cynthia. "I'm not sure."

"I was afraid of that."

"Look . . ." His mind was working, trying to find a way. "This is a homicide investigation. You can't expect that you're not going to be in the middle of the investigation. Maybe your lawyer can get you a deal, but you're going to have to come clean on this other—"

"Oh, clearly." Cynthia was nodding agreement. "We know that, I think. Right, Frank?"

Frank looked uncomfortable in the extreme. "What about immunity? Couldn't Elaine work out some kind of immunity or—"

"She'll work out what she can work out." Cynthia turned back to Tim. "Here's the deal to you. We'll turn ourselves in, let Elaine do whatever she can do, but she won't help with the children. We can't turn it over to her until we have them taken care of, or she'll just hand them right to the INS. Maybe she won't represent us on those terms, but there are other lawyers, if we have to go that route. You don't have to know what happens to the children. If we can just get in touch with the right people, I'll take care of the rest of it, and if I have to go to jail, then fine. I still need a few days."

"Cynthia, even if you gave these guys the money they're asking for, they're still not out of the country yet. They may not make it. Or they may get the money and still think they have to eliminate all the witnesses. See what I mean?"

Cynthia nodded. "I guess the question is, what are *you* going to have to do? Nobody knows where we are or where we're going. That plus a hefty dose of money ought to be good enough to get us a few days, at least."

Tim looked away again, thinking. Finally, he looked back at Cynthia, and this time, he wasn't equivocating. "I have to tell the L.A. cops something. I can say I got it from an informer named Hans, which would be true enough. They'll let me hide the source of the information for a few days. Just a few."

That seemed to be what Cynthia was waiting to hear. She nodded to Tim, then leaned forward, her elbows on her knees so that all of their heads were closer together in the aisle of the bus. "All right. Buy me that few days, that's all I'm asking."

She looked at Frank. "First, you need to tell Hans that we're going to pay the money. Tell him we're paying, understand? And he's got to tell that to the smugglers."

Frank nodded, readily agreeing. "Sure. Okay, I'll tell him that."

"But then we've got to do it. We can't take a chance with these people, so don't go fooling around. You and Jack do whatever you have to do to get that money together, right?"

"Yes, right. Jack's mainly the one for that."

"Okay, second, you have to talk to the people in Belgrade who put us in touch with Rita in the first place. You remember who I'm talking about?"

"Yeah. The first people we dealt with."

"Right. You can contact them, right?"

"I'm sure. I'll talk to the Princess, she'll have the numbers."

"Those people have to know somebody else in the States who does what Rita did, right?"

"Yes, that's right. There were other people. They didn't want to tell us more than we needed to know, but there were others."

"Those are the names I need. Can you call them now?"

Frank took out his phone and looked at the screen. "Still no service. That's what I was talking to the driver about. He thinks he knows where the relay stations are and he said he'd let me know when we're getting near one."

Cynthia nodded, the General approving of the efforts of a Lieutenant. "We might have to wait until we get to a landline phone, unless you think you can hold a sustained conversation on an international call while we're passing a relay station."

Frank shrugged. "I don't know. Our driver goes this way all the time, I'll ask him."

He got up and went toward the front of the bus. Tim went with him, needing to make his own calls.

Vicki looked at Cynthia. She was sitting back again, distracted, one hand on Charlotte's car seat.

Vicki spoke to her, keeping her voice low.

"Maybe when Frank calls those people . . . where are they?"

"Belgrade."

"That's in Yugoslavia?"

"Yes, it used to be."

"Julia went there when it was off-limits?"

"Yes, once or twice. I think she made the important contacts there at first, but later she dealt with people in Macedonia. I'm making it sound too complicated, like some huge conspiracy. For us, it was simple. All we had to do, basically, was supply some money in cash and the kids showed up later in Los Angeles. I know how that sounds. If someone had just told me about it like that I would have thought they were being awfully naïve. But it worked very well. Several times."

Vicki nodded and watched her. In spite of the efficiency, the apparent businesslike toughness of this woman, there *was* an element of naïveté about her, about her involvement in this, that even Cynthia recognized herself.

So it must have been Julia. With Julia, the children were the driving force, at least to begin with. Then maybe it was her romantic lover, the one who was in the business, as Julia must have seen it, of saving refugee children from starvation. For Cynthia, the children were important, but her incentive was probably more the need to see Julia engaged in something outside of herself.

At some point, Cynthia's child must have seemed hopelessly lost to her—an addict, going through rehab, despondent to the point of being suicidal. But then Julia, still young and, in spite of everything, still fresh, found the children. Concerned with something she could do about the children, Julia began to come alive again. Julia must have made an enormous effort, a total dedication to worthwhile work—truly worthwhile, in spite of the dangers. Oh yes, the dangers must have been obvious to Cynthia, too. Maybe that was the reason she was able to stick to thinking about business now.

Maybe Cynthia didn't want to think about the other part of it. She didn't want to ask herself what she was thinking when she let Julia go off and do this thing.

Twenty-three

They only stopped at one more rest area before they reached Bakers-field, where they rolled into the parking lot of a chain discount store to buy supplies. Vicki stayed on the bus with Consuela and the children. She tried the phone again, but there was no answer at the ranch. She glanced at her watch. Mid-afternoon, he was probably out work-ing the horses.

Vicki saw Tim coming back ahead of the others. He threaded his way through the cars, carrying a bag of new clothes and talking on his phone like some ambitiously self-important broker or lawyer. She smiled, watching him, knowing how little like that he was. She got off the bus to be able to talk to him in the relative quiet of the parking lot. He smiled when he saw her, as if he didn't have a care in the world, as if he were enjoying this. He closed the phone and put it away in an inside coat pocket. Vicki could just see the edge of his holster with the movement of the jacket, and then she saw his eyes narrow and sweep the parking lot around them, even a quick glance over his shoulder where he had just been. The cop was still in there, too.

"You okay?" His question took in everything—the children on the bus, Peter's death, leaving her practice for a weekend without notice, the descent on her father's peace and tranquility—everything. He was genuinely concerned.

"Everything's fine, so far."

He tapped the phone through his jacket. "That was LAPD. I'm going to take the Jag from here and go directly to their office downtown. I'll wait until you're back on the freeway."

"We're surely okay here. Don't you think?"

"Yeah, but I thought . . ." He let the idea drift off.

"Yeah, Peter."

"Right. I would have thought the hospital was safe, too."

"Tim, what are you going to tell them?"

"I don't know yet. I'm going to have to play it by ear, I guess." He watched the cars driving slowly through the parking lot, not looking at her. "Maybe you better call your friend, that lawyer."

"Yes. You're right, I will."

"Tell her I'm in touch with the police down here, so . . . I don't know, maybe she can think of something." He looked down at her and frowned. "You're not going to have anybody with you that's armed."

Vicki had already thought of that. "We're in a bus, on the freeway. Unless someone was following us—"

"I wouldn't have missed them. I'm sure nobody was following."

"Okay." She waited for him to say more, to tell her what he was thinking. His mind was going a mile a minute while his eyes were scanning the parking lot, looking into the cars that drove near them, looking in the distance at cars coming into the lot from the street from two directions. He was trying to make up his mind about something, she thought, but she couldn't tell what it was, if he was so sure nobody was following them.

Finally, he looked down at her and caught her watching him. He started to laugh, embarrassed that he'd been caught, then his eyes were serious again. "What the hell is it about these people?"

"Cynthia?"

"All three of them. You get the feeling we're getting about half the story?"

She was not ready for that question. "Maybe. I'm not sure."

"But something, right?"

"Yes, something. You got that feeling, too?"

"Yeah. I just don't see what it would be, though." He frowned down at the pavement, then looked directly into her eyes.

"They don't seem dangerous."

Quickly, Vicki shook her head. "No, not at all. I'm not worried about them. Not like that."

"I was thinking the same thing. I honestly don't believe they knew Julia was murdered. I don't think they could have faked that."

"No." Vicki knew that was right. She didn't have to even think it over. Cynthia and Jack could never have faked the scene she saw them go through when Tim told them about that. "Whatever it is they're not saying, it's not about homicide."

Tim let out his breath in a sigh that said it all. They both knew that Cynthia and her crew were lawbreakers, that they could lie, at least by omission, to the FBI. But that didn't make them dangerous. Vicki couldn't believe that they were, and she could tell that Tim didn't believe it either, but he was having trouble leaving her with them.

Vicki saw him glance at the busload of children, then scan the cars in the lot once again. Vicki could almost see him thinking, following the same pathways that her own mind was taking. Dangerous people did not harbor a busload of orphans and reject every opportunity to dump them on someone else.

Tim's voice sounded matter-of-fact, stating his plans. "I'll see if the cops have got any more information, if they turned up anything. Hell, they might even have it figured out, but I doubt it. Frank is going to wait and try to call overseas from your father's house so he doesn't get cut off in the middle. That reminds me—I already said this to the rest of them. Be careful who you call from your father's house, and don't leave a number for people to call back, okay? That's the last thing we need—all anybody would have to do would be to run his number on a reverse directory and they'd get the physical address you're calling from. Understand?"

"Okay, sure."

"I asked Frank, but he didn't know if Europe has such a thing as caller ID. That could be a serious problem with any calls they're going to be making—"

"Not a chance." Vicki was sure about this one. "As soon as that technology came out, my Dad had it blocked on his phone. No way he was going to call some store and get a thousand calls back from salesmen."

"Really?"

"Absolutely positive. If my phone rings and there's no number on the screen, I assume it's probably him. Don't worry about that."

Tim looked at her, obviously pleased with this news. "Fortune smiles. That's another reason to use your father's telephone. Better than the cellulars, because those can be traced to the nearest relay station." He kept looking at her.

She couldn't think of anything else to say. She didn't much like the idea of him taking off to downtown L.A. by himself but she couldn't say that.

She looked back at him and suddenly just said it. "Do you know the people you're dealing with? In the LAPD?"

He shook his head. "No. Don't know any of them personally."

She thought about that, and realized that he must have already thought of the same thing. Still, she couldn't help saying it. "Be careful."

When he didn't answer, she looked up again and found he was staring at her hard, his eyes suddenly intense. His expression softened just a little as he spoke. "I would like to hug you."

For a second she was so startled, the comment so out of context of anything she was thinking about, that she didn't know how to react. Then she saw he was grinning, embarrassed at his own words. She smiled, felt a glow of response to this awkward, childlike side of him. She cocked her head and smiled back at him.

"Well?"

But he was looking over her head at the bus, still grinning as though embarrassed. She glanced back and it seemed as though every single child on the bus had found a spot at a window and was staring at them.

Vicki laughed softly as she impulsively slid her arms around his waist and pressed her face against his chest. "Won't hurt 'em a bit."

She felt his arms move around her tentatively, then with a deep sigh he gently pushed her away by the shoulders. Her hands on the sides of his chest, she could feel him vibrate with silent laughter. Then she heard the children, too, several squeals and one with an unmistakably American expression. "Eeeew!"

She could feel his chest shake as he laughed, thoroughly embarrassed. She looked up quickly at his laughing eyes looking at her. Then she pulled her hands away, suddenly afraid she would grasp his head and pull it down to her level. When he met her eyes again she smiled, almost laughing. "Some psychologist."

"I know. Waste of a good education."

"Later. I would at least like to kiss you once, for real."

He whispered. "Me, too."

They stared at each other, but the sounds of the children squealing and gawking at the two of them could not be blocked out.

Once they were back on the freeway, Cynthia filled Jack in on what they had discussed while he was in the Jaguar, and went over what they had to do. Jack showed no hesitation about starting to work immediately to transfer funds so they could have the money ready at the beginning of the business day on Monday. Frank would have to talk to Hans again to hold the smugglers off that long, at least, and then they had to figure out how to turn over the money without letting the smugglers know where they were.

Cynthia was ready to start calling whoever might be able to take the children to place them in new homes. Frank had to get those names from Europe as well.

The bus arrived at the ranch late in the afternoon. Little Nadya had stretched out on the back bench with her head on Vicki's lap. All of the children were tired, some sleeping; curled in the seats, tucked under jackets and sleeping bags that they had acquired in Bakersfield, some staring glassy-eyed through the windows at the bleak chaparral of the countryside now that they were not whizzing by it on the freeway.

Vicki eased out from under the sleeping child, and walked up front to direct the driver through the final two miles of back roads to her father's place. She got out and opened the gate at the driveway to let the bus through. The driveway, still graveled up by the gate, went up a low rise and then dropped down; from the gate, she could just see the tip of the roof to the house. She could see the hills on the other side, green with recent rain. She caught herself searching the hills looking for Candy. Oh, yeah. She felt her chest fill with unexpected disappointment as she remembered. Her old mare had died two years earlier. She kept forgetting that.

The bus rolled by her and stopped, noisy and diesel-smelling and full of shouting little invaders to this peaceful vale of her father's, of hers to the extent that she had grown up here and still felt like she was coming home when she stopped and opened the gate. When she came by herself she always paused by the gate and savored it for a few moments, breathing in the smell of horses even though they were not close enough to smell, soaking up a little of the quiet before she drove over the rise and then down to the house itself.

She heard the children and glanced up at the windows to the bus. Cynthia was watching her patiently. Vicki sighed and closed the gate.

As she climbed back on she could see through the windshield a pair of dogs racing from the direction of the house. One was small, a woolly, furiously animated white toy with black nose and eyes for emphasis. The other was a hound with an easy lope and extravagant, flapping ears. The hound bellowed once, then reversed direction to lope ahead of the bus, a canine guide to the obvious. The small white dog, voiceless, saving his breath for athletics, circled the bus and then continued his orbit in an earnest, chugging blur, as though his sole duty were to expend energy; his job description, an otherwise useless, wildly extravagant display of miniature exertion.

Vicki pointed for the children and named them: "That's Elsie and that one's named Dan O'Bannion." Dan O'Bannion scooted across the bow and continued his revolution a third time around. Elsie bellowed once again without turning around, as if more concerned about announcing the new arrivals than acting as a watchdog.

As they stopped in the yard in front of the house, Vicki could see a third dog as he emerged from the interior of the barn. The dog was not familiar to Vicki, and obviously had not absorbed the inherent good nature of the other two. This one was mostly German shepherd, but with a heavy, shaggy, black-brown coat that made him look bigger than he already was. The dog emerged, stiff-legged, tail up and rigid, head low, eyes glowering. He sniffed, seemed to gauge his angle of attack, then rushed in low, silent intensity at the bus, just as Frank stepped down, a small boy right on his heels. Vicki grabbed the next child as she watched the oncoming dog.

"Frank!"

Frank turned, saw the dog and then immediately grabbed up the little boy at his side. As the dog got closer, it let out an audible rumble that seemed to catapult Frank backward onto the bus with more alacrity than Vicki would have given him credit for with his bulk.

The door to the bus slammed shut just after Frank made it back inside. The dog smashed against the glass of the door, and the rumbling snarl erupted into fire and thunder. Teeth flashed as small flecks of foam went flying, sticking to the glass.

The bus driver held his hand on the door control lever as if he thought the dog might try to pry it open. He stared at the animal through the glass. "Uh-uh. Nobody is getting me off this bus."

The dog suddenly turned and rushed at the rear of the bus, as though looking for another way in. He immediately whirled and scrambled back to the front, roaring out eternal damnation and chomping at the glass next to Frank's feet in the door well, causing Frank to back up another step, even with the door closed.

Vicki saw her father emerge from the barn waving his arms and carrying a lead rope. Vicki couldn't understand what he was saying for the noise that the dog made, but his warning to stay on the bus was as clear as it was unnecessary.

The dog finally broke off the attack when Vicki's father snapped the lead onto his collar. The beast looked up at him and whooshed his tail back and forth, obviously proud of having captured a whole busload of intruders, all at once.

"Sorry! I got a pen out back. Let me lock him up before you let the children out."

They waited a moment until her father reappeared, coming out the front door and half-trotting with a rolling, bow-legged gait, grinning apologetically.

"Sorry about that!" he shouted.

Vicki jumped down from the bus and threw her arms around his neck. He gave her a brief squeeze, but was too full of apologies to do more for the moment. "That damn dog just showed up a few months ago. Thought I had him tamed down, but I guess not." He looked at Cynthia and Frank as they peered out from the bus door. "Don't worry, he can't get out of the pen."

Vicki introduced Frank, Jack, and Cynthia as they stepped down from the bus. Cynthia was carrying Charlotte, holding her against her shoulder as though afraid she would get too near the dirt in the driveway. Vicki thought it might take a while for her to be able to loosen up.

The children, though, swarmed out of the bus in a stampede with San Juana and Consuela right behind them, trying to keep up. The children had already spotted the corral with a half-dozen horses in it, all staring at the children coming at them. The horses had a look of curious trepidation that Vicki thought was well advised.

Nadya lagged, gamely swinging the slow left leg, but focused on the horses with undiminished delight. Elsie dropped back from the mob to walk next to the little girl, whipping her tail in response to the child placing a hand on her back and using the hound for added support.

Cynthia, Jack, and Frank were looking around cautiously, as though not sure what other kind of wildlife might suddenly emerge. The bus driver would not get off the bus.

"Dad trains young horses for people to use on the trail," Vicki said.

Cynthia looked at Vicki's father, the horses, then back at him, at the age in his face. Vicki thought he hadn't changed since she was in high school, but she knew what he looked like to Cynthia by the incredulity in her voice. "By yourself?"

He grinned at her, enjoying the attention. "It's okay. I don't have to wrestle with 'em."

He looked at Frank. "Let me show you around and we can figure out where to stash everybody. I got some ideas, but anywhere you want is fine with me."

Frank nodded. He was smiling, but the smile was looking a little strained. "You can't actually see the road from down here, can you?"

"Dad, we've got one more coming in a car. He had to make a side trip."

Cynthia was looking at the corral with the children lining the pipe fence staring at the horses. The horses were staring back at them. One of the smaller children ducked under the lowest bar and started for the herd, but Consuela was after him in a flash and snatched him back through the fence as if the horses were polar bears. A sleek young mare approached the crowd at the fence to check the prospects for treats, and Consuela pulled the children away from the inquisitive snout. When a small hand reached for her face the mare jerked her head upright and the mob backed off even more. She stuck out her nose again; trying to find the food that experience with Cody's brood had taught her was probably there somewhere.

Cynthia's voice was courteous, but, Vicki thought, a little urgent, too. "I wonder if we might use your phone?"

"Oh, sure, I'll show you."

"You expecting somebody?" Frank had walked back up the dirt drive, where he could see the gate to the road.

Vicki's father looked up and started up the driveway. "Somebody here?"

"A blue pickup."

"Oh." He stopped, seemed undecided, then cast a sheepish glance at Vicki. "That's just a neighbor."

It didn't take Vicki two seconds to scramble up the small hill to look for herself. She could see two people in the pickup; as they got closer, she recognized Roger Dorr's silhouette in a black cowboy hat on the passenger side. The driver was a woman. Vicki had forgotten all about the woman until her father looked sheepish. She thought, *Jesus! A blonde!* She was prepared to dislike the woman immediately, then caught herself at it as the truck came to a stop. Not blonde. Her hair was white.

Vicky turned away and looked for her father. He was watching her, waiting uncomfortably for her reaction. Of course. He didn't know about any of the other business. He would think this was the most important thing going on. She felt as if she were being rude to him—the last thing she wanted to be. But still . . . "Dad, it's kind of urgent about the phone."

Cynthia was barely containing her impatience. Her father looked around and saw it, too.

"Oh, yeah, okay. Right this way." He led her toward the house and Vicki turned her attention to the new arrivals. She walked to the passenger side door as it opened and Roger Dorr slowly climbed down, his hat obscuring his face until he looked up at Vicki standing in front of him.

"Mr. Dorr, how are you?"

"Hi." He grinned and his face crinkled in a thousand places, his eyes dancing as he looked her up and down. "You looking great."

He was normally so reticent that she felt truly complimented. She was trying to think of a way to keep them all outside, away from the telephone, so Frank could get started without being interrupted. Maybe she could just keep them talking for a while and her father would come back out to join them.

"I feel great. What about you?" She watched him taking slow, careful steps. "Are you all right?"

He slapped his skinny flanks. "New joints."

She stared in surprise. "Hip replacements?"

"Both sides, brand new. Get to try 'em out on horseback, end of this coming week."

She watched as he gingerly took a few steps toward the house. "Do they hurt?"

"Just 'til I get rolling, then they're fine."

Reluctantly, knowing he might want to go sit down, she plucked at his sleeve to stop him. She whispered, "Who's your driver?"

He seemed to think he might have been rude. "You haven't met her yet? Maureen?"

"No. I . . ." She looked around, distracted, trying not to be obvious. Frank and Jack had gone inside to the telephone with Cynthia. Okay, they must be getting started. She wanted to hear what was being said, but she couldn't be that rude to these people, obviously geared up for her arrival, not a clue about the urgency of her situation.

Roger changed direction slowly. "Well, got to do that first." He dropped his voice to a confidential level. "You can't put this off now." He leaned toward her as he turned, listing on the new hips and forcing her to turn with him.

Vicki was suddenly deeply chagrined that he had misinterpreted her tone for impatience. But when Vicki looked, Maureen was closing in on her. Maureen approached with a determination and directness that Vicki had to notice.

"Hi, Vicki. I'm Maureen Knowlton."

Vicki extended her hand, too formally, she knew. "Hello, Mrs. Knowlton. Cody and Beth told me about you."

Maureen took the hand and grinned. "Oh, dear. Is my reputation entirely ruined?"

"We just call her Miz Maureen." Even Roger was working on her, trying to make her like the woman, or at least relax a little.

Vicki was embarrassed in the face of all this effort at friendliness. She wasn't doing this well. She was distracted with the need to get other things done, but this was important to her father. She needed to give it her attention, he deserved that from her, and, after all, it was the others who needed to be doing things on the telephone, not her. She looked at Maureen again, trying to force herself to respond with some friendliness.

"They had nothing but good things to say about you. I'm very pleased to meet you."

Maureen beamed, looking at Vicki for a long moment. Vicki suddenly realized from the way Maureen looked at her just how important this meeting was to her, that the woman had been thinking about it a great deal in advance—and that she was in love.

With Vicki's father.

Good God!

Quickly, behind the façade of a friendly greeting, Vicki lectured herself. She would have to get used to it. She decided she would like the woman, after all. She felt a sudden need to like her.

Maureen indicated the back of the pickup. "I brought a bag of carrots. Your father was running low and I thought the little ones would get a kick out of giving the horses treats. We can carry the bag together, but it'll take two of us."

Vicki looked around, but Roger had already made his way to the house and was about to go in the door. Well, it couldn't be helped. Maybe Frank could do his business in Serbian or something anyway.

The back of the pickup was crammed with grocery bags and smelled of fried chicken. The carrots were stuffed against the tailgate. Between them, Vicki and Maureen lugged the fifty-pound bag to the back of the crowd of children at the corral. Maureen turned her attention to the children as she untied the bag with a practiced twist of her hands. "Who knows how to hand a treat to a horse? Anybody?"

San Juana almost laughed, but contained it. "They don't speak English."

"Oh." Maureen blinked, and then shrugged. "I didn't teach public school for nothing." She turned to the children and started giving the same instructions in Spanish. Then San Juana did laugh. "No *habla Español*, either."

Undiscouraged, Maureen continued talking to them. "That's okay. You can figure it out, right?" The children stared, not understanding the words but vaguely sensing this might be important. Maureen started breaking the carrots into bite-sized pieces and handing them out, one to each child. When one started to eat it, she grabbed the child's hand and pointed to the mare, whose her nose had homed in on the carrot smell. "That's for her."

Vicki looked back at the house, hoping to see her father and Roger coming back out. No luck yet. Maybe she should go get them, make some excuse to bring them outside. She glanced at Maureen, attentively giving instructions to the children.

The other horses had picked up the carrot scent and plodded en masse towards the children.

"Okay, now, hold your hand out flat like this, see?" Maureen demonstrated. "The horse can't see your hand when he eats, so you have to keep your fingers out of the way. Like this." Maureen took a child's hand and flattened it so the other children could watch. They dutifully balanced carrot chunks on the palms of their hands and held them out toward the fence, but at such a safe distance none of the horses could reach them. Soon, there was a line of horses, necks extended, and an opposing knot of children, hands extended just out of reach.

One little boy inched closer, stretching his arm until several horses went for it at once. It looked as if they might have a horsey riot on the other side of the fence.

Maureen shouted, "Okay, let's spread out so they don't have to argue so much."

While the women were engaged in spreading the line along the fence, Vicki finally turned and started walking back toward the house. She hoped she could pull her father to one side and talk to him soon, even though she didn't know what she was going to say to him. This was a huge invasion of his normally quiet preserve of peace and harmony. After thirty years as a Los Angeles police officer, he put a high value on peace and harmony.

Vicki heard the bus start up. The driver was exercising his option to go to a quiet motel on the freeway. She stopped and watched the bus as it went up the rise toward the gate, then saw it stop before it went over the top.

Vicki saw the Jaguar come over the rise from the direction of the road, maneuver around the bus then park near the house. Tim frowned, looking around. He looked toward the corral and there was a quick grin, relieved and delighted, when he spotted Vicki coming toward him.

Twenty-four

"They didn't know squat." Tim answered Vicki's question without her needing to ask it.

"Nothing?"

"Not a damn thing new that they didn't know yesterday when I talked to them. I told them my informant said that the killers were the people that were in that border shooting."

"You didn't tell them they were in San Francisco?"

"Oh, yeah, that, too. They'll be talking to the feds to see what they might know about their fugitives, getting physical descriptions, if they have any. My boss is going to be looking for me when they talk to him." He thought about it. "He won't worry about it if he can't find me over the weekend, but he's going to be serious about it Monday morning." He looked at his phone. "Did you notice that you can't get coverage on your cell phone here?"

"I always considered that a good thing."

"Maybe it used to be."

"You don't want them to be able to reach you, do you?"

"No, but I could always turn it off. I would like to be able to call for help, if we need it."

Vicki stepped back and looked at him seriously. "You don't think we're safe here?"

He shrugged and nodded at the same time. "Yeah, we should be."

"You don't sound all that sure."

"I'm never that sure about anything, are you?"

Vicki stared at him and waited until he noticed, then she waited some more. When she spoke, her voice was quiet, personal. "Sometimes I am."

He stared back her. Their eyes met and neither would look away to break the stare. Tim reached up with one hand and cupped her cheek gently with his palm. She raised her face toward his, didn't quit watching his eyes.

As he leaned closer, she whispered, "You don't have to change anything you're doing, but that *is* my father watching."

He froze.

"You don't have to stop. That was just if you wanted to know."

He didn't turn his head away. Just his eyes shifted and then he looked at her again. "Which one?"

"With the pipe."

"Oh." He lowered his hand. Vicki sighed and took his arm to lead him over.

Vicki's father was tilted back in a wooden chair on the porch, puffing on the identifying pipe. Roger Dorr sat next to him in a padded rocking chair with a cigarette and a glass of iced bourbon, the two of them trying to look like a pair of old, worn-out cowboys. Vicki thought they looked convincing. She was gratified that they had come outside on their own, apparently not even curious about what business was being conducted on the telephone inside. She could talk to them and keep them out here almost indefinitely.

"Dad? This is my friend Tim Murphy. This is my father, Will Shea, and our good friend Roger Dorr."

Roger didn't stand because of the new joints, but he leaned forward and politely held out his hand. "You in the business?"

Tim nodded, grinning in understanding at the old man. "Yes, sir. San Francisco PD." He didn't have to ask how the old man knew. Vicki didn't have to guess, either. Roger Dorr had spent his career with the DEA, and the old narc may have detected Tim's gun, maybe smelled it through the jacket, or saw something else about Tim that would give it away to his eye only.

Vicki looked at her father and caught him looking back, a quiet smile in his eyes. Had he seen something? What was she thinking? Of course he had. The crinkles around his eyes were so familiar, the smell of the pipe.

"Dad, I hope all of this is okay with you."

"Sure. 'Course it is." He put the stem of the pipe in the corner of his mouth, the smile lingering in his eyes as he watched her.

She suddenly felt self-conscious. "What are you smiling at?"

Will looked away from her, glanced at his old friend, then worked on tamping the tobacco in his pipe with a roofing nail.

"Roger and I been talking about how to give these kids a ride."

"Oh, Dad, nobody's expecting—"

"No, now, you got to give 'em a horseback ride when they go to all the trouble to visit a horse ranch."

"Dad, we weren't even thinking about . . . these kids are from Europe somewhere. They might not even want to ride on horses."

Will leaned to the side to look past Vicki, up toward the corral. "Aren't those children? Did you bring a bunch of short people? I could have sworn they were kids."

Vicki laughed. "Yes, of course."

"Then they want a ride. And they've got it coming to 'em. They deserve it, don't you think?"

"But Dad—" She stopped and stared at him. For a moment she thought she might have told him more than she had. "What do you mean they deserve it?"

"For being kids!" He looked at Roger.

Roger, a dutiful straight man, nodded agreement. "Right."

Will looked at Tim Murphy. Tim hesitated only briefly before he understood what was expected of him, then he nodded, too. "Oh, sure. Absolutely."

"Okay, now, don't argue with an old man. We still got to think about the practical side of it. Okay?"

Vicki laughed, glad to give in. "Okay."

"Okay. Now about the only horses around here I would trust with an untested child on 'em would be your mare and my gelding, but I can't use him because he's got a shoe loose. Tried to get hold of the far-rier, but he hasn't called back. Even if I did reach him, though, it would take him a couple a days to work it into his schedule."

"Have you got the tools?" Tim's voice was almost apologetic for intruding on the conversation.

Will looked at him. "Tools?"

"For shoeing."

Will gave him a tentative, speculative smile, as if he wasn't sure he understood the question or that Tim knew what they were talking about. "You done this before?"

Tim shrugged. "Couple a hundred, anyway. I'm probably not as good as your farrier, but I won't hurt your horse and the shoe will stay on." He hesitated, a quick glance at Vicki as though trying to get a cue. "Of course, you might want to stick with somebody that—"

"I think I still got all my stuff." He looked at Vicki, no longer smil-ing but thinking about what was going to be needed. "I know where the forge is because I used it to cook on when the power went out last year. Sure you wouldn't mind? He's mostly pretty quiet, but some-times he can be a handful."

"That won't be a problem if you don't mind me doing it."

"No, that'd be great. I'll show you where everything is after dinner." He looked back at Vicki. Again there was that slight smile in the eyes.

"Here's the deal. Roger's got five or six old nags—no offense, Roger—five or six equine senior citizens that would be perfect for children, but they're over at his place. People keep retiring their horses in his pasture with the cattle, so he's got some really old ones. We could pony 'em over, but Roger's not supposed to ride for a couple of weeks yet."

"End of next week."

"Whenever. We were just talking about taking the kids over there on that bus."

Vicki felt as though she were shriveling up just at the thought of loading all those kids into the bus, taking the time for another outing when they had so much to do in so little time. "Daddy, we really . . .

this is awkward, but could we just take a rain check on that? It's hard to explain, but this isn't entirely a vacation trip."

"Oh, sure. Just an idea."

He had seen that she was close to being upset. Damn! "I think it's a great idea and I'm sure the kids would love it, but as it happens we do have to do some things on the telephone." That sounded lame. "See . . . well, it's hard to—"

"Sugar, you don't have to explain. It's perfectly all right, whatever you want to do. This is your place, too."

"We'll see how this other stuff goes tomorrow. Maybe then, huh? Can we leave it up in the air?"

"Sure." He looked at Roger. "Okay with you?"

"Oh, yeah. Don't even have to give any warning, just show up and we'll give 'em a ride."

Will looked back at his daughter. "I'm going to go stay over at Roger's so there's more room for people to sleep here. I'll be back early to feed, so don't worry if you hear me making noise."

Vicki stared at him. It hadn't occurred to her that it might be possible to get him off the place. Quickly, she spoke up, trying not to sound too enthusiastic.

"Dad, we can handle the feeding in the morning. You don't have to hurry. Take some time off."

"Well . . ."

"Sir, I believe I remember how to do the rest of that stuff." Vicki thought Tim was probably smoother than she was at this.

Will grinned, this time bigger. He and Tim both knew that raking and shoveling was involved. He glanced at Vicki, then regarded Tim briefly before he spoke.

"Well, if you really wouldn't mind."

Vicki was surprised that he consented so easily. He was such a creature of routine that she expected him to refuse her offer of time off, with no room for discussion. But, no . . . he had seen something else. That must be it.

Tim was almost a little too much. "I wouldn't mind it a bit. Believe it or not, it would be a nice break for me to do a little real work. It's been a while."

"Me, too. Been a while since anyone else has done it on this place, I can tell you."

Vicki thought there was a glint in his eye. He didn't look at her. Maybe, she thought, he really was tired. Maybe he really could use a few days off from the routine of working almost continuously. She knew he worked the young horses every day, even through the weekend, to instill a sense of what was expected of them. She also knew that it wouldn't hurt the horses to take a few days off, too. She just didn't expect her father to give it to them.

Vicki went inside while they were still talking, pleased that they were so easy to get together. She thought she should have realized that anybody that competent with horses and not afraid of a little manure was going to get along with her father and Roger Dorr just fine.

Cynthia was stacking paper plates next to boxes of fast-food chicken. She pointed to the kitchen.

"The pen where that wolf is, is right outside the back door. Make sure the kids don't make the mistake of going out that way, they'll be right in there with him."

"Okay. Frank make his calls?"

"He's trying now. It's four o'clock in the morning over there. If he gets through, we probably ought to make sure Tim's in here in case he wants to feed him questions or something."

Vicki looked around the corner into the dining room where her father kept the telephone. Frank seemed to be groping for words in a language that was completely unfamiliar to Vicki. It was apparently not that familiar to Frank, either. She heard him try French and German before he settled on English. Tim came into the room and stood there, listening.

"We've had a couple of problems here. We need to know how to contact the people who brought the children into the country. Can you possibly help us with . . . ?" Frank glanced at Tim as he listened to the voice on the other end.

"Tell him one of the children was sick and you need to find out what happened on the way over."

Frank nodded at Tim, still listening to the voice on the other end of the phone. "No, not that kind of trouble exactly. I don't think. One of the kids is sick. He had to go to the hospital." He looked at Tim and shook his head. He clearly wasn't getting anywhere with that line.

"Well, yes, see, that's the other problem. The children are with us right now. We need to find the people who set up the adoptions, too; that make the connection to the new parents?"

Frank's voice was friendly, but his face was serious, intent. "Mrs. Fairchild isn't available. She can't do anything . . . No, I can't talk to her. See, we have the children and I need to find out who else besides—" He squeezed his eyes shut in frustration and then tried again. "No, I can't talk to Mrs. Fairchild. She's dead." He rolled his eyes as he listened to a commotion on the other end of the line that was audible even to Vicki.

"Yes, it's a terrible tragedy. A good woman." He listened for a moment as the party on the other end of the line calmed down. "Yes . . . the children are with us, but here's the question. We need to find someone else, someone besides Mrs. Fairchild that did the same thing that she did, understand?" He listened a moment longer. "Yes. That's exactly right. That's who we need to find."

Frank looked around at Cynthia as he listened to the voice on the other end. When he made eye contact, he raised his eyebrows, an encouraging expression. His attention was brought back to the conversation on the phone by something the other had said. "Yes, that's the person we need to find . . . better make it somebody in California, if you can. Could you?" He listened. "Oh. All right. When should I call back?"

Cynthia pointed at the pad and pen in front of him. He ignored her. "Okay, yes, that will be fine. Two days is fine."

Cynthia grabbed up the pad and nearly hit him with it, whispering but with so much power she was about to scream it.

"Get the name and number! Anybody!"

He looked at Cynthia and shrugged. "Listen, Yosef, why don't you give me the name of that other lady. Yes, we might as well . . . okay, good." He wrote on the pad. "Okay, I got it. California would still be much, much better if you could try to find that for us. Thank you, Yosef. Thank you very much."

As he hung up he kept looking at Cynthia. "Couple of days he should have the other names. Two or three people in California, he thought." He looked at the pad. "This one's in Alabama."

Jack sounded dubious. "Alabama?"

"Mobile."

"Does he know how far that is?"

"Doesn't have any idea. He'd have to cross ten countries to go that far, but he's checking on California."

Cynthia took the pad and looked at the writing. She reached for the phone. "I better call before it gets any later—"

Jack got the receiver in his hand first and pulled it out of her reach. "Sweetie, I've got to get this money started. I've got a twenty-four/seven number here, but it's going to take them a while to get this moving."

"Okay, honey, as soon as I talk to this lady." She reached for the phone in his hand.

Vicki looked around, suddenly aware that Tim was not standing there. She put her head in the kitchen and looked around for him. The back door was standing slightly ajar. She whispered, "Oh, shit!"

Quickly, she went to the door and looked out, half expecting to see the dog clamped on his throat, but at the same time realizing that she wasn't hearing anything—there was no killer-dog commotion.

The "pen" was a wire fence, six feet high, enclosing a fairly large area. Her father had put it up years before so he would have a place to turn out Dan O'Bannion at night occasionally, where it wouldn't be so convenient to the coyotes to snatch him away for a snack.

Tim was standing at the far end of the enclosed area, apparently surveying the landscape seeing what there was to be seen from there. One hand hung down and negligently scratched the ears of the German shepherd terrorist as if he were just another docile pet. The dog's tail was slowly wafting back and forth.

Hearing her, the dog turned his head and looked directly at Vicki. The tail stopped. His ears came up and there was an alert intensity in his eye that was enough to make her close the door and go to the window to watch.

Tim walked along the edge of the fence, craning to see, and the dog turned and followed him, watching, but without even a hint of hostility. Vicki was amazed. After a moment, Tim looked back at the house and saw her face in the window. He gestured for her to come out.

She pointed at the dog.

Tim shrugged his shoulders and scratched the dog's ears.

Finally, Vicki went to the door and took a tentative step outside. The dog ignored her. She took a few more steps, ready to turn and run for the house if she had to, but not feeling particularly afraid. When the dog continued to ignore her, she relaxed and walked out to where they were standing.

Tim pointed. "That's not the road I came in on, is it?"

"That's the back way. You came in from the other direction. That road goes into Sunland, eventually."

Tim nodded. "Okay. Where does that go?" He pointed to a trail through the chaparral going up a hill several hundred yards from the house. With the sun going down, Vicki could barely make out what he was pointing to.

"That goes over to Roger Dorr's place. His house is about three miles that way, by horseback."

He nodded, thinking about it. "Okay."

"Tim. What did you do to this dog?"

"Pardon?"

"When we drove up in the bus this dog tried to attack it like . . . like the worst, most ferocious . . ." Words failed her.

"This dog?"

"Yes! He had everybody terrified!"

Tim grinned and scratched the dog's ears again. "You wouldn't hurt anybody, would you?"

The dog wagged and stared at Tim's face as though waiting for instructions.

Tim looked at Vicki. "Your father's dog doesn't know you?"

"He's new. Dad said he just showed up a few months ago. People abandon animals out here sometimes."

Tim nodded, remembering his own experience, living outside of town. "Feeds the coyotes."

"But what did you do?"

"Oh, nothing. I just assume dogs are friendly and they are, mostly."

"But why would he have attacked the bus?"

"Probably thought he was supposed to. Maybe somebody trained him to do that."

"To attack a bus?"

"Anybody that he doesn't know, coming in on the road or just showing up on the place. He probably thinks if you come through the house where Will is, then you must be okay."

"He scared everybody to death!"

Tim nodded, thinking about it. "Might be handy."

Vicki stared at Tim a moment, then looked back at the big dog. "Yeah. He might be, huh?"

Tim looked back at the road, then toward the hills where the path through the rocks and scrub oak was fading from view with the sun. Vicki looked with him and saw the faint wash of pink on the underside of a wisp of cloud above the dark hills to the west. That's what he was staring at.

"Why would anybody leave this place?"

Vicki smiled and slid one arm around his waist. "I keep asking myself that whenever I come back."

She felt his arm encircle her shoulders, but he didn't look down at her.

"Do the children bother you?"

She felt his chest swell and subside unevenly as he sighed. He lifted his arm from around her and patted her shoulder gently. "Vicki, I got to tell you about something."

"You don't have to."

"Yes, I do." He walked a few feet away from her, not wanting to look at her. It was almost full dark now. He walked to a stump in the middle of the yard and sat on it, his elbows braced on his knees, his head down.

"I caused an accident."

"Tim—"

"A bad one. A really bad . . . I was on duty in a day watch car, heading north on the bridge about seven in the evening, daylight in the summer. I thought I saw . . ." He stopped himself as though realizing that the details were just in the way. He kept his face turned toward the ground, not looking at Vicki, avoiding looking at her.

"I did something completely reckless, completely inexcusable. I did a U-y into traffic on the Golden Gate Bridge—during rush hour. There wasn't even that good a reason. I did it without thinking, impulsively, hot-dogging like something on television. It was completely unforgivable." There was a short pause, as though for emphasis. "I killed two small children."

He sat perfectly still, his head down, his hands hanging.

"Tim—"

"I've tried to think what could have made me do something so stupid. But it wasn't just that one thing." He raised his head and looked into the darkness, still not looking at Vicki. "There were a lot of times, I did stuff when I was lucky and nobody got hurt, but this was one time I wasn't lucky and somebody else had to pay, not me. The day watch car wasn't even touched." He looked back down.

Vicki approached him. She started to reach out a hand to touch him, then held back.

He seemed to be aware of her nearness but only because he lowered his voice, almost talking to himself.

"Angelino and Maria Duran." He paused as if she might know who he was talking about. Then he just pushed on ahead, maybe not even talking to her anymore.

"The boy, Angelino, was five years and two months old. It was in August. He was ready to start kindergarten in one more week. Maria was three and a half, exactly three years and six months old. Both their parents worked, so the kids stayed with the mother's sister in Marin City for day care. Made that trip over the bridge twice a day. Back and forth, the mother driving an old station wagon, a Chevy. The car seats for the kids were second- or thirdhand, so she was always careful, always 'extra-special careful' was the way she kept saying it, but she was anxious to get home."

Vicki could just see his features in profile, saw his eyes seeing the mother, talking, saying the words. He closed his eyes and sighed, then opened them again, looking toward the dark ground.

"The little boy lived for two days but he never woke up. That little girl—Maria—came out through the windshield like a dart, hit on her head on the pavement, and died right then. Right there. Just that fast, and it was all over. That quick, it was too late to do anything. I couldn't do anything at all."

She waited to see if he would go on. She could see him in the ambient light from the house, where they had turned on the lights. He didn't move. Finally, Vicki sat next to him and placed her hand softly on his back.

"It was a long time ago, Tim."

He shook his head quickly. "Eight years, you would think so, but it's not. It's just like it was right now, right this minute. And it doesn't change. It's still too late to do anything to make it different."

"Tim . . . it's okay." When he didn't answer she spoke again. "I already knew about it."

It took a moment for the words to sink in, then he turned his head to look at her. He looked away again.

"I used to know tons of people in the police department. Still have quite a few friends over there."

He shook his head. "Doesn't matter who told you."

"It's not exactly a secret."

"No, it's not a secret."

Vicki laid her cheek on his shoulder. "I'm still glad you told me."

He nodded but didn't look at her. Finally, Vicki turned and put both arms around him, nestling her face in his neck. Slowly, she felt him turn under her embrace until his arms came around her, too. She held him tight, kissed his ear, his jaw, found his mouth and forced her tongue in until he responded. After a long moment, locked on his mouth, she took his hand and placed it on her breast.

He was suddenly so hungry, so eager for her, that she opened her blouse and then had to help him pull up her bra and even then had to pull his head down to her bare breast.

The dog growled. A deep rumbling voice, so full of menace that Vicki jumped and had to look. There was a car moving slowly, lights out, up on the back road. The dog rumbled again, more insistent, ready to bark.

Finally, Tim had to turn around, too. Instantly as soon as he saw the car, he was on his feet, crouching low to keep out of the light, pushing Vicki ahead of him toward the deeper shadows near the fence. Vicki was closing her blouse as she moved, watching the car. It had almost stopped.

Then, as if the whole thing were a mistake, the headlights came on and the car picked up speed, moving on over the hill away from them, the sound of rhythmic cymbals fading with it. The three of them at the fence, man, woman and dog, stood and watched. Tim holstered his gun and Vicki realized she hadn't even seen him take it out.

He looked down at her and grinned.

"Probably neighbors. Local kids, trying to see what's going on at your father's place with all the children running around."

"And a couple of people necking in the backyard."

He put his arms around her again and she snuggled into him. They heard the back door open and Maureen's voice.

"Anybody hungry? Dinner's on."

Twenty-five

Vicki surmised that Jack and Cynthia had broken off the attempts to use the phone while her father was around. They were doing their best to keep their host out of their problems. It was obvious to Vicki that Cynthia was unhappy about the results of her first call, but Vicki hadn't had a chance to find out why. She pictured a scramble back to the one telephone as soon as her father, Roger, and Maureen left for the night.

At dinner, the adults sat around Will's dining room table, a huge, round oak piece that had been his mother's. The children were collected in the living room, sitting on the rugs and furniture, scarfing down the food and negotiating with Dan O'Bannion to get him to stand up on his hind legs for pieces of roll. Elsie was too big for successful bargaining by the children, so she was banished to the outdoors.

Maureen reached across to touch Cynthia's arm. "Are these children in your class?"

Cynthia looked at her, wide-eyed. "Class?"

"School. Are you a teacher?"

"Oh. No, we just wanted to give them an outing. Vicki thought . . ." She looked to Vicki for help.

Vicki knew that any teacher could see that this group of kids, with the broad range in ages, was not a "class." Maureen was curious to know what this was about, but too polite to ask directly. Vicki kept her voice light.

"I just suddenly realized that I knew the perfect place to take a bunch of children for a few days of true Americana." She turned to her father. "I knew you wouldn't mind."

"No, of course not."

"Dad, I think you ought to take a few days off."

"Just thinking that."

Vicki stared. "You were?" She had been trying to shift the topic of conversation, but she hadn't expected that answer from her father.

"Well, might be nice to have a break." He glanced at Maureen quickly, then away, and turned his eyes back to Vicki, suddenly smiling.

Maureen spoke up. "He hasn't taken a day off as long as I've known him. You should take a cruise or something, Will."

Will shook his head. "Every morning I wake up, it's like being on a vacation." He looked at Vicki again, his face too placid. "Not to say a break wouldn't be nice, though. I was just thinking, I might take a couple of days, let you-all have the run of the place. You know everything that needs doing, and Tim can work all he wants."

"You sure you don't mind?"

He looked behind him at the other room, where the children were, not meeting her eye but still smiling. "Not a bit."

Vicki glanced at Maureen, but Maureen wasn't looking at her either. Oh. Light dawned. *Roger's house, my foot.*

Well.

She didn't know how she felt about that. It wasn't entirely lost on her that she was being pickier about what her father did than he had ever been about what she was doing, even when she had lived here.

She nodded and looked down, avoiding everyone's eyes. "Dad, take a few days. We're going to be around for probably two days, at least. Maybe longer."

"I'll leave you Roger's number, in case you can't find something or one of the horses acts funny."

She glanced at Tim and caught him grinning at her. He looked away, turning to Will. "You were going to show me where your tools are."

"Oh, yeah. Right." He looked at his daughter. "You haven't been in the barn yet, have you?"

"Not this trip. You change it around?"

"Got a new tenant."

"Another horse?" She wondered what was new about that.

Will got up. "Come on, both of you. The tools are out there, too, I hope."

The barn was more like a long stable, Will's only extravagance in his retirement. There were four stalls on each side, solid plank walls between them. There were broad, barred windows to the outside and between the stalls, so the horses could see and smell each other unobstructed, but a new horse could be introduced without being chewed on too much right away. At the far end there was a tack room with a work bench. Hay was stored under cover in another big shed, open on the sides to keep it aired and, Vicki had always suspected, to let the deer and rabbits take what they wanted. There were also a few half-wild cats that hung around, the dogs having been taught to leave them alone.

Will stopped in front of the second stall on the right and looked at Vicki shyly. "What you think?" He rolled the big, sliding door open and stood to one side.

For a second, Vicki was shocked. She thought she was looking at Candy's face looking back at her, but another second and she could see it wasn't her. Candy had died out on the hills, probably of heart failure, during a mild summer night. Although the law said he was supposed to call the knacker, her father hadn't done it. Instead, he had hired a kid with a backhoe to bury her in the side of the hill where she died.

Vicki had grieved for her mare as though for another family member, even though she had ridden her very little in the last half of her long life. Candy's death had meant an end to something valuable, and her father had understood.

But this new quarterhorse looked remarkably like her in the head and coloring. Vicki approached the stall and looked in to see if she had the stockings—Candy had had three. This one had two in front.

"Daddy, she looks just like . . ." Tears came to her eyes and she laughed apologetically.

"It's her granddaughter. Candy's. Looks like her, doesn't she? A little?"

"A little? She's almost . . . I mean . . ."

"Yeah, that's what I thought when I saw her. She's ten years old, real quiet like Candy was. I bought her for you when the lady that had her called and said she was going to sell her."

"A while ago, you said something about my mare . . . I thought you forgot that Candy wasn't around anymore. I didn't want to say anything."

"No, I just forgot I hadn't told you about this one."

"What's her name?"

"They called her Banjo, but you can—"

"No, that's a good name. Hi, Banjo. Hello, girl." She reached out and stroked the horse's neck. Banjo turned and inspected the arm, sniffing at Vicki's shoulder, then lowered her head to be scratched.

"Oh, Dad, just look at that eye. She's so sweet! Do you ride her every day? How long have you had her?"

"Got her a few months ago. I get on her two, three times a week. She likes to go over to Roger's. Look back there. She's got those big, round haunches—loves to run, just like Candy did when she was that age."

Vicki saw a couple of brushes on the floor of the stall. It was not like her father to leave things lying around, so she knew that he had been in here grooming her horse for her when the bus drove up and the commotion with the dog started. She grabbed up one of the brushes and stroked it gently down the mare's withers, down the flank. The horse dropped her head, enjoying the attention, just like Candy used to do it.

For a moment Vicki was lost, taken over with attention to this new animal, so much like her old one, reveling in the stroke of the brush the gentle hand on the throat, stroking the big muscles of the foreleg. After a few moments, she turned to look for her father, but he had already gone to the tack room, showing Tim where things were, finding the right shoe and setting it aside for the morning. The two of them were talking easily, joking about something as Tim put a hand up and touched her father's best saddle, admiring the workmanship, the smooth, worn leather.

Tim had left his jacket in the house, but the holstered automatic did not draw her father's curiosity. In a flash, she remembered her father around civilians on the few occasions she saw him out among local people. Church on Easter, dutifully smiling too much and speaking quietly and politely to people who knew him by sight but talked to him maybe twice a year. She remembered the intrusive sound of metal on wood when he sat back in the pew and the gun made itself known, no matter how he had kept his one baggy suit coat buttoned to hide it, to try to make sure it didn't attract people's attention.

She closed the door to the stall and slipped the latch in place. She bent and kissed the horse on the broad dry nose, reached through the bars and swept her hand smoothly along the big jaw. Then she turned and just stood there, watching her father and Tim talking—or rather, her father talking, Tim nodding—understanding of something, both of them easy and relaxed.

They walked toward her still talking, and she felt her heart lurch, turn over. She almost said it out loud, "Oh, my God." And then, "Oh, lord." A prayer, almost.

When they were near she clutched her father around his neck while he patted her back. "Thank you so much. Oh, Daddy, she's beautiful."

He patted her back and she couldn't see his face, but she could picture his expression of pleased embarrassment. It was in his voice as he spoke. "Thought you'd like her."

She pulled her head back and had to look at him, stare at his face up close. He *was* getting old. There were more lines or they were deeper or it was the set of his grin, the strip of white between the hat, where she had pushed it back on his head, and the tan line of his leather-creased face. No, the grin was the same as it had always been when he looked at her, the same. It would always be there, wouldn't it? In his eye she could see the little girl that he saw, that he would always see.

She turned with him and held his arm in both hands as they walked back to the house. He crooked his elbow, awkwardly accommodating her grip on him, and cleared his throat. Tim stared at the ground as they walked. She was embarrassing everyone. She didn't care. Quickly, she swiped at her eyes with one hand and then clamped it back on her father's arm.

As they left the barn, Will, almost unconsciously, an automatic reflex, reached across behind Tim and flipped the switch to turn out the lights. They walked, then, in the darkness of the yard no more than a hundred yards to the lights in the house and Vicki found herself clinging to her father's familiar arm and slowing her steps.

She had almost forgotten the children. She'd been absorbed in the familiarity of horses, the gift from her father that seemed familiar, and really was expected, although she hadn't consciously thought about it.

She knew the horse would be useful to him, the calm, older horse among the jittery, excitable green ones that were brought out here by rich people for him to train. He needed a second reliable mount. It was also something that he owed to his own gelding, Dragonfly. He needed another permanent resident, a companion, who with any luck at all would bond with him, and give him something familiar and comfortable in the midst of the comings and goings of the younger horses. Even horses needed that kind of stability, that kind of reliable, unquestioned, and unquestioning companionship.

But there, behind the lighted windows of the house in front of them was another thing, something that her father didn't know anything about, and wasn't even concerned enough to ask about. Was she bringing him trouble for his devotion?

This stop was just a short time to try to at least make the effort to get these children to some semblance of home of family, of some chance to grow up whole. How could that be bad? It couldn't be wrong, she was sure of that.

Elsie had managed to get herself back inside. She was sprawled on the floor in the middle of the children, eyes closed, luxuriating in the attention of many small hands.

Will crossed the room and peered under the brim of Roger's hat. "Wore out already?"

Roger's head came up and he blinked. He looked around, reorienting, spotted Vicki, and smiled.

Maureen's voice was soft as she put a hand on Roger's shoulder. "You as tired as I am?"

"No, I'm fine. You tired?"

Maureen looked at Will and he nodded. "I'm ready to go if you are."

Roger lurched forward, held up his arms, and, one on each side, they leveraged him upright. He flexed his hips one at a time, adjusted his hat, and looked at Vicki. "Good to see you."

"I'll walk out with you."

"All right." His first few steps were tentative and short, but then he picked up speed and a modicum of fluidity as he went. He paused in the open door. "Good to meet you-all." He went outside as though he couldn't hear their responses.

Vicki walked slowly next to him. "Everything working okay?"

He laughed then, as though he had needed to get outside to relax. "Don't look like much, but they're a lot better than before."

"Before the surgery?"

"Hell of a lot better. Be back in the saddle in no time."

The old cowboy climbed into the cab of the pickup, declining assistance, and scooted to the middle as though from habit. Maureen continued to talk to Cynthia for a few moments at the front door to the house while Vicki's father stood in the open door to the truck and watched her.

When Maureen came toward them, he climbed in and Vicki, suddenly seized with an impulse, grabbed Maureen with a quick hug, then backed off. "I'm glad I met you."

Maureen smiled, pleased and self-possessed. "Well, I feel like I've known you for a while. It's so good to meet you in the flesh." She paused, her voice kept low. "Your father's a wonderful man."

"I know. I agree." Vicki glanced at the men waiting in the truck.

"I left Roger's number, and mine, too, by the telephone. If you really need anything, you probably better call my number."

Vicki laughed out loud, suddenly thoroughly enjoying this woman. "Sure, of course."

Okay, she thought. *It's okay, it's okay,* all the way into the house.

Twenty-six

Vicki could hear Cynthia's voice before she was back in the house, even over the noise of the children. " —then call your secretary. What is it, seven o'clock there?"

Then Frank's voice. "Right. Nine hours' difference. She's not usually in the office much before ten, especially if I'm not going to be there."

"Well, wake her up!"

As Vicki entered the dining room, she could see Jack trying to use the telephone with his hand over the other ear. There were notes, debit cards, and papers on his lap and on the floor around his chair.

Cynthia seemed exasperated. She looked at Vicki, coming in the door, but hardly saw her. She looked back at Frank. "Okay?"

"Sure, Cynthia. As soon as Jack gets off the phone."

Cynthia took a deep breath and let it out, finally looking around and focusing on Vicki. "I just now realized you can't get cellular phone reception out here."

Vicki nodded. "Well, not down here, but you could probably get it to work up on one of the hills near the house, if you don't want to drive closer to Sunland."

Cynthia shook her head. "That's not the point. We don't have Hans's number. He has Frank's cell phone number to stay in contact with us, but if Frank can't get calls. . . . See the problem? We need be able to tell the guy that we're getting the money together." She turned on Frank and raised her voice.

"Come on, Frank! These guys are killing people just to scare us and we need to let them know that we are already, by God, scared. Am I making sense or have I got it confused? The point of you and Jack raising the money is to give it to them so they can leave us alone and go on to Canada, right? How are they supposed to know we're doing it?"

"I'll talk to the Princess, he'll be calling the office. Calm down, Cynthia."

"Well, Frank—"

"Calm down."

Cynthia took another deep breath and slowly let it out.

Vicki sat down at the dining table, trying to put a calmer face on things. "Okay. How's Jack doing? And how did you do?"

Cynthia sat opposite her. "I think Jack's getting it together okay. I only did so-so."

"Did you talk to the woman in Mobile?"

"Yes, I did. Frightened her to death, I'm afraid."

"What did you say?"

"It's not so much what I said, just the fact that I called her up late at night and started talking to her about kids from Europe. Think about that. Can you imagine how we would have felt if some total stranger called us up in the middle of the night and started asking about smuggling aliens? I would have been pretty frightened, too."

"Did she turn you down?"

"Well, she denied knowing what I was talking about. Don't know what I expected, but that response made a lot of sense to me."

San Juana came into the room carrying Charlotte, sound asleep after a long day of entertainment. Cynthia raised her arms. "Let me hold her awhile, San Juana. It'll settle me down."

Vicki watched her. She did seem to relax with the baby in her arms, but Vicki still didn't know the answer to her question. "So she won't be of any help?"

"I didn't say that. She didn't exactly get friendly, but she did talk to me for a while. Let me put it this way. It was clear to me that I had the right person, and she knew that I knew and she didn't hang up. Finally, I told her I would call her back tomorrow after she had a chance to call some people we might both know, and she said that would be all right. It could have gone worse."

"Well . . ." Vicki groped for something positive to say. She couldn't think of anything. "What . . . Let's think about this, okay? What are we going to do if she says, 'Fine, bring 'em over?' "

"Well, it beats not having any place to take them."

"Yeah, but Cynthia . . . to Mobile? We just going to go out to the airport and load 'em on the next flight? How far ahead do you have to book twelve children and a couple of nannies to make sure they all fly at the same time?"

Jack hung up the phone, finally.

"One or two more calls in the morning should do it."

"Banking on Sunday?"

"Depends on how much you're talking about."

Cynthia gestured at the phone. "Okay, Frank."

Frank checked his watch.

"Frank, for heaven's sake, just call her. It's going to make it worse if Hans tells them we're frightened and running away instead of getting the money together."

"Okay, I'm going to. He'd be right about that, though. I am definitely scared."

Vicki spotted Nadya standing at the doorway, changed into shorts and a T-shirt and now peeking in as though she thought she might not be welcome. Vicki held out a hand to her. "Come here, Nadya. You can come in and calm me down."

Nadya swung her thin left leg and did a double hop with her right, immediately accepting the invitation. Vicki lifted her onto her lap, beaming at her. "I bet you're not afraid, are you?"

Nadya spoke to her in a high, soft, almost inaudible voice. Vicki turned her ear toward her and gestured with an upward motion of her other hand. "Say it louder." She pointed to Frank's ear. "Say it again."

Nadya picked up the cues enough to restate what she had said, in Russian.

Frank stopped dialing and looked at her. "Aw, honey." He spoke to her quickly, and turned to see three other children who had come up and were watching from the doorway. He repeated what he had just said to Nadya. Two more joined them from the other room, their eyes guarded and solemn, apparently intimidated by the adults' strange behavior.

Frank looked at Cynthia. "She said they wanted to know if we were going to send them away."

Vicki had her arms around the little girl already. She gave her a squeeze and gently caressed her head, inadvertently feeling the scar in her scalp beneath the hair. "We are not just sending you away, sweetie. Why did you think that?"

Frank translated, then listened to her reply, his face looking sympathetic now, his voice showing concern. Nadya spoke toward her hands as she picked at a cuticle. Her voice was high and clear, although her volume was low enough that Frank had to lean toward her and turn his head to make sure he got it all.

"She says, they were listening to us arguing, and some of the kids thought it was because they were being too loud or too much trouble. We should be more careful. That one's picking up English pretty fast."

Frank spoke to the children at length. Vicki didn't need a translation to tell that he was giving them lots of reassurance. She cradled the little girl and gently rocked her.

Vicki glanced up at Tim. He was standing, leaning against the wall with his arms crossed, watching the child. He saw Vicki looking at him and gave her a small, discreet smile.

Nadya spoke again and Frank nodded sympathetically. He looked at Cynthia. "She says she's tired and wants to go to bed." He shrugged.

Cynthia spoke to the child, nodding her agreement. "Of course you are. It's been a long day, hasn't it?"

Jack put a hand on Frank's arm. "Make your call while we tuck 'em in. Tell the Princess that Hans has got to give us a number where we can call him."

Cynthia's voice cut in. "Frank, if you have to, give him this number."

Tim shook his head quickly. "No. No numbers."

Cynthia looked from one to the other, but she could see that she wasn't getting any support. "All right, but get a number and talk to him. Tell the Princess to be very, very conciliatory. Just try, okay?"

Vicki stood up, shifting Nadya to her hip. "We got all the sleeping bags out of the bus, didn't we?"

Cynthia rose with the sleeping baby on her arm. "They're all set up. They all wanted to be in the living room together, so they're sort of packed in there with San Juana and Consuela."

"Really?" Vicki walked to where she could see into the living room. "San Juana? That doesn't seem very comfortable."

San Juana had already put on a flannel nightgown, brand new from the store in Bakersfield. "Your father showed us a couple of cots. I guess your brother's family uses them?"

"Oh, right. Forgot about them."

"We're fine. That way if any of them wakes up, we'll be here."

Vicki nodded, observing the efficiency of the sisters' layout. They were way ahead of her. She saw that Frank was watching her, waiting for instructions apparently. "That didn't take long. You make your call?"

"Yeah, I told her. I told her I needed a number from Haus, but if I had to I'd sit on a hill in the morning."

Vicki watched him, thinking about it. That fast?

Frank smiled. "Where should we . . . ?"

"Oh, sorry." Vicki looked around. "Okay, Cynthia, you and Jack take the master bedroom. You keeping Charlotte with you?"

"Yes, that'll be fine."

"Frank, you get Cody's old room at the far end of the hall." Keeping her hand hidden from the others, she moved close enough to Tim to pinch him on the butt. His face went blank. He got it. He turned around and walked back into the kitchen.

Cynthia had picked up a pair of shopping bags from the mound of supplies that had been unloaded from the bus, squatting awkwardly, still holding the baby. Vicki went to her and started to lift the bags off of her hand.

Cynthia glanced at her and then looked down at Charlotte. "Here, why don't you hold her a minute and I can find what we need."

Vicki put Nadya down, took the baby from Cynthia, then sat on the rug near the other children. Nadya stood next to her, one hand on Vicki's shoulder. The child reached out and gingerly stroked the baby's head, gently felt the scars.

Watching her closely, Vicki realized she must have seen from a distance that the baby had those wounds, seeing it for the singular thing that it was, a head so much like her own. Up close for probably the first time, Nadya touched the baby's right hand, then her right leg, the affected one. She understood what she was seeing. She looked at Vicki, the question imprinted on her face.

"It's all right. She's going to be all right."

"Ahright?" She was going to struggle with English "Ls."

"Yes. All right."

Nadya touched her own bad leg, the atrophy clearly visible with the child in shorts. "Ahright?"

Vicki stared at her and didn't answer.

Nadya put the hand to her head, fingered the scars. "Ahright?"

She thought that the word meant injury or handicap or something. Vicki swept an arm around her and pulled her onto her lap next to the baby. "You are all right. Nadya's all right now. All right means good, understand?"

Nadya shrugged, only seeing that she didn't understand. She sighed contentedly and leaned her head on Vicki's breast. She touched Charlotte's fisted hand again. "Bebe."

"Yes, that's a baby."

One of the other children called out and Nadya answered in Russian, her voice suddenly as loud as the next kid's. She jumped up and swing-hopped her way into the middle of the pile of sleeping bags, chattering and laughing. She wasn't self-conscious around the other children. Well, not yet.

Charlotte, awakened by the shout, began to fuss until San Juana appeared, bearing a fond smile and a disposable bottle. Vicki let herself be relieved of the infant and got to her feet.

Tim came through the front room holding the German shepherd on the lead rope, his hand close to the collar. The dog, though, showed no interest in the children. He seemed anxious to get outside, out the front, where he had the run of the place. Elsie squeezed through with him, but Vicki noticed that Dan O'Bannion was huddled among the sleeping bags. He was not likely to leave of his own accord.

Having only one bathroom for all of them was a problem, but at least the men were willing to walk out to the corral. Frank took two of the older boys with him to demonstrate. In short order all the boys had it figured out, so that took some of the pressure off of the indoor facility.

Vicki brought Tim into her own room and closed the door. He stood still for a moment, looking around the room. Vicki had to put her hands on him to get him to look at her.

"This is where you grew up."

"This room? Yes, I guess so." She thought about how long ago that had been, then quickly tried to push that idea out of her head.

She watched him staring at the details, the furniture, the drapes, the small closet, all of it largely unchanged from the last time she had actually lived in it in residence, as it were. The last time she had lived here, without another "home," had been when she was in transition, that period after Mary had died and she had divorced her husband and dropped out of her first residency program when she was only twenty-five years old. She stayed here eight months before starting law school in New York.

Even then she hadn't changed anything around. This room hadn't changed very much from when she had lived here in high school, doing her homework at the desk late into the night, then sleepily dressing in the morning to catch a ride with her father and brother. The room hadn't changed at all if she didn't look too close.

It was almost a shock to realize that, although she had visited and stayed in the room many times, she hadn't looked closely at these familiar surroundings in years, maybe decades. The room had been cleaned recently, at least dusted and swept. She pictured her father with the once familiar implements in his hands. He had been as good at those tasks as the mothers of most of her friends, but they had given him absolutely no credit for the effort, assuming and so observing only his rare shortcomings.

She could remember when he had brought the dresser home from a yard sale and then refinished it—the harsh smell of the stripper, the tedious scraping, and then, finally, the new-looking bureau. But if she looked too closely now, it was chipped and cracked. The drawers no longer rode smoothly on the riders, the middle one always stuck until she bumped it with her knee a certain way. If she looked too closely, the drapes seemed to be ready to fall of their own weight, worn and stretched almost transparent at the rod.

Looking at it anew, because Tim was looking at it, she was suddenly more than a little self-conscious. Bringing him into the room like this was more intimate than she had realized it would be. He seemed to understand, maybe better than she did. The look in his eye was not critical. He was seeing not so much the way it was now as the way it had been for so long, as if to prove it wasn't only in her own mind.

It was suddenly too much. Too much to think about, to let herself be absorbed in all at once like this.

She tried to stop what she was saying, she hadn't had time to think it through, to go through the gradual process of getting used to a new, very profound idea. But the words wouldn't stop. It was as if she were hearing somebody else talking. "I could adopt Nadya. If we knew who it was that managed to do whatever they have to do to get the paperwork . . . I . . . I don't know . . . I haven't thought about it enough, but if it was the difference between sending her back or letting her stay . . ."

Suddenly, Tim's arms were around her, her hot face pressed into his chest. She gripped him as if holding on to a life buoy, or a piece of floating debris in a deluge hanging on. She could hear his voice from just above her head.

"I thought that's what you were thinking."

"I didn't even know I was thinking it."

She put her hands on the center of his chest and stepped back to be able to see his face better, to look at his eyes, so kindly and warm. It was more than just the psychologist's professional warmth. This was personal, and he was looking at her like that, not terrified of the fact that she might come prepackaged with a little girl—oh! She stood there a moment lost in thought, staring at him while he watched her patiently. Such a radical idea, an adoption. But it was possible she could do it. She could! And he wasn't scared off. That's something.

Vicki turned out the light in the room and moving confidently in the dark, went to the window and opened the drapes. Her room faced the front of the house; her window shaded by a huge live oak in which she'd hung bird feeders and baths when she was little so that she could watch the activities while she did her homework. At some point she had removed the screen in one of her windows so that she could come and go that way, sometimes getting up in the middle of the night to go sit with the horses, if she wanted to; the dogs grateful for the nocturnal company, eager to play. Her particular favorite had been a collie named Scooter, a male version of Lassie. Scooter was not friendly to strangers, but would follow Vicki and her friends everywhere, constantly on guard, ready to attack any hapless snake they might come across. Scooter had been buried for many, many years now, but she could almost see him out in the yard, on a flat-out run after one of the multitude of rabbits that he never quite caught.

At one time her father had installed an arc light on the end of a twenty-foot pole, not so much to see by, but to discourage the skunks and coyotes who didn't like the light. Vicki had complained about it so much that he had turned it off, and, at least when she was home, it never came on again. She wondered if it still worked. She opened the window and checked to see that the screen was still missing. She wondered if her father even knew where that old screen had gone, or if he had ever noticed that she had removed it and hid it in the hay. He'd never said anything about it. He must have known, though. Of course he did.

Standing in the dark, a forty-five-year-old adult, she had a sudden revelation. He had probably done the same thing. He'd been raised on a farm in Missouri, had not even seen California before the end of World War II, when he'd been dumped off a troop ship in San Francisco, an eighteen-year-old hard case, and stayed. But before that, on the farm that she had never seen, he must have had his own window, and so was wise enough to leave it alone when he found the screen missing in his daughter's room.

She heard Tim sit on the bed behind her. She turned, but she couldn't see him in the dark interior of the room, except for the glint of his eyes, a dark shadow on the lighter bedspread. He could be anybody, in the dark.

She whispered. "Come on."

Getting through the window was not as easy as she remembered it. She had to sit on the windowsill and slide off to drop the fourteen inches or so to the yard under the tree. It took Tim a second or two, then he was with her, walking next to her without any questions, headed toward the horse corral in the dark. She took his hand.

Elsie joined them, wig-wagging mindlessly, trotting in front as though she always had to lead the way, checking over her shoulder to see that they were still following. They could see the German shepherd up on the low hill toward the road. He watched them from a distance but didn't come down to where they were.

They kept walking past the barn, past the hay shed. Vicki heard one of the horses nicker, either to one of his buddies or to them, the humans, who just possibly might have lost track of the time and decided to feed them early. She smiled at the sound in the dark. Hope springs eternal in the horsey stomach.

They continued up the trail that led to the bridle path to Roger Dorr's place, on an uphill grade now, but walking faster. Finally, they were at a crest, a gentle ridgeline, the chaparral dropping in a long deep slope, off into the dark, the quarter moon providing little illumination. This close to Los Angeles, they couldn't get the brilliance of stars that you could farther out on the desert, but this was still good, much better than you could see from anywhere in San Francisco.

They stood for a long moment with their arms around each other, staring at the distant outline of the hills in the night, absorbing the quiet and the gentle blessing of the stars, the only visible evidence of eternity. When they kissed, the urgency was slow in returning.

Vicki removed her blouse and bra, holding to him then, shivering a little as he touched her, not entirely from the cool night air. Outside, out here, she didn't have to see the cracks in the bureau, the decrepit state of the drapes at the window of her childhood room. Out here it was timeless and dark and the passing of years was not so cruelly evident. She didn't mind the cold against her skin, and in a moment shed her pants, as well.

Suddenly feeling his tension, she was pleased, gratified by his hunger as she held him and felt his touch. She undressed him and pressed against him for a long moment, enfolded and held against the dark and the cool air. He sat on the pile of clothes and she straddled him, her arms wrapped around his neck and her mouth tasting his. She felt his involuntary thrust, his energy quickened. She raised herself enough to mount him, guided him to the spot and lowered herself onto his penis.

He gripped her until she could feel his strength, feel the hunger of his need, and then she moved gently, thrusting until he tensed, spasmed, and held on to her as though with utter desperation. She felt him slowly relax, his breath gradually coming easier.

He whispered. "It's been a while. I—"

"Shhh." She stroked his head, his shoulders, and kissed him gently. He held her, almost rocking her, turning gently, slowly side-to-side. His gratitude was palpable, and she thought there was a little worship there, too. At least for now. For now was enough.

When the dog's cold nose touched her bare shoulder, she jumped. Elsie stood over them, wagging nervously, then thrust her snout between their faces and slurped until they squirmed their faces away, laughing. She could feel him with his laugh and snuggled her hips down tighter on him, knowing he could feel her laughing, too. She had to use one hand to hold off the dog's head while she kissed her new lover, lingering in his lap and in his quiet laughter. She laughed with him, holding her mouth on his, not at anything particularly funny, but for the pure joy of being there, laughing softly, feeling his laughter inside her.

Finally, they rose and dressed without speaking, Vicki thinking about her warm bed, eager to get him into it.

He lifted her easily to the window and then made an inordinate amount of noise getting himself in, too. Vicki hauled on his arm, grinning until her cheeks hurt, thinking until she caught it, caught the words in her mind, *My young man.* Oh, lord.

Undressed again, they snuggled under the blankets, getting warm for a moment before he began stirring again. She stroked his back, feeling his muscles tense and relax in little ripples, thinking all at once of how she had imagined, longed for this very thing in this very spot and not done it—how she had longed for a lover here when she didn't even know what it meant except for the actual, physical steps and those she had known only in theoretical outline. So long ago, but not changed really. Not essentially different. The need was basically the same, except now he was here. She could feel him, feeling her.

She knew, suddenly, that she would be in this bed again alone, except that she would have this moment with her then. It would be different then. She tried to force the thought out of her mind, to concentrate on the sensations of the moment. It was almost impossible until she felt his mouth on her body and she gave up the effort. As she quit trying, she began to fall and closed her eyes. She was soaring, dropping, falling away with just the focal point of her lover's mouth. She heard herself gasp far away. She heard a cry, somewhere between passion and despair, between love and pain and knew it was her voice, but she couldn't tell if she had cried out loud. If it was audible, her young man did not hear it or he did not care, either, who knew. All of her mind, all of her body, every sensation of her being was focused on that tongue, and she didn't know if it was hers or his until this time the cry *was* audible.

She pulled him up to her, wanting to hurry, but her limbs were heavy, moving languorously, not fully back in the room. When his head was next to hers she held him tight, listening to the sounds of the house and hearing only the hammering of her own heart against his chest.

The house was quiet. Either the others hadn't heard or they were listening for a repetition. She had to giggle, stifling it in his neck, feeling him vibrate, alive, smelling of her own smell. Quietly, she rolled over him and fit him into her, moving quietly, aware of every squeak of the bed. Giggling under their ragged, held-back breath, trying to be quiet, they made it last a long time.

Vicki woke in the dark, and without a pause for thought knew where she was and whose chest her head was lying on, whose hairs were tickling her nose. He was lying on his back, his breathing deep, one arm draped along her back, his hand on her waist. She tried to touch his chest without waking him. She could feel a warm pool where she had drooled on him in her sleep and had to smile. Gently, with her fingertips she took up some of the saliva and smeared it on the head of his penis. He stirred and came alive immediately, but he, too, seemed to take up where they had fallen asleep without having to pause to wake up and wonder.

Their lovemaking was warm then, warmed with the sleep-heated bed, the slow, not-quite awake sensations of skin and sweat and drool and quiet, slippery passion.

The next time, he woke first, and she swam to consciousness under his caress, yielded and enwrapped him without having to wake up entirely, almost weeping with the strength of sensation, even half conscious. Surely, this would never stop, never end this night.

But it did. The children's voices, whispering, were right outside their door. Vicki twisted her head around to see if she had thought to slip the bolt to lock the door, knowing she hadn't done it, not even sure if the bolt worked anymore.

In a flash, Tim was out of the bed, naked, grabbing for his pants and backing up, until his bare butt was braced against the door to hold it shut while he tried to get his foot into the leg of the pants without making any noise. The children's voices moved on down the hall toward the bathroom.

Their eyes met, crescents of silent merriment. It was barely beginning to be light enough to see each other in the room.

One of the horses whinnied, a tentative early morning sound. The first voice was answered by another, less patient voice, a long, insistent, demanding trumpet of hunger, of near desperate starvation, then a tremendous bang as someone kicked the solid wall of his stall. They watched each other's eyes, listening to the horses. No way to put off getting up now. They each knew that the other didn't want to. Vicki thought she'd just had more sex in one night than in the last five years put together. And she was horny. She was suddenly lusting after this man, staring at her in the half-light of predawn, lust in his eye, too.

He reached over his shoulder and slipped the bolt to lock it. He dropped his pants on the floor and came to her, his erection already bobbing with his step. Vicki reached out and grabbed it as he slid into the bed next to her. She used it as a handle to pull him on top of her and then gripped him in a full body embrace, holding him, gripping him as if she were afraid he might levitate off the bed away from her. She slid up onto him and locked on, her arms and legs and vagina suddenly steel bands, capturing him and holding him inside her. She heard him growl, his face against hers. He pushed his face into the pillow to muffle the sound he couldn't stop making deep in his chest, rumbling an animal grunting. Vicki pressed her face hard into the side of his neck, her lips pushed back by the pressure until her teeth were on his skin. She bucked, the sudden urgency overwhelming her and him, too.

The horse called again and she recognized the voice of her father's gelding, bellowing in anguished extremis, close to collapse from starvation. The call was so pitiful that she laughed just as her lover was bursting, grunting into the pillow next to her ear.

Twenty-seven

The two of them turned the young trainees out into the near pasture to kick at each other and race around at random after being cooped up all night, then they did the feeding, raking, and shoveling. When they were nearly finished with the chores, they were considering a literal roll in the hay but several of the children came out to watch, putting a stop to that idea. Vicki put her father's gelding on the lunge line to work out his kinks while Tim set up the forge and got ready for shoeing. She left him performing for a small audience while she took her turn in the shower.

Vicki could hear the other adults talking in the dining room while she dressed, but she couldn't tell what they were saying. Tim came in, sweating and as happy to see her as if they'd been parted for days, but she wouldn't let him get close until he'd gone to the shower himself. Yes, civilization could be a pain.

Three of the children were still eating at the round table when Vicki walked in. Jack was holding a mug of coffee and watching Frank, who was on the phone. Cynthia was drying plates and putting them away in the wrong place while she kept one eye and both ears on Frank. All three of them were tense.

Frank was trying to keep his voice calm as he talked to Yosef. "Yes, that's what we need to do. We talked to the lady in Mobile, did she call you? Would you mind calling her for us? Just to verify that we're all right?"

Cynthia was shaking her head and trying to get Frank's attention. He held up one hand to indicate for her to keep quiet.

"Here's the thing, Yosef. If the lady in Alabama is the best you can do, okay, but . . ." He looked up and rolled his eyes. "I know, she did seem nice. But Yosef, Mobile is a very long way away from where we are. We really have to get somebody in California today. Can you do that? Today? Oh, that would be wonderful!" He gave a thumbs-up sign and Cynthia sat down in relief.

Vicki sat next to her. "Any luck talking to Hans?"

"Maybe."

"What happened?"

"He's supposed to call the Princess back with a number where he can be reached, then Frank will get it from her and call."

"Hans agreed to do that?"

"It's four million dollars. I guess he'll do it."

"I keep forgetting that."

Frank finished his call and looked up. "Okay. He has to go to his office to get the names and numbers, but he's going to go right now. He should have them in another hour or two. I'll call him back at"—he checked his watch—"nine forty-five our time."

"Okay, now the Princess."

Jack reached for the phone. "Just a couple of calls. I don't think they'll take more than a few minutes and I can have this part wrapped up."

Frank was handing him the phone when Cynthia stood up. "It won't do us a bit of good unless Hans knows that you're doing it. Call the Princess first."

Frank took the phone back. "Okay. All right, I'm calling."

Vicki looked at Cynthia, at the tension in her face. Everybody needed to calm down. This was going to take more than a few minutes. "Why do you call her the Princess? Is she . . ."

"Oh." It worked. Cynthia almost laughed. "No, she's definitely not nobility. She's my age, about as unkempt as anyone you can imagine. She wears cotton housedresses and sweaters to work, but she's marvelous with languages, even better than Frank, and she can get absolutely anything done. She knows how valuable she is, so she rules the roost around that office."

"I see. So they treat her like royalty."

"I hate to tell you, but she gets paid more than most executives. You really would think she could afford a business suit. But yes, she's treated in accord with her value."

"*Très, très, très richement!*" Frank was gushing. "Okay, give it to me." He wrote the number on the pad. When he had the number, he gushed some more in a language Vicki could not identify and then hung up in satisfaction.

"Okay, she got a number." He held it up on the pad. "Eight o'clock his time, which will make it eleven here. Perfect." But while he was talking, he kept looking at the number on the pad. He didn't look at Cynthia or anybody else directly. Vicki thought his enthusiasm seemed a little forced, tight-voiced, even when he was speaking in the other languages. Well, okay, maybe she should cut him a little slack. They were all tense. It was a bad situation, that's all.

Jack was already back on the phone, punching in numbers from one of his notes, balanced on his knee.

Cynthia put her hand on Vicki's arm. "You still have to call Elaine about the status of the children who have family here."

"Oh, yeah." Vicki was not looking forward to that call. Elaine would give her a hard time for doing this. Then she thought Cynthia might be thinking of more than that. "You want to talk to her, too? You might want her to get started . . . to go ahead and open negotiations . . ."

Cynthia shook her head quickly. "We'll get to that soon enough. But for right now . . . I suppose you might want to tell her where we are just in case she has to be called in a hurry, but I want these kids safely in someone else's hands before I talk to her. If I talk to her before that . . . well, she's already told us what she wants to do. Right?"

"Yes, okay." Vicki watched her. Cynthia's mind seemed to be on thoughts of her own. "Is there something else?"

Cynthia stared at her without seeing her, then turned her face away. "Maybe I'm afraid I'll lose my nerve."

Oh, yeah. Vicki wondered why she hadn't given that any thought. These people might very well be looking at prison time. Cynthia understood that she wasn't helping her cause by working so hard to disperse the children before she turned herself in.

For a moment they watched Jack on the phone, making notes and dictating numbers back. Both of them were so impatient they could hardly look away, watching for a clue that he might be finished.

"Does your father have call waiting?" Cynthia looked at Vicki as she asked, her face bland, innocent.

"No, I'm sure he doesn't. Cody says we're lucky to get him to keep a telephone. Cynthia, who do you think might call? You didn't give somebody the phone number, did you?"

"Just the bus driver. He's supposed to call in and let us know where he is, but he hasn't done it." She saw the way Vicki was staring at her. "Well, when I gave him the number I wasn't thinking about reverse directories and all that business. He was going to go to someplace that was on a list he got from the bus company, but he didn't know who might have a vacancy. I had to give him the number so he could call and let us know how to reach him when we're ready."

Tim, fresh from the shower, was standing in the doorway to the dining room. "He hasn't called in?"

"No, but if there's no call waiting, he'd just be getting a busy signal most of the time."

They all looked at Jack, who was ignoring them, reading a string of numbers off another note into the phone.

"Did he write the phone number down or memorize it?"

"I had Will write it out for him." She saw them all staring at her. "It's just the bus driver. He already knows where we are, right? Look, I wasn't thinking about what you said—"

"Okay, it's probably all right."

"Sorry."

"Forget it." Tim poured himself some coffee. "Maybe when Jack gets through we can stay off the phone for a little while and give him a chance to get a call in."

The children who were still in the room suddenly sat up straight and looked at each other as though startled. They tumbled from their seats and ran for the outside. Then when she listened, Vicki heard it too. All of the children in the yard were yelling. At least one child's voice was screaming.

Vicki scrambled for the door, moving as fast as she could but still a step or two behind Tim. They went out the door and kept running, heading for the children. Tim was slapping at his hip and Vicki realized what it was. No gun. He hadn't put on his gun.

Most of the children were in the yard up by the barn, a few just coming out of it, with San Juana and Consuela in calm, dutiful attendance. The children were shouting, gleefully jumping up and down and looking up the hill toward the trail leading to Roger's place. There was a small herd of horses up there, several riders leading other horses on lead ropes. A posse with remounts, going at a slow walk.

The children seemed to mass together briefly, then charged the posse, yelling and jumping. The children knew what was up, why the horses were being brought down, long before Vicki recognized her father, Roger, and Maureen, and figured it out. Even most of the horses without riders had saddles.

Little Nadya hopped and skipped and swung her leg as fast as she could, but still lagged farther and farther behind the main mob, just barely ahead of the toddlers and the patient women.

Vicki groaned inwardly. Just when she needed for them to be left alone, just when they needed to be on the telephone, getting their business nailed down, here was her father coming to do them a favor. She reached out and took Tim's arm.

"Look, I better stay and try to keep them outside. Go on back, tell Cynthia they're out here, but just keep on making those calls, okay?"

"Got it."

Will dismounted and led them, except for Roger, into a large, round exercise pen and then closed the gate.

"Everybody's going to get a turn. Calm down now, don't run up behind 'em like that."

Vicki thought there was unlikely to be much danger. These horses looked ancient, with swollen knees, broadened, bowed tendons, ribs showing in front of pelvic bones, clearly defined.

"Good morning!" Vicki's father was grinning at her.

She smiled a greeting in return. "Dad, you didn't have to—"

"No, now, you let the old ones have some fun, too. We wouldn't have been so late, but we had to take 'em at a slow walk." He leaned close to her. "Roger wouldn't stay home either."

Vicki looked around at Roger. She waved and smiled at him from a distance. "Dad, if he should fall and loosen one of those prostheses—"

"Oh, he knows it. Just let him alone. He's going to do it anyway." He turned back to the children. "Okay, now, everybody hold it down so you don't wake 'em up too much. Who wants to sit up on old Thunderbolt here? Let's make a line over that way, okay?"

Vicki wasn't sure if he was aware that the children didn't speak English. But the children watched his face, stared at his gestures, chattered at each other, and then conformed as if they understood every word, they were so eager to ride. Vicki reached down, grabbed a child at random and put him on the back of a decrepit mare. She handed the reins to the little boy and showed him how to hold them properly, with one hand poised just so over the pommel.

She looked over her shoulder at the house. Jack was standing in the doorway, looking at them. He disappeared back inside and the door closed. Vicki looked back at the boy she had just placed on the horse. He straightened his back and sat there with an expectant grin that threatened to split his face. The horse stood still, staring at nothing.

All of the other horses were soon occupied. Will and Maureen kept a hand on two that were without saddles, but the other horses slowly milled about the exercise ring, blowing and sniffing the sand for evidence of who had been there last and for any scraps of food that might have been overlooked.

The little boy on the mare that Vicki had picked for him looked around in bewildered consternation as the other children seemed to be able to move their horses around. His had slipped into a catatonic state, four hooves rooted in the ground. The little boy frantically scooted his rear end in the saddle, trying to push the horse forward and calling out an impressive array of commands in Russian. The mare went into a deeper coma, her head sinking lower, her eyes half-lidded and glazed.

Patiently, Vicki took the boy's foot and showed him how to touch the horse with his heels, explaining, but knowing he wouldn't follow the words. "You have to give her a little nudge, here. Like this, see?" She pushed his heel against the horse's side. Catching on, he drew his heels across the horse's flanks. The mare didn't notice.

"Maybe a little harder." Vicki demonstrated a small kick with her own heel and then pointed at his. The little boy promptly straightened both legs, raised them high, and then brought them down with a resoundingly hollow double thump against the horse's ribs.

The startled mare's head came up. The emphatic signal seemed to take a half second or so to register, but then she remembered. She went from stuporous immobility through a kind of stumbling lurch to full-body motion in about two strides. The kid continued to hold the reins just so with one hand, grabbed on to the saddle horn with the other, hooted with all his might, and kicked her again.

The mare painfully hauled her carcass around the perimeter of the exercise pen, at first in a kind of continuous forward fall, but gathering momentum as she went. Gradually, her undercarriage caught up with the rest of her and she began to organize the stiff-legged stumble into an honest-to-God canter.

In another few seconds it was obvious that she was about to run right over a pair of urchins in diapers who had ducked into the pen under the lower rail. She would have ground them to road dust if they had not been scattered like pigeons by Consuela, who was suddenly sprinting, shrieking Spanish lamentation, in front of the lumbering mare. Consuela held a one-length lead for a few seconds, but the mare was finding her stride and Consuela began to lose ground. At the last split second, just as the mare's nose was parting her hair in back, Consuela dove between the rails and rolled in the yard on the other side.

In full gallop now, eyes wide and glaring, the mare took to the outside rail and tore into a second lap, ears back, head surging in time to the quick rhythm of lunge and gather. She seemed to quicken her stride as she warmed into it.

All those years simply disappeared. They magically fell away as though she were actually outrunning her infirmities. She seemed to focus entirely on the act of running. She didn't need a goal, a destination—the physical motion, the run itself, was enough for a wild, if momentary, rejuvenation.

Going as fast as a five-year-old now, she shot by Will's outstretched hand and ripped off in a cloud of dust, heading into the next furlong. Her old companions in hitherto somnambulant retirement had to jump to get out of her way, nearly spilling several children onto the ground. The mare never altered her stride; she didn't appear to even see them as she pounded ahead past the crowd, whipping by the fence posts and off into another lap.

As they rounded the far turn and thundered down the home stretch, the expression on the little rider's face began to change. It seemed to occur to him that things were not right. Heading toward them now, he saw the terrified faces, heard the screaming and yelling, and knew he was in trouble.

Finally, horrified by the shrieking children and bellowing adults, the boy dropped the reins to hold on to the horn with both hands, nothing visible in his face but two huge eyes.

As soon as the reins began to fall, the old mare knew it. She had learned that command so long ago that she could not remember a time when she did not have to obey it. The signal of the falling reins was as much a part of her instinctual repertoire as eating and breathing, learned so young that it was a part of the chemical anatomy of her brain. As soon as the reins began to drop, she stiffened her forelegs, squatted on her haunches, and went into a perfect slide as though she could actually see the calf on the end of the rope.

The diminutive Russian, continuing on his own, shot over the horn, took off on a launch that would have been destined for a far distant glide path, except that the mare's head had pulled back with the effort of the stop.

The kid hit the horse's head dead center, the ears flattened at the middle of the boy's chest. He instantly clamped on with arms and legs both, dragging down the animal's neck until he was gently deposited on the sand.

There were several seconds of silence as the spectators absorbed the near catastrophe and then recognized the fact that everyone had survived.

Then Will's voice, quiet, but loud enough to be heard. "We probably better just lead 'em."

Twenty-eight

Vicki listened to the telephone ring at Elaine's house. Cynthia, staring at her, was so tense that Vicki had to look away, down at the pad of paper and pen she had automatically put in front of her before she punched in Elaine's number. Vicki thought Cynthia was overreacting. The woman was upset because she couldn't locate the bus driver, and she was stewing more about that than she had about any of the rest of their problems.

Jack was acting like it was no big deal, but Vicki thought Frank seemed upset, as bad as Cynthia. Jack said he thought the driver would probably just call them when he got around to it, but Cynthia insisted that he should have called long before this. If the line was busy, he should have kept calling until he got through.

Vicki, listening to the ringing of the phone at the other end of the line, looked up, and her eyes met Tim's. He looked grave, his eyes leveled at hers without expression, their shared knowledge already enough to convey meaning through a blank expression. By helping these people out—good people that were Vicki's friends now and that she knew Tim was growing to like—by helping them do this they might very well be sending them to prison instead of probation. But the children—Tim was thinking of the same things. She wanted to reach out and touch him, but she didn't.

"Cohen's residence." It was Karen, her voice sounding British and friendly. Vicki almost relaxed.

"Hi, Karen. It's Vicki Shea."

"Well, hello, you. Want to speak to Mrs. Cohen?"

"Please."

"Right, then. Hang on." Vicki glanced at Cynthia, but the older woman's stare was so intense that she had to look away. She glanced around for Tim's face but couldn't see him. She looked around. He had been right there a second ago.

"Vicki?"

"Hi, Elaine."

"What's up?" She sounded impatient, as if she were in a hurry.

"Did I call at a bad time? I just have a couple of questions, but if you're busy—"

"You caught me as I was heading out the door. Time to buy shoes for the kid again. That comes up about every four days at this age."

"Well . . . can I just ask about a couple of things?" Vicki avoided looking at Cynthia by staring at her blank pad. Cynthia was radiating tension.

Elaine sounded a little better. "No, that's all right, no hurry, really. What's the question? Something about those aliens?"

"The children, yes."

"Still aliens. Never mind, what's the question?"

"First I need to tell you where I am."

"Uh, you're not at the clinic? On a Saturday?"

"I took the weekend off."

"Good for you . . . I guess. Where are you?"

"I brought everybody to my father's ranch in Los Angeles."

There was a pause, then Elaine's voice seemed cool. "Vicki, who's 'everybody'? What does that mean?"

"Cynthia, Jack, Frank, the kids. Tim's here—"

"Are you out of your fucking mind?"

Vicki was shocked for a few seconds, then started searching for excuses. "I was just—"

"Vicki, for Christ sake! Examining the kids as a doctor is one thing, taking them off for the weekend is something else entirely. Don't you see that?"

"I guess I just wanted to give them a chance to get out. You've been here, it's a great place to take kids. They've been cooped up in that basement—"

"Vicki!" There was a pause as Elaine's brain whirred and clicked, sorting information and not liking it. "Vicki, what are you doing? Those kids are going straight back to Latvia or wherever it is they came from. Why can't I make that clear?"

"Well, that's one of the things I wanted to ask about."

"They came into the country illegally! What's to ask?"

"Some of them have relatives in the States. They have family here, if we can just figure out—"

"Makes no difference."

Elaine seemed so positive, so final in her opinion, that for a moment Vicki couldn't believe it. "You're kidding."

"Not a bit. In fact, if they're adults and they came in illegally and get deported, they can't come back for some period. I'm not sure, but it's like five years or some damn thing, even where they got relatives here and even if they had an application pending before they came in. I'm not positive about juveniles, but it's probably not any different."

"Why?"

"Why? You think there has to be a reason? Didn't you go to law school? There has to be a rational relationship to a legitimate governmental purpose—no matter how stupid that relationship may seem to you. There's no legal requirement to be fair or even to make any sense. Vicki, listen to me—"

"But if they have relatives here?"

"Vicki!" Vicki could hear her take a breath and let it out. She sounded like she was trying to explain to a child. "Vicki, you have no idea how long the line is to get relatives in from Eastern Europe. It's like years."

"Even a close relative?"

"I'm talking mothers separated from their children. I'm talking

years." She took another deep breath and let it out. "Are you somewhere where you can talk?"

"Uh . . ."

"Oh, Christ. Are they all sitting around staring at you while you're
talking?"

"Mm-hmm."

"Okay, then, just listen a minute. Okay?"

"Okay."

"Vicki, as you know, lots of people harbor aliens. It's illegal, but it's
not nearly as serious as this smuggling business. You listening?"

"Yes."

"I've been talking to some other immigration lawyers, people who
deal more with the gritty side of it than I do. Immigrant smuggling
has become big business. I mean, big, organized business. These gangs
are making more money than you can even imagine, and they are
unbelievably ruthless. They make the Mafia look like gentlemen. You
are getting yourself tied up with some people who are very serious
trouble. Understand? Maybe your friends are just philanthropists, but
the people they've been dealing with are very hard-core dangerous. Do
you understand what I'm saying?"

Vicki didn't answer. She sat and stared at her pad to keep from
looking at anyone, as if she were still listening. And she was. She was
hearing the silence of disapproval and condemnation from the other
end of the line. Elaine didn't get it. She didn't understand.

"Vicki, what you don't seem to understand is that by getting
involved in this, by doing something more than just what a doctor
should do, you can get sucked in, too. It could be very difficult to convince the feds that you just got into it after the fact, understand?
Believe me, they take this smuggling business very seriously. People
get killed, lots of people die because of these gangs. If they're convinced that you are involved, the feds will definitely come after you.
Understand? They *will* come after you. This is very, very serious."

Vicki looked up from the pad, saw Cynthia's glare, and quickly
looked back down. "Well, we're here now."

"Not for long."

"What?"

"I've got to call somebody. I've got to report this right away or I'm going to look like I'm part of it, too."

"Elaine! What? You can't—"

"Vicki, if we do this now, right now, it won't look so bad. It'll be like as soon as you realized how serious it was, you got your lawyer to get ahold of the authorities, so that—"

"Elaine, stop it! You are not going do that!" God, why hadn't she seen this coming?

"Vicki, it's for your own good!"

"Elaine, no! I mean it, now. The answer's no!"

"Vicki—"

"Elaine, you do that and I will never, ever speak to you again. You hear me?"

"Vicki—" But her voice had lost some of its conviction.

"I mean that, Elaine. I'm dead serious."

"Oh, Vicki, I know. It's hard . . ."

"Elaine, I mean it!"

"Oh, Jesus, okay. Calm down."

"You hear me?"

"Okay, I said okay. I just want you to think it over."

"I don't have to think—!"

"Calm *down*! Jesus, Vicki, just give yourself time to think. You're one of the smartest people I ever met. You can think. Now just do it for a change."

"Elaine, promise me. I want your promise. You're not going to call anybody, right?"

"I'm going to go buy shoes."

"Okay."

"Okay." There was a pause while Vicki could hear Elaine breathing into the phone. Then Elaine's voice sounded calmer, more somber. "Listen, I've got your father's number in my book. I'll call you this afternoon, okay?"

"Okay."

"You don't hear from me, call here. I might miss you if you're out with the horses or something."

"Okay."

" 'Okay, okay.' Jesus, Vicki. Don't just say 'okay.' Think about this. I mean it, understand?"

"Yes, I understand what you're saying."

"All right, then." She still sounded angry. "Talk to you later." She hung up.

Cynthia's voice was flat. "That didn't sound too promising."

"I guess she doesn't think going away for the weekend was a very good idea."

"I gathered." Cynthia looked around and found Jack. He looked unhappy under her gaze. "Where do you suppose that idiot went with the bus?"

Jack shrugged and looked at Frank. Frank raised his hands. "Don't look at me. I didn't pay him in advance."

"Well, it seemed like a good idea."

Vicki closed her eyes and then opened them. "Why don't you just call the bus company and see if he checked in with them?"

Cynthia stared at her. "Finally, a sound idea. Okay, I can do that. Don't know where my brain went."

"Where are you going to go in the bus anyway?"

"Nowhere. I just want to make sure we can if we want to, that's all."

Vicki looked around and still couldn't see Tim. Where the hell did he go? She looked back at Cynthia. Cynthia was staring hard at her. So was Frank. Only Jack seemed to find something else more interesting, unless he was looking out the window to avoid looking at her.

"What is it?" Vicki's question was directed at Cynthia.

"What? Oh, sorry." She shook her head and closed her eyes. "I was thinking about something else. Let me call the bus company and make sure we still have transportation, and then maybe I can relax and think about something more productive. Sorry."

Vicki stood quickly and walked out the front door. She was half expecting someone to say something, to try to stop her. Why the hell was she thinking that? She decided Cynthia must be making her jumpy. The woman was suddenly so tense she was difficult to be around. Just because she couldn't locate the bus driver? Jesus, these people could just go buy a bus if it was that important.

Wait a minute. Were they thinking about running? Well, if they could pay off the smugglers and get rid of that danger . . . Where were they going to go with a busload of kids? Okay, maybe it was just normal to think about it, but really they knew there was nowhere to go. Didn't they? Besides, they were making progress. They were about to get the names of some people in California—that was it. That's why Cynthia was getting so jumpy. They really were that close.

Vicki's father was in the exercise ring, patiently leading two horses, one lead rope in each hand. The children, having sampled the Wild West, were beginning to drift out of the ring to wrestle and chase over the open ground.

Vicki stood outside the pen to watch. Tim had brought her father's gelding out and was saddling him. Apparently, her father was going to ride back to Roger's place with Roger and Maureen. Well, okay. She would try to find some way to sit down with him and visit after they knew more about what they were doing. Now, there was just too much to worry about to give him the attention that she wanted to give him. She felt a little guilty about it, but she really wanted her father out of the way.

Oh, Jesus, that shouting match with Elaine. Leave it to Elaine to try to bring back reality.

Wait a minute. Was that right? Was Elaine right all along? What was she, Vicki, doing, thinking that she could just take a weekend off and change her whole life around? But they were getting so close. Just get the names and numbers, find the bus. . . .

But what was wrong? Vicki suddenly knew that if she were thinking straight, she would be saying the same things Elaine was saying, following the straight and narrow, protecting what she had and not taking such insane chances. But, at this point, what else could she do? She had held that poor dead child, tried to breathe life back into his broken little body—now she couldn't just send the rest of them back, even if she weren't thinking so much about Nadya. But it was a warning, a promise of what those people would do to the rest of them. They had to either call the cops or stay here where it was safe, at least for a short time, at least for now, until they got the names.

Okay, she had to admit it. She was scared. They all were. Of course they were.

She wiped her hand over her eyes. Just this morning, she had felt so good about all of it. What had changed, except Elaine gave her a dose of reality? But Elaine just didn't see it all, the whole picture, the way she, Vicki, saw it. Elaine's voice was the voice of duty, of a corrupted sense of good, conservative citizenship. It wasn't the voice of her conscience, especially when all Elaine could offer for an alternative was the proper, legal course—just ship 'em all back. All Elaine could do was to tell Vicki to do something that Vicki knew, deep down, was wrong. Just wrong.

Vicki leaned on the rail of the pen, her chin on her crossed hands. She stared at the animals and the three children that stayed in there with them, but she didn't see them.

She wasn't just floundering. There was a plan, right? Frank was going to call this guy back, this guy in Belgrade who was going to give him the other contacts, who, with any luck, would be able to help them get the kids to adoptive parents, *and* who would get Vicki in touch with whoever the forger was that could help her come up with papers for Nadya so she could do the adoption.

It would be illegal. What if somebody figured it out? What the hell would they do? She could imagine a U.S. attorney telling a federal judge he was bringing charges of criminal adoption. Okay, right. Nobody would look beyond the papers. Probably not ever. She was sure of that. Almost. Well, probably.

Was that so crazy? If other people did it, she didn't see why she couldn't. Elaine might not like it, she might even break off their friendship over it, but Vicki didn't think she would rat on her. If the kids got dispersed, then that problem was gone. As long as Elaine didn't know where they went, Vicki didn't think she would pursue it, and they had been friends long enough she was sure she wouldn't say anything to anybody about her adopted daughter, once it was a done deal.

Suddenly, Vicki straightened up and stared. She had been looking right at Nadya without realizing it until the child saw her and waved with a cheerful, "Aunt Vicki!"

The other two children were climbing down with Will's assistance, ready to go play at something else, but Nadya was crimped on the back of an old gelding, so skinny his bones stuck up through his ragged coat, his old knees swollen to twice the size they should have been. Nadya grinned hard, her eyes shining, as she leaned forward to stroke the side of the old boy's neck.

When Maureen offered to help her down, using sign language, the little girl shook her head, gripped the scraggly mane in front of the saddle with both hands, and appealed with a look to Vicki.

Immediately, Vicki called out, "It's okay, Maureen. I'll take her. I don't think she wants to get down yet."

Maureen was laughing and shaking her head. "No, she doesn't. You're going to have to serve her dinner on that horse. She may try to sleep up there tonight."

Vicki held the lead rope and walked over to the edge of the pen where her father and Maureen, on the outside, were just mounting up. Vicki shielded her eyes with her hand to see them. Tim was standing next to her father's horse, getting last-minute instructions about one of the green trainees he apparently wanted Tim to do something with. Tim was holding one of her father's hackamores and Will was pointing to a hot-looking gelding that he obviously wanted Tim to ride. The man had to be right if her father trusted him that much already.

Maureen looked at Vicki and smiled conspiratorially. Vicki couldn't help but grin back. She liked her. Yes, she decided, she definitely liked this lady.

Maureen spoke. "Didn't you bring a hat?"

Will turned his head. "Hat? You must have half a dozen of 'em around here. I know there's a couple of yours in the tack room."

Tim headed for the barn. "I'm going there anyway. I'll bring you one."

"Bring one for Nadya, too."

He grinned and waved. "You bet." The picture of stability. What was she afraid of?

She looked at her father, wanting to say something serious to him. It was so good of him to let her do this, to make so much of an effort to bring these horses over so that the children could ride, and she'd been so distracted she had hardly even thanked him.

But Will was not looking at her. He was looking at Maureen. "You ready?" He turned farther until he could see his old buddy. "How about it, Rog?"

Mr. Dorr touched his hat to Vicki and walked his horse in the direction of home. Her father and Maureen followed, talking to each other.

Oh, well. She could talk to him later.

Nadya said something to her in Russian. Vicki looked up at her and grinned. "Okay, we're going."

She stepped off across the sand ring and the old horse obediently, patiently trudged after her. Vicki picked up the pace until she was running and got the horse to trot along behind her, its head even with her head. She looked at Nadya over her shoulder and the little girl was hanging on, grinning with her mouth open, her eyes shining as though there were tears.

Vicki slowed to a walk, turning around to walk backward so she could see the child as she went. She noticed the horse's limp and stopped. She hoped Nadya had not detected it. She didn't seem to, the way she was grinning. Vicki tried walking her very slowly and the gelding dutifully stepped along, just a slight hitch in his step. No question, his arthritis was bad.

"Why don't you try this one?"

Vicki turned around and saw Tim. He was holding the reins to Banjo, all saddled and ready for her. She all but hopped up and down. "Great! Did you take the kinks out of her? She's been in that stall for a full day, at least."

Tim didn't move, standing there, grinning at her. "She's probably okay."

"Just try her out before I get Nadya up there."

"Okay." He still stood there, grinning.

"What?"

"There's a Mrs. Lynch, in San Diego. Wouldn't you know she'd be Irish?"

"Who? Oh! Oh, my God! Tell me!"

"Cynthia talked to her just a minute ago. They've got lawyers, papers, everything, about two and a half hours from here on the bus."

"Oh, my God!" Vicki couldn't move for a moment. It was possible. More than that, it was going to happen. It was there, right in front of her now. It was going to work. Tim was grinning. He was with her on it. He was watching her and grinning. It really was about to happen!

She turned and looked at the little girl. "Nadya, you hear that?" She swept her out of the saddle and spun her around, squeezing her until Nadya squawked. Vicki pulled her head back until she could see the child's face.

"Oh, baby. Oh, Nadya!" She could feel tears hot behind her eyes and see the look of bewilderment on the child's face, trying to smile, but not sure what it was all about.

"Oh, I've got to calm down." She clasped the child to her breast and looked at Tim. "We still have to find the bus driver, right?"

"Cynthia's working on that now."

"Aunt Vicki?" Nadya's voice was so small, intimidated by the unexplainable rush of emotion. She held out her hand toward the horse she'd just vacated.

"Oh, I've frightened you, haven't I?" Vicki laughed and put the child back on the saddle, then turned to look at Tim, her face glowing.

Tim almost seemed embarrassed. He glanced at Banjo. "Okay, I'll give her a spin."

With a quick, fluid movement, he was up in the saddle and they were off at an easy jog. As she watched him, Vicki was making a supreme effort to calm down, get back in control. This wasn't over yet. There were still several more steps. Okay, be patient. So close.

In another moment Tim brought Banjo up to an easy canter and they went off past the barn, made a lazy turn, and came back.

"How's she doing?" Okay, much calmer now.

Tim winked. "Push-button. You gonna like this one."

"Take Nadya up there with you for a minute."

He looked at her and smiled, but he shook his head as he dismounted. "You can do it." He handed her the reins. "Here."

Quickly, Vicki mounted and held out her hand to Nadya, still sitting the other horse. "Come on with me. Come on, we'll go for a ride."

Nadya understood the gesture. She held out her two hands to Vicki and leaned toward her. Tim quickly stepped between the horses and lifted the child off, intending to pass her immediately up to Vicki. The little girl wrapped her arms around his neck and gave him an unexpected hug. Tim gave her an awkward squeeze, and then lifted her up to Vicki's waiting hands. Vicki could see the look of surprise on Tim's face, then the glow of his smile as he looked at the child sitting on the pommel in front of Vicki. He stepped back out of the way.

Taking it easy, Vicki walked the horse up the trail, following the path that her father had taken a few moments before. She crossed the low ridge and headed slowly down into the broad valley.

She was working at calming herself down. Still more to do. They weren't there quite yet.

At the deepest part, she turned off the path and followed what she thought was a game trail until she remembered that this was what passed for a streambed on those rare occasions when it rained enough to fill it with a little water. She was going uphill, gradually remembering more about where this path led. There was an outcropping of rocks, boulders that formed an obstacle about a half a mile up ahead. There used to be ways around it by horse, but she remembered that it got complicated so she turned back and went downhill instead. There would be time later. She could take Nadya all over this place, all over the countryside like this.

Vicki was eager to get back to check on the progress of locating the bus driver, but she also wanted to savor this moment, draw it out so that she would always remember it. This would be the moment of a new start, of something entirely new that was going to make her whole entire existence different and richer by far than it had ever been. In twenty years, if she was still alive, she wanted to remember this ride with her child, for the first time realizing that this *was* her child, actually realizing that it was real, that she could really do it.

Nadya had both hands on the saddle horn until Vicki picked up her left and got her to hold the reins just above Vicki's own left hand.

"This is how you steer, see?" She moved her hand to the left enough to make the rein lay across the right side of the mare's neck and she obediently moved left. Then she did the same thing to the right. "See? You push her head over with the rein and she goes that way."

Nadya laughed out loud with delight. Vicki kept a hold on the ends of the reins but let the child take over the controls. Nadya giggled maniacally as she steered the horse one way, then the other, then around in a tight circle. Vicki softly held her hand in the center so they could go back up the path.

"Now, here's the brakes." She pulled the hand back gently and the mare stopped.

"Okay, now look at my foot." She tipped the little girl's head down and then pointed at her foot. "See it? You watching my foot? Here we go." She brought her leg in sharply and the mare jumped ahead, going into an easy trot. Nadya seemed to go up with the saddle, but then stayed there while the saddle went down and back up. She would have kept bouncing, except Vicki had a good hold on her and kept her down in the saddle so they could jog on back toward the barn.

With one arm wrapped around the child's middle she leaned her head out and turned it to try to see Nadya's face.

"You okay, baby? All right?"

"Ahright!" She shouted to the sky. "Ahright!

Vicki wrapped both arms around the little body, still so skinny. Remembering to be gentler, she held her tight, pressed her face against the side of the child's face. She knew if she let herself, she would be crying.

As soon as they cleared the ridge, Vicki saw that all of the adults except San Juana and Consuela were gathered around Tim by the exercise pen. As they got closer she could see that he was frowning. He was wearing his gun.

Closer still, she could see Frank scowling, his face red. Jack was pacing, his back to Vicki. Cynthia looked up at her as she approached on the horse. Cynthia's face was pale, her mouth a straight line of . . . what? Anger? No. She was frightened. Vicki could see it in the rigidity of her back, the stiff movement of her arm as she gestured toward Tim.

"Found the bus driver."

Vicki dismounted and lifted Nadya down to stand next to her. Vicki kept watching Cynthia's face; her intense expression of imposed calm with the fear behind it. Cynthia was filled with urgency to tell her something, but was having trouble saying it. Vicki glanced at Tim, trying to catch his eye but failing as he turned suddenly and headed for the house. "Tim found him?"

"No, I found him, he's just going to call the police and get the details." She seemed to have to steel herself to push on. "The bus company told me their bus turned up this morning off the side of some freeway."

"Where's the driver?"

"He was on the bus."

Cynthia glanced down at the little girl, seemed to remember that she didn't speak English, and then tried to continue. Her voice, pitched a little lower, caught, so that she had to say it twice before Vicki could be sure she heard her clearly, with no mistake about what she said.

"He was stuffed under a seat."

Twenty-nine

"If they were coming here, wouldn't they be here already?" Jack's voice shook in spite of his attempt at logic, at reasonable rationalization. He didn't believe what he was saying. He stared at Tim, who was just coming back from the house.

Tim stared back at him, his mind working behind the calm eyes. "I don't know. Two bullets to the head sometime last night between the time he left here and midnight. His wallet was taken, but this is not a simple robbery—"

"No, it's too much for coincidence." Cynthia was doing her best to calm down. At least she looked and sounded calmer. Vicki realized that she was exercising a tremendous effort to stay rational, analytical, and, as much as possible, in control. Her voice did not shake. "It would have been fairly simple if somebody was watching our house and saw us leave in the bus. They could have contacted the company yesterday afternoon to find out where we went. To me, that makes more sense than a coincidental robbery of a guy on the freeway on a bus."

Vicki's stomach turned over. Now, even Cynthia was making up her mind, girding herself for the rational decision to surrender. She was talking herself into giving it up.

Jack's face was sour in frustration. He was becoming more agitated as his wife calmed down. "But why kill the driver if they know where we are? That doesn't make sense to me. To kill our driver and give us warning that we're next? Why would anybody do that?"

Frank kicked hard at the ground and turned away. He wasn't saying anything but his face was terrified, a deep, dark flush, making his eyes look luminous in fear. Vicki saw Cynthia glance at him and then away. It was a quick look, as if she didn't want to be caught looking. She saw it, too.

Tim stayed concentrated on Cynthia, watching her and not looking at Vicki at all. It was as if he thought, if he didn't look at her, at Vicki, he could be all cop. Tim's voice was calm and devoid of inflection. It was simply business, matter-of-fact, what he would have called, in the psychologist's jargon, a flat affect.

"Okay, Mrs. Wilkins, we've got to quit fooling around. We have to get the kids out of here, that's the immediate thing. We have to assume the worst and then, if it's not that bad, at least everybody will be safe." He looked at Vicki, or rather toward her, without looking directly at her, at her face. "How far is Sunland on the back road?"

"I think it's less than ten miles. Maybe more like seven. Where do you want to take them?"

"There's a Los Angeles Police station in Sunland. They're sending somebody."

He looked at Jack, directly into his eyes, forcing Jack to pay attention to business and calm down. "How many can you get into the Jaguar at one time?"

"Kids? If we pack 'em in, maybe six or seven."

Tim looked at Vicki, this time at her eyes. With an effort that Vicki thought only she would be able to see, his face was still all business. "Do you have the keys to your father's pickup?"

"I know where they are." She watched him carefully. He was telling her something by not looking in her eyes before then. Now, he was expecting argument from her.

He looked away from her, turned and concentrated on talking to Cynthia. "Okay, we can get the rest of the kids in the pickup. Have to take it easy, driving—"

"Wait a minute." Vicki got it. Her hand reached out involuntarily to touch the top of Nadya's head as she stared at Tim. Her voice boiled out of her with the realization of what he was saying. "We're just giving up? Just like that?"

Tim looked at her. He stared at her hard, his mind churning. Finally, barely perceptibly, his expression seemed to soften as his eyes searched hers. "That's all I can think of that's safe."

She could see that he was telling her the absolute truth. He was trying to appeal to her to be rational, to think. His question was direct and personal, putting it back to her.

"What do you want to do?"

"I don't know." She kept her body still but she felt as if her mind were flailing in the air, trying to grab on to something, some better idea, something solid. "We don't know for sure we're being threatened, do we? Why are they giving us all this time, if they're trying to harm us or get at the children? Is that even rational?"

Tim shook his head quickly. "No, but look at what happens if we're wrong about that."

Vicki hesitated. Was he willing to give in to her because she made it personal? The policeman side of him wanted to be practical, mechanical, quit playing games and just take care of business in the way you normally took care of business, but he was hesitating, waiting for her to agree. And there was something else going on, wasn't there? Her thoughts swirled in desperation. She couldn't give up if there was anything else she could come up with.

Wait. Something. What was it? Damn it! She looked at Frank. What was it?

Frank stood with his back to the rest of them, staring in the direction of the pasture. She spoke to his back, her voice suddenly hard. "Frank?"

He didn't respond.

Vicki scowled, staring at the back of Frank's head. The whirling in her mind stopped. She turned deliberately to look at Cynthia. Goddamn it! She'd been so caught up, she'd missed it. Right in front of her, and she hadn't thought it through. Goddamn it! Cynthia—was it Cynthia holding out?

Vicki heard her own voice go hard. "We are missing some information here, aren't we? Something else we might want to know about?"

Cynthia stared back at her, her face an open look of puzzlement, looking at Vicki directly, meeting her eyes. "What?"

Vicki looked back at Frank. "Frank? Goddamn it, Frank!"

He turned his head and struggled to meet her gaze, then broke it off, turning toward Jack with a look of appeal. As soon he broke off trying to make eye contact Vicki knew she'd hit it, she'd guessed right.

Jack looked from Frank to Vicki and back again at Frank. "Like what? What else is there to tell you?" He was speaking to Vicki but staring hard at his partner, who was staring back at him, but then broke off that look, too.

Vicki stepped around to where she could see Frank's face. "Okay, Frank. What is it? Frank? This doesn't make any sense. It has never made much sense, but now . . . they're torturing us, terrorizing us. Nobody else knows why, but you do, right, Frank?"

He tried to turn away, but Vicki stepped in front of him again. "This whole business of a teenage kid coming to you, demanding blackmail—just to you and not to the Wilkinses—it never made any sense. It never happened, did it?"

"Yes, it did. It did happen, walking right into my office—"

"But there's something else to it. I know there is. What was it?"

Cynthia's voice was cold. "Frank?"

He started to look at her, then didn't. He couldn't look at her. He looked at Vicki instead, terror and appeal in his eyes. "All of that was true."

"That part of it?"

"Yes . . . no, not just . . ."

Cynthia again. "Nobody's buying it, Frank."

Vicki glared at him. "What was the part you left out? It was the dope, wasn't it?"

"Okay, yes. I didn't think that—I didn't know that everything was going to happen that way."

Jack, this time. "Jesus, Frank. Why?"

Frank was gaping, opening his mouth, trying to make up the lie, but nothing was coming out. He was too scared.

It had been right there all this time. Vicki's voice was hard but she lowered the volume. "We just kept forgetting about the heroin. It was the dope, right? You had something to do with the— When they got to the border, was it still opium or had they turned it into heroin already?"

"They did that in Mexico." He stared at the ground, at Vicki's feet. "Opium from Turkey and Afghanistan, cocaine from Colombia. Assembled everything, combined it all with the human cargo in Mexico."

"And you were in on that. Right? What did you do, finance it up front?"

"Part of it." He shook his head, still looking at the ground. "It was so much money, so quick. It looked so easy."

"But they tried to put the squeeze on you, knowing you couldn't go to the police because this was a lot more serious than a few orphans, right? They thought that you could be tapped for a whole lot of money, an easy shakedown, right? Just you. And this was before the shooting at the border. That's right, isn't it?"

"Jack, Cynthia . . . they didn't know anything about it. I couldn't just come up with millions of dollars like that."

"Okay. So what did you do? You set them up to avoid paying off? You tipped off the police about when and where they were coming into the country? Was that it? You called the border patrol from Belgium?"

"The Texas State Police."

"Okay, you did set them up at the border. They were right about that, figured out that it had to be you, right? You set them up, but it didn't quite work out because most of them still got away. And Julia was the payback? That was their revenge on you for setting them up? And Mrs. Fairchild? The heroin was to let you know what it was about, wasn't it?"

Cynthia sounded more disappointed than anything else. "Frank, was there ever anybody named Hans?"

He turned to her quickly, this time looking at her. "Yes. That part really is true. It's just that he wasn't closely connected to the drug people and he can't control them. Hans thought if we gave them all this money—a million for the Canadians, the rest for them . . ."

"Well, I guess they were too pissed."

Frank nodded. "Too late."

Tim's voice was flat, all business, nothing personal in it. "All right. That's it, we have to move. No more time to fool around."

His voice stopped as he looked at Vicki. Suddenly, the clarity was gone, seeing him look at her like that. With that look of compassion, the realization, her rationality was destroyed. *Oh, shit! No, not now! Not right now!* She was staring at Tim, trying to make her mind work. No bus, no way to get to San Diego, no way to avoid the arrests, the INS—time running out. Right now. Everything was falling apart in front of her. They were going to have to abandon—what, her child? Her little girl? To the INS, an institution, again? She couldn't move. She couldn't even think.

Cynthia turned abruptly. "I'll get San Juana moving, see how many we can get into the Jag."

Okay, Vicki thought. She could feel a numbness, a creeping paralysis in her legs as well as her mind. She had to do something practical. Follow Cynthia.

"I'll get the keys." Vicki thought her voice sounded surprisingly normal. It was schizophrenic.

In spite of the normal voice, her legs felt wooden as she stepped out toward the house. She was aware that she'd left Nadya standing in the yard. All of her instincts told her to go back and pick her up, keep her close as long as she possibly could. She couldn't do that. She had to follow this practical woman in front of her, had to go through her father's house to his bedroom, open the dresser, and get out the spare keys. No time for anything else. Be practical, damn it!

The keys were not where she thought they were. She went through several drawers, feeling ridiculously as if she were violating her father's trust. She'd already violated his trust by bringing all this trouble down to him. Jesus, quit it! She had to be practical.

She thought of a utility drawer in the kitchen filled with all kinds of odd junk, old pocket knives, can openers, string junk. As she went through the living room it was empty and quiet, strewn with sleeping bags and the detritus of children on a holiday. Her eyes blurred as she went into the kitchen, and she had to swipe at them impatiently with her hand to see into the drawer. The spare keys were there.

Vicki came back out into the too-bright sunlight of midday. The Jag was packed with children and already rolling slowly up the drive. Jack was driving, leaning forward to see past waving arms and legs. As far as the kids were concerned, they were still on a holiday, an outing, a fun trip to the Wild West. They did not understand that they were going to jail and then back to where they came from. What had Frank said about the Russians? An orphanage? What would an orphanage be like in Russia?

There were four kids in the back of the truck with Frank and San Juana, who seemed to be trying to keep a hand on each of them to hold them down. Consuela was in the cab with Cynthia, Charlotte on Cynthia's lap, Consuela holding one of the toddlers.

There were too many in the back of the shortbed pickup. They were having a problem finding a place to sit down. Vicki motioned to San Juana with the keys.

"You better drive. Turn left on the road when you go out the gate and then take the very next left turn. Just follow that road all the way into Sunland."

San Juana climbed over the tailgate and took the keys. She looked back at the truck bed. "I don't know how you're going to get in there." She pointed past Vicki's shoulder. "And we still got one more kid."

Vicki turned around and saw what he was talking about. Nadya was next to Banjo, her little arms wrapped around a foreleg, staring at Vicki, a look of open alarm on her face.

Vicki moved toward her. "Come on, Nadya. You have to go, sweetheart."

But Nadya was staring at her face, at her eyes. She read what was going on, could see her whole future in Vicki's face, the misery in the adult's eyes.

Nadya gripped the horse's leg and began to cry out loud. It wasn't the cry of a stubborn child who wanted to play, who was spoiled by the adults' attention. It was that of a terrorized little human, a small but perfectly comprehending being, crying out in true hopeless anguish, in helpless desperation, near panic and in utter, mile-deep disappointment. She stared at Vicki's face and wailed at what she saw.

Vicki stopped. She felt a cold core deep in her center. She was letting her child down again. She was. Vicki was. Nobody else had promised this child anything—probably never in her short life—but Vicki knew that she had promised, that the child knew she had promised and now she could see that the adult was going back on it, backing out.

Nadya stared, eyes wide open as she cried. Hope was going out of her with every breath, and it made a sound of mourning, musical in pitch and tone, a wild lament, the sound of escaping hope—dreams escaping the child and turning to nothing but vapor and empty sound.

Vicki had to turn away, to turn around and look at the adults. San Juana and Tim staring at her, waiting for her to do something about the wailing child. They didn't see it.

"We can't all get in there, anyway. I'll wait with Nadya. I can call my father—"

Tim lifted a hand toward her as he spoke to San Juana. "You go ahead. There's a police car coming to meet you on the way. Just have him send another one for us."

San Juana nodded. "I'll send him on out here."

"No. He's your escort. I want that car to go with you and he can send another one out here. Better yet, I'll call them and get them to send another car for us. Go ahead, get going."

He had seen it. Tim understood. She watched his back as he headed into the house to the telephone.

Vicki watched the two vehicles as the truck took the lead, going up and over the rise toward the gate. She couldn't make herself turn around and see that little face again. She kept staring at the road to the gate, unable to move for a long moment until Tim came back out of the house. She kept staring until Tim was close enough to Vicki to put his arm around her shoulders and pull her tight up against him. She hadn't imagined it. He understood.

Behind her, Vicki could hear that the crying had stopped. How long had it been stopped?

Vicki put one arm around Tim, but twisted her head around to look. Nadya was grinning again. Her tear-streaked face was open and worried, still alarmed, but the pleading grin was back, missing tooth and all.

Vicki wanted to smile back, but all she could feel in her face was a spasmodic tic for all the effort. Her face felt numb. But the little girl kept smiling, grinning; the only means she had, the only appeal she could use, and she knew it. Vicki managed to turn her mouth up but she knew it was not going to be convincing. Nadya was watching her eyes. She held on to the horse's leg, gripped it, her face half buried in the angle of the mare's chest.

Vicki could feel Tim turn with her and look. She felt his gentle laughter as he gripped her shoulders with both arms now. She could feel the rumble of his voice in his chest when he spoke. "I think she likes that horse."

Vicki's answer came so fast that she was almost surprised, first at the sound of her own voice and then at the idea at what she had said. The idea must have been formed already, fully grown and developed, because the idea burst out of her without her having to think about it at all.

"On that horse, she's not crippled."

She could feel the sob coming up, struggling to get out of her. She could feel the swelling tightness of her throat, the sudden heat in her eyes.

"There's got to be a way. Isn't there? Maybe they don't have to tell the police everything. Cynthia's good at that. At not telling everything."

Tim sighed. "Maybe. We'll see." But she knew he didn't believe it.

Thirty

Vicki made herself move. She stepped out from under Tim's protective arms and approached Nadya, trying to smile at her but knowing that she was screwing it up. Her mouth felt twisted.

She wanted to pick her up and hold her, squeeze that little body to her breast and cry. She couldn't let herself do that She stopped in front of the child, next to the horse.

Nadya watched her, the edges of the grin wanting to start again with the slightest encouragement, but transparently tense, wide eyes taking everything in, the little forehead worried about the adult's expression, the obvious grief. She held to the mare's leg, the side of her face against the hair, her little fingers clutching the horse's skin.

Vicki patted the saddle. "You want to sit up here? She's good, she'll just stand there, for you."

The child held up her hands to be lifted and Vicki put her into the saddle. Vicki tied the reins so they wouldn't fall and handed them to the little girl. "Remember how to hold them?" She held her own hand up, demonstrating.

Nadya remembered, adjusted the reins in her hand, and looked back at Vicki, grinning again, this time genuinely. This kid would be no effort to teach to ride. She wanted to so badly, she would have it down in a week, if she could keep her. She knew she should quit thinking like that, that she was just making matters worse. She spoke to Tim, to help her quit thinking.

"Are they on the way?"

"More than you know."

"Why do you say that?"

"Your buddy Elaine blew the whistle. They got FBI all over 'em at Sunland now and they'll all be coming out here."

"Oh, God!" Her voice was more of a whisper than an exclamation. But she wasn't surprised. Elaine was determined to rescue her, and so she had capped off her doom instead.

Vicki realized she was staring at Tim and he was staring back at her. He was going to speak, and she knew instantly what he was going to say.

"We can try to do it. We can still try."

"Try? An adoption?"

"Sure, why not give it a try? We could get married. That might make it easier, huh?"

She wasn't surprised at all. It was a practical suggestion. "It might."

He grinned, then stowed it. "I love you and I want to marry you. Is that how you say it? Ask it?"

"I don't know. What do I say?"

"Just say yes. It's for the good of the children."

"Child."

"Okay, child. That mean yes?"

"We could try, huh?"

"You want to, I'm ready to mount up and head for the mountains. We can probably reach the Doc Larsen Trail around here somewhere and then we'd be in a national forest."

She stared at him and thought for a long moment. "You know we can't."

"Yes, I know." He hesitated. "But we could still do the first part."

She caught herself nodding, almost an immediate agreement, then caught herself just as she was about to vocalize it. "Yes, well . . . let's talk about that. Ask me again later, okay?"

"Sure."

Quickly, she turned away and saw Nadya watching her as if she had never quit watching.

"Shall we walk her around until we have to go?" She reached out, and with a hand on the cheek strap walked the mare away from Tim, away from the future that was coming too fast to think about it.

She heard the vehicle behind her and pictured the police car without turning around to look at it. She didn't want to see it now.

Once, a police car had been where she could look for her father. She never passed one then, when she was young, without scrutinizing the policeman inside, looking for her father. Twice, she had actually seen him and he had stopped to make a fuss over her before sending her on her way with her friends, suitably impressed.

But now she could hear the car and couldn't bring herself to turn and just look at it. She was aware of Tim approaching her, his voice a low murmur. The sound of the car was another low rumble, thunder in the far distance—no, a machine noise, valves moving in rhythm. Why couldn't they come back later? She didn't want to see them, didn't want to hear Tim tell her they had to go.

Tim's voice was still going on so quietly that she finally realized that he was keeping it down on purpose. The words. What had he said?

"Mount up. Vicki, get on the horse. Hang on to the kid."

It wasn't a police car.

Tim had his gun in its clip holster in his hand, holding it in front of him, out of sight of the van in the driveway. He had a second clip of ammunition that he was cramming into his front pocket. He shoved the holster and all into the front of his pants and quickly pulled his shirttail out to hide it. He was still talking. "May not be anything. We don't know the neighbors."

"Oh, shit!"

Vicki got her foot in the stirrup and swung up behind Nadya.

Hardly looking at the van, Tim crossed to the corral and took the hackamore in his hand. He slipped through the rails and worked at putting the hackamore on a young gelding, a skittish youngster, tossing his head with energy. He brought the colt out and tied him to the outside of the corral, and only then turned and looked directly at the van.

A man got out on either side. Not policemen. Not FBI. They were both wearing sport coats without ties. Vicki immediately thought they were dressed that way for the same reason that policemen dressed that way off duty: an easy way to hide a weapon.

The two men walked toward Tim. One of them reached under his coat to hitch his pants, and Vicki could see Tim's hand go to his front and then idly scratch at his belly, keeping the hand there.

The man closest to Tim spoke first. "Anybody else home?"

Tim shrugged. "Don't know."

"You don't?"

"Haven't looked lately."

The man grinned. It was not a friendly grin. His eyes shifted to look at Vicki and then shifted back to Tim.

Then there was another car, a Ford Explorer this time, rolling slowly in and parking behind the van. Four or five men got out this time. Vicki lost count, but it was obvious that they knew the first two.

The man closest to Tim pulled a pistol out and pointed it at Tim, standing close, the gun almost touching Tim's belly.

Tim's move was so fast that he never had a chance to fire. With his right hand, Tim had the man's wrist pushed to one side, at the same time he came up with the left to grab the barrel of the gun and twist it backwards over the man's shoulder. There was an audible sound of snapping finger bones, and a yelp.

Without letting go, Tim swung him in front of the other man near him and then hit him twice. His fist made sharp cracking sounds on the man's face and he went backward, showering blood. Tim hit the second man while he was trying to get out of the way. As he went down, Tim went right on over him, stomping on his head with his heel, twice, three times. His voice yelling, "Go! Take off!"

Vicki started to turn the horse, but hesitated and stopped, looking back for Tim. Before she could make up her mind to do anything, Vicki saw Tim run for the gelding at the corral. As he passed the barn door, a black-brown shape came hurtling past him, heading for the men from the other car. The men, startled into immobility, were suddenly moving, drawing weapons, running to head Tim off before he could get mounted.

The German shepherd swerved a streaking arc to intercept them, running so fast, with such determination, that he seemed to levitate as he got close to them, rising from the ground in deadly savagery.

He hit the first one without slowing down. He knocked him backward, slashing at his face, hit the ground and sprung at the next one, finally a snarling roar coming out as if he had been saving it up. He got the man's ear as he tried to turn his face away, and the ear ripped.

Two guns were firing at once, point-blank, but the dog hit the ground and leapt again, this time getting his teeth solidly into the cheeks of the man before he could move.

Tim was mounted and the gelding running before the dog died, running right at Vicki and Nadya on Banjo. Tim's mouth was moving and, as though in slow motion, Vicki made out the words, "Get moving!" and then "Go, damn it! Go!" She wheeled Banjo and took off.

They raced over the ridge and down the other side into the valley. Riding bareback, Tim had to haul on the lead rope tied to the hackamore, the only control he had, to keep from running away from the mare. The young horse jolted to a halt, lowered his head, and kicked out with both rear hooves. Tim stayed on, thrashed the horse with his heels, and spun him in a tight circle.

As his face went by he was yelling at Vicki, "Lead! You know where you're going. Someplace they can't drive!"

Okay. She didn't even have to think about that. Banjo plunged down the path until they hit the streambed, and then Vicki turned her sharply uphill. In that direction the valley was less even, more rutted with old water erosion so that they temporarily disappeared and then reappeared, higher up. Just as they came to the pile of boulders that Vicki remembered she could see the van appear at the top of the ridge behind them. Shit. They'd been seen.

She had to slow Banjo down, searching for the path through the rocks. She couldn't remember where it was, right or left. Finally she had to stop entirely. She moved the horse to the right but ran into a dead end. As she brought the horse around the front of the pile of boulders, she could see that the men had already brought the van as far as it could get in the streambed, and they were climbing out, all of them armed with what looked like rifles or shotguns.

She urged Banjo to the left, trying to find the path around the rock pile, but it wasn't there. She was either misremembering it or someone had managed to move the rocks to block it off, to keep people from using it as a horse trail. There wasn't any way to keep going. The ridges on either side of them were too high to take the horses up. They would have to head back toward the van to get out.

Tim's gelding was dancing and kicking, flecks of foam along his flanks, his eyes rolling wild. Tim saw her expression, saw the rocks, saw the men running at them from the van. Somebody fired and the flat, sharp crack of the ricochet powdered rock behind them.

Tim was yelling then. "Get off! Take her on foot! I can hold 'em a while."

In a second, Vicki was off the horse and carrying Nadya over the rocks. Twice more, she heard the sound of a rifle firing and the answering crack-slap in the rocks around them. She spotted a hole, a gap in the boulders, and shoved Nadya down into it. She got on top of her, blocking the hole with her body, and turned to see what Tim was doing.

He had moved further to their right, wedged into the seam between two round boulders. He leveled his automatic over the top of the rock, took his time to aim carefully, and fired. Once, twice, three times in quick succession.

Then silence.

She heard the voices of the men in the distance, but she could not see them and could not make out the words. She was shaking.

By the way Tim was twisting and craning his neck she could tell that he had lost track of them, too. He glanced up at the pile of rocks, saw Vicki, and waved at her to keep going, if she could.

Carefully, Vicki crawled higher, trying to see what was there before she got Nadya out of the hole.

A rifle fired from behind her, from the direction of the van, and Vicki quickly got back down. Where the hell were the rest of them?

She saw Tim raise up enough to look at her, size up the predicament, and then motion for her to stay down. He was in the act of turning back to look back toward the van when they shot him from two sides.

Vicki almost never heard the firing. The sight of Tim shuddering from high-velocity impact, his blood flying and spilling, falling forward onto the rocks, lying still, filled her consciousness and stopped her cold. She could not move, could not breathe, begged for her sight to be wrong.

He did not move. He was dead. That fast, too late. Nothing she could do.

She snarled as she leaped over the rocks and scrambled down to him. Her feet were slipping on the rocks, and her knee banged as her ankle wedged into a crack and she went down. She was up again and scrambling, trying to get to Tim as though that's all she had to do. If she could get there, she could . . . she didn't know. She fell again, and again scrambled back to her feet, and finally the last few yards on her hands and knees over the rocks, not even feeling them anymore.

The men were close, one of them coming at her from the other side of Tim right in her vision. Tim's gun on the rock right in front of her. She grabbed for the gun and the man in front of her dropped out of sight.

Vicki could hear the men now, hear them yelling and hear their footsteps. Then she had the gun in her hand and came up firing. She fired fast, all six rounds that were left, shooting at the sounds, at the voices, hearing, finally, her own voice screaming, roaring ferocity and rage.

The next second she was sprawled among the rocks, the breath knocked out of her, the man who had kicked her from behind climbing down to her. She tried to move but she was stunned, her arms barely moving before the man had grabbed her by the throat, raised her off the ground, and hit her in the face with his fist.

The blow from the rock where she hit her head was harder than the one from the fist. She lay still, trying to see, trying to get up. She couldn't tell if her eyes were open or not. She could taste blood. She felt her blouse torn open, then a wrenching pain as one of the men tried to rip off her bra. She couldn't move her arms. She heard laughter, hard and mean. She tried to listen for Nadya. Tried to tell if they had found her or if she had stayed hidden.

She felt a hand grip her crotch, fingers probing her.

More voices. The hand was gone. Loud voices. No, one voice. A radio? No, an amplifier? She could hear individual words.

"—right where you are! Nobody move! Hands out in the open, asshole!"

She couldn't make sense out of it. Then the next voice was closer, more normal, not amplified. A woman's voice, but sounding as mean as anything Vicki had ever heard. "You move one finger and you're about to have a hell of an accident, motherfucker. Just give me a reason, shitface."

Then a man's voice. ". . . little girl up here. Scared to death."

Then the woman's voice again, but Vicki couldn't see her. "It's okay, honey. It's going to be all right." Vicki couldn't get her eyes to open. "Don't try to move, honey. You might be hurt. Be a stretcher up here in a minute. It's going to be all right, now."

Her eyes would not open.

Thirty-one

The woman was large and she was black. She guarded Vicki, sitting on the edge of her cot and talking continuously. Vicki, at first, decided it was like a radio, a sound that she could take or leave, listen to or tune out at will. The woman's voice didn't seem to need or expect a response.

She knew she was in jail. She knew she couldn't move without pain racing through her. Both knees seemed to be as tight as sausages in their casings, but when she finally could see them, they were not bandaged. Her pants were torn, her blouse all but nonexistent, so she lay wrapped in a blanket on the cot and tried not to think.

At some point, possibly in the middle of the night, she was taken to a shower and held by two sheriff's deputies until she was thoroughly rinsed and then dressed in an orange jumpsuit. Then she was back on the cot, not sure if she had dreamed of the shower until she looked at her arm and saw the orange evidence of change.

Then the black woman was gone and there was a teenager instead, who was obviously afraid of her, afraid of Vicki and everything else in the jail. She could not remember if she had slept or if she had been offered food. If she let herself think or tried, deliberately, to sleep, she saw Tim's head, the back of his neck as he shuddered and fell. She tried to keep her eyes open, but all she could see was the man she loved, and he was dead.

Then, mercy. She couldn't remember. Her mind would grow numb again, her feet gone, the aches in her knees and her head as deadened as the ache in her hollow chest.

She could feel only the pounding of her heart, a hollow, mindless, insistent thudding that shook her chest and would not quit. Oh, why? Why not quit, stop that brutal pounding? What could it possibly matter now?

Then it was Elaine. Elaine's voice. "Oh, Jesus Christ!"

Vicki tried to open her eyes. She seemed to be seeing things at a distance. She tried to sit up on the cot. Her head was ten feet across, stuffed with wadded newspapers.

Elaine's voice, still. "My God, Vicki! Have you seen a doctor? Have they taken you to a doctor? Vicki? It's okay, babe, lay back down. I got to get a doctor for you here."

Now Elaine was like a radio that she could choose not to listen to, unless she wanted the distraction so that she could go back to sleep. Elaine was almost screaming.

"A doctor! Haven't you ever heard of a doctor? Jesus Christ, this woman is seriously injured! Do you have anybody working here with an IQ over thirty? If you do, could I speak to her now, please?"

Then Elaine's face was close again. "Hang on, babe, I'm going to make sure you get medical attention."

"Elaine."

"You can talk?"

"Elaine, don't bother. I'm all right."

"Oh, right, sure you are. Have you seen a goddamned mirror?"

"Don't . . . I can sleep here, okay?"

Vicki closed her eyes again and there was a pause in the conversation. She didn't realize that Elaine had been gone until she heard her coming back.

"Babe, listen to me. They don't have a doctor on the premises at the moment, but they promised, okay? You have to be transported to San Francisco. They let me talk to you just for a minute to tell you what's going on. We're going to get this worked out, okay? That's why we got venue changed to San Francisco, so we can deal with a judge we know, okay? Okay, babe? Can you understand what I'm saying?"

"Yeah, it's okay."

"Oh, Christ! Vicki, we're going to get this worked out. We will do it, I promise you. I got to go. Meet you in San Francisco, okay? Okay, Vicki?"

"Yeah, fine, okay."

Then Elaine was gone and the teenager was gone and she slept. Every time she woke, she thought it was the middle of the night because she couldn't see a window and the same brilliant light was on in the hallway outside her cell. She understood she was in a cell, on a cot, under a blanket. She was hot, but she wanted to be under the blanket.

"Vicki Shea? Vicki? Time to go to the doctor, sport."

Vicki didn't want to open her eyes.

"Come on, sport. Looks like you pissed off the cops, huh? Can you walk?"

She found she could walk. She kept the blanket, clinging to it when they tried to take it away, finally relinquishing it when she realized she was in a small clinic. They stripped her and it was cold. Two of them were in there with her, a male and a female deputy.

The doctor looked to be about ninety years old. He looked in her eyes repeatedly until Vicki wondered if he was forgetting between times that he had done that already. Poor old guy. He should have been retired somewhere instead of having to do this menial and thankless task, examining prisoners for the county. She wondered if he had grandchildren, and if they had all abandoned him so that he had to keep working.

"Miss Shea? Is that right? Is that your name?"

"Yes."

"You been beat up a little, huh? I want to get some films of your head. Did you lose consciousness?"

"No, I don't think so." She understood the questions, the thinking behind them. He could see enough with his flashlight in her eyes that he was pretty sure she didn't have a brain injury, but he wanted to look for fractures anyway.

323

"Can you tell me what hurts? Where it's the worst?"

"Everything."

"I can see that. Any particular part that's worse than the others?"

Vicki managed to shake her head.

"Miss Shea? Can you understand me all right?"

"Yes."

"What do you do? What kind of a job do you do?"

"A doctor."

"Yes, I'm a doctor. Can you tell me what your normal occupation is?"

"I'm a doctor."

She could hear him chuckle. "Okay, fine. Looks like somebody's been operating on you, though."

After the X rays she was outfitted in manacles, chained to four other prisoners, and put on a bus. It was night, the middle of the night on the freeway. The other prisoners, all women, looked at her with alarm, tried to keep their distance from her, as if she might start throwing up. No, that wasn't it. They were concerned. One of them finally sat next to her and touched her shoulder, the chains rattling with each movement.

"Honey, you want to try to lay down?"

"Thank you. I'm all right."

"You sure?"

So nice of you to ask . . . She had thought the words, but then realized that she had not said them out loud.

She spent the remainder of the night on another cot, she supposed in San Francisco. She did not recognize the jail from this perspective, although if they were in San Francisco, she had been in here many times questioning witnesses. Long time ago. Many, many years ago it must have been.

Elaine again. "Vicki? Feeling better?"

She could only look up. No, that wasn't true. Suddenly she knew she could sit up and she could talk, that she wasn't paralyzed, just slow. Her head was now only about a foot across.

"I'm okay."

"Well, that remains to be seen. Jesus! Here, sit up. They let me bring in some wipes and a comb. We're going to court."

"Court?" Suddenly, Vicki felt naked. "Oh, Elaine, I can't."

"You don't have to do anything. We got it worked out, okay? We have to go before a federal judge for about two minutes and they'll dismiss the charges, that's all." Elaine smiled brightly. "You even know where you are?"

"Jail?"

"You're in the Federal Building, San Francisco. You're just going to go downstairs to court, then you're going home with me, okay?"

Vicki nodded and then lost focus. What could it possibly matter where she was? Now she had seen it all, and that's all there was.

"Vicki?" Elaine kept trying to engage her. Couldn't the woman see she didn't care?

"Vicki? The children are all okay. Did anybody tell you? All the children were . . . none of them were hurt, you understand?"

Suddenly, Vicki was wide awake. Her eyes were fully open and she raised her head to stare at Elaine, trying to get out the words in a form and order that would make sense.

"Nadya? Nadya's okay? Where is she?"

"I don't know her. Is that one of the children?"

"Yes, a little girl with a partial hemiparesis. A little girl . . ."

"They're all okay. None of them hurt. Just scared a little, I think."

"You saw them?"

"Well, no. They were on the way to New York before I got down there, but I talked to several—"

"New York? Elaine, why?"

"Immigration, Vicki. Remember?"

"Immigration? They're going to deport them?"

"Already have, I'm sure. From the way they were talking, they're halfway to Moscow by now. But they're okay. They're just going home, back to where they came from, Vicki. They're none the worse for wear, and you even got some vitamins into them, right?"

But Vicki couldn't answer. She lost the focus that she had gained, and lost interest entirely in what Elaine had to say.

"Okay, ready for court? I'll meet you downstairs, okay?"

"Okay."

They removed the shackles from her feet but left the manacles on her wrists, a cable connecting them to a belt. Vicki was not even curious as she was led between two federal marshals through the prisoner's door into the courtroom. She was steered by her elbows to a chair at the counsel table. Standing next to her was a distinguished-looking man, silver hair in abundance, slightly curly and styled so that it came down below his collar in meticulous waves. He wore rings on both hands and a prominent gold watch.

Elaine appeared from behind her and took the chair on the other side of Vicki. "This is Jim Gonzales, one of our partners? Remember, I told you about him?"

Mr. Gonzales leaned toward her, a self-satisfied smile that wasn't exactly directed at her. "How do you do, Dr. Shea. This will just take a minute."

Everyone rose as the judge came into the courtroom, so Vicki struggled to her feet.

"Oh, my Lord! Dr. Shea?" It was the judge talking to her, a judge she knew very well. She had to look at the nameplate. Judge Angora? Vicki wasn't even aware that she had been elevated to the federal bench.

"Off the record a moment. Vicki?"

"Yes, Your Honor."

"Have they let you see a doctor? You look horrible. For heaven's sake, sit down before you fall!"

An extremely young man from the U.S. attorney's office was standing at the other counsel table. "She was examined by a doctor in Los Angeles before her transport, Your Honor. Bumps and bruises, but she's basically all right."

"That, Counsel, is not going to wash. I'm not a doctor, but I can see!"

"Your Honor." Elaine was on her feet. "We're going straight to UCSF when we finish here."

The judge looked at Jim Gonzales, ignoring Elaine. "You got this all worked out?"

"Yes, Your Honor."

She looked over at the assistant U.S. attorney. "That right? This is the case with the child smugglers, right? And that rogue cop was involved in it somehow? Is he in custody?"

"He's in intensive care, Your Honor. They stabilized him enough to get him up here to SF General, but they're not sure if he's going to make it."

Vicki's back went rigid as she jerked upright, lightning flashing through her head. Everything was suddenly crystal clear. The sounds, the coolness of the air, the smells, even her own smells, were suddenly, vividly clear. Judge Angora's face . . .

The judge was smiling and nodding. "That's right, I remember. Okay, got it worked out?"

"Yes, Your Honor, this part of it. The other defendants completely exonerated Dr. Shea in their confessions."

Vicki started to rise, not sure where she was going. She could hear a sound starting in her chest. Elaine gripped her hand, pulling on her arm to keep her in her seat.

"As I understand it, you are dismissing all charges against Dr. Shea, right? With prejudice?"

The assistant U.S. attorney answered like an adult. "Correct, Your Honor."

Vicki was looking at Elaine, her eyes staring, her mouth open, still wanting to get up and run out.

Elaine held on to her, leaned to her ear and whispered, "Sit still! You're about to have the charges dismissed."

"Jesus, who cares!"

"Shhhh!"

The judge looked at Vicki. "Are you okay?"

Elaine half rose, one hand on Vicki's shoulder to hold her down. "She's having some pain, Your Honor."

"Okay, I'll speed it up. Now, Dr. Shea, I'm sure you know you have to cooperate, right? Oh, never mind, I know you will." Her smile broadened as she looked back at Jim Gonzales and the kid acting as a U.S. attorney. "I suppose you don't realize you are in the presence of one of the very best trial lawyers in this city." She looked back at

Vicki, positively beaming. "I'm sure you're just as good as a doctor. You're a pediatrician now?"

Elaine spoke up. "She is, Your Honor."

The judge continued to ignore Elaine and stared at Vicki, her smile changing to a look of concern. "Well, I hope you check out okay. Ready? Let's go back on the record."

In a swift, scripted recital of legal magic, the deal was done.

Somewhere in the middle of it, Vicki had been hoisted to her feet again. She was aware that the blood had drained out of her face. She could feel the prickly sensation of fever in her scalp and in her cheeks.

"Okay, off the record. Vicki? Understand? You're free to go. Vicki? It's okay now. You're free."

Vicki would not agree to be admitted to the hospital at UCSF. She insisted on going to San Francisco General, where they had Tim, and Elaine finally got her to compromise by having her admitted there.

It was dark by the time they finished with scans, films, blood, and urine samples. She was examined by three different trauma residents, none of whom she knew. She waited a few minutes after they turned out her light and then disconnected herself from the IVs. In the hospital gown and bare feet, she walked down to the ICU.

She didn't know what to expect. No one could tell her what his wounds were. She kept hoping there were no head wounds—please, no brain damage!

But his head, when she saw him, was not bandaged.

The nurse, aware that Vicki had come in the room, glanced at her, then did a double take. "Dr. Shea?"

"Yeah, hi. How is he?"

"Are you a patient here? My God, you're a mess!"

Vicki tried to smile, knowing she would not remember the nurse's name. "It's a long story. How's he doing?"

"Better than yesterday. This is one tough son of a bitch." The nurse peered at Vicki closely. "Too old to be one of your patients, right?"

"He's my fiancé. Nobody will tell me his injuries."

"Oh! Well, congratulations! I mean . . . Dr. Shea, I think he's getting better by the hour. He's loaded on Demerol, is why he's asleep. Had his third surgery this morning, lost a part of his liver and his spleen. He's got some atelectasis so we're watching his O sats, might have to put him on a ventilator if it gets any worse, but tell you the truth, I think it's clearing. Oh, just have a seat. I'll get you the chart."

Vicki turned the light down and sat on the nurse's stool, staring at Tim's face. She glanced up at the monitor and could see his oxygen saturation was holding at about 96 percent. No ventilator for him.

She had to put both hands on him, on his arm and his face. Then she lowered her own face until it was resting on his shoulder, her eyes pressed closed by his flesh.

The nurse came to the doorway, the chart in her hand, then put it down and discreetly backed away.

His voice was dry and breathy. "Vicki?"

"Yes, Tim, I'm here."

"Tell those doctors for me . . . tell 'em to hurry up . . . the treatment."

Vicki raised her head and smiled down at him. His eyes were closed. She stroked his face with her fingertips. "What's the hurry?"

"Tell 'em . . . I got to ride a bull on Sunday."

She smiled, almost a laugh, and put her face back on his bare shoulder.

"Vicki?"

"Yes, Tim."

"How long do you think . . . before I can get out of here?"

She didn't lift her face up again. "No idea. Weeks, maybe. Your liver's the most important thing. No booze for you, for a while."

"Damn!"

She smiled against his shoulder.

"Well, give me an idea. How long before I can travel?"

She shook her head, barely moving it. "Where?"

"Well, I figure first stop is somewhere in Russia." He paused, hearing her.

"Here, now." He tried to touch her hair, but he couldn't move his hand that far so he had to give it up.

"Vicki? Come on, we got to plan this."